The Sunflower Girl

The Sunflower Girl

Sara Hylton

St. Martin's Press New York

Library of Congress Cataloging-in-Publication Data

Hylton, Sara.
    The sunflower girl / Sara Hylton.
        p.   cm.
    ISBN 0-312-15667-7
    I. Title.
    PR6058.Y63S85   1997
    823'.914—dc21   97-6854
                                                       CIP

First published in Great Britain by Judy Piatkus
(Publishers) Ltd

First U.S. Edition: July 1997

10   9   8   7   6   5   4   3   2   1

The Sunflower Girl

Book One

Marie Claire

1

The view from the long windows was famous. Paintings of it hung in galleries all over the world, books about the glories of English gardens would never have existed without it, but its beauty was largely wasted on the young man slumped in his chair and staring out dejectedly through the open window.

Emerald green lawns edged with stately beeches swept down to where the gentle river meandered under two ancient stone bridges, and swans glided gracefully in and out of the feathery branches of the willows that lined its banks.

It was the end of June 1894. The trees were filled with bird song, and the sun shone radiantly from sunrise until it set in a blaze of glory beyond the distant hills. It seemed incredible that bitter thoughts should ever be allowed to intrude upon such a day but Andrew Martindale's thoughts were bitter indeed as he reflected on the anger he had just been subjected to from his father.

Of course over the years there had been many such scenes: never his father's favourite, he had had to listen to long harangues about his inadequacies, while his elder brother's misdemeanours had been largely ignored and his younger brother had been protected by a doting mother.

Being the middle of three brothers hadn't been easy, particularly when John, the eldest son, was clever enough to be a faithful copy of his sire and Daniel the youngest son had had the good sense to join the Indian army straight from the schoolroom. All his mother's tears had been unable to persuade him against this enterprise and Andrew was left with his mother's recriminations and his father's disfavour.

The slamming of a door brought him out of his reverie and he turned to look into the amused eyes of his sister Lady Vivienne.

She would never have the delicate gentle beauty of her mother, but she was none the less striking. A tall slender girl wearing a long black

3

riding skirt and velvet riding jacket. The white lace ruffles round her throat accentuated her smooth skin and dark auburn hair.

She perched herself unceremoniously on the edge of a table, her long legs crossed under her skirt, her riding crop on the table top along with the roll of newspaper placed beside it.

'What was all the shouting about, you could be heard all over the house?' she demanded.

Andrew scowled. 'Father giving me his usual exhortation which I could have done without.'

'What have you done now?'

'Nothing.'

'Oh come on now. He walked out of here with a face like thunder, still shouting the odds. I'm used to his tantrums, what brought this one on?'

'Something and nothing. Mother's decision to hold the family re-union at the house in Bath and my not being there.'

'Why aren't you going, you've known about it for months?'

'Because I promised Mirandol I'd visit him in France at the beginning of July and stay on for the Wine Festival.'

'That's months away, why can't you come back for the reunion?'

'Because I don't want to. You can manage without me, the aunts and grandmother'll be here. You'll be here and John and Daniel will be on leave. What's in it for me except for father to keep going on about my joining his wretched regiment and pointing out how well the other two are upholding the family tradition. I've had it up to here, I want to get away.'

'What will you do in France all that time?'

'See something of France, meet old friends, do some painting. When I told him about that he said I'd never be any good, that I'd always be an amateur and that I'd be wasting my time. Unless you're flying a banner, making money out of what you do, dying on some foreign field, in his eyes you're nothing.'

'Oh well, since you're so disenchanted with life you might as well sink further in the mire,' she said tossing the newspaper across to him.

He stared at it where it had fallen into his lap.

'It's all over the front page, not a story to be missed somewhere in the middle of the paper. Geraldine Fallon will be supremely gratified at the spread *The Times* have given the announcement.'

Curiously he spread the paper out across his knees while his sister watched intently for the reaction to show on his face.

There was a photograph of a beautiful smiling girl arm in arm with a much older man in army officer's uniform standing on the front steps of a stately pile and under it the announcement that Miss Constance Fallon had just announced her engagement to Lord St Veep of Effingham Court. Miss Fallon is the only daughter of Mrs Geraldine Fallon and the late Colonel Giles Fallon of London. Voted the Debutante of the Year Miss Fallon is a keen rider to hounds, a great help in her mother's many charities and a product of one of Switzerland's most famous finishing schools.

Unaware that his sister had gone to stand behind him he stared down morosely at the newspaper.

'He's old enough to be her father,' she commented, 'but he is a baron and she's missed out on several more blue-blooded young studs, largely because her mother has pushed too hard.'

'You've never liked her, have you?' he said in some irritation.

'Not really. She's a fortune-hunter fashioned by Mummy. I agree with Father about the Fallons. The fact that you were besotted with the girl didn't exactly endear you to Father. How many times have you asked her to marry you?'

'Several. I lost count.'

'And each time she turned you down.'

'Yes.'

'Did you ever ask yourself why, when I'm quite sure she told you she was terribly fond of you.'

Andrew scowled.

'Fondness is not sufficient reason for marriage,' he said stiffly.

'If you'd been the eldest son rather than the middle son she'd have said yes so quickly you'd still have been spinning from it,' his sister said dryly.

'He's too old for her,' Andrew said grumpily.

'Unimportant when she'll be Lady St Veep. One thing is sure, father'll heave a sigh of relief when he reads this.'

'You mean he hasn't seen it already?'

'No. I got to the paper this morning before it was put on his breakfast tray – Molly Jarvise told me the announcement would appear in *The Times* this week. I knew what he'd make of it if he read it before the rest of us. You can be sure he'll raise it over dinner this evening, now you're prepared.'

'I suppose I can thank you for that.'

She smiled down at him as she took hold of the newspaper. 'Why don't you come out for a ride over the downs, it would cheer you up, give you some courage to face your next meeting with him.'

'Why is it you get along with him and I don't?'

'I've learned to talk the way he talks. One has to practise being the sort of person he expects one to be.'

'I don't want to be that sort of person.'

'Couldn't you even pretend a little?'

'He'd see through it, he always does.'

'Well he hasn't entirely seen through me. In public I'm his little girl who does as she's told and agrees with every word he says, in private I'm my own woman, I go my own way.'

'One day he'll find out.'

'I'm clever too. I cover my tracks very well.'

'You'll slip up one day.'

'No I won't. I have a great aptitude for make-believe. You could learn from me Andrew if you weren't so busy making waves.'

'I'm going for a walk. I feel a pressing need to get him out of my mind,' Andrew said rising to his feet and making for the open French window.

His sister watched him go with a faintly contemptuous smile on her face. Of her three brothers Andrew was her favourite but she had precious little time for any of them. A strong-willed girl and undoubtedly her father's favourite child, she had grown up with a strong sense of injustice. Vivienne had never come to terms with the fact that sons succeeded their fathers and girls were expected to find husbands looking for blue-blooded girls competently able to fulfil the role vacated by their mothers.

She had had her year as a debutante, curtsied prettily before her Majesty and run the gamut of suitable swains with the same sort of contemptuous regard she meted out to her brothers.

She picked up the newspaper from where Andrew had left it and looked down at Constance Fallon's face staring up at her from the front page.

They had been schoolgirls together and debutantes in the same year at the same court. Vivienne had watched with amusement as Constance's mother had begun her machinations to find her only daughter a husband. The balls and garden parties, the tea dances and dinners where only the noble sons of titled aristocracy were invited, little realizing that it was Geraldine herself who was the stumbling-block in attracting the man she wanted for her daughter. Geraldine had a reputation as a pushy domineering mother. Fathers warned their sons off and in the end Constance had had to settle for a man old enough to be her father.

Andrew was in love with the girl and she with him, but her mother had cautioned her to look around. Andrew was only the second son of an earl, there were better fish in the sea.

She strolled out through the window keeping to the path that edged the house and walking in the direction of the stables. She walked thoughtfully and it was one of the gardeners who passed her, raising his cap respectfully, who brought her out of her reverie.

'Is my father at the stables?' she asked him.

'No milady, he's in the conservatory lookin' at the orchids.'

'Thank you Raynard.'

She strode off towards the conservatory. Orchids were her father's passion and tending to them would no doubt have put him in a gentler frame of mind.

She smiled as she found him in conversation with his head gardener. A stranger could well have believed that it was Jamison who was the earl and her father the gardener since Jamison was wearing country tweeds while her father was attired in a disreputable old jacket and wearing his bedroom slippers. They both looked round as she joined them and the gardener smiled as she embraced her father and planted a kiss on his cheek.

'What do you think of this one?' her father enquired holding up a stem from which sprouted an orchid whose exquisite petals were shaded from pale blue to glowing purple.

'It's beautiful, Father. Is that the one you intend to show?'

'If all goes well. We've brought it along well and there won't be one like it. Now we need a name for it.'

'And have you got one in mind?'

The two men smiled at each other. 'I'm thinking of calling it The Lady Vivienne. What do you think of that my girl.'

She threw her arms around his neck, beaming happily. 'I think it's wonderful and I hope it takes first prize. Have you nearly finished in here?'

'Why? Is there anything to go back to the house for?'

'There's tea, and I've something to show you.'

'What is it? Something that's going to cost me money I'll be bound.'

'No Father, something in the newspaper.'

'You can show me that in here.'

'Oh no. Back at the house with tea and crumpets and where you can sit back in comfort.'

'Is your mother back?'

'I don't think so.'

'Oh well then, I'll leave you to it Jamison. You've done very well, I think we've got a winner there.'

Father and daughter sauntered back to the house, her arm in his, and the gardener smiled as his eyes followed them. She was the one who brought out the best in her father, there was no doubt about it.

A little while later His Lordship sat back in his favourite chair with a satisfied smile on his lips as he read the announcement of Constance Fallon's engagement.

Laying the newspaper down on the table besides his chair he beamed across at his daughter. 'Has Andrew seen this?' he asked.

'He has.'

'And how did he take it?'

'Not too well. He's walking her out of his system.'

'Perhaps now he'll stay here for your mother's reunion in Bath. I'm convinced he was going away because she'd turned him down yet again.'

'I think he'll still go to France Father,' Lady Vivienne demurred. 'He's promised his friend he'll spend the summer there and I can't think he'll change his mind.'

Her father scowled. 'It's time he found himself a job instead of dabbling in dubious racing stables and painting pictures nobody would want to buy. We've got a houseful of masterpieces by famous artists. Have you seen anything he's done with any merit at all?'

'Some. You don't bother to look at them.'

The Earl snorted contemptuously. 'He has two brothers in the army that's where he should be.'

'I'm not sure you're entirely fair about Andrew, just because the other two have decided to follow your advice and serve in some regiment or other doesn't necessarily mean that Andrew is less of a man.'

'Sticking up for him, are you?' her father retorted.

'Well he does seem to cause you more annoyance than the other two simply because he doesn't always agree with you. You were delighted when John married Charlotte Blaine, but I've seen that you're not nearly so enchanted with his choice these days.'

'You're too astute, Vivienne, that's your trouble. She fits the bill, but it's necessary for my second son to choose wisely and I'm not very sure that he'll do that. Are you getting my drift, girl?'

'Not entirely.'

'Well, as Charlotte's presented my eldest son with three daughters, spoilt, mewling children unlikely to add any lustre to the family tree, it may rest with Andrew to sire the next Earl of Westmond.'

'I see,' his daughter mused. 'But don't you think it will take him a little longer than a few weeks in Bath to get over Constance Fallon?'

'Your mother's got all sorts of things planned there. Tea parties and garden parties, and she's got a list from here to eternity of people she intends to invite.'

'Perhaps Andrew will meet someone in France, a relative of the Mirandols.'

'Some descendant of the nobility who was lucky enough to escape the revolution do you mean? I don't want a French daughter-in-law, I never could master their lingo and the French haven't forgiven us for Waterloo. Good British stock is what we want. You don't think there is somebody there, do you?' he asked in some alarm.

Vivienne threw back her head and laughed delightedly. 'Oh Father, you really are an old grouch, of course there isn't, but now with Constance out of the running who knows.'

She went over to the table. 'More tea, Father?' she enquired.

'No. I'll have a scotch, never could understand the English absorption with afternoon tea.'

He watched his daughter as she poured out a generous helping of whisky from the decanter at a side table. She was a comely looking girl, high-spirited and with a good figure and his expression grew grim as he thought to himself that she was the best of the bunch. Who would she marry? he wondered.

She'd come through her year as a debutante without making a choice. He'd watched her at all the balls and bun fights surrounded by a host of young eligibles but there'd been nobody special and he'd been reluctant to ask any questions.

What sort of man was his daughter looking for? There had been a surfeit of army and naval officers, ambitious politicians, young men who were doing things in the city as well as wealthy landowners, so where was Vivienne looking for a suitable husband?

She brought the glass over to him, staring directly into his eyes, seeing the speculation there, but she smiled airily saying, 'Here's mother, for heaven's sake let us not have a scene just yet about Bath.'

'She'll have to know sometime.'

'Well, later then.'

Vivienne's mother was still a very beautiful woman with fine fair hair now sprinkled with silver, and eyes as blue as English summer skies.

Her figure was pleasantly well rounded but her smile was warm and sunny and as her smile embraced them both before she bent down to pet her spaniel, her husband reflected that he had chosen very well when he first encountered Clarissa Graham at her débutante's ball thirty-five years before.

Lady Clarissa Graham had proved to be beautiful, intelligent and of a delightful disposition, a disposition she had had to call upon a great many times over the years to accommodate her irascible husband.

Vivienne presided over the tea trolley while her mother chatted about her day out.

'Is Andrew out then?' she asked.

9

'Yes, and feeling sorry for himself.' His Lordship couldn't resist saying this, in spite of the cautionary glance he had from his daughter.

'Why is that, what has happened?' asked his wife.

'That Fallon Girl has announced her engagement.'

'Oh dear, poor Andrew, he was so besotted with Constance, I felt sure she would accept him one day. Who's the lucky man then?'

'The unlucky man is some baron old enough to be her father. He must be somebody her mother approved of.'

'Well yes,' she said seriously, 'Geraldine would have to approve, how is Andrew taking it?'

'Gone for a walk across the park. We'll know at dinner.'

'Of course it was Constance's mother who was the problem, I could have told Andrew so, immediately I was aware of his interest in her. I've known Geraldine Fallon since we were children. Her father was a terrible gambler, they never had any money, why I remember that she was happy to wear hand-me-downs from a great many older girls in my family and in other families we knew. Perhaps that's why she's been so sure somebody rich had to be found for Constance.'

'Andrew is hardly likely to be a pauper,' he retorted.

'No dear, I know, but she also wanted a title for Constance and the Honourable Mrs Martindale wouldn't have been good enough. When Andrew gets over it I'm sure he'll think he's had a lucky escape.'

She did not see the glance her husband exchanged with his daughter as she went on to say, 'Perhaps Andrew will spend the weekend with us in Bath and go on to France from there, surely he'd be willing to do that?'

Nobody spoke, and after a few minutes she said, 'Well I'm going to mention it at dinner; if he's not prepared to do that, I shall let him see that I am very annoyed with him indeed.'

2

The atmosphere over the dinner table was crusty in the extreme.

His Lordship was decidedly sullen whilst his son was still smarting from their scene of the morning. Lady Clarissa, annoyed with him, chattered to her daughter about trivialities and Lady Vivienne waited expectantly for the subject uppermost in all their minds to surface.

Unable to bear it a moment longer Lady Clarissa said, 'Your father tells me you are going to France Andrew, and that you've chosen to go when I wanted us all to be together in Bath.'

'I arranged to go before I heard about Bath, Mother.'

'I'm sure if you told your friend how important it is to be with your brothers when they come home on leave he wouldn't mind you postponing your holiday.'

'I rather think he would, Mother. Besides, I want to go. I want to do some painting in the French countryside and I can't honestly think that my brothers will care whether I'm in Bath or not.'

'Well, of course they would care. I care. I want us there as a family. Heaven knows, we don't spend all that much time together.'

Andrew's face was mutinous. He didn't think that it was fair, evidently both his father and his sister had acquainted his mother of the morning's confrontation.

'Darling, I'm so sorry about Constance,' his mother went on. 'We all know how much you wanted to marry her and her engagement to somebody else must be an enormous blow, but the world is full of lovely girls, with Constance out of the way who knows who you might meet.'

Andrew was silent and his father said testily, 'I suggest we leave Geraldine Fallon and her machinations out of this argument. If he thinks going to France more important than doing what you wish, let him get on with it. Go ahead with your plans and leave him out of it.'

'But it won't be complete without Andrew. Can't you manage a long weekend, dear, and then go to France, at least you'll have made the effort.' his mother pleaded.

He was trapped. He knew his mother would have her way, and meeting his sister's eyes across the table he knew that she knew it also.

'We can go to Bath early on Friday morning,' his mother was saying. 'I do so love the house in Bath, it's so much cosier than this one for a family reunion and Daniel always loved it, he was always so well in Bath when he was small. When we came here he got one chill after another.'

For the first time he could look at his father with some degree of sympathy.

The entire household had suffered as a result of Daniel's ailments. There had been a procession of nannies, physicians and tutors all primed with remedies for Daniel's deficiencies while the rest of them had to tiptoe about the house, play well away from the windows and take holidays with friends and relatives because their mother felt unable to leave her youngest son.

That Daniel had elected to take up a commission in the army and serve the last five years in the heat of India had astonished all of them. Andrew felt he should be curious to see how army life had shaped his younger brother, but all he wanted to do was get out of England, particularly now when the papers would be filled with Constance Fallon's approaching wedding. Her mother would see to that.

'Andrew, darling, surely you can manage a long weekend, Friday until Tuesday, and then you can go off to France and enjoy yourself?' his mother said persuasively.

'I'll see what I can do Mother.' he said. He couldn't get out of it, and across the table his sister grinned, more than a little amused at his scowling expression.

Five days were neither here nor there, but until then he would have to read about Constance, listen to people talking about Constance. Being well away from it in France would have been much better. His mother was saying, 'How is your French friend, Andrew, such a very charming boy, such beautiful manners. Will you be staying at the château?'

'I expect so, either there or in a cottage on the estate.'

'Why a cottage, aren't you the Vicomte's guest?'

'Yes, of course, but I don't want to be a part of all the wine festivals, the banquets and such, Mirandol knows that. I want to see something of Burgundy and do some serious painting.'

His father sniffed derisively. 'There are artists all over France, all over Europe doing serious painting, usually with an eye to earning their living by it. You're dabbling, both with painting and your life.'

'If you say so, Father,' Andrew retorted, 'but it is my life. I should be allowed to live it the way I want to.'

'You should make it something worthwhile while you're about it, and now I suggest we get on with our meal and forget about France and Bath. I'm heartily sick with mention of both of them.'

The rest of the meal passed in silence.

In the weeks that followed his wishes were obeyed. The countess went about her plans without interference. Servants were instructed to prepare the house in Bath so that it was ready for the family to occupy it, and she exchanged long letters with her daughter-in-law Charlotte, and although she deliberately refrained from any mention of the weekend to either her husband or son, she informed Vivienne that the children would be on holiday and were looking forward to being with them, and that everything was going according to plan.

As expected Constance Fallon's picture together with her fiancé and her mother filled the newspapers. Constance was making the most of her engagement from garden parties to hunt balls, sailing regattas and race meetings and Vivienne wondered where she was getting the money for the array of gowns she was pictured wearing. The Fallons were not exactly rich, but for Constance no expense was being spared.

Her name was never mentioned, but Vivienne took an impish delight in leaving magazines and newspapers around for her brother to read, and she always knew when he had seen them from his morose expression.

They went to Bath in the second week of July on a day when the sun shone bright and golden on Bath's exquisite squares and crescents. The stone house surrounded by green lawns and Italian gardens welcomed them with its pillared portico, its lofty rooms hung with priceless paintings, carpeted in pastel colours, chairs and sofas covered with delicate chintz and everywhere the sheen of walnut.

The countess loved the house, far more than she loved Blaire, the seat of the Earls of Westmond. Mortlake House in Bath had always seemed more like home than the famous stately pile so beloved by artists from many lands, and as she entered its portals her spirits lifted.

She was aware that Andrew had come with bad grace, that Vivienne had not looked forward to it and that her husband had come to please her but without any real enthusiasm. It would be different, she reflected hopefully, when they had all arrived and were sitting down together for their first meal.

Her two sons were expected on Saturday morning but Charlotte would be arriving later in the afternoon with the children. She saw very little of the three little girls since Charlotte spent a great deal of time with her parents in Scotland and the girls were at an age when they had a private governess.

Her husband thought it nonsense that they had a governess at all. They were in danger of being spoilt, and more and more now the children of the aristocracy were going to school instead of being educated privately. Charlotte had had three daughters in three years, always with the hope that one of them would be the boy they longed for. Now she was proclaimed delicate and her doctor had said she must not have any more children in the immediate future. Sadly it seemed that the future of the Martindale family might rest with Andrew or Daniel: a fact that Geraldine Fallon seemed to have overlooked when she cautioned her daughter to look elsewhere for a husband.

The servants had laid out a buffet for them in the dining room, and after they had eaten Andrew and Vivienne went out into the city in search of familiar sights.

'I can understand Mother's long lasting love affair with Bath,' Vivienne said, gazing enraptured at the crescents of stone Georgian houses and tree-lined squares. 'Where is there a more elegant city?'

Silently Andrew agreed with her even though he was wishing he was miles away.

They dawdled around the city's parks and streets and by the time they returned to the house it was mid-afternoon.

Servants were trying to cope with a pile of luggage inside the hall, considerably hampered by the antics of three small girls, two of them armed with skipping ropes while a third jumped round on the polished surface of the hall on a hobby horse, making quite a noise.

At that moment two women came running down the stairs, an older woman wearing a snowy white apron over a dark blue dress, still wearing her felt hat pulled firmly over her hair, and a young maid, evidently anxious and flustered.

'Now then girls put away those toys, the nursery is upstairs. This is no place for jumping around.' Then turning to Andrew and Vivienne she said, 'I'll take the children upstairs now. I'm Nanny McFarlaine. I hope she didn't disturb you.'

'Fortunately no,' Lady Vivienne said with a wry smile. 'I am Vivienne Martindale and this is my brother Andrew. Where is their mother?'

'In the drawing room with the Countess. I've been inspecting the girls' bedrooms m'lady, now come along girls, you go with Janet, Amanda. You two come with me.'

The girls complied in sulky silence and Vivienne said with a grin, 'Come on, let's get it over, you've only a few days of it, have some sympathy with the rest of us.'

Their mother and their sister-in-law sat over the afternoon tea. There was no sign of their father.

Charlotte came forward to meet them, holding up her face for their kiss of greeting. She was tall and willowy, her pale face surrounded by a halo of brown hair prematurely streaked with grey. She was not a pretty woman; but she had an undeniable aristocratic aura of superiority in her bearing.

'You look very well, Charlotte,' Vivienne said in an endeavour to stop Charlotte short before she could embark on a list of her maladies.

'Well, I'm feeling a little better,' she said, 'but I am rather tired after that long journey and the girls were fretful. They hate trains, and we had so much luggage.'

'I'm sure the girls would have found the nursery upstairs very adequately equipped,' Vivienne said dryly. 'We've met your nanny, she seems a very competent lady.'

'Oh yes, indeed. She's been with us since Amanda was a baby. I really couldn't cope without her, the girls are all delicate and I spoil them, it takes Nanny McFarlaine to be firm with them.'

'Are they looking forward to seeing their father?' Andrew asked.

'Well of course. John keeps on and on at me to spend time wherever the army chooses to send him, but I can't leave the girls, and Mother and Father simply can't cope with them.'

There followed a long discourse on the rights and wrongs of bringing up children, the fors and againsts on schooling, the advantages and disadvantages of foreign travel and the apprehension of living with foreigners.

'Your mother tells me you are off to France in a few days, Andrew?' she said, in a tone of voice which conveyed to Andrew her surprise that he should even think of such a thing.

'Yes, it was arranged some time ago, something I can't get out of.' Andrew explained.

'How very sad,' Charlotte said, 'particularly as it's such a long time since you've seen either of your brothers.'

Andrew decided that that remark did not require an answer but he knew that the issue would be raised again and again over the next few days.

The first occasion occurred that evening. His two brothers had arrived. John had been first, along with his batman, whom he cheerfully left to cope with his luggage whilst he disappeared with his wife into the nursery.

'Your batman can eat in the kitchens with the servants,' his mother said adamantly. 'I'm not giving the man an opportunity to say he's been treated badly in your parents' house.'

15

Daniel arrived in the early evening in the company of a brother officer, both of them looking as smart as paint in their officers' uniform, and both of them so obviously enchanted with each other's company his father was inclined to put the worst possible construction on it and retired to his study in disgust.

'Well isn't this delightful,' his mother said as the adults sat down to dinner that evening. 'How many years is it since we were all together as a family?'

'I hear you're off to France in a few days,' John said, fixing Andrew with a sardonic smile.

'Yes. Something arranged some time ago.'

'Is Mirandol married yet?'

'No, but I believe there is a lady in the offering.'

'Oh well, the French are good at having it both ways, a wife and a mistress,' his brother remarked, and looking at him in scandalized annoyance his mother said, 'Really John I'm sure André isn't at all like that. I always thought him absolutely charming.'

'How about you Daniel, anybody in mind?' John persisted.

His younger brother merely smiled, and John proceeded to hog the conversation by talk of his military acumen. 'We're being shipped out to Bombay at the end of August,' he announced. 'Evidently the War Office feel our publicized Indian Army needs a booster from home to sort out the mess India's in.'

'If India's in a mess it's hardly the army's fault,' Daniel demurred.

'Well of course it is, we should let those blighters know who's boss. We're letting them run rings round us and they know it.'

Meeting Andrew's cynical gaze across the table Vivienne murmured, 'T'was ever thus,' and immediately John turned his attention on to her.

'I thought you'd have announced your engagement or been married long before this,' he said. 'You're letting the pick of the crop slip through your fingers. I'll bet Vivienne's coming out cost you a fortune, Father.'

'No more than the commission I bought for you and Daniel in the army, no more than keeping your brother Andrew in indolence while he makes up his mind what he wants in life,' the earl said testily.

It was to be a foretaste of lunch and dinner throughout the next few days. Breakfast was the only meal which escaped the presence of the entire family but just when Andrew believed there was not going to be any mention of Constance Fallon's engagement, his sister-in-law remarked, 'I met Constance Fallon in the park this morning, I didn't realize she was in Bath but apparently she and her fiancé are visiting his aunt who lives here.'

There was an uncomfortable silence, and John chortled merrily,

'You've put the cat among the pigeons m'dear. Don't you know that Andrew is nursing a broken heart over the girl's engagement?'

Andrew remained silent and Charlotte said unhappily, 'Oh dear, it really is most unfortunate, I asked her to come for tea this afternoon so that she could see John and Daniel. She'll be bringing her fiancé with her.'

'You really don't need to be here,' his mother said quickly, favouring Andrew with a sympathetic look.

'If he's not here it'll advertise his broken heart,' John said heartily. 'Stay here and face it, that's my advice,' he persisted.

They arrived promptly at three and Andrew stayed in the drawing room with the rest of them, wishing he was miles away.

Constance looked ravishing in pale green, a pale straw boater on her pale blonde hair, her fiancé wearing civilian clothes and looking down at her with obvious admiration.

She was charming, receiving their congratulatory wishes with dimpled smiles, looking up at Andrew shyly, hopefully sympathetic in case his disappointment still showed, whilst Andrew manfully hid it behind a charming smile and warm hand clasp, both hiding an ardent wish to kick her smiling colonel out of the room.

The children were paraded in front of them and Constance kissed each of them in turn. She presented the countess with a bunch of carnations and said she hoped to see Vivienne at the tea dance one of their friends was giving in London at the end of August.

'Not me,' Vivienne said sharply, 'I'm sick of tea dances, I hope to be in Scotland, anywhere but London at the end of August.'

'You're missing out on all the fun,' Constance said gently.

'It isn't my idea of fun,' Vivienne said adamantly. 'I find my fun in other ways.'

'Oh well, I still think you're missing out,' Constance persisted. 'There are still a great many men just waiting to be charmed by the right sort of girl.'

'I know, but it isn't a criterion for me Constance, I suppose it was for you.' Vivienne said and was rewarded be seeing the other girl's cheeks suffuse with colour. She did not deserve Constance Fallon's hints that it was time she found herself a husband – she would find one when she was good and ready, and hopefully not one who held on to her every word as if it was a proclamation from God.

'I hear you are off to France for a few weeks Andrew?' Constance said looking up at him with a bewitching smile.

'Yes, to stay with Mirandol, an old friend of mine from childhood days.'

'Did I ever meet him I wonder?'

'I don't think so.'

'I do hope you enjoy it, Andrew, it's so good for you to get away just now. Are you hoping to do some painting there?'

'That, amongst other things.'

'Bertie and I are still having thoughts about where we should spend our honeymoon. We both had thoughts about Italy but Mother says it's not very clean. We'll probably settle for something far more mundane, Scotland perhaps.'

'Scotland is very beautiful.' he said stiffly.

'Isn't it? All those lovely lochs and the mist on the braes. Have you met Bertie, Andrew, I must introduce you.'

'I met him earlier on, and now I must make my excuses, I have some packing to do, I'm off early in the morning.'

'Really, so soon?'

'I'm afraid so.'

Across the room he watched his mother and sister coping with the three little girls who had come down to parade their pretty dresses and later he watched their tantrums when one received more attention than the others.

Andrew was glad to escape to his room and start to pack. Tomorrow at this time he would be in Paris boarding his train for Dijon.

3

Andrew was not in a good mood. The steamer had been delayed because of bad weather in the Channel and he had missed the early train to Dijon on which his reserved seat had been booked. Consequently he must now travel on a later train and take pot luck with regard to seating.

A long argument at the ticket office had assured him that it was a very busy train. No, there were no reserved seats left, all the same a generous tip had persuaded his porter that there might just be one first-class carriage with room to spare and no children.

He strode along the platform in the wake of the perspiring porter pushing a trolley piled with his luggage. People stared at him curiously. He was so obviously an Englishman with his immaculate tweeds and deer-stalker hat, blond and striking, and wearing an air of authority. Due deference was paid to him by those who stepped aside to afford him a straight passage through the crowds.

The porter came at last to a compartment where two fashionably dressed women were conversing at the carriage door, and the porter indicated that this was the carriage he should occupy. An elderly cleric was already slumbering peacefully in the far corner, while Andrew piled his hand luggage on the rack overhead and took his place in the corner at the other end of the seat. Obviously one or both the women would be joining him, he only hoped they would finish their chattering on the platform instead of continuing it throughout the journey.

He could hear their conversation quite clearly from where he sat. Holidays in France since schooldays had given him a good grasp of the language, and listening to the two women talking he couldn't help repressing a smile. It would seem human nature was much the same all over, and it was evident the two women were sisters.

'Why don't you and Paul come home for the Wine Festival this year,' the stouter of the two was saying, 'Everybody wonders why you never come home, Surely he can't be busy all the time.'

'Oh but he is, and we like to take our holidays in the mountains. Really, Elise, I love you to spend some time with us in Paris but there is nothing now in Dijon for either me or Paul.'

'There is what's left of your family and your old friends. Monsieur le Vicomte has invited us to the château for the night of the Wine Festival. Everybody in the area who's anybody will be there, if he knows you're visiting he would extend his invitation I know.'

Her sister smiled dismissively. 'Like I said Elise, I doubt if Paul could be persuaded to come. Have you got all your parcels, that dress you bought at Marcel's will be just the thing for dinner at the château.'

'I doubt if it will be grand enough for that, you have no idea what it's like there, all the rich aristocratic people who are invited, and the gowns are sensational.'

'All purchased in Paris I have no doubt. There's nowhere to compare with Paris. Now you really must get into your compartment. Let me know what sort of a journey you have and give my love to everybody.'

Elise was more or less pushed into the compartment, and Andrew got to his feet to help her stow her parcels on the rack overhead. She took the opposite corner, and gave him a bright smile. Within seconds the train was pulling out of the station and she was waving her hand until her sister was lost to sight, then she settled back in her seat and he was left in little doubt that it was her intention to talk.

'This is always a busy train,' she commented, 'but I prefer it to the early one, there's always somebody on this train I can chat to. Are you staying in Dijon?'

'No, a few miles further on.'

'Really, so you will have to change trains at Dijon or perhaps you are being met.'

'I shall have to change trains and I expect to be met at the other end.'

'I hope this isn't a short visit and you are staying on for the Wine Festival. We make such a big thing of it in Burgundy. Have you been to the Dijon area before?'

'Yes, many times.'

'Then you will know the Château Mirandol. Oh but Monsieur le Vicomte makes much of the festival with house parties and banquets. Indeed my husband and I are invited to his banquet on the eve of the festival. My husband is the mayor of Dijon.'

Andrew smiled.

'You do know the Château Mirandol.'

'Yes of course.'

'And Monsieur le Vicomte, you perhaps know him also?'

'Yes, I have had that pleasure.'

'I was trying to persuade my sister to visit us at the time of the festival but it is impossible she tells me. Her husband is a policeman, very high up at the Sûreté Génerale of Paris. A very busy man no doubt, but my poor sister misses so much.'

So in a very short time the lady opposite had acquainted him with the fact that her husband was the mayor of Dijon and her brother-in-law an officer of considerable rank at the Sûreté. He groaned inwardly, but the lady had not done with him yet.

'I am intrigued, Monsieur, why does a young Englishman journey to the Dijon countryside at this time of year unless he visits friends. I know everyone there. I was born in Besançon, it could be that your friends are mine also.'

There was no help for it. 'My friend is the Vicomte de Mirandol, and his family.'

The lady beamed her pleasure. 'And I am Madame Grolan, mention my name to the Monsieur le Vicomte and he will confirm that he knows both my husband Maurice and his wife. Then we shall meet at the château, Monsieur, but you are travelling alone, does that mean that you are unmarried.'

'Yes Madame, I am unmarried.'

'Then we must see that you meet many pretty young French women. The Vicomte invites a great many of them to his house parties, you will not lack for feminine companionship, Monsieur.'

That was the moment that Andrew decided he did not want to stay at the château. There were many cottages near the château that the Vicomte made available to his friends. Indeed Mirandol's mother preferred to stay in one of them rather than with her son and his bevvy of friends at the château.

Madame Grolan was disposed to chatter on without his need to respond apart from the occasional word. He learned more about the prominent citizens of Dijon and the area from her than he had learned in many years of visits to his friend, and he was relieved with the Abbé came out of his slumber and she turned her attention on him.

'You've been sleeping since we left Paris, Monsieur l'Abbé, have you had a very tiring time there?' she said coyly, intimating that she knew the Abbé and possibly his reason for visiting the capital.

'Alas yes,' he said. 'The conference was trying, now I go home to my little church to relax.'

Turning to Andrew she said, 'Monsieur l'Abbé is well known in our district and he too will be a guest of Monsieur le Vicomte. This young

21

Englishman is a friend of Monsieur le Vicomte. You have not told me your name, Monsieur.'

'Andrew Martindale.'

'How charming. Mr Andrew Martindale?'

'Yes of course.'

Andrew had no intention of elaborating on his name. That he was the Hon. Andrew Martindale would have had her chattering to all her friends about him before he had the time to unpack his bags.

He was glad the Abbé had awakened since now they were able to converse without any participation from him. He leaned back against the cushions and closed his eyes. He was not asleep and in a little while he heard Madame Grolan say, 'Our companion is fast asleep, he has travelled a long way and must be very tired.'

He opened his eyes when the attendant came to inform them that lunch was being served in the dining car, hoping fervently that he might be permitted to dine alone.

The Abbé rose to his feet saying, 'Are you joining me, Madame Grolan?'

'Why no, if you will excuse me. My sister has made up a picnic for me. We have a very important function this evening so I did not wish to eat a large meal on the train.'

'Then you will not mind being left alone for a little while?' he said with a smile.

'Not at all. Will you be lunching also, Monsieur?' she asked Andrew.

He smiled. 'Yes, it is quite some time since I had something on the steamer.'

He walked behind the small rotund figure of the Abbé to the dining car and they were ushered to a table where they could sit opposite each other. The Abbé said apologetically, 'This is a very crowded train, I'm sorry if you would have preferred to dine alone.'

'No of course not.'

The Abbé's eyes twinkled behind his gold-rimmed spectacles. 'Madame le maire takes her duties very seriously indeed. Her husband is a worthy man and this is his third time of office, a most gratifying situation for his wife who has largely had to live in the shadow of her sister for many years.'

'The sister with the police officer who is very important at the Sûreté?' Andrew added with a smile.

'That one, yes. He was a young man in the police service in Dijon, very able and ambitious. He has done well to rise to such heights in Paris, and I have little doubt that his wife relishes his success.'

22

'This sort of thing happens in a great many families,' Andrew said, and the Abbé smiled. 'Alas yes. Humility is a great leveller, it is a pity that not all of us recognize it. May I be permitted to invite my English guest to a glass of excellent Burgundy?'

The meal passed pleasantly. The Abbé was a mine of information about Dijon and its environment and Andrew enjoyed his wry sense of humour and the mischief that twinkled in his sharp blue eyes.

They dawdled over their lunch, both of them seemingly reluctant to return to the chattering of Madame Grolan.

'What brings you to Burgundy?' the Abbé asked presently.

'The Vicomte de Mirandol is an old friend, we've known each other since we were children, and he has been a visitor at my home and I to his a great many times over the years.'

'And what do you intend to do to pass your time?' the Abbé persisted.

'I want to do some painting. I'm very much an amateur but I enjoy it and I've never attempted anything outside England.'

'The countryside is beautiful, but then so are the gardens of the Château Mirandol.'

'Yes of course, but I'm more interested in the countryside. I never feel the urge to paint the views or the house in England, better artists than I could ever be have done it justice.'

'Then you must make sure that Monsieur le Vicomte gives you time to yourself. He is a great one for entertaining and the Wine Festival gives him every opportunity. It is not for some time yet so when it happens you may be glad to lay aside your artist's palette and join in the festivities.'

'Perhaps.'

The Abbé did not need to probe as Madame Grolan had probed. This man was a student of human nature, he did not need to be told that Andrew was running away from a terrible disappointment, or a father's anger.

'I shall hope to see you again during your stay,' the Abbé said courteously. 'Are you interested in architecture, surely as an artist you must be?'

'Well yes. The château is very beautiful.'

'And the churches, Monsieur. There is the church of St Michel with its cupolas and its loggia, but you should go to the church of Notre Dame, a Gothic church, delicate in its structure like a jewel from whose terrace you can look out across the miles to where Mont Blanc sparkles in the distance.'

'I shall do that with pleasure, Monsieur l'Abbé.'

They finished their lunch in contented agreement then reluctantly

23

returned to their compartment where Madame Grolan greeted them with a bright smile.

It was four o'clock in the city of Dijon and at the Convent of St Agnes, Sister Emelda was already ringing the bell set high up in the soaring tower to denote that school was over for another day, and indeed for that summer term.

The army of girls walked decorously down the stone steps from the classrooms to the sunlit square where Sister Marthe waited to give them her usual stricture.

'You will walk in an orderly file until you need to separate,' she admonished them. 'There will be no shouting, no laughter, you will demonstrate to the good people of Dijon that you are St Agnes girls,' and if the girls smiled and nudged each other her shortsighted eyes were unaware of it behind her spectacles.

Two other nuns stood at the gates to open them, then the girls filed out in an orderly procession, a pretty sight in their light navy dresses and white organdie collars, each girl wearing a cream straw boater on her head adorned with a navy-blue ribbon which cascaded on to their shoulders; some carrying their valises, carriages were waiting to pick up some of them, whilst others walked sedately on until the bend in the road, when they broke up into laughing groups and ran joyously along the street.

Here they went their separate ways to their homes and only one girl ran towards the railway station to await the arrival of the little country train that would take her to her home. Joyously she snatched off her hat and her glossy blue-black hair caught the breeze and blew its shining halo around a face so beautiful that all who passed smiled in admiration.

Marie Claire was in love with life: with the people strolling along the streets of the old town; with the bells ringing from the old churches, and the late afternoon sunlight falling on cobbled squares and red tiled roofs.

There were so may things to be happy about. Her family who lived in a pretty farmhouse in the shadow of the Château Mirandol, parents who rejoiced in her beauty and her cleverness, because Marie Claire had been the winner of the scholarship to study at the Convent of St Agnes and she was amongst its brightest pupils. She was ambitious. She wanted to go to university – to the Sorbonne, no less. It had been known for a few women to do this. And she had so many friends at the convent, girls who admired her beauty, her sunny disposition and her brightness.

On that golden afternoon not a single cloud appeared to dampen

24

her enthusiasm for life as she ran down the station steps, clutching her valise with one hand, her straw boater with the other. Soon now the train from Paris would come steaming into the station on its way to Switzerland, and this was the moment she had looked forward to all afternoon.

One day, she told herself, she would live in Paris. She would be a passenger on that train arriving home from Paris. She would be wearing clothes from some expensive salon, and her arms would be filled with gifts for her family from exclusive shops on exclusive boulevards.

She loved to watch the passengers alighting from the train. Visitors and citizens alike, they had a glamour for the country girl who had never ventured further than the city of Dijon from her small village.

Only a few people waited on the platform and Marie Claire knew most of them. There was Madame Piccarde the dressmaker who came regularly to Dijon to buy thread and material for her trade, and Henri Gasparde who was a little younger than herself and a student at a boys' school in Dijon. He favoured her with a toothy smile, and to her relief showed no interest in joining her. Marie Claire preferred to travel alone and daydream about what she would do in Paris in some distant summer. At fifteen years old dreaming came easy to the girl whose only problems were exceedingly trivial.

The long transcontinental train steamed slowly into the station. All along its length doors were being opened and porters were walking the platform in anticipation that some passenger might require them.

Where did they all go to in Paris? the girl wondered: men carrying leather portfolios, women with children looking round eagerly for friends or family, then one woman in particular caught her attention, a plump woman in grey moiré silk, wearing a large dark rose hat on her dark hair, assisted on to the platform with her luggage by a tall slender man in tweeds and the smaller figure of the Abbé Fauriel who came often to the convent of St Agnes.

She watched them shake hands formally, the tall man bowed courteously, the Abbé took several of her parcels and walked beside her along the platform. He smiled at the girl, recognizing her instantly as one of the girls who decorated his church most charmingly whenever the convent's choir sang there. Eyeing the subject of his smile Madame le maire frowned at the straw hat swinging nonchalantly in her hands, and hastily Marie Claire placed it on her head and lowered her eyes in her blushing face. The Abbé smiled, and his companion swept onwards, still frowning. Really there should be some sense of decorum. That scholarship girl should observe the rules which governed young ladies: you never took off your hat in the street.

Madame Grolan served on the Board of Governors of the convent school and kept abreast of everything that went on there. She had been averse to a scholarship going to a girl who did not live in the city, she had been overruled, but that did not mean that the girl could run wild – discipline had to be adhered to.

Marie Claire waited until the Mayor's wife passed through the ticket turnstile before snatching off her hat for a second time. To the girls of St Agnes, Madame le maire was a figure of fun with her large ornamental hats and overbearing manner. Now compartment doors were being slammed shut and slowly the train crawled out of the station, gathering speed as it reached the bend in the track on its way to Lausanne. Only a handful of people waited now for the local train to Autan. The tall man who lounged gracefully against a lamp standard, in his immaculate tweeds, and with his air of superiority. He reminded her of Monsieur le Vicomte de Mirandol whom she had seen often riding in his carriage along the lanes near the farmhouse, she smiled to herself thinking that her mother would label him instantly as an aristo.

In only minutes the country train arrived and Marie Claire ran to a compartment far enough away from Henri Gasparde. She reached the door at the same time as the foreign gentleman, who courteously held it open for her. He had the most charming smile, a smile that made her feel suddenly grown up. They were joined by a woman carrying a crate of pigeons and a ginger-haired boy who promptly put out his tongue at her. As a product of St Agnes Convent she knew that she should have ignored him contemptuously, but she waited until he was settled next to his mother before she responded in kind. The exchange of insults might have gone on had she not caught sight of the gentleman's amused glance, so she turned her head and stared resolutely out of the window for the rest of the journey.

At Autan the door was once more held open for them to alight. The crate of pigeons was taken from the woman and placed on the platform while the boy, ignoring the steps, jumped down. After an impatient shake by his mother they walked together to the station's exit and Marie Claire hung back to see where the gentleman was going, not entirely surprised to see that an open carriage awaited him outside the station and that the driver immediately helped him load his luggage before they drove off quickly in the direction of the château.

A visitor for the Vicomte, now that would be something to tell the family when she got home, that a visitor for the Vicomte had held open the carriage door for her and helped her down from the train.

Her sister Margot would say she was giving herself airs as usual, but the rest of them would smile, her father in particular. Marie Claire was well aware that in her father's eyes she could do no wrong.

4

Jules Moreau leaned over a fence and gazed contentedly across his fields, thinking that God had indeed been good to him. Here he was with his own farm paid for by his own industry and worked by his willing wife, himself and their children.

It is true he would like to have been blessed with sons instead of three daughters, but Jeanne the eldest had married a local boy who was a good worker and true son of the soil. His daughter Margot's husband was a different kettle of fish, a layabout, with too much fondness for the village wine cellars and the wenches who worked in them.

Margot was blind to his faults and in the cause of domestic harmony he seldom showed his annoyance in her presence, but he still had a great deal to be thankful for.

As he sauntered down the lane towards his farm his eyes fell on the stretch of yellow sunflowers, so tall that they seemed to vie with the intense blue of the summer sky. Every year he vowed to sow a different crop, so that he could plant potatoes, but Marie Claire wanted her sunflowers, the first thing she looked for when she walked from the station to the farm. She would never forgive him if he changed the crop.

She would be home soon. He liked to sit outside the farm house where he could look down the road and see her climbing over the stile, waving her hand gaily, her hair a raven halo around her rosy face. How could he and his pleasant homely wife ever have produced anything so beautiful as Marie Claire with her porcelain skin and jade green eyes, her delicate slender grace and her cleverness. When he listened to her telling him that one day she would go to a university he believed her. When he saw the enthusiasm shining in her jewelled eyes, as shining as chipped jade, how could he not believe her.

He sat in his old comfortable rocking chair gazing out across his fields, smiling at his wife who came to place a glass of red wine on the table by his chair.

Marie Claire walked to where she could see her brother-in-law Marc Perréz working patiently in the fields. His round rugged face lit up with a smile when he saw her and she went to pat the old horse standing in front of the piled wooden cart.

'So school's over for the next few weeks, you'll be helping me to dig potatoes now will you?'

When she laughed he went on, 'But of course not; not Marie Claire who is going to go to a university!'

'You don't think I can, do you?' she smiled.

'I think, Chérie, that you can do anything you set your heart on. Did you see that brother-in-law of mine as you passed through the village?'

'No, but then I wasn't expecting to see him.'

'Two and a half hours he's been away, shopping for provisions or so he said, he's more likely to be found in the wine cellar with his light of love.'

'Don't say that Marc, you don't know, and Margot would be hurt by it.'

'I wouldn't say it to her, would I, but here am I working my fingers to the bone and he's out there doing nothing. I can't understand why your father doesn't get rid of him.'

'How can he without hurting Margot?'

'I suppose not.'

'You'll get your reward one day Marc.'

'How? How will I get my reward?'

'The farm. Papa'll never leave any of it to Marcel and I don't want any part of it. It will go to you and Jeanne.'

'You've got it all worked out have you, Chérie. I never count my chickens before they're hatched and that Marcel is a plausible rogue.'

'And Papa is no fool. He knows how hard you and Jeanne work, you'll see. One day he'll reward you.'

He grinned at her, his round cheerful face shining with perspiration. 'You get off home now,' he advised her, 'or your father'll be thinking it's me that has kept you chattering here. He'll be waitin' for you, sitting in that old rocking chair of his.'

With a gay wave of her hand she was off, running across the fields, her black hair streaming in the breeze.

Her father sat with closed eyes and she bent down to kiss the top of his head.

'You're not asleep Papa,' she said. 'I know you've been watching for me.'

He pretended to snore, and giving him a little shake she said, 'All right then, I'm going into the kitchen if you won't talk to me.'

The threat was strong enough to make him open his eyes and favour her with a broad smile. His beautiful Marie Claire who could always bring a smile to his face and joy to his heart. She sat on the wooden stool beside his chair talking about the convent, the nuns who taught her and her many friends, and all the time he sat smiling and sagely nodding his head.

'And who got off the Paris train today?' he asked with a wry smile.

'The Abbé Fauriel. He smiled at me, he must have remembered me from the choir at Christmas, oh and Madame le maire, with so many parcels and wearing a very large hat. You knew her once, didn't you Papa?'

'Oh yes, I knew her, but she wouldn't want to remember when she was plain Elise Surec living in that old clockmender's shop at the end of the street. That's what her father did, he was a clockmender and now his wife has so many airs and graces because both her daughters have married well. I knew them all, the sister's husband when he was a humble gendarme walking the streets of Dijon, and Maurice Grolan long before he was made mayor.'

Marie Claire loved to hear her father talking about the old times and the people he had known before they were somebody. She often wished that her father had aspired to being somebody better than a farmer, but once when she had voiced her views to her mother her mother had said sharply, 'You should be ashamed of yourself Marie Claire, and your father with his own farm, his own fields and not owing a centime to anybody.'

Her father asked, 'And who else got off the Paris train, nobody else of note?'

'There was a man who caught the country train and sat in my carriage. I don't think he was French and he was met at the station with a carriage from the château.'

'He's come early for the Wine Festival then.'

'He was very handsome.'

Her father laughed. 'And what would you know about foreign gentlemen being handsome or not. If he's up at the château we're not likely to be seeing him.'

'No, I suppose not.'

She gazed out across the fields thoughtfully. They seldom saw the visitors to the Château Mirandol but they heard about the revelries from servants and gardeners who lived in the village and when Madame la Vicomtesse visited her son they saw her driving in her carriage or walking her dogs.

Once Marie Claire had rescued one of her dogs when he got caught up in the brambles below the bridge and when she returned him to his mistress, the Vicomtesse had thanked her charmingly and reaching in her purse had presented her with the most exquisitely embroidered handkerchief Marie Claire had ever seen. She had never used it and it remained pressed between the pages of her prayer book.

'And did you see either of my sons-in-law working in the fields?' her father enquired.

'Marc was there, Papa. He works so hard and so cheerfully,' she enthused, 'not like Marcel who is never around.'

Her father nodded but said nothing. When be berated Marcel for his indolence he had to reckon with his daughter Margot's temper and because she was still besotted with her wastrel of a husband, even after six years of marriage, it made life very uncomfortable.

One day, after he had gone, Marc would be rewarded for his industry. The farm would belong to him and to Jeanne and it wouldn't matter if there were sulks and ill feeling, he wouldn't have to listen to it. As for Marie Claire, well she wouldn't have to listen to it either, Marie Claire would be somebody in Paris, somebody everybody else looked up to.

The girl jumped to her feet, favouring her father with her warm sweet smile.

'I'd better see if I can help in the kitchen,' she said, 'or Margot will say I never do anything around the farm.'

'Just tell her you can't be in two places at once Chérie, school and here,' he said, and with another smile she walked quickly on into the house.

She placed her suitcase on the floor, hearing sounds of activity coming from the kitchen at the back. Her mother was busy at the sink while Jeanne was setting out crockery on the long pine table. They both looked up when she entered and her mother said briefly, 'Oh here you are, school finished for the summer then? The eggs need collecting Marie Claire. You're late home, aren't you?'

'I was chatting with Papa and I spent a few minutes with Marc in the field. Where's Margot?'

'Gone down to the village,' her mother said shortly. 'It's a fine thing when a wife has to go looking for her husband who is supposed to be bringing home groceries I asked for hours ago.'

Jeanne smiled at Marie sympathetically. The evening ahead of them promised to be anything but harmonious. Their mother looked harassed, her face was flushed, and her dark hair hung in bedraggled tendrils around her once pretty face. She looked more careworn than usual, Marie Claire reflected as she took the basket her mother handed to her and set out for the poultry roosts.

Life during the week at the convent of St Agnes was a haven of peace but at weekends there was seldom anything peaceful about life at the farm. It was always Marcel and Margot. If they were not at loggerheads with each other they were quarrelling with some other member of the family, either with Marc or with herself.

Margot had always resented her. That she was going to school in Dijon, that she was doing well there and that she was pretty. Margot had forgotten how to be pretty. Most of the time there was discontented frown on her face and she had put on so much weight recently all her clothes seemed far too tight for her.

Jeanne said she ate too much, largely as a comfort against her husband's shortcomings, and then of course she had been jealous of Jeanne's baby boy. Marcel did not like children, and adamantly said there was enough wailing in the house from one child he had no intentions of fathering another.

Marie Claire who occupied the bedroom next door had heard their quarrels, as she tried to sleep with her head buried in her pillow, her hands over her ears.

Margot called him a fool. Saying it was Jeanne and Marc who would be rewarded for producing an heir to the farm, but Marcel screamed at her, saying he didn't give a toss about the farm, and when the time came they'd be well out of it.

She paused on her way to gaze down at baby Henri sleeping peacefully in his cot outside the side door. He was such a beautiful baby, she could not imagine how Margot or Marcel couldn't help but love him. She was only halfway across the cobbled yard when the gate opened and Marcel came through, wearing a sulky expression and followed by Margot saying sarcastically, 'Doing something useful for a change then!'

When she got back to the kitchen her father had already taken his place at the head of the table and her mother had placed a large platter in front of him containing a still sizzling piece of veal and as he picked up the carving knife they took their places round the table.

Marcel sat next to her, a fact that brought a glower to his wife's face from across the table. As the plates were passed around she became aware that under the table his leg had made contact with hers and she edged away so violently that the bowl of potatoes she was holding almost spilled on to the table.

'What is the matter with you?' Margot said angrily, 'If you sat up straight in your chair you wouldn't spill things.'

His leg moved away and they started to eat, then surreptitiously she became aware of his hand exploring her knee and she sprang to her feet crying, 'I need a handkerchief, please excuse me.'

She was trembling as she ran out of the kitchen. She didn't want to go back but what could she say to the others? It had happened once before when he had come across her in her favourite place in the sunflower field, then he put his arms round her and kissed her mouth, rubbing his hands against her breasts, then he had told her if she told anybody he would say it was her fault, that she had asked for it.

She looked up startled when Jeanne entered the room and she opened her satchel and started to rummage inside it.

'Is something wrong Marie Claire?' her sister asked quietly.

She hadn't realized how much she was trembling, and her sister came to put an arm round her shoulders. 'It's Marcel isn't it?' she said.

She nodded mutely.

'Do you want me to tell Papa?'

'Oh no please, it'll be trouble. You know what Margot's like about Marcel.'

'Then perhaps I should tell Marc.'

'No please Jeanne, perhaps he'll stop now.'

Together the two girls went back to the kitchen and after glaring at Marcel with a long hard look, Jeanne sat down and Marie Claire resumed her place at the table. He turned his head and grinned at her so that she lowered her head, aware that her face was blushing furiously.

Marcel was aware of his wife's dark hostile eyes across the table and he forced himself to stare back airily before saying lightly, 'Have you had any more thoughts on the sunflower field then? That field's capable of producing some fine crops.'

Marie Claire looked up in dismay. 'Papa you mustn't,' she cried, 'You promised.'

'We don't get much for the seed,' Margot cried, 'Marcel's right, the land could be put to better use.'

'Since when have either you or Marcel been concerned about what the fields are used for?' Marc cried adamantly.

'Well of course we care,' Margot said firmly. 'They're Papa's fields, he can do what he likes with them.'

'Well, up to now he's been content to grow sunflowers,' Marc retorted.

'And he's not making as much money as he could – turnips would pay better,' Margot went on.

Distraught, Marie Claire leapt to her feet and ran out into the farmyard. There were tears in her eyes as she ran helter skelter down the hill and across the field until in the distance she could see a field glowing yellow in the evening sunlight, a field where tall golden sunflowers reached up against the bright blue sky, great showy flowers standing tall and straight above their dark green leaves, their waxen petals hardly stirring in the warm wind that swept across the fields and she ran across to the stile from where she could gaze out across the most precious vista in her entire life.

Ever since she could remember this was the place to which she had come to weep or celebrate, to pour out her joys and her woes to the field of bold yellow flowers.

She loved her family, she loved the farm, but the sunflower field was always her special place. Without it the summer would not seem the same. She sat looking miserably across the field, unaware that she was not alone, until she felt her hand being taken in her father's deeply furrowed one.

'In a few years, love, when you get to Paris and become something big there, you'll forget about the sunflowers, there'll be other things to make you happy. Until then we'll always have our sunflowers,' he said firmly.

'You mean that Papa, you really mean it?'

'When have you even known your papa to say something he doesn't mean.'

'But Marcel could persuade you perhaps.'

'Not him. Do you really think anything Marcel could say would make me break my promise to you? He's no good at working the fields as they are, anyway.'

She smiled through her tears, throwing her arms around his neck and kissing his cheek.

'Oh thank you, thank you Papa. I don't like sitting next to him at the table.'

'Why, what has he done?' her father asked sharply.

Gathering her wits together she answered, 'He's mean and sarcastic. Like he was about the sunflowers.'

'Take no notice of him then. Tomorrow you must sit next to me, and he must sit next to his wife.'

Her heart lifted. Tomorrow would be like old times before Marcel had come into the family. She would ignore him and there was nothing he could do!

Innocence and experience were a long way apart and Marie Claire had a great deal to learn about life and people, particularly men.

Marcel was not one to give up lightly. When she went to collect the eggs he was behind her, when she went into the village he accompanied her on some pretence or other, and finally it was Jeanne who threatened to tell her father if it continued.

'What are you talking about?' he said sulkily. 'I've got a wife who is a woman, you surely don't think I'd be bothered with a silly schoolgirl. I'm trying to look after the girl, and if she's said anything different she's lying.'

'I'm warning you,' Jeanne snapped. 'If you touch her again I shall tell Marc, he'll soon sort you out.'

'And what will he do? Nothing. He'll not risk a family squabble, there's too much at stake.'

'I'm warning you Marcel, Papa will listen to Marie Claire and Marc even if Margot refuses to hear anything's wrong with you.'

'She's a good loyal wife is Margot, worth a hundred of you or Marie Claire.'

'Try to remember it then when you're chasing round after half the girls in the village, and laying your ugly paws on my sister.'

Marie Claire had watched him slamming out of the kitchen, his shoulders hunched, his face dark with anger, and she counted the days ahead before she need return to the convent.

Her escape and her joy was the field of sunflowers. Here she could dream her fantasies. The apartment in Paris on one of its fashionable boulevards. The galleries and the salons, the perfumed fashion houses the opera, and the Friday afternoon journey on the train to Dijon to see her family. There would be convent girls standing on the platform watching the passengers alight, and she would smile at them graciously. They would know who she was of course, Marie Claire Moreau, the famous Marie Claire Moreau who had once been a convent girl herself and was now . . . She hadn't quite made up her mind about which path her future would take, but it would be something wonderful and unique in a man's world, that much she was sure of.

Madame le maire would be enchanted to invite her to her soirées when she entertained other local dignitaries, and it was she Marie Claire who would be invited by the Reverend Mother to present the end-of-term prizes to her special pupils, not the lady mayoress.

It was heavenly to dream in the warm golden sunlight surrounded by stately sunflowers. Marie Claire had no difficulty in pretending they were her admiring audience.

5

André had been looking forward to greeting Andrew but it had not taken him long to realize that his friend was not a happy man.

Across the table laden with silver and crystal he surmised that his friend was hardly in a holiday mood. For most of their meal he had listened to Andrew bemoaning the fact that the love of his life was to marry another, a man old enough to be her father, but a baron, and that he was not measuring up to what his father expected of his son.

He allowed his thoughts to wander, aware that Andrew would hardly notice if they did. They went back a long way, since they were nine years old when he had met Andrew on holiday with his mother and younger brother in Trouville.

André had been there with his mother who loved Trouville, while his father was elsewhere happily spending time with whatever light of love he delighted in at the moment. At Trouville his mother could indulge herself at the fashionable race tracks, in the ballrooms and salons and always on the arm of some suitable gentleman who afforded her the adoration so lacking in her spouse.

To their hotel had come the Countess of Westmond with two of her boys. The younger recovering from an attack of measles, the older boy largely ignored and left very much to his own devices.

The two ladies exchanged pleasantries. The French lady was more than delighted that her son had a found a friend, particularly as his tutor was a very personable young man who seemed nothing loath to transfer his attentions from her son to herself.

The English lady seemed totally concerned with her younger son, a sickly boy who clung to her for attention and showed little interest in leaving her side.

Together André and Andrew rode their horses along the sands, and explored the shell pools left by the tide. They sat on the cliffs and told each other stories of their respective lives, lives cushioned by aristocratic wealth but with totally different ways of spending it.

Andrew talked about his home, a vast mansion crippled by death duties where his father was forever moaning that there was never enough money to keep it up! That he had an older brother who would one day hold the title and who was hoping to go into the army in his father's old regiment.

He talked about Winchester where he was at school and winters when the local gentry hunted the fox and summers when the men played cricket and the women played croquet on smooth green lawns, or went on holidays where there were sailing regattas or polo matches.

André talked to Andrew about his father's château which would one day along with the title belong to him. He spoke of snow-clad mountains and winter days on the ski slopes of Chamonix, of the wine festival when the rich red grapes had ripened and the full bodied wines of Burgundy were identified into famous vintages.

At the end of the holiday they made promises to each other that their friendship would continue, that they would visit each other's homes, spend other holidays together, and their mothers looked on indulgently.

Andrew was unsure that his friend would enjoy a holiday in England. His father was stern, had a lot to say about foreigners from anywhere under the sun and his older brother was an undeniable braggard, while Daniel was a mother's boy. Still he hoped André would accept the invitation, he had liked being with the French boy who had seemed a relaxed and uninhibited individual.

André wasn't sure what Andrew would make of the free and easy atmosphere of the château. His father liked entertaining his guests, guests which more often than not included his lady friend of the moment, and his mother who unpredictably could receive the lady with considerable charm or cynical detachment. Like Andrew, however, he hoped their friendship would continue. Now twenty years on here he was, albeit a little bored, listening to Andrew's list of calamities.

He had spent summer weeks visiting the country seat of the Earls of Westmond and Christmas holidays in their London home in Belgravia. Andrew had explained to him the intricacies of the game of cricket which bored him to tears, the long intervals when it seemed nothing happened, and then the sudden bursts of excitement that seemed to André to come so seldom.

He had ridden with the local hunt on a cold December morning when frost clung to the branches of the trees and his breath froze on the still air. He had been caught up in the excitement of hunting pinks and yapping fox hounds, impatient steeds and red-faced waiters from

36

the local hostelry carrying laden trays to the riders clustered in the yard of the inn. He had sat on the river's bank watching river races, white flannels and blazers, straw boaters and girls in frilly white dresses, and he had wondered what Andrew would make of the informal gatherings for the wine festival.

Andrew had loved the mountains and become an expert skier. He had told André on many occasions that those holidays in the snows of Chamonix had been among the happiest of his life. He had loved the dense fir forest and the grandeur of the snow-covered mountains. He had loved cooking fresh trout over charcoal fires outside a log cabin but always at the end of their time together it was Andrew who had been the more reluctant to return home.

André was trying to remember if he had ever met Constance Fallon. Andrew's description was that of a man in love; a goddess, blonde and beautiful with eyes the colour of sapphires and a figure of matchless grace. His bitterness was painful to see, but a more sophisticated André could not understand how he had continued to idolize a woman who was only interested in marrying a man for his title and his money, a woman who had turned him down because he didn't have either.

When he had more or less said as much, Andrew had looked at him pityingly, saying, 'I knew you wouldn't understand, you French are different!'

They were different. He thought about Andrew's father who asked his sons to address him as Sir. A stern hard man who laid down rules for all his sons, and for his wife. Even Daniel had gone into the army at his father's instigation, and strangely enough it had been Andrew who had refused to conform.

His own father had laid down no rules that he had failed to obey himself. He was not the ladies' man his father had been, but if there had been women in his life he had not as yet found one he wanted to marry. Andrew's father had pushed his eldest son into marriage in order to secure an heir, the fact that there was as yet no heir from that union was ironic to say the least.

Daniel had shown little interest in women and Andrew was mourning the loss of a girl his father had considered unsuitable anyway. His thoughts strayed to Lady Vivienne.

He had enjoyed a long hot summer dalliance with Vivienne and had been enchanted by her. She was beautiful and spirited, and too much like her father. Materialistic André knew he would not ask her to marry him, and by the same token he knew marriage with him would not please her father. He was foreign, he was French, besides, her father would want a hand in his only daughter's choice of a husband.

They had gone their separate ways but he often thought about her, far more than any other woman he had known. One day when Andrew had talked enough about Constance Fallon he would ask about Vivienne.

He yawned delicately and Andrew said quickly, 'I'm sorry André. You must be bored to death listening to all my woes. I have gone on a bit, haven't I?'

André merely smiled, and Andrew went on, 'Have you made any plans for these next few days?'

'Not really. I realized when you wrote to me that you had a reason for coming here. I'm busy on the estate at this time of year, but you do whatever you wish. The grape harvesting isn't for some months yet.'

'I'm not sure how long I can stay, I don't want to put you out, but at the moment I'm hardly in the mood for festivals of any kind.'

'I have a great many guests staying here at the château, and guests who come to dine. We could shake you out of your lethargy.'

'I met a woman on the train who assured me you could.'

'Oh, who was that?'

'She told me her husband was the Mayor of Dijon.'

'Ah, Madame Grolan. Yes, she would delight in looking round for a suitable lady and she knows everybody in Dijon she considers worth knowing. Her husband is decent enough, she is a formidable woman.'

'There was a priest on the train also, an Abbé Fauriel. They seemed to know one another.'

'But of course. The Abbé Fauriel will also be a guest here, but perhaps not on the same evening.'

'It is most decent of you to invite me, and please don't think I am being ungracious but I came here to do some serious painting. My father says my paintings are rubbish, I thought that perhaps just once I might paint something worthwhile. The countryside here is beautiful, the views of the distant alps are wonderful, I might find some inspiration to do something even my father would approve of.'

'And if you enter into the spirit of the wine festival you couldn't do that? Is that what you are saying my friend?'

'I remember that your mother liked to stay at a cottage on the estate and I am risking your thinking it an impertinence of me if I ask for one also.'

André smiled. 'My mother's cottage is vacant and will be for some time. My mother is not coming for the festival, she is in Paris and enjoying herself. The cottage is charming and I can let you have servants and arrange for meals to be taken down there for you.'

'No indeed, I wouldn't ask you to do that. I don't need a servant, and I can cook whatever I need. Perhaps there is a farm that can supply me with produce?'

'Of course, there is the Moreau farm nearby. They would supply you with milk and eggs, indeed anything else you require, and if you get lonely the château's here and I'll be glad to see you.'

Andrew beamed his pleasure.

'I can't thank you enough André. You have no idea how much I shall enjoy just doing the things I want to do, even looking after myself.'

'I'll send somebody down to clean the cottage although I'm sure it is perfectly habitable now. I'll have fires lit, it's months since my mother occupied it. Your room here is ready for tonight, tomorrow you will have your own abode. You will forgive me if I don't go down to the cottage with you but this is a very busy time for me. Unfortunately I must go to Paris, my visit there is long overdue.'

'What do you do in Paris?' Andrew asked with a smile.

'Talk business with my lawyer and my accountant, spend some time with my mother.'

'How is Madame la Vicomtesse?'

'Very well. I marvel how much energy she has for her vast array of interests. My mother enjoys perpetual youth.'

'She's wonderful.'

'Even more wonderful since my father died. They went their separate ways and seemed happy to do so, and yet when he was ill for two years before he died she was totally devoted. Very cynically I told myself that it was remorse, but now I really believe their affection for each other was genuine. Who am I to stand judgement?'

'There have been many times when I have wondered how my mother could ever have married my father. He's always been a despot. She's never been able to instil any tolerance into him against his will, but still she makes excuses for him, against all her better judgement I feel sure.'

'Shall we take a turn around the gardens, the Italian gardens are particularly fine this year,' André said, and the two men rose to their feet and walked out of the room. They were both tall, both handsome, but very different. Andrew had all an Englishman's Saxon fairness, while André was dark with a thin whimsical face and intense dark eyes. Vivienne had once remarked to her brother that he had the most romantic profile in the world and Andrew had accused her of being in love with him.

They strolled along the paths of the Italian gardens while the domes and turrets of the château rose behind them like some medieval enchanted castle in an old fairytale.

They stood at last looking back from the brow of the stone bridge that crossed the stream and Andrew said musingly, 'I can imagine knights in shining armour riding up to the château and waiting for them would be beautiful women in tall pointed hats and floating ethereal draperies.'

André smiled. 'That's how I saw your home in England. Jousting on the downs below the house and some brave knight riding forward to receive his token from the fairest lady in the land.'

'You have the Château Mirandol André, Blaire will never be mine. One day it will go to John and God knows where I'll go.'

'You resent that, don't you?'

'I shouldn't. I've always known about it, but I can't help it. I love the house, it's my home. Whether I marry or not one day I've got to find somewhere else. Suppose you'd had an elder brother, wouldn't you have minded?'

'I've never thought about it. It never occurred to me.'

'I suppose not.'

'The problem applies equally to your brother Daniel and to Vivienne. Do you know how they feel about it?'

'Daniel won't mind. He doesn't particularly like the house, he prefers the one in Bath. Vivienne will marry, it's up to her husband to provide her home.'

'And who will she marry, has she made up her mind?'

'One never really knows with Vivienne, I thought perhaps that one day you and she might get together.'

'Ah no my friend, much as I adore her and admire her, I am a lot like my father. When I marry, if I marry, it will be to a woman with all my mother's tolerance, or long-suffering acquiescence.'

'You are expecting rather a lot from some poor woman.'

'Hardly. She will live in this beautiful place, I shall shower her with jewels and anything else she may require, all I ask in return is that she allows me to be myself. I should hate to be smothered with attention.'

Andrew laughed. 'Why is it the French and the British see life so differently. We brush things under the carpet that a Frenchman or woman might think perfectly natural.'

'Well of course. And how you agonize over trivialities my friend. Life would be so much gayer all round if you didn't take yourselves so seriously.'

His eyes were gleaming mischievously and Andrew smiled. His friends words were full of banter, but in them he recognized a certain degree of truth. His father wouldn't know gaiety if it stared him in the face, and he would want a similar sort of man to marry his only daughter.

'Will you take up residence in the cottage tomorrow evening?' André asked. 'Everything will be ready for you then?'

'Yes, that would be splendid.'

'Then I suggest we return to the house and drink a glass of my most prized red Burgundy. I expect you're tired after your journey.'

Andrew had to admit that he was tired. Not so much from the events of the day but as a result of the few days that had gone before. His mother's insistence on the party atmosphere at the house in Bath, the forced conversations with people he had little in common with, and behind it all his father's disapproval that he was leaving for France and the uncertainty of how long he intended to stay here.

He drove to the cottage with André the following evening just as the sun was sinking in a great red ball in the west. They had dined together and André had informed him that his luggage had been taken down, there was food in the cupboards and a housemaid would change his linen and bring it up to the château for laundering. He had asked that the local farm should supply him with anything he needed and he would be left alone to do precisely what he wanted. If he did want company he knew where to find his friend.

He thanked André warmly, and sat back to enjoy the drive along the ordered paths lined by willows and oleander. The cottage, if one could call it a cottage, was more in keeping with a small manor house. Built in warm stone it stood surrounded by a garden of flowering shrubs and stone arbours covered with climbing plants and there was a pretty summerhouse with leaded windows.

Andrew's face beamed with pleasure.

'It's beautiful André. I must have seen it before.'

André shrugged his shoulders. 'Perhaps you wouldn't remember it. We never had occasion to come here and when you stayed at the château most of the time the cottage stood here quite empty.'

'I can understand your mother liking it.'

'You may find that she has left something behind, just put it aside or ignore it.'

'I shall enjoy painting in the garden here.'

André looked around him curiously. 'What will you paint? There is the garden of course, and the cottage itself, but you would be well advised to wander the countryside. Inside the cottage you'll find that a good many people have painted the garden, their efforts are hung on the walls.'

Andrew laughed. 'I never wanted to paint Blaire, it had been done so many times and so well. My father would have compared my poor efforts drastically.'

He watched his friend's carriage drive away before he let himself

41

into the cottage then stood for a few minutes looking round him with evident delight.

Brought up in large lofty rooms where the warmth of the fire never seemed to reach beyond the hearthrug, rooms hung with portraits of long-dead ancestors and priceless paintings of gloomy Scottish lochs or long naval battles by famous artists, rooms filled with marble busts of Ancient Roman senators or more recent composers, with priceless porcelain and gleaming with polished walnut, and now here was a room with gentle delicacy. Walls hung with water-colours, carpeted in pale green and everywhere pastel chintz. Undeniably French, and overall there lingered a floral perfume which Andrew immediately attributed to its last occupier, the Vicomte's mother.

Delightedly he wandered through the rooms of the cottage. The large serviceable kitchen and the bedroom where he found more mementoes of André's mother, her cashmere shawl draped over the back of a chair, her heavily embossed silver brushes bearing the initials H de M, Hélène de Mirandol, and here again he was aware of the delicate fragrance of mimosa.

The only sounds came from the birds singing in the trees outside the windows and he unpacked quickly so that he could explore further the delights of his home for the next few weeks at least.

In the kitchen he discovered fresh milk and bread. In the cupboards were potatoes and cheeses, coffee and a ham, certainly enough to make a modest meal for himself and he had already dined well at the château.

He laid out his artist's equipment on the kitchen table. He had brought several canvasses with him and oil painting equipment and new brushes, enough at any rate to keep him busy for several days, all he had to do now was find a subject to paint, and he wandered out into the living room to look at the water-colours adorning the walls. They were good, all of them by accomplished artists and Andrew was honest enough to know that he had accomplished nothing half as good as any of them. For a few minutes he began to accept his inadequacy, then squaring his shoulders he vowed silently to prove himself.

He took a stroll around the garden in search of some ideal place to erect his easel but quickly realized there was no aspect in the garden which he wished to paint. The summer house was pretty with its climbing tendrils of clematis. Honeysuckle ran riot across the hedges and water lilies bloomed profusely across the pond. It was scenery that had all been painted again and again, expertly and sympathetically.

He strolled back to the cottage in time to see a man he recognized as a servant from the château carrying a crate of wine. The man smiled, setting down the crate at the door and enquiring where he should leave it.

Andrew thanked him, saying that he would attend to it himself, but as he made to enter the cottage other footsteps came along the path and this time his gaze encountered a large man accompanied by a lurcher dog. The man touched his beret respectfully saying, 'I'm Jules Moreau, Monsieur, from the farm. I was asked to supply you with anything you need and already I sent milk and a ham and cheeses, is there anything else you wish for?'

'Well yes, eggs I think, and I take it you will supply milk every morning and anything else I should need?'

'Yes of course. I'll send the eggs tomorrow.'

The man's gaze was sweeping across the garden, taking in the easel Andrew had left leaning against the fence and with a little smile said, 'You're an artist, Monsieur?'

'An amateur of modest talent.'

'My daughter Marie Claire would tell you where to paint, she goes out into the field with her water-colours every day.'

'Then I must talk to her and find out where I can expect to find some view to paint.'

'My son-in-law will bring the eggs. As for Marie Claire, she's a will-o'-the-wisp, we never know two minutes together where she can be found.'

Andrew smiled. It was obvious that Marie Claire was the apple of her father's eye and needed to be shielded from such as he.

In the days that followed Andrew made several attempts to sketch in the garden but, discouraged, he left his oils alone. Again and again his eyes scanned the water-colours on the cottage walls, water-colours depicting the garden in every season, the gold of summer, the red of autumn, the green of spring and winter when frost sparkled in the trees and the pond lay frozen.

He never saw who delivered the produce from the farm, they came very early and after the first week it seemed to Andrew that he was living in a world devoid of human habitation, a cool green world where he lived with his memories and where the future lay shrouded in uncertainty.

6

In the days that followed Andrew tramped the poplar-lined country roads, beside gentle undulating fields, and lanes around the château, and craggy outcrops from where he could look down on the great house and small homesteads. It was on a day where the morning mist lingered and he sat with his back against a rock while he ate his modest lunch of bread and cheese. He had with him a small sketching pad and a pouch filled with pencils, disappointed that he had discovered nothing worthy of his oil paints.

Suddenly the sun burst forth in a blaze of gold, and the mist evaporated in its glow so that below him the fields with their grazing cattle came suddenly to life and in the distance he became aware of a field glowing with gold. He thought it was a field of rape, but something drew him towards it. The startling difference between the fresh green of the fields, the darker green of the trees and suddenly the piercing yellow.

He scrambled down the hillside, his footsteps quickening in anticipation and it was only when he crossed the stile and the field lay before him that he stared at it incredulously. Never in his life had he seen a field filled with sunflowers, tall and proud, their golden heads open to the sun, huge yellow flowers adorned with golden centres amid their dark green leaves.

He circled the field suddenly aware of the familiar feeling of disappointment that there was nothing here he wanted to paint, sunflowers were hardly his favourite flowers. He walked on towards the gate and then he saw her sitting on a bank, her black hair flowing softly in the breeze, her arms hugging her knees, her face gazing raptly out across the still flower heads.

He paused, enchanted, thinking that this was a picture he had been searching for all his life, a picture no artist had ever painted, a picture that could make him famous.

He stood still, hardly daring to breathe in case the girl vanished and he was left with the feeling that she had only existed in his imagination. She sat so still, totally absorbed by the showy flowers spread out before her and then she turned to pick something up from the grass and he saw that it was a small sketch pad similar to his own which she laid on her lap and with a pencil poised in her hand she stared thoughtfully at the flowers.

He strolled over to where she was sitting, anxious not to startle her and as his shadow fell across the grass she looked up into his face. In that split second her beauty made him draw his breath sharply. She possessed the most exquisite face he had ever seen. Dark raven black hair vied with eyes the colour of chipped jade, and a mouth curving exquisitely over small even white teeth in an enchanting smile.

'Good morning Monsieur, you have come to sketch my flowers?'

He smiled. 'You speak to me in English, why is that?'

Her smile widened. 'But you are English Monsieur, I saw you on the train from Dijon, I remembered you.'

'Of course. The lady with the pigeons, you and the boy. You live here?'

'Yes, my father owns the farm which supplies you with milk and other things you need.'

'You speak remarkably good English.'

'Thank you Monsieur, you are most kind. I learn it at school.'

'And school is in Dijon?'

'The convent of St Agnes.'

'And you are Marie Claire?'

She stared at him in surprise. 'How do you know my name?'

'Your father told me he had a daughter who went into the fields every day to paint. I can see that you've brought your water-colours.'

'My father talks about me to everybody he meets, I am sometimes afraid that he asks too much of me.'

'I'm sure he doesn't. Would you mind if I join you?'

Smiling she made room for him on the bank beside her.

Instead of drawing, he watched her pencilling a solitary flower and after a while she looked up to say, 'You're not drawing Monsieur.'

'I prefer to watch you.'

'It is not very good.'

'It is very good, do you intend to paint it in water-colours?'

She shook her head. 'Water-colours are not right for sunflowers, they are too bold, but I suppose I will paint them. Why aren't you working?'

'I would like to paint them in oils, oils would do them more justice but I do not have them with me this morning. Perhaps tomorrow I'll bring them and make a start on a picture.'

Her eyes shone. 'Oh yes, that would be wonderful, a great big canvas all bright yellow and green.'

'I would really like to paint you sitting here gazing out across the field, would you mind?'

'I'm not sure. Would it not take a very long time to paint a picture like that? I do not know if I could come here every day.'

'I could do some sketches of you sitting here, you shall tell me if they are good enough.'

'How long will you be staying in the cottage?' she surprised him by asking.

'I'm not sure, weeks, perhaps months, I'm not sure.'

'You are a friend of Monsieur le Comte.'

'A very old friend.'

'Why do you not stay with him at the château then.'

'Because I came to paint something like this. If I had stayed with him at the château I doubt if I would ever have found this field or an enchanting young lady to inspire my picture.'

She laughed. 'What will you call your picture?'

'I'm not sure, perhaps you will help me, "Girl amid the Sunflowers" perhaps.'

'The Sunflower Girl. That is what I would call it.'

'Then that is what it will be, The Sunflower Girl.'

The new incentive in Andrew's life brought a smile to his lips and a spring to his step as every morning he set off with his oils and canvas for the Sunflower field. Marie Claire was always there, helping him to set up his easel and chair, sitting on the grass at his feet, watching avidly as he worked.

None of his pictures had come to life as this one did, and the summer days passed by. Marie Claire was as enraptured with his work as he was himself and the canvas came alive with colours of gold and green, the summer sky a haze of blue, cloudless as the sky above them.

'What do you think of it?' he asked her anxiously, 'I want you in the picture but I'm not sure where I can put you.'

'On the little hill where you first saw me,' she volunteered.

'I'm not sure. The flowers would be overpowering, and I want you to be the focus in the painting.'

'Perhaps the stile, sometimes I sit there where I can feel the wind in my hair.'

'Then let us try the stile by all means.'

So Marie Claire took her place on the stile and her pale blue cotton dress flowed around her ankles in the breeze and the breeze caught her hair in a raven halo around her lovely face. Andrew caught his breath sharply, she was too beautiful this girl who had brought the

46

laughter back to his lips and the benison to his wounded pride. Marie Claire was not popular with her sister Margot.

'Where do you go to every morning when you could help in the house or on the land. There are beds to be made and vegetables to prepare, it is unfair that you have everything and do nothing in return.'

Marie Claire had looked at her doubtfully, but her father had said 'leave the girl alone, she'll be returning to her studies soon enough.'

So Marie Claire made a parcel of her school books and whenever she went out she took the parcel with her. Her parents smiled approvingly at her industry.

Andrew made sketches of Marie Claire sitting on the fence, and in the evening after his meal he looked at his picture anxiously for the right place to introduce her. He was working on it one night when he heard the sound of thunder rolling across the countryside and sudden flashes of lightning spasmodically lit up the room.

Before he retired for the night he heard the pattering of rain on the windows and outside in the garden the trees rustled angrily in the sharp wind that had arisen. Above the sound of the rain and the thunder he heard the sound of a horse's hooves and carriage wheels, and before he got to the door it was flung open and his friend was inside laughing and shaking the rain from his cape.

Andrew was glad that he had had the foresight to put away the picture. He did not want André asking questions about his model, amused that he had found a beautiful companion to help him idle away his days.

'You are comfortable here my friend?' André asked as Andrew handed him a glass of burgundy. 'I am sorry not to have seen more of you but I have unfortunately to go back to Paris in the morning. Why don't you come with me?'

'A large city is the last place I wish to be in right now,' Andrew prevaricated. 'I am happy here, I love the solitude and I am painting.'

'You found something worthy of your talent then?'

'My modest talent. I have found several things I wish to paint. Why do you have to go back to Paris?'

'To see my lawyer, and my mother. I could not go without reassuring myself that my guest was happy here.'

'Well now you can go with good grace, and my blessing.'

The two men sat chatting for an hour or so, until the thunder that rumbled overhead retreated in the distance and the rain lessened.

'This is the season for summer storms,' André explained. 'There are likely to be more of them, but they are good for the vines and between the storms the sun shines as warmly as ever.'

Andrew stood at the gate until his friend had driven away then he went inside the cottage and locked the door.

He lay on his back looking through the window. A pale moon had risen over the tree tops illuminating the garden with silver, but the rain came again and dark clouds obliterated the stately moon. If the storm persisted into the morning there would be no meeting with Marie Claire and he felt strangely disconcerted that he minded so much.

At the farmhouse Marie Claire sat in the window seat in her bedroom gazing out across the fields. She was hating the rain, pleading with God to stop it long before the morning so that she could see Andrew, finding an excuse to go out when the paths were muddy and the sunflowers would be hanging their heavy heads dejectedly under leaden skies.

It was still raining when she heard the farm around her coming to life, the crowing of the rooster, the lowing of the cattle and from the kitchen below the homely sound of crockery and occasional voices. She jumped out of bed and ran to the window.

Dark clouds hung low over the fields and then she saw Marc crossing the yard accompanied by the old dog. He was wearing a raincoat and an ancient sou-wester, and the dog slunk inside the barn out of the driving rain.

Her father would be pleased that the rain had come. The land was dry, the fields crying out for rain, but although she knew it would be short-lived she hated everything and anything that might keep her away from meeting Andrew. Marie Claire had never been in love before and even now she hardly recognized it as love. She only knew his sudden sweet smile made her heart race, bringing the rich red blood into her cheeks, a tremble to her hands.

She refused to think that one day he would go away, back to England and a life far different from her own. He would come back, hadn't he said he had visited the Vicomte a great many times, but where would she be the next time he came to Burgundy? She had told him about her ambitions and he had encouraged her but what were ambitions when her heart was crying out for him to love her. To Marie Claire at sixteen ambitions had suddenly become trivial while love was paramount. She sat on the window seat hugging her knees. She had huddled with her friends at the convent, as they imagined what it would be like to be loved. There had been whisperings and giggling, and occasionally one of the nuns had entered the room telling them sharply to keep quiet, glaring at them angrily so that they felt contrite, ashamed of thoughts that no nun would ever dream about.

She had talked about love without any vision of who she would love. Someone tall and dark, very handsome. The girls all had the same ideas, but when she saw Andrew stepping off the Paris train she had known then that this was the sort of man she would love, and fate had been kind in bringing them together.

Marie Claire was a great believer in providence. The nuns had taught her to pray for the good and decent things in life. She had prayed for her parents and her sisters and their husbands, for the animals on the farm and the prosperity her father was working so hard for. God had answered her prayers. Her parents were healthy and happy, the farm was prospering, and if Margot and Marcel were not exactly what she had hoped for, at least Margot could see nothing wrong with him. Now it would seem God had brought Andrew into her life and it was blessed to love, or so she had always been led to believe.

Without ceremony her bedroom door was thrown open and Margot was there saying acidly, 'You won't be able to go out this morning, it's raining. There are a good many things you can do here.'

'It won't rain all day.'

'Well it's raining now and I want some help in the bedrooms.'

'I'll be glad to help you Margot.'

'Breakfast is ready. What are you doing sitting there staring out at the rain, the fields are crying out for it.'

Obediently she followed her sister down the stairs and into the kitchen where her mother and Jeanne were busy at the stove and the men were seated at the table.

She helped carry food to the table, taking care to sit next to her father and disdaining to meet Marcel's cynical grin.

Watched over by her sisters she swept and dusted and made beds, but always with an ear to the sound of rain against the windows, and anguished stares at the pools in the farmyard and the steady downpour that enlarged them. It seemed only the ducks were happy as they waddled noisily towards the pool where once stagnant water was turning into a rippling pond.

She visualized Andrew sitting at the cottage window staring dismally out at the leaden skies, disconsolate and hating it as much as she was.

In actual fact Andrew was philosophical about the weather. He was more concerned that his sketch of Marie Claire was hardly doing her justice. The pose was right, the colouring of her hair and costume fair enough, but there was something missing. He had yet to capture the haunting delicacy of her face.

Sketching Marie Claire from a distance was not enough, he needed to study her face more closely so that her beauty became the real subject in his painting, not the sunflowers. Meanwhile at the farmhouse Marie Claire was being given petticoats to mend and socks to darn and in some desperation she said, 'I'm so tired of being indoors, can't I deliver milk or eggs or something?'

'And get drenched at the same time.' Margot snapped.

'I can wear my raincoat.'

Nobody spoke and biting her lip angrily she went on with her darning, wishing her father would come home.

It was late in the afternoon when the rain abated somewhat and her mother said, 'If you want to help with the deliveries Marie Claire, there is milk wanted at the cottage and eggs. Do you know where it is?'

'Oh yes Mama, the Vicomte's cottage through the trees?'

'Yes, but hurry back. If the young man is out leave the basket on the doorstep.'

Marie Claire prayed that he would not be out. It was hardly likely on such a day but he might have grown tired of sitting in the cottage looking at the rain.

Andrew smiled as he took the basket from her, inviting her in, where she stood looking at the picture and his sketch of her.

'You are happy with it?' she asked him.

'I'm happy with the picture but not with the sketch I did of you. I would really like you to sit on the arm of that chair as if it was the stile, and I can draw that elusive something that is missing. Can you stay for a little while?'

'No. Mama said I must hurry back.'

He smiled. 'Is there an art shop in Dijon where I can purchase one or two things I'm short of. You know Dijon, don't you Marie Claire?'

'There is such a shop in Rue le Creseau. When will you go to Dijon?'

'Tomorrow perhaps if the rain continues.'

'Perhaps I could go with you.'

He smiled ruefully. 'And how do you propose to do that, what would you tell your mother?'

'I can think of something. I will try. Will you go in the morning?'

'Yes. There is a train at ten o'clock.'

'Then I will try to be at the station before then. I could show you where to find the shop, I could show you all Dijon.'

He laughed. He thought it highly unlikely that Marie Claire would be allowed to go to Dijon, and recognizing the disbelief in his expression she said quickly, 'I have many friends in Dijon, I would tell my mother that I am tired of the rain and I would like to visit them.'

'I really don't want to be a part of such a deception my dear.'

'But it is true. I am tired of the rain.'

'And your friends?'

'You are my friend.'

She smiled at him and in the next moment she was running down the path towards the gate, turning to wave to him as she let herself out.

Flattered and troubled in turn, Andrew was unsure how he could handle this friendship with a girl young enough almost to be his daughter. That she had a girlish infatuation for him he was well aware but he had no conception of the depth of her feelings. He was sure she would not be able to go to Dijon with him the next day, she had already told him that her parents were strict with her and that her sisters, particularly her sister Margot, were constantly demanding that she do more at the farm to help.

Marie Claire had no such misgivings. She broached the subject over the evening meal, directing her request to her father.

'I'm so tired of the rain Papa, I would like to go into Dijon tomorrow to see some of my friends, please may I go?'

'Have they asked you to visit them?' her mother asked sharply.

'But of course. All of them on the day we left for the holidays. We shall miss you Marie Claire and September is such a long time away they all said, particularly Diane. She is my best friend.'

'But what about her parents, they have not asked you?'

'But they have Mama, so many times. All I shall need is my train fare.'

'You cannot expect your friends' parents to feed you when they have not invited you tomorrow. Write to them, ask them if you can visit next week.'

'Oh Mama, next week the sun could be shining and I love it here, it is only because there is nothing to do here when it is raining. In Dijon there are the parks and the museums, the art galleries and the beautiful churches.'

'And here there is the cleaning to be done, and the cooking, the poultry to be cared for and all the things we are expected to do,' Margot said angrily.

Marie Claire turned her beautiful eyes upon her father appealingly. 'Please Papa, this is my holiday, all I am asking is just one day, the dusting and the cooking will be here waiting for me.'

Her father smiled indulgently. 'Let the child go, but you shall not go without money. Your train fare and enough for your food if you are eating with your friends in the city.'

Marie Claire rejoiced that it had all been so easy. Tomorrow she would spend all day with Andrew, she would show him all the beautiful things in Dijon, Notre-Dame church and the church of St Michel, the narrow winding streets behind the Grande Taverne where he would buy his artist's materials, and she prayed that the rain would end so that from the terrace of the cathedral they could look upon the white pristine perfection of Mont Blanc, omnipotent among the distant range of mountains.

51

7

There were many times in later years when Andrew looked back on the day he spent with Marie Claire in the city of Dijon, and always his expression grew tender, his eyes warmer.

She had danced by his side like quick silver, her beautiful face alive with joy, her lilting voice enchanting him with her enthusiasm about the city.

Marie Claire thought that she had never spent such a day. It had all been so different with her schoolfriends, watched over by Sister Teresa, their history teacher. Now she was the teacher, showing Andrew all the things she had found interesting, delighted that she knew enough about them to be informative.

They ate in Dijon's best hotel and he smiled at her expression. Large green eyes surveyed the opulent dining room with excited wonder, and all around them the hum of conversation went on and Marie Claire smiled at him across the table. Andrew was aware that they were the object of interest to many of the other diners, but then Marie Claire would always be an enchantment and even the women at the nearby tables were smiling indulgently at her smiling face and wide-eyed excitement.

It was only when they were boarding their train for the journey home that her enthusiasm waned. Her beautiful day was over, Andrew would return to his cottage and she to the farm: there might never be another day when he could belong to her exclusively.

In desperation she told herself that she had lied to her parents once, if she lied to them again God's punishment would only be the same.

'I could come with you to the cottage, you could do that sketch of me sitting on the arm of a chair, you know, the one you told me about yesterday.'

'But your parents will expect you to go straight home, Marie Claire, they will be worried about you.'

'No no, they will think I have stayed with my friends, they expected me to stay with my friends.'

If there were suddenly warning bells ringing in Andrew's head he ignored them. He would do his sketch, work on the picture, and while Marie Claire slept in the small bedroom he would finish it so that she could see it completed in the morning. Then she would watch while he signed his name on the finished result and he would cook breakfast for them so that she could go home as if she had stepped off the morning train.

As they left the train Marie Claire whispered, 'I will wait until everybody has left the station then I will come to you, do not wait for me please, Andrew, there is no need.'

He felt strangely amused. He had never expected at his age to be nonchalantly ordering a cab to drive him to the cottage, knowing that somewhere in the background lurked a pretty schoolgirl determinedly ignoring his existence.

In the meantime Marie Claire was anxiously trying to avoid the eyes of the station master who was a friend of her father. She walked in the shadow of Monsieur Cladel, hoping that his considerable bulk would disguise her presence, but she need not have worried, the station master was in deep conversation with an elderly lady who was a shopkeeper in the village. She was not worried about Monsieur Cladel. He was shortsighted, and only recognized people he bumped into.

Outside the station she took to her heels and ran along the road, never stopping until she reached the tree-lined path that led eventually to Andrew's cottage. By the time she got there Andrew had made tea and brought out a large chocolate cake cooked for him by the Vicomte's cook up at the château.

It was excitement she had never dreamed about. They chatted and laughed together, and the lies she had had to tell gave an added excitement to the adventure. Before the night was over she would know if Andrew loved her as much as she loved him. She had no thoughts of where they would go from there, there was nothing in Marie Claire's thoughts beyond the passions of the moment. Neither of them could look into the future and see the anguish and trauma that lay ahead.

While she washed the cups and saucers and Andrew put out his easel and all he would need for an evening's work she fantasized to herself that this is how it would be. She would be his model as well as the lady of the house and he would be a famous artist acknowledged by the world.

It would be the picture of her in the sunflower field that would make him famous, but he would never tire of painting her, in the garden, on the beach at Trouville, in the Lavender fields of Provence. Her face would smile back at the world from a hundred pictures. Poor Papa, he would have to forget his ambitions for her. He would have to be happy that fame had come to her in a far more womanly way.

He set her up on the arm of a chair so that he could visualize the stile with her voile dress drifting in the breeze, and his pencil began to capture all the enchantment of her face.

She watched him work, the concentration that brought a frown to his brow, and then the sudden swift smile when his drawing came to life.

He looked up and she asked breathlessly, 'Is it right, are you pleased?'

He nodded. 'It's almost there, now I can put it in the picture and the colour will bring it to life. You can come and look at it if you like.'

She jumped down and went to stand beside him.

In a small voice she asked, 'Am I really so pretty, is that really how you see me?'

'I'm only afraid that I haven't made you pretty enough.'

'Oh, but it is beautiful, the picture will be beautiful.' She was gazing up at him and in her eyes was all the love and admiration he had been telling himself for days he had imagined.

He looked away quickly, busying himself with the sketch pad and pencils, and in a small hurt voice she asked plaintively, 'Andrew, do you never want to make love to me?'

He stared down at her disconcerted. He would not have been a man if he had turned away, but some vague threat of chivalry still remained: she was too young, too vulnerable and too untried. He thought about Constance, then in the next moment he thought about her older fiancé for whom she had scorned him. It was that sudden recollection of them together that made him reach out for her, and then she was in his arms and he was kissing her mouth, her eyes, her hair.

This was how she had imagined it, the ecstasy, the sweeping passion, even the hurt when they lay together on the couch and she screamed with pain as she felt the hardness of his maleness before he entered her.

It was not perfect. She wept with the pain, while he soothed and petted her, assuring her that it would be better the next time, and then with her heart soaring with joy she could only think that there would be a next time.

The pain was still there in the morning, but by the time she had walked to the farm it had gone, and she felt a great sense of relief that there was nobody in the kitchen. She was not ready yet for their questions, they would come later when she felt composed to deal with them.

In her room she flung herself on her bed but all her thoughts were on the night before, his passion and his tenderness. All sorts of silly thoughts entered her head: had she been a good lover or had she been too untried, too afraid? Had there been other women who had pleased him more?

When she heard the sound of voices below she changed hurriedly out of her best city dress, stuffing her underwear in the bottom of a drawer and quickly changed into clean cotton underwear and a dress she wore around the farm. Her face looked pale in the mirror so she pinched her cheeks to bring the colour into them then after lightly brushing her hair she went downstairs.

When the eyes of her mother and sisters appraised her it seemed to Marie Claire that they already knew her secret, but Margot merely said, 'So you're back, you didn't say you intended to stay in Dijon all night.'

How easy it was becoming to lie and lie and lie. To chat about friends she had not seen, to enthuse about an overnight stay in one of their houses and her mother smiled indulgently while Margot continued to scowl, unimpressed by the tales of the welcome she had received.

Andrew had finished his picture and it was drying in the sun-filled room. She looked at it every day, admiringly, and he stood with his arm around her, delighting in her praise.

They seldom met in the sunflower field now because she preferred instead to go to the cottage. There they could sit in the summer house and she would talk about all her father wanted for her. It was only when he encouraged her that she became unsure because nothing now was important, only her love and the things they would do together in a future they would share.

All Marie Claire wanted was to talk and make love, to make his meals and watch him eat them, loud in his praise of her cooking even on those days when the pastry was burnt and the chicken could have done with extra cooking. Food was unimportant, Marie Claire's mission was to get it over quickly so that they could make love.

She longed to ask him how long he would stay at the cottage – he had told her he would probably stay as long as the wine festival lasted, but would he take her with him when he left, or how long would it be before he returned?'

Her summer holiday was nearing its end and there was talk in the farm about what awaited her at the convent of St Agnes. Marie Claire neither knew nor cared. Andrew would explain to her parents, and they would warm to his charm, to the sweetness of his smile, hide their disappointment and give them their blessing.

All she knew about Andrew's home was that he had parents and two brothers. The brothers were in the British army and serving in India, that much he had told her, but he did not want to talk about his home or his family. This little time, he told her, was for her alone.

The sunny weather had come back to the fields of Burgundy and her feet hardly seemed to touch the ground as she ran towards the cottage. She was later than usual. Margot had insisted that she sweep the bedroom floors and help her fold the newly laundered sheets. Even Jeanne had remonstrated over her sulky face, but in the end the work was done and she had run away from the farm as though her very life depended on it.

At the cottage gate she paused uncertainly at the sight of the Vicomte's horse tethered to a tree trunk. She knew it was his horse because she had often seen him riding it across the fields, now she had to wait in the hope that he would conduct his business quickly and leave.

She walked back along the path, sitting sheltered by the trees where she could not be seen, and time passed so slowly, what could they have to talk about that would keep him there so long?

Inside the cottage the two men sat over a glass of wine, and Andrew stared down dismally at the message his friend had brought. It was in the form of a cable, terse, uninformative, but saying simply. 'Imperative you return home at once. Martindale.'

It was like his father to give no explanation. A few words from him and he thought they would be sufficient to send Andrew scurrying back, and it was probably something and nothing, merely a ruse to make him conform and toe the family line.

When he said as much to his friend, André seemed unsure.

'What would you have done if you'd received such a cryptic message from your father?' Andrew demanded.

'My father would never have sent such a message, he would have explained why I had to return. This is typical of your father's highhanded attitude.'

'Don't I know it.' Andrew muttered. 'I suppose I'll have to do as he asks, does it put you out at all?'

'Actually I would have had to ask you to return to the château at the beginning of September. My mother is arriving.'

'Then perhaps it is opportune that I leave you, you'll have me again I hope?'

'Of course, whenever you wish to come here. Will you return to England tomorrow?'

'I suppose so. It won't take me too long to pack, the afternoon train I think and I'll get the over-night steamer from Dieppe.'

The two men shook hands and André said, 'I'll send the carriage round for you in the early afternoon. Leave everything as it is here, there will be servants to clean it and remove any food you leave uneaten.'

Andrew thanked him warmly, before accompanying him to the door. He stood there while his friend mounted his horse and cantered through the gate and along the path leading to the château.

He was still standing there when Marie Claire emerged from her hiding place and ran towards him. For the first time a feeling of alarm traumatized him. Ahead lay the tearful farewells he anticipated, the parting he had refused to contemplate in his heart but which had suddenly been catapulted into the present.

One look at his serious face told her that something drastic had happened. Without speaking he handed her his father's cable, waiting for the astonished misery to cloud her expression, and the jade green eyes to suddenly fill with tears. In a small breathless voice she asked, 'Will you go?'

He took the cable from her and laid it on the table, then bringing her into the shelter of his arms he said softly, 'I must, Marie Claire.'

'But he has not said why you must go,' she argued. 'How can you obey without knowing why?'

'If you knew my father you would understand why. If the command is trivial and I had no need to return home then I'll come back. If it was necessary then I'll come back another time, soon, I promise you.'

'When will you go?'

'Tomorrow afternoon, the Vicomte will send his carriage for me.'

'So soon?'

'We have today, Marie Claire. Today we'll do whatever you wish.'

There was nothing she wished only the urgency of love and the ecstasy of their love-making made her forget the time, forget everything except that tomorrow there would be no Andrew, it was over.

She ran along the leafy lane when the moon was already high in the sky and as she neared the farm her misery at his leaving was replaced by the fear that her family would be deeply worried by her absence. Long before she reached the gate she could see her father and Marc walking along the path carrying lanterns and she ran towards them, her mind already frantically searching for excuses.

Her father took her by the shoulder, spinning her round to face him, and although there was relief in his voice there was also anger, and with her words tumbling one after the other she said, 'Papa I'm sorry, I fell asleep in the sunflower field and when I awoke it was already dark. There were strangers on the paths so I hid, waiting for them to go. They were quarrelling, it took so long, and then when I started to run along the path I sprained my ankle and had to limp.' For the rest of her journey home she had to remember to limp and Marc took hold of her hand, holding it firmly in his to help her.

The tale was repeated to the rest of them in the farmhouse, and her mother said sharply. 'What are strangers doing on the road near our fields, they could be stealing from us. Marcel and Marc must go out to see that everything is safe.'

Marcel was quick to say, 'If we'd heard anybody prowling about we'd have gone out, all we heard was silence. She probably fell asleep and imagined it.'

'I did not,' Marie Claire insisted. 'I saw them and I heard them.'

'Who were they then, men or women?' he demanded.

'Men, that is why I was afraid, why I hid and waited until they'd gone.'

After Marcel and Marc went out with their lanterns, her mother said, 'You've had nothing to eat since breakfast, sit there and eat, there is plenty of food on the table.'

'I'm not hungry, I don't want anything.'

'What have you eaten outside then?'

'Nothing, I'm not hungry, I'm just very tired. I shall go to bed.'

Four pairs of eyes were looking at her curiously and in a rush of contrition she said, 'I'm so tired Papa and I was so afraid out there, I took pears and an apple. My ankle hurts, I should go to bed and rest it.'

'What about your ankle?' her mother demanded, 'Let me see it.'

She held out her foot reluctantly, and after she had examined it her mother said, 'It isn't swollen, where does it hurt?'

'It aches all the time,' and placing her weight on it she winced and started to limp towards the stairs.

'I'll bring you a warm drink,' Jeanne assured her, 'Get into bed.'

She didn't want the warm drink, she wanted to be alone to wallow in misery and her memories of this last day with Andrew. She wanted to relive the joy of his arms around her, how she had matched sensation for sensation, touch for touch. As long as she lived there would never be anything to match the passion they had shared; to Marie Claire it was a unique thing, a passion he would never experience with any other woman, and one he would remember as long as he lived.

Marie Claire thought about Andrew lying awake at the cottage where he too would be reliving their last day together. His thoughts would be tender, anguished, thinking of a thousand reasons why he must return to France quickly, desperately praying that his father's command would turn out to be trivial.

Andrew was not asleep but he was not lying in his bed plagued by uncertainties. He sat slumped in his chair, a half-filled bottle of wine on the table in front of him, a glass filled with rich red Burgundy in his hands. He was not thinking of Marie Claire.

He was thinking back on the years of his childhood, followed by his schooldays when his overbearing father had ruled their lives like some medieval despot, when obedience had never been enough, when there had to be only blind obedience and when family pride had been all that mattered to his father.

Now he was going back to it, for some unknown reason his father had no doubt dreamed up to show him who was master. He looked bleary-eyed at his painting and the beautiful girl sitting on the stile looking out nostalgically across the sunflower field. It was then he thought about Marie Claire, her soft young body in his arms, her joyous youth and the worship in her eyes and the for the first time a feeling of guilt swept through him. He had made her love him, a sweet untried country girl whose only dream of love had been taken from the books she read, the girlish stumblings into an adult world she shared with other girls in that convent she attended. The young heal quickly, he told himself complacently. She would go back to the convent and her studies, fulfilling her ambitions so that in time she would forget his existence, and as she grew older and more sophisticated she would find other loves.

He decided it would be a great many years before he returned to Burgundy, when Marie Claire no longer lived at the farm across the fields, and when, if they accidentally met, she would look at him with a faint smile of surprise and a vague feeling that perhaps she should know him, that somewhere they might have met.

With that comforting thought he decided to finish the wine in his glass and go to bed. In the morning he would pack his suitcase and his painting materials. He would have to pack the picture very carefully, perhaps he would ask André if he had something at the château. The picture was good enough to persuade his father that he had not been wasting his time in Burgundy and that he might just have something to offer the world after all.

His sleep was entirely dreamless.

The next morning Marie Claire went out immediately after breakfast, much to the annoyance of Margot and the remonstrations of her mother who said she should not be walking about on a sprained ankle. She was careful to limp until the farm was hidden from her view then she ran as fast as her legs would carry her towards the cottage where she hid among the trees in the place where she had hidden the day before.

She saw servants arriving from the château, a man and two women, then she saw rugs being brushed outside, and shortly one of the women came out to hang sheets and other household linen. The man-servant left carrying Andrew's picture, returning in a little while carrying a slender box which she felt sure contained the picture expertly packed away. She longed for Andrew to come out into the garden so that she could look at him just once more, even when she must not go near him in case the servants saw her.

Andrew remained strangely elusive. In the early afternoon the servants went and then the Vicomte came riding his big bay horse and went inside the cottage.

She visualized the two men saying their farewells, then she heard the rumbling of carriage wheels and an open carriage arrived and pulled up at the front door. The driver went inside immediately returning minutes later to loan Andrew's luggage.

Her heart missed a beat when she saw Andrew and the Vicomte emerge into the sunlight. He was dressed for travelling, looking as he had done the first time she saw him waiting for the train at Dijon. Immaculate in English country tweeds, chatting amiably to his friend before they shook hands, then he was sitting in the carriage and she stood staring at him through the trees, waiting with tears rolling down her cheeks until the carriage was lost to sight through the quivering trees.

The Vicomte mounted his horse and rode back towards the château and Marie Claire strolled slowly along the lane until she came to the sunflower field. They did not know those brassy golden flowers, they did not care that they had been the start of all the trauma and tragedy that came after. Perhaps it was a blessing that at that moment Marie Claire was not aware of it either.

8

His father's autocratic demand that he return home immediately seemed hardly appropriate when Andrew viewed the peaceful park surrounding his home. Geraniums bloomed profusely in the great stone urns along the terrace, deer grazed peacefully under the trees and in the distance the tarn sparkled in the sunlight. It was a scene that had enchanted him since childhood.

He had told himself constantly over the years that he was apathetic about it, wearied by its sameness, but he knew in his heart he was only blasé about Blaire because it would never be his. This morning was no different, he viewed the great house and its gardens with studied boredom, coupled with an acute wariness that soon he must face his father with some degree of anger.

He paid the driver of the ramshackle carriage he had acquired at the railway station, leaving his luggage on the terrace to be collected later. Before he could find his doorkey the door was opened and Bayliss, the head footman, was holding it wide.

'I saw you arriving, my lord,' he said. 'I will see to your luggage.'

Andrew stared at his curiously. The 'my lord' could only be a slip of the tongue but Bayliss was running down the stairs to collect his luggage so Andrew crossed the hall towards the drawing room where the family usually congregated in the morning.

He opened the door, staring across the room at his sister sitting on the window seat looking out of the window, and his mother sitting on a couch gazing forlornly in front of her, and occasionally dabbing her eyes. His sister looked round, and getting up from her seat went over to her mother saying 'Mother, Andrew is here.'

His mother turned, then she was rushing across the room to throw her arms around him, her voice throaty with tears, 'Oh Andrew, thank God you've come, your father had to go up to London, he'll be back tonight.'

Over his mother's head his eyes met his sister's and Vivienne shook her head sadly. He drew his mother back to her seat and sat down beside her, holding her hands in his.

He waited patiently for the tears to subside. His sister had gone back to her seat at the window but her eyes were on them, waiting. At last his mother composed herself and holding his hands tightly in hers she said. 'We've had terrible news Andrew, it's John. Almost as soon as he got back to India, he caught cholera and died. There's been a most devastating epidemic there. Many of his fellow officers have also succumbed.'

Stunned, Andrew shook his head. 'Will they be buried there?'

'Yes. They have all been buried already. There is to be a memorial service here on Sunday, Charlotte and the children will be coming here tomorrow.'

'How is Charlotte?'

'Well of course she is absolutely devastated as we all are. You know what this means don't you Andrew, now you are a Viscount.'

Vivienne had left her seat at the window and stood behind them looking down. Her eyes suddenly hard, cynically amused. 'With all this and heaven too,' she said softly.

Ignoring her, Andrew said, 'Why is father in London, something to do with John's death?'

'There were things to see to, but he had to go to the House of Lords, some big debate going on he said. He'll want to talk to you as soon as he gets back.'

'I'm sure he will,' Andrew said dryly.

The tears flowed anew and Vivienne said evenly, 'How is André? Is he still escaping the bonds of matrimony?'

'For the moment. He is well, looking forward to the grape harvest and a houseful of guests. He spoke of you several times.'

Before she could think of an answer his mother said, 'How is Hélène, I should write to her?'

'She is well Mother, visiting very soon but she doesn't stay at the château.'

'I'm so very tired,' his mother went on. 'I haven't slept a wink since we heard about John and I don't want lunch. I shall go and lie down, there will just be the two of you for lunch.'

Lunch was a silent meal and Andrew was not hungry. He had eaten an early breakfast on the steamer and now the sight of the food placed in front of him only succeeded in nauseating him.

Vivienne too played with the food on her plate, pushing it on one side irritably. 'It isn't John,' she said sharply. 'Heaven knows we never got on, but he was my brother, I can't forget we were children together.'

'Any news of Daniel?'

'He represented father at John's funeral. He isn't coming home. I don't suppose he can get leave and things are pretty hectic in India.'

When Andrew remained silent she said, 'Are you thinking about all those years when father went on and on trying to persuade you to pick up the white man's burden. Why for heaven's sake, to surrender your youth to an impossible climate in the mistaken dream that you are helping the heathen, only to leave your bones rotting in a foreign field. How right you were to refuse to conform.'

'I don't feel very right at this moment Vivienne, I only feel I've fallen into shoes that were never meant to be mine.'

'It's fate Andrew. Remember when Grandfather died after that fall on the hunting field. I've never forgotten the bishop's words at his funeral "There is no armour against fate, death lays his icy hand on Kings."'

Across the table their eyes met and she smiled, and she reached out so that he could clasp her hand in his. 'Tell me about Burgundy,' she said. 'Does the château still stand like something out of The Sleeping Beauty; and do his eyes still smile in that dark attractive face. I loved him you know, and there were times when I thought he loved me.'

'Then why didn't you do something about it?'

'I thought he would be too much like his father, in love with too many women, too mercurial, and I couldn't have been like André's mother, accepting it, expecting it.' She smiled, her dark attractive smile that Andrew had always felt set her apart from other women that he knew. Vivienne would never settle for second best, she would go on looking for something and someone different, and as if she read his thoughts she said softly, 'Like I said Andrew, Hélène accepted it, I would have either killed her, him or myself.'

'I didn't see a lot of André, I stayed in the cottage and he was busy on the estate.'

'What did you do all day? You must have been terribly bored.'

'I told you I wanted to do some painting.'

'And did you?'

'I painted a picture. I've finished it but it will need varnishing and framing. I'll show you later.'

'Show me now. Are you pleased with it.'

'Yes, it's the best thing I've done.'

'Come on then, show me, then we'll take a turn around the park.'

His luggage had been taken up to his room where a servant had unpacked for him and put everything away. The case containing the picture lay unopened with his other materials on the floor.

Vivienne watched as he carefully opened the case, easing the picture out slowly before standing it on a low chest across from the window where the light fell on it. For a long moment they stood in silence, then Vivienne exclaimed, 'Andrew it's beautiful, wherever in Burgundy did you find a scene like that, and the girl, who is she?'

'A young girl from the farm, I found her sitting in the field looking at the sunflowers and trying to sketch them.'

'And such a beautiful girl,' she said softly.

'Yes. She was at school in Dijon.'

'A schoolgirl?'

'Yes,' he answered shortly, putting his artist's materials away in one of the cupboards while Vivienne went over to the picture, picking it up in her hands.

'She doesn't look much like a schoolgirl to me,' she said dryly.

'That's because she isn't wearing her school uniform. She went to school at the convent of St Agnes in Dijon and she had wonderful ambitions to be somebody someday.'

'You got to know her well.'

'We talked.'

'And you met every day in the field, she looked at the sunflowers and you looked at her?'

'Of course.'

'What did she think about it when you'd finished it?'

'She thought it was very good.'

'And André, what did he think about it?'

'He didn't see it, like I said, I saw very little of him and he wasn't interested in my painting anyway.'

'Wouldn't he have been interested in somebody as enchanting as this sunflower girl living on his land?'

'She didn't live on his land, her father owned the land the farm was built on. They were industrious, proud, but Marie Claire was the one receiving a really good education. They were all expecting great things of her.'

'Marie Claire! It's a very pretty name.'

'Yes.'

'Will you show the picture to father?'

'Not immediately, not at this time. Perhaps one day I'll show him.'

She looked down again at the picture. 'I've never seen sunflowers growing in a field like that, I've never really liked them. I always thought they were too loud, too big, but it's the girl, isn't it? They're so big and brassy and she's so delicate and elusively beautiful. Is that how you saw her Andrew?'

'Yes, that's exactly how I saw her.'

She replaced the picture on top of the chest. 'I need to get out for a while, Andrew, the house suffocates me and tonight Charlotte will be here with the children. It will be unadulterated gloom, nobody can engender that better than Charlotte.'

'I suppose the memorial service means that the church will be filled with all sorts of people on Sunday?' he said, ignoring talk of Charlotte.

'Well yes, there'll be representatives from John's regiment, friends and family as well as all those people who come to things of this sort because it's the thing to do.'

They were halfway across the lawn when they saw Charlotte's carriage coming through the gates and Vivienne said feelingly, 'Mother will cope. They'll be able to weep together, it's hard lines on the children who are probably too young to have taken it all in. If they'd had a son, you realize you wouldn't be the Viscount Darnley?'

'Well of course I realize it, and it wouldn't have mattered.'

'Well of course it would, Andrew, this is Vivienne you're talking to. It's always been there with both of us, the fact that one day John would have everything, you and Daniel wouldn't exactly be paupers and I would have to see that I married well, enough to keep my end up at any rate.'

'You're too cynical Viv, that's your trouble.'

'I know, but we both know, don't we, that I am speaking the truth.'

For a while they walked in silence then for a time they stood near the boat house watching the antics of the cygnets sailing in the wake of their parents.

'That would make a nice picture,' Vivienne remarked.

'I tried to paint them often, but somehow or other they never turned out right. Painting birds and animals is a field on its own.'

'But painting Marie Claire was a joy?'

'Well, the results are very gratifying.'

She smiled. She would get nothing out of Andrew, on the subject of Marie Claire perhaps there was nothing more to tell, but she was remembering the beginnings of a smile on the girl's exquisite face and the promise in her jade green eyes.

I'm getting to be a vindictive bitter old maid, she admonished herself, what does it matter where Andrew loves, or André for that matter.

Dinner that night was a harrowing affair. John's wife and her mother-in-law ate like sparrows and they wept copiously. The servants moved about on silent feet with morose expressions and when the butler addressed Andrew as 'my lord' Charlotte dissolved into such a flood of tears she abandoned her dinner and ran out of the room. She stayed out for several minutes, returning with tear-drenched eyes and an expression of stoic endurance.

'Were the children very tired when you arrived here?' Vivienne asked her.

'They were very distressed, it is only weeks since they saw their father alive and well, now he's dead. How can I make them understand?'

'Perhaps it's too soon Charlotte, in time they'll understand.'

'But they have to know, I want them at that service on Sunday, they have a right to be there.'

'Well of course, but isn't it all rather over their heads. Children won't really know what it's all about, it could be far too traumatic for them to cope with,' Vivienne persisted.

'That is for me to decide,' Charlotte persisted, and Lady Clarissa, said cautiously, 'We shouldn't influence Charlotte, Vivienne, she knows best how her children can cope.'

Vivienne personally didn't think Charlotte had any idea how to cope with her children. One minute she molly-coddled them so that they were impossibly spoiled, and in the next she was pushing them willy-nilly into an adult world in which they were bemused strangers. Her father might have something to say about the children going to the service, she hoped so.

Andrew viewed everything going on around the dining table in some sort of haze. In two short days his entire life had changed, two days ago there had been nothing beyond the cottage sheltered by tall trees and Marie Claire alive and ecstatic in his arms. His future had seemed like a wilderness unless somebody somewhere recognized his talent in the picture he had painted, now it really didn't matter. One day Blaire would be his and all that went with it. All the priceless treasures that Blaire contained and he could paint because it was something he liked to do, not something he relied on to bring him in an income.

Marie Claire would be unhappy but she was so young, in no time at all she would be thinking of examinations, the excitement of seeing more of the world, and she would not be untried in the ways of men. Marie Claire would not settle for a ne'er-do-well, not when she had been shown gentleness, tenderness and generosity at the hands of a British aristocrat.

Andrew was not a snob, but he prided himself on being an English gentleman, capable of showing a girl only the best things in life, and that day in Dijon had been an introduction to all that was best. His eyes warmed as he remembered her smile of delight as she had sat opposite him in Dijon's most exclusive hotel. That day he had been wishing with all his heart that he could show her Paris, Lauzanne and the mountains of Switzerland. One day she would see them with somebody else, and she would remember him.

The ladies had retired to bed but Andrew was still waiting for his father to arrive. He heard the sound of carriage wheels along the drive, just before midnight and braced himself for the meeting to come. The door was flung open unceremoniously and his father called out, 'I'll have a rum toddy in here,' and then seeing Andrew he said testily, 'So you've come back, have you?'

Andrew rose to his feet and the two men stared at each other across the room, then his father said testily, 'Put another log on the fire, these late summer evenings can get chilly.'

Andrew obliged, then his father said, 'Are you joining me in a rum toddy?'

'No Father, I'd prefer a whisky.'

'Oh well, help yourself, I suppose you've been put in the picture about events. Has Charlotte arrived?'

'Yes Father, this afternoon, with the children.'

'She should have left the children at home, grief and children are poor bedfellows.'

'The news about John is terrible, Father.'

'Terrible. Only been in the God-damned country a few weeks. Still I suppose it's on the cards if one goes into any of the services, I'd thought one day it might happen to Daniel, the boy never had the stomach for the army, but that it's happened to John is something none of us expected.'

'John was your favourite, Father.'

'I never had any favourites. It's only that John always conformed. He knew what he wanted out of life and he went all out for it.'

'He was born into it, Father. There never needed to be a choice.'

His father stared at him sourly, 'Wasn't that all the more reason why my second son should want to show us that he could do it on his own, but not with an artist's palette, lad. I tried to encourage you to join the army or the navy, and heaven knows you were always better than either of the other two at sport or riding.'

Andrew decided silence was the better part of valour, and his father went on. 'Even Daniel joined the Indian Army and I expected him to be the milk sop of the family. Sit down, I can't do with you standing there staring at me without saying a word.'

Andrew complied. 'There's to be a memorial service, Father?'

'Yes, and the church will be crowded with people who never even met him.'

'They'll be here out of respect to you and Mother, Sir.'

'I suppose so. I'll be glad when it's all over. I don't want the children at the service, I hope she's more sense than to suggest it.'

For several minutes there was silence, then the Earl said sharply, 'How's Mirandol?'

'Very well, very busy.'

'Not married?'

'No, Father.'

'Oh well, we all know what the French are like, he won't be short of women in his life.'

'I don't know. He's expecting his mother for the Wine Festival.'

'Handsome woman, Hélène. Went their own ways, Mirandol's parents, and somehow or other it worked for them. She liked Paris and the life at Trouville, he preferred Monte Carlo and Switzerland, shallow sort of existence they both led, how is she occupying her time now?'

'The same as ever I should imagine, flitting between Paris, Trouville and Burgundy.'

He was surprised at hearing his father's soft chuckle, 'And not alone I should imagine. Your mother used to tut-tut at all her escorts, all considerably younger than herself, all of them totally bemused by her. She certainly knew how to flatter and flirt, I'm surprised she isn't insisting that Mirandol finds himself a wife, he needs an heir. Who will it all go to if he dies young like your brother John?'

'He has cousins I believe, Father.'

'Cousins!'

'Well yes, several of them.'

'It's his duty to marry and sire a son. Surely there are some ripe blue-blooded French girls attending the vintage festival.'

'I expect so, I don't really know.'

'Well, I shall go to bed,' said the Earl. 'the next few days will be in limbo I'll be glad when they're over. I couldn't tell you in that cable what had happened, I could only ask you to come home immediately.'

'Yes Father, I see that now.'

'Goodnight then.'

'Goodnight, Sir.'

He stood on the hearthrug while his father walked to the door, thinking that he had aged in some strange elusive way since he walked with bowed shoulders, shuffling a little on the heavy oriental carpet. At the door he turned and fixing Andrew with a keen glance he said, 'That Fallon girl hasn't married her doddery baron yet, that mother of hers will be kicking herself now that she turned you down.'

Andrew didn't speak, and with a sardonic smile his father said, 'Don't be surprised if she doesn't come around, but remember that it won't please me if you rise to the occasion. Keep your pride lad, and show Miss Constance Fallon the door.'

'I hardly think she'll be within miles of Blaire, Father, she'll be too interested in her approaching marriage.'

'Let's hope so. Any man who marries that girl will have her mother like a millstone round his neck. That woman's simpering sweetness covers an ambition as wily as it is ruthless.'

The door closed behind him and Andrew realized that it had been weeks since he had thought about Constance Fallon, and it had taken a French schoolgirl and her field of sunflowers to obliterate her memory.

9

The cathedral was already crowded when the family made their way down the centre aisle on the morning of John's memorial service.

Andrew sat between his father and his sister-in-law who had insisted that the children should attend the service in honour of their father. Already they were fretful, the youngest entertaining herself by kicking the front of the family pew, the elder one standing up so that she could look at the congregation behind them.

Their piping trembly voices carried, and if those around them smiled indulgently the Earl's scowl of annoyance deepened.

The sermon, delivered by the bishop in his deep stentorian voice, eulogized dramatically on John's many virtues, his bravery, his modesty, his dedication to family, duty and love of country. Andrew failed to recognize many of these traits in his memory of his older brother. Modesty had not been one of John's strong points, indeed Andrew wryly suspected that the people who remembered him would be thinking of his pomposity, and his dedication to family had been given mainly from a distance.

That John had shown bravery in the face of danger he did not doubt and the bishop made the most of a young man being cut down in the flower of his youth in the cause of empire.

The children became more restless, the younger one started to cry so loudly that her nanny came from the back of the cathedral to take both girls out of the pew.

At last it was over, the last hymn was being sung, the final prayers said, and they were walking back along the aisle to the far distant door and all around them in crowded pews the congregation stood respectfully with bent heads. Outside the cathedral a strong wind was blowing and at the foot of the steps the carriages to take them back to the hall were already waiting.

The two little girls were brought back to their mother and the Earl said testily, 'They should have been left at home, this has been no place for children.'

'This is the morning they will remember when they're older.' Charlotte retorted, 'it is probably the memory of their father they will remember most of all.'

People known to them were now coming forward to express their sorrow and there was no time for further talk among themselves. Andrew was shaking hands with so many people he failed to put a name to a great many of their faces, then suddenly a voice he remembered made him look down sharply and he was gazing into Constance Fallon's china blue eyes, eyes moist with tears and he was holding her slender gloved hand in his.

'This is so awful Andrew,' she was saying in her soft breathless voice. 'Mother and I had to come to pay our respects, poor Charlotte she must be simply devastated.'

'Yes, I'm sure she is. Thank you Constance.'

Her mother was already in conversation with his mother, and catching his eye she smiled, nodding her head graciously and Constance was saying, 'Will you be staying on here Andrew or will you be moving into John's house immediately?'

'I haven't even thought about it. Obviously Charlotte will be consulted.'

'Oh yes, of course.'

'I do hope that when things get back to normal for you we shall see you in London. You were always so bored with a great many of the functions.'

'Yes. You will be very busy yourself Constance.'

'Busy?'

'Well yes, with your forthcoming marriage.'

Constance merely smiled, and after squeezing his hand again she moved away. Her mother favoured him with a further gracious nod, then they walked down the steps to look for their carriage.

His sister smiled cynically in his direction and his father fixed him with a disconcerted glance that spoke volumes.

Over dinner that evening Charlotte indicated that she was prepared to move out of Upcott House as soon as possible, as soon as she could find a property in Scotland that was to her liking.

Andrew assured her that she could stay there as long as possible because he was in no hurry to move in to the official residence of the Viscount Darnley. He was of the opinion that it was a feudal system anyway. If Charlotte had had a son then she would not have had to contemplate leaving the house.

Unconcerned his father said testily, 'I noticed that the Fallon women were there in force, where was the groom do you suppose?'

71

'I have no idea, Father, probably with his regiment, I don't think he knew my brother.'

'Perhaps not, but he didn't accompany his fiancée either.'

'In a couple of months she's due to be married,' Vivienne said dryly, 'not even Constance can be expected to find an excuse not to go through with it at this late hour.'

'Why should she want not to go through with it?' Andrew asked.

His sister smiled maddeningly across the table. 'I could spell it out for you by saying a viscount and future earl is preferable to a baron any day. A baron is as far as he'll go, you have potential Andrew.'

'And I find this whole conversation totally irrelevant,' Andrew retorted.

It was much later when only he and Vivienne were left together playing chess on a small table in front of a roaring fire.

'You refuse to hear anything bad about Constance Andrew, even now,' his sister said quietly.

'I don't see why we have to talk about her at all.'

'What a pity that your little sunflower girl wasn't a year or two older, then you might have fallen in love with her and forgotten Constance totally.'

Andrew was glad of the glow from the fire lighting up the room, hiding the warm rush of blood into his face. He was remembering Marie Claire pulsating in his arms, telling him how much she loved him, that she would always love him, and he had never told her once that he loved her in return. She had been so sure that he did.

It might be years before he could go back there. He had to sort out his life here, bury himself in those responsibilities that had so suddenly been thrust upon him, and he would be pressurized into finding a suitable wife.

He could never think about Marie Claire in that role. She was a young girl with her way to make in life, and it could not be his life. His memories of her were joyous and she was part of a golden summer, a carefree summer when he could indulge himself in what he liked doing best in the world. The summer was coming to an end and with it a youth he had tried to hold on to too long.

Marie Claire would forget him. She would go back to the convent of St Agnes and the good sisters, and one day if he went back to the château Mirandol he might accidentally hear of her. He smiled gently, perhaps the country girl who had become famous in a man's world, or more likely as the wife of some man who would cherish her intellect as well as her beauty.

Vivienne saw the smile. Her brother's thoughts were tender, his memories happy. Andrew had said all he was prepared to say about those weeks in Dijon, but there had been something, she was sure of it.

One day she would accept André de Mirandol's invitation to visit him at his château. She had always decided against it without quite knowing why. Surely she knew how to handle her feelings for André, hopefully as light-hearted and mercurial as his own, but she would look for the sunflower field and the old farmhouse, recognize instantly the black-haired beautiful girl in Andrew's painting.

They would have been surprised if they had known that they were both thinking the same thing, 'One day, one day . . .' then Andrew said quietly, 'Your move Vivienne.'

Charlotte set about looking for a new residence quickly and in no time at all Andrew was moving into Upcott House several miles from his father's residence. His mother and Vivienne were helpful in deciding replacements for the hundred and one things Charlotte had elected to take with her.

Memories of her life with John, she called them. It was a large stone house covered with virginia creeper, surrounded by formal gardens and extensive lawns. John had had no interest whatsoever in horses so the stables had been allowed to run down. Charlotte had had a considerable army of gardeners and oddjob men however, and Andrew gave his mother and sister full reign around the house while he concentrated on the estate.

By the end of October he was fully installed and for the first time in his life free from his father's larger-than-life presence. The old man had come to view the house the day after he moved in, poking and prying into every corner, remembering things that had been in the house when he had lived there and demanding to know what had happened to them. When Andrew said Charlotte had taken them, he snorted angrily, saying she should have been told to return them, that they belonged to the next viscount not the deceased one.

Needless to say, Andrew did not pass on his father's comments to Charlotte and watched him depart with some relief. He had purchased two excellent hunters and employed a groom and a couple of stable hands. He was invited to become a member of the local hunting fraternity and invitations quickly began to arrive to sit on various committees in the area for various pursuits. He was invited to hunt balls and dinners, weekends in country houses and his sister advised him that it was time he started entertaining in return. He had an excellent housekeeper who had stayed on from his sister-in-law's time and the house ran like clockwork.

It was at one of the hunt balls that he came face-to-face again with Constance Fallon. She was quick to inform him that she was a guest of one of the hunt members and that she was alone.

'Why is that?' Andrew asked pleasantly, 'Is your fiancé unable to be here?'

Giving him a rueful smile she said gently, 'Oh Andrew I'm nearly always alone these days, Bertram is always with his regiment, either abroad or on duty.'

'You don't sound very happy with your engagement.'

'No. I thought we would be everywhere together but it hasn't been at all like that.'

'He was a serving soldier when you got engaged Constance, surely you must have know what it would be like?'

'Oh Andrew, I was so very foolish. I had mother telling me that Bertram was so good for me, that I needed an older man to care for me, that young men were selfish and too demanding, now I find myself engaged to a man old enough to be my father and whom I see very seldom.'

Andrew looked down at her beautiful face, and the tendrils of golden hair and the wide blue eyes, at her mouth which smiled tenderly and something of her old enchantment for him came to tantalize him anew. He had thought he was over her. When he had held Marie Claire in his arms with her bewitching youth and beauty he had been so sure, but Marie Claire was a world away, besides she had been too young, it had been beautiful, exquisite joy, but it had been a dream, nothing more.

He invited her to dance, and as they whirled around the room he could smell her perfume, the delicate perfume of jasmine he had always associated with her so that even in the gardens of the cottage its scent had brought her teasingly close. Now once more she was in his arms and forgotten passions resurfaced, and those about them who watched them dancing together smiled knowingly.

They ate supper together and danced again, but this time it was Constance who made herself agreeable where hitherto it had always been Andrew. He had made a vow that she would never hurt him again and he meant to keep that vow, if she wanted him now all the moves should come from her he decided.

At the end of the evening he bowed politely over her hand and watched her leave with her friends, she had smiled tremulously saying 'I hope we'll meet again very soon Andrew,' she said softly. 'Will you be at Lady Cheston's ball in November?'

'I'm not sure. I may be in France.'

He knew very well that he would not be in France, but he was aware of the swift shadow of disappointment in her expression and he rejoiced. This time Constance would do the grovelling, the pain of her refusal was still raw; he would not risk it again.

With another smile she left him and, as he turned away, his hostess joined him, saying with a little smile, 'I don't think poor Constance is entirely happy with her engagement. Of course, everybody knows she was pushed into it by her mother. You were always very fond of her Andrew.'

He smiled.

'I think even Geraldine thinks now that it was a mistake. The girl is always on her own and in any case Bertram is set in his ways. Even without the regiment. He's a bit of a gambler, likes being with the men, and, quite honestly I don't think he'd be too bothered if she ended the engagement tomorrow.'

'You mean it's not exactly the love story of a lifetime?'

'Well of course not. Constance is at a great disadvantage with that mother of hers, she's scared a great many eligible young men off and I can't see anything coming of the engagement.'

In the weeks that followed Andrew lived life to the full but he did not accept his invitation to Lady Cheston's ball. His sister Lady Vivienne informed him that Constance was there alone, undeniably forlorn, and had seemed even more so when Vivienne informed her that her brother was unable to attend.

'She's after you,' Vivienne said with a wry smile. 'Didn't Father tell you what would happen. He's astute enough to see this sort of thing.'

'I don't want you talking about Constance to Father, Vivienne.'

'So things really are moving that way then?'

'She's engaged to somebody else.'

'Unhappily engaged, and if she gets any encouragement from you she'll end it.'

Constance, ably abetted by her mother, did end it just before she and her mother embarked on a cruise to the South of France and Madeira at the end of November, returning to London in time for the Christmas festivities. Andrew's invitation to a country weekend was waiting for her when she got back and on Christmas morning she went with Andrew to his father's house for Christmas lunch when their engagement was announced.

It was accepted with forbearance on the part of his mother, cynical amusement from his sister and the utmost resistance from his father. Nothing was said in Constance's presence, indeed it was reserved for Andrew the following day.

'Didn't I tell you that this is what would happen,' his father stormed. 'You're a step up the social ladder, and one day she'll be the Countess of Westmond. You'll have her mother round your neck like a millstone and the world and his wife knows what she's about.'

'It has nothing to do with the world and his wife.' Andrew said stonily.

'I never thought you'd be such a fool. It'll be a marriage made in hell.'

'You're entitled to your opinion, Father,' Andrew said coldly, 'I love her and she loves me. We'll prove you wrong, that's all I'm prepared to say in the matter.'

Andrew and Constance were married at St Margaret's in London at the beginning of March. It was a cold day with a pale watery sun shining as, on the arm of her uncle Brigadier Royston, the bride walked into the church, a vision of loveliness in her cloudy white chiffon, her long train held by two exquisitely dressed page boys in cream velvet and followed by two bridesmaid in pale peach chiffon. One of them her cousin and the other Lady Vivienne.

Lady Vivienne reflected silently that it was undoubtedly the wedding of the year, but since the year was still in its infancy, others would follow even if they would have a hard task to supersede her brother's.

Geraldine Fallon on the arm of the Earl of Westmond left the church wearing a triumphant smile under a large hat trimmed with sweeping osprey feathers. She was well aware of her escort's unsmiling face and air of truculence but she smiled serenely, gratified by the sight of Constance and Andrew standing on the church steps while all around them the crowd called out their good wishes. Andrew's mother on the arm of her younger son who had got leave from his regiment to attend his brother's wedding dabbed her eyes occasionally, but none of the Martindales could reasonably find fault with Constance's beauty or poise. She had carried out the occasion with the serenity expected from the new viscountess.

André de Mirandol, Andrew's best man, stood on the steps with Lady Vivienne feeling not entirely sure that his friend had married wisely after so many rejections from the woman he had made his bride. He watched the day's celebrations with a degree of cynicism that was not lost on Andrew's sister.

It was much later after they had watched the happy couple depart for their honeymoon in Switzerland that she stood with André in the drawing room of her father's London house overlooking one of the capital's most exclusive squares.

Carriages containing theatregoers were passing under the long windows, and the gas lamps shone eerily in the thin mist that had drifted from the river. Reflectively André said, 'This is how I always remember London, gas lamps shining through the mist, the sound of carriage wheels and the clip clop of horses hooves.' He smiled down at her. 'I thought you looked very beautiful today Vivienne.'

'Thank you André. Where you very surprised when Andrew told you he was going to marry Constance Fallon?'

'He talked about her and I gathered he was unhappy that she'd rejected him. I really didn't see a great deal of Andrew when he came to Burgundy. He preferred to stay at the cottage and I was careful not to intrude.'

'Did he show you anything he painted?'

'No. He seemed preoccupied and I thought he wished to be left alone. Tell me about you, Vivienne. You had your season as a débutante, apparently no man emerged to sweep you off your feet.'

'I'm pretty unsweepable André.'

'I remember that you are.'

She laughed. 'Even to your Gallic charm which is not inconsiderable!'

'Why have you never been to visit me at the château, Burgundy is very beautiful and we could spend some time in Switzerland before the snows have gone. Aren't you tempted?'

'Yes I am, but I like my life as it is André. I'm the mistress of my fate. I don't want to get involved in a situation where there are doubts and perplexities.'

'And you think there would be in France?'

'I think there might be, yes.'

'So you are afraid?'

She stood beside him gazing out across the square, a small frown on her face, aware that he was looking down at her with that faintly derisive smile on his face, darkly handsome, confident that he could cope with any calamity, armed against the wiles of women.

She resented his inference that she was afraid, that he should feel that he had the power to make her afraid, and abruptly she turned and walked back into the room. She went to sit on the couch in front of the blazing fire, picking up a magazine from the long low table in front of her but he did not immediately go to join her.

He continued to watch the activities in the square below, waiting while she turned the pages of the magazine, and then unhurriedly taking the chair opposite he stared at her calmly while he watched the delicate colour suffuse her cheeks, aware that he was disturbing her.

She looked up and met his gaze. He smiled.

'When will you return to France?' she asked him.

'Tomorrow afternoon. I shall spend some time with my mother in Paris, she was disappointed that she couldn't come with me for Andrew's wedding.'

'I love Paris in the springtime, another month and it will be beautiful.'

'Of course, but by that time I shall have returned to Burgundy.'

Again there was silence, then André rose to his feet with a little smile said, 'I shall go to bed, aren't you tired, it's been a long busy day for all of us.'

'No, I'm not tired, I'll stay and read a little.'

He walked across to the couch and stood looking down at her. She felt bemused by him, he attracted her as no other man had ever attracted her, but all the old tantalizing reservations were there. Vivienne liked to think that she was a woman ahead of her time, a cool emancipated woman who frequently scoffed at the vapid anxieties of her contemporaries yet faced with André de Mirandol's easy sophistication she recognized her inadequacies.

She was as much a slave to the conventions she had sworn her life to defy as all those girls she had professed to despise. Calmly he took the magazine out of her hands and laid it on the table, then he reached out and pulled her to her feet.

'I didn't simply come to Andrew's wedding, much as I wanted to,' he said softly, 'I came to see you, to see how much you'd changed, to see if I still admired you and I find that I do. Are you always going to be afraid Vivienne?'

'I'm not afraid,' she retorted, 'I'm disinterested,' she snapped.

'In that case I'll say goodnight Vivienne, fear I can understand, reluctance I can live with, but indifference is something else. Goodnight Chérie.'

She watched him walk out of the room without a backward glance and she sank back on to the settee trembling. There would never be another time.

André would dismiss her as a naïve coward and he would forget her. She would go on pretending to be sure of herself, worldly and confident with her life, and it would be a lie. She rose to her feet and hurried to the door.

The lamps were dim in the hall and André was staring up at one of the portraits in the hall. He turned towards the stairs and unhurriedly started to climb the shallow steps. Lights from the room behind her shone out across the hall and he turned to stare down at her.

He waited while she crossed the hall and started to climb the shallow steps, he smiled, holding out his hands, and she hurried upwards towards him. Drawing her closely into his embrace he said softly, 'So you are interested after all, Vivienne?'

She smiled tremulously.

His kiss at first was gentle, then more demanding, and even in the beginning she was discovering in herself a sensuality she had not thought possible. Before she was aware of it she was in his bedroom and they were embarked upon a night filled with such passionate abandonment it left them both satiated and drained in the hours before the dawn.

10

Letters were few and far between at the farmhouse. Marie Claire wrote dutifully every week and occasionally Jeanne's friend who lived in Lyon wrote to her. The letter was from Dijon and Margot threw it unceremoniously on the kitchen table where the family sat eating their breakfast.

'Who's the letter from?' her mother asked, and Margot answered briefly, 'Marie Claire.'

'There was a letter from her yesterday,' Jeanne said.

'Then she's wanting something,' Margot snapped.

Her mother picked up the envelope and stared at it. It was not Marie Claire's usual plain white envelope. This was endorsed with a black cross and underneath in black letters 'The Convent of St Agnes'.

'This isn't Marie Claire's handwriting,' her mother said quickly. 'Open it Jeanne, something's wrong with Marie Claire, perhaps she's ill.'

Jeanne picked up a knife from the table and slit the envelope open. 'You read it for me Jeanne, her mother said, I never had much schooling, I don't read well.'

'It's from the Mother Superior,' Jeanne said quickly. 'See her signature.'

By this time all eyes were fixed on her.

'It is addressed to you, Papa, Dear Monsieur Moreau, I would ask if it is possible for you and Madame Moreau to visit me here at the Convent at your earliest opportunity. I know that you are very busy people but this is very important. Perhaps you will be kind enough to let me know if you are able to come and when that will be. Yours most sincerely, Sister Maria, Reverend Mother.'

They stared at each other in amazement.

'She's never asked us to go to the convent before, only for

prize-giving and we refused so often she stopped asking us. This must be very important,' Madame Moreau said.

'You must write, Papa, and say when you can go,' Jeanne urged him.

'We'll go tomorrow,' he said firmly. 'This is to do with Marie Claire's future, it is important.'

All day Madame Moreau agonized on what to wear. 'I never go beyond the village,' she complained. 'What sort of clothes do I have for Dijon and all those other mothers with their fashionable clothes.'

'Mama, you don't know that,' Jeanne said gently. 'The Reverend Mother has asked to see you and Papa, you don't know if other parents will be there.'

'Well of course they'll be there,' her husband said shortly. 'This visit is to do with Marie Claire. It is to tell us how well she's done in her exams and to tell us where she is to study further.'

Madame Moreau wore her Sunday best dress and shoes, and with them Jeanne's best hat worn only once for her friend's wedding, and her best coat in finest hopsack. The rest of the family watched them setting out in the buggy driven by Marc, with Papa Moreau in his best suit and trilby hat, looking ill at ease in clothes he disliked, but with a proud smile on his face.

In high good humour Monsieur Moreau decided they would take a cab from the station to the convent. His wife looked out of the cab window with interest, at the soaring spires of the churches and the citizens of Dijon going about their business. They would eat at one of the modest restaurants in the city and hopefully he would allow her to look at the shops. He was in a congenial mood; afterwards they would buy small gifts for Margot and Jeanne.

At the huge, brass-studded door to the convent, they pulled the bell chain. They could hear its echo along the silent corridors, then after what seemed like an eternity, the sound of bolts being drawn back, then the door was opening and two elderly nuns were staring at them curiously.

Monsieur Moreau produced his letter. Looks were exchanged between the two sisters, then they stepped back and held the door open wider so that they could enter. No words were spoken, and they followed the nuns along the corridor and across a small enclosed garden to the building ahead of them.

With every step Madam Moreau's anxiety increased, with the stillness and the distant chanting of voices, the nuns' darkly clad figures and the absence of smiles on their faces. Did nuns not smile a greeting or was that forbidden? she wondered, but now they were walking along stone corridors, their footsteps echoing sharply on smooth flagged floors, and if she had thought to hear the sound of girls' voices in those hallowed rooms there was only silence.

The walls are too thick, she reassured herself. The girls are in the chapel where the chanting is coming from. Then, before she could speculate further, the nuns halted outside a door and knocked. A woman's voice bade them enter and the two nuns stepped aside, indicating that they should enter the room.

The Reverend Mother was sitting at her large desk with her back to the window which overlooked a garden. There were several chairs set about the room and the walls were decorated with dark icons. Sunlight flowed through the windows, falling in a shaft across the desk and with a smile she rose to her feet and beckoned them to sit. She looked at them enquiringly and Monsieur Moreau produced the letter once again.

She smiled. 'Forgive me, we have met only once and that was several years ago. I am pleased that you have come so quickly in answer to my letter. Perhaps you would like coffee?'

'No thank you, first we would like to know why you have sent for us. Marie Claire is not ill?'

'No. She is well.'

'You wish to tell us about her exams, she has done well we hope?'

She sat back in the chair and regarded them silently. There was something in her attitude that made Madame Moreau feel vaguely uneasy, but not so her husband who was beaming genially in anticipation of the good news he expected hear.

'Marie Claire's examination results were everything we expected of her,' she said gently. 'She received the highest marks in her class.'

'So what have you in mind for her Reverend Mother?'

For a moment her fingers drummed idly on the desk in front of her, and her expression was one of great sadness. She was not relishing the news she had for these two people who had come in anticipation of hearing nothing but good news. Prevarication was not the answer, no words of hers could shield them from the truth or make it easier to bear.

'I am sorry to have to tell you that the news about Marie Claire is very grave. I fear there will be no further education for her, Monsieur Moreau. Your daughter is pregnant.'

The silence in that sunlit room was one of shock. Nothing she said could assuage the hurt their daughter's condition had caused them, she could only sit in silence until the enormity of her news had registered in their numbed minds. Monsieur Moreau was the first to speak.

'But that's ridiculous,' he said stoutly. 'Marie Claire has no man friend, we would have known, she would not have kept it hidden from us. What has she said.'

'Nothing at all, Monsieur Moreau. I have questioned her very seriously about everything that happened to her during the summer holiday but she remains silent. You may be able to talk to her, I could not make her speak.'

'You say it happened when she was at home with us in the summer?'

'That is so. It did not happen here, Monsieur. This is a convent, the girls are supervised closely. There was undoubtedly some boy she has not told you about.'

'But her studies, she has to go on with them.'

'No, Monsieur Moreau, she must return home with you and in the months to come she will need all your forbearance, understanding and forgiveness you can find. We are none of us perfect human beings, if we were we would sit among the angels. Try to forget that you had hopes that one day Marie Claire would do great things for women, and remember instead that she is little more than a child and that she is your daughter.'

His eyes met hers, filled with gentleness and very wise, but in his she read only disillusionment and anger. Marie Claire would have no easy passage in her father's house.

His wife was watching him covertly, taking her cue from him and from a marriage where she had always obeyed him, even when his rules had been harsh.

Poor woman, thought the reverend mother, she is a subservient shadow of all his dreams and aspirations, and poor Marie Claire who was to be the living answer to his failures and inadequacies, now so unfortunately fallen from grace. Over the last few days she had thought long and hard about Marie Claire's future and only felt great sadness at the waste of it all.

Her hand reached out for the small brass bell on top of her desk, and almost immediately the door opened and a young novice stood looking at her enquiringly.

'Bring Marie Claire Moreau to me and ask that her suitcase be put in the courtyard,' she said.

Jules Moreau stared at her in surprise. 'Does that mean she will never be able to come back here, Reverend Mother?'

'Ask yourself, Monsieur. She will have a child. Do you not agree that her schooldays are over?'

'But it is months before the child is born.'

'I cannot keep a pregnant girl here, and the end results will be the same. She will have her child, nothing else is possible. Perhaps one day Monsieur a woman will find completion as a mother and success in the world outside, I very much fear that day is not yet. Surely you must know that.'

He was saved from answering by the return of the novice bringing with her a sad-eyed, wan shadow of the happy girl he had seen departing for Dijon at the end of her summer holiday.

She was very pale, and there were blue shadows under her eyes. She stood within the doorway looking at her parents, but neither of them went forward to embrace her, at last she said in a trembling voice, 'I'm sorry Papa. I'm sorry I have disappointed you.'

'Who is he?' her father demanded. 'Tell me who he is, I have a right to know?'

Slowly she shook her head. 'I can't tell you, Papa.'

'Why? Why can't you tell me? Is it some village boy, some man who raped you in the fields around the farm. You're afraid that I'll kill him.'

'I'll never tell you who he is, Papa, not if you ask me every day of my life.'

Her voice was defiant, but it was a defiance born out of the certainty that Andrew would come back, at Christmas, in the springtime. There would be smoke rising from the cottage chimney, she would see him striding along the lane, carrying his easel and the case containing his oil paints, heading for the sunflower field, his eyes searching eagerly for a sight of her. Then it would be Andrew who would tell her father. He would ask for his blessing and they would be married in the tiny village church and she would go with him to England.

The Reverend Mother watched the changing emotions on the girl's beautiful face, willfulness and anxiety, then suddenly the small secret smile that was a promise to herself, a promise that in the end all would be well, a promise that she had ultimate faith in the fairness of life.

How had she failed this sad lost beautiful girl? She had been taught to pray for friendship and love, for success in her studies and godliness in her everyday living, but she had never been warned of the unguarded passions that could destroy her, or that love was the most devouring passion of all.

Without a backward glance Jules Moreau strode out of the room, and the fact that he did not have the courtesy to say farewell to the Reverend Mother was indicative of his disappointment and blistering anger. His wife turned and bobbed a quick curtsey, then Marie Claire came forward and stood with bowed head.

The Reverend Mother embraced her quickly, saying, 'God bless you, my child. Remember us with kindness and bring your child to see us in the springtime. May God go with you.'

Outside the convent her parents waited beside the waiting cab. Her suitcase was already stowed on the rack and she climbed inside to sit opposite her father's frozen angry face while the tears rolled mercilessly down her mother's cheeks. There would be no shopping for presents in the streets of Dijon, no happy conversation over the coffee cups in some small café. Instead they would sit on some form on the platform waiting for the next train home.

She was dreading the evening ahead of them. Margot would be scathing, her sharp tongue would find a thousand and one things to say about the disgrace, that this was the way she had repaid her parents for all their hopes of her, hopes that had always prompted her father to put her above any of them because she was clever, more intelligent than the rest of them put together. And Jeanne and Marc would be sorrowful and Marcel would gloat.

In her imagination she could see his handsome face leering at her knowingly, and even in her imagination she squirmed with embarrassment.

The long green fields slipped by and the trees lining the railway were already shedding their red gold leaves so that they drifted against the windows, caught up by the speed of the train in a flurry of autumn gold.

She had never thought that she could look at her father's face without seeing it relax into smiles, and hear his voice flushed with pride. Now he sat across from her sternly, never once looking into her eyes, like a figure carved in stone, emotionless and filled with silent anger. Her mother's tears were easier to understand. They were tears for herself and Papa, tears created by fear that she would bear the brunt of his anger, and that for a time the farm which was her domain would suffer for it.

All her mother's joy in simple homely things would be put aside to await the return to normal of her husband's whim, but how long could he go on nursing his anger, his humiliation and his need to repay hurt with hurt.

Marie Claire thought she would never forget the night of her return to the farm. Margot's eyes narrowed with scorn and malice, her sister Jeanne's disbelief and her anxious attempts to comfort her mother. Marc had looked at them with the same incredulity displayed by his wife, but on Marcel's face was only amusement, ribald amusement. Through it all her father sat impassive, his face etched in stone. She longed for him to upbraid her, to punish her. Anything was better than this impassive silence.

She had been afraid of his anger, the threats he would make, the ranting and raving she expected of him, but not this cold aloof face she could not reconcile with the face of the father she had loved, who had loved her.

Long after she was in bed, she could hear her sisters' and mother's questioning, shocked voices downstairs, but never her father's voice, it was as though he had no further interest in her, that overnight she had become of no account in his life.

It was much later when the house was quiet and she had heard most of them passing her room on the way to bed that her door opened and her sister Jeanne came in. She sat on the edge of her bed, her face sad and tearful, her voice kind.

'Why won't you tell us who has done this to you?' she urged. 'What will you do, what can any of us do?'

Marie Claire remained silent, and fearfully Jeanne asked, 'Was it Marcel?'

Marie Claire's eyes opened wide with astonishment.

'Marcel! Oh Jeanne, how can you think that?'

'I've seen him groping at you, he has a bad reputation in the village, if it is Marcel you must speak out.'

'I would not let Marcel make love to me Jeanne, you must not even think it.'

'Then tell me who! Will he marry you Marie Claire?'

She took hold of her sister's hand and pressed it. Her voice was confidently gentle. 'Please Jeanne, I can't tell you anything, not yet at any rate, but in the end it will be all right, you'll see.'

Jeanne stared at her. 'He'll marry you?'

'No more questions, please Jeanne. I'm so tired. I've been worrying every since the Reverend Mother said she had written to Papa, now I just want to sleep. Don't worry, I promise everything will be well.'

Jeanne kissed her, then left her alone, but Marie Claire did not sleep. She lay on her back staring up at the ceiling, at the tracery made there as the full moonlight filtered through the branches outside her window. Occasionally she could hear the eerie hooting of an owl and the barking of a fox.

She knew that her parents would probably be sleepless too and she was sorry that their sleeplessness could be laid at her door, but she believed optimistically that in the end they would rejoice for her.

Andrew would come back to Burgundy. He had said he had found the perfect place to paint his pictures and the perfect model. He would go on to paint better more perfect pictures in the autumn when the leaves were falling or in the winter when snow carpeted the fields.

This was the place he would come back to, and he knew that he would find her here waiting for him. There were no doubts in Marie Claire's mind and in time her parents would come to admire him as she did. He was an English gentleman, a friend of the Vicomte. Perhaps the Vicomte would give them the cottage as their first home; they would be guests at the château and her father would be as proud of her on that score as he would have been had she gone to university.

In the days that followed she would help on the farm. She would try to ignore Margot's spiteful remarks and Marcel's taunts. She would work in the kitchen and help to care for the livestock, and she would show them that she could do any of the things they did. If only she didn't feel so nauseous in the early morning, and unable to face the food on her plate.

The rest of the family watched her movements, waiting for her to show any interest in wandering off to the village, but she seemed content to stay in the farmhouse and its surrounding hotchpotch of buildings.

They speculated amongst themselves as to where she had found some boy from among the village boys she had never appeared to be interested in, and the more they speculated the more Marie Claire regarded them with stolid silence.

Her mother's woe-begone face and air of despondency made her very unhappy, but it was her father's sullen resentment that troubled her the most. She tried talking to him and was ignored, she waited on him at the table but he never looked at her, and once when she heard her mother chiding with him to speak to her he said coldly, 'I have only two daughters, I have a stranger living in my house, I do not have to converse with a stranger.'

It was one night when they were sitting down to their evening meal that her father announced. 'There'll be no more sunflowers.'

She looked into Marc's eyes helplessly and knew that he was aware how much unhappiness her father's words had caused her. She lowered her eyes which were filled with tears and quietly pushed away her plate. For as long as she could remember the field of sunflowers had been her joy.

The sunflower field had been part of Andrew, she only had to think of it to conjure up his face smiling at her over his canvas, now there would never be a sunflower field again she prayed that it was not an omen that Andrew was going with it.

Several days later she wandered along the lane in the direction of the field. It had been ploughed and lay bare, leaving only desolation and ugliness.

11

In the days leading up to Christmas snow fell and the cattle were brought down to the barns to shelter them from the driving snow and high winds.

Marie Claire had always loved Christmas at the farmhouse, when the thick walls shut out the elements and curtains were drawn in rooms rosy with firelight and the smell of cooking.

Her mother scolded her because she had no appetite, but food nauseated her and when she looked in the mirror she realized that she was now merely a travesty of the girl Andrew had admired. It was one afternoon when the snow had stopped that she let herself out of the farmhouse and wrapped in a heavy shawl and with her stout boots on her feet she decided to walk along the country lane.

'Where are you going?' her mother demanded.

'I need some air, Mama, I won't be long,' she said.

'Jeanne will go with you,' her mother said firmly. They would not let her go out alone, they had to be sure that she remained alone, or if she met somebody, then they had to know who it was. She felt like a prisoner, but she could not refuse to have Jeanne with her.

They walked in silence, slipping and sliding on the icy road until Jeanne said petulantly, 'Really Marie Claire, why did you have to come out today, it's very cold and it isn't easy walking on this road.'

'Just as far as the stile, then we'll go back,' she replied.

From the stile she could see the cottage through the trees, and for days she had been telling herself that he might come back to Burgundy for Christmas. There would be signs that the cottage was being prepared for him, smoke rising from chimneys, servants coming with logs and linen, all the things the Vicomte considered necessary for a guest. She suggested that they sat for a while to rest on the stile and Jeanne looked around her with interest. 'Do you often come this way?' she asked.

'Hardly ever. I like the fields better but the snow is deep there.'

How adept she was becoming at avoiding their questions and seeing them for what they were.

On their arrival home Jeanne would no doubt report as to what they had done and where they had been. Nobody asked her questions now, they had decided long since that she would tell them nothing, and yet they speculated amongst themselves. They kept their distance from the people in the village and their neighbours at the other scattered homesteads, all the while contemplating the village boys and the sons of their friends and neighbours. Was it one of these who had brought Marie Claire such disgrace?

Marie Claire smiled to herself when she thought about the village boys, swaggering loud-mouthed yokels she had thought beneath her notice, and they in turn had disliked her, thinking she was too full of herself.

Now her family thought it was her air of superiority that had brought her down and one of these boys she had despised had taken his revenge.

One day they would learn the truth, one day when Andrew came back to the château.

It was Marc who raised the mystery of the shuttered cottage one evening as they sat down to eat.

'The cottage is still all shut up. I don't think there'll be anyone there this Christmas.' he said. 'If they want us to supply milk and other produce you'd have thought they'd have asked for them long before now.'

'It's quiet at the château this year,' Margot said thoughtfully. 'I'll ask Thérèse, she'll know if they're expecting guests.'

Thérèse was Margot's friend and worked at the château in her role as junior housemaid. Thérèse was the one who informed most of the village of forthcoming events, the comings and going for the wine festival and any other of the Vicomte's adventures, true or imagined.

The cottage remained shuttered against the snow and the cold winds that swept from the snowclad alps. Margot was able to inform them that the Vicomte and his mother were visiting friends in England and Marie Claire was sure she could have told them where they were spending Christmas and with whom. Now surely it would be Easter before Andrew came back to Burgundy.

Speculation was rife around the château when the Vicomte failed to return home immediately the Christmas holiday was over. It was said he was spending time with his mother in Paris, he was with friends in St Moritz, or more indolently inclined at some expensive hotel on the Côte d'Azur, and Marie Claire fretted and fumed that his absence meant that Andrew could not come back to the cottage in the absence of his friend.

At the beginning of February the Vicomte returned and in no time the entire area was buzzing with excitement that he had informed his staff that he was to marry an English aristocrat's daughter in England just before Easter. The celebration of their marriage would be held at the château on their return from their honeymoon.

Alone in her bedroom Marie Claire wept tears of disappointment and frustration. Her child would be born in the spring and Andrew would still be oblivious of the fact that he was the child's father.

She remained confident in the outcome. He would come back to the château expecting to find her unchanged, but would be delighted with the child, how could he not be?

Marie Claire knew nothing of the recent events in Andrew's life.

That his sister had decided to accept the Vicomte de Mirandol's proposal had been something of a surprise to the entire family. His father had told her she should have had the sense to settle for a titled Englishman, heaven knows there'd always been enough of them around and if Mirandol was anything like his father she'd live to regret it. The French were notably flighty, before she knew what was happening she'd be doing exactly the same sort of thing the Vicomte's mother had done, separate holidays, a string of fawning escorts and with a cynical disregard for the multitude of women her husband was dallying with.

Lady Vivienne treated his ill humour with tolerant amusement. She loved André. He was handsome, charming and he made most of the men she had toyed with seem unimaginative and boring. She was honest enough to admit that her fianceé was a great charmer where women were concerned. He liked to flirt with them and flatter them, and even Andrew warned her that she should think carefully.

Vivienne was convinced that she would love living in Burgundy. She would adore the château, and only a train journey away was Switzerland and the shops and salons of Paris.

The Vicomte's mother was delighted at her son's choice of a wife. Vivienne was beautiful, intelligent and lively. She would know how to handle that part of her son that was so like his father and she was quick to inform Vivienne that for the time being she should indulge herself in the pursuits he enjoyed like winter sports, the gambling tables of Monte Carlo and Trouville. Riding to hounds was something the French hardly ever indulged in and in any case it was usually the women who was expected to make sacrifices.

Vivienne smiled, thinking wryly that the Vicomtesse had hardly ever made sacrifices, they had simply elected to go their separate ways.

Her father on the other hand said shortly, 'You keep your end up, my girl, let him see that you enjoyed the things you did here and the life you led here, if there are any changes to be made, let him make them.'

'But you'll come to Burgundy for the celebrations, Daddy?' she asked plaintively.

'I'm not sure. I like England in the springtime, why couldn't you have them here?'

'Because we're having the wedding here to suit you and Mother. It's only fair that his tenants and the people at the château should join in some of the festivities. If Andrew were marrying a French girl you'd have had the wedding there and hopefully some sort of celebration here.'

'That's what I was afraid of, that he'd pick up with some French girl Mirandol knew.'

'Well, he hasn't, has he? He's married Constance.'

Her father snorted. 'And don't think I'm any more pleased about that,' he retorted.

Andrew too was none too sure that his sister had chosen wisely. He wasn't certain that she would fit in with those friends of André he had met at the château, friends André met on the race tracks of Europe and those others whose only interests were the growing of grapes and vintage wines.

André had never lacked for a beautiful woman on his arm and he had been cynical about marriage and too fond of his bachelor freedom. Vivienne had attracted him with her liberated spirit and wholesome beauty, but when the first rapture was over would he flinch at her high-flung independence? There was a lot of his father in Vivienne: was his friend so blinded by love that he failed to discover it?

The wedding was celebrated in great style at Blaire. A ball was held on the week before the wedding when everybody who was anybody was invited to attend and the wedding which took place in London attracted royalty and aristocrats from England and France.

Vivienne and Constance had never been exactly compatible and he found himself constantly having to listen to his wife's innuendoes on the fuss and expense, and Vivienne seemed to thrive on the envy she engendered in her sister-in-law's opinions.

Constance wasn't at all sure that she wanted to go to Burgundy for the second lot of celebrations. She was two months' pregnant and in a delicate state of health which she said would interfere with any enjoyment there was to be had. Andrew was eager to return to France without really understanding why.

He had put Marie Claire firmly out of his mind. After all, it had been charming, a beautiful episode with an enchanting girl but he was now a married man with responsibilities. Men were entitled to sow their wild oats. The days of Marie Claire had been superseded by all he had ever wanted, he was now the heir to his father's earldom and Constance was his wife. The Gods had indeed been good to him, for never in a million years had he expected both those blessings to be his.

He looked upon those few days in France as a voyage of nostalgia, but when he suggested that they should stay in the cottage Constance said irritably, 'I don't want to stay in any cottage, I want to stay at the château and be waited on properly.'

He pointed out that the Vicomte's mother preferred to stay at the cottage and Constance was quick to retort. 'She will probably wish to stay there in this case then. If we don't stay at the château I shan't go.'

When he told his sister she laughed, 'Well of course Constance won't want to stay in the cottage Andrew, how obtuse of you to suggest it. I'm sure the cottage was the scene of a little romance you had?'

'That's none of your business Vivienne.'

Her smile tantalized him.

'You're very fond of giving me advice, Andrew. Allow me to give you some,' she said softly. 'Never go back, never try to capture something that has gone, remember it kindly and let it go.'

'You're telling me to do something you've failed to do yourself,' he retorted.

'But it isn't the same, is it, Andrew? I'm as whole-hearted now as I was when André and I first met. You, on the other hand, are a married man, expecting to become a father. You chased around Constance for years, now that you've caught her, why poison it?'

'I have no intention of doing anything of the kind.'

'Then you should stay away from the cottage.' And with another enigmatic smile she left him to his thoughts.

The Mirandol honeymoon extended from Venice to Istanbul, then on to Samarkand, returning from Bombay at the end of May. Her father thought the entire enterprise a considerable waste of time and money but it fulfilled every dream of romance that Vivienne had ever had.

She couldn't think of a single Englishman who would have agreed to take such a journey with her so that when her father's testy letters caught up with them she merely smiled at their ill humour.

Their return to the château was welcomed by smiling villagers and children in their Sunday best shyly presenting the new Vicomtesse with posies of flowers wherever she went. They drove through the villages and the parkland lined with smiling faces. There were lanterns in the trees and the gardens were already glowing with spring flowers.

Tables groaned under the food they provided for their array of guests and flags blew in the breeze from every turret of the château. The Earl, in spite of his many prejudices, was impressed, and Constance, in her element, gave everybody the benefit of her considerable charm and her many costumes, meant to outshine her sister-in-law, made Andrew groan with dismay at the cost.

There were so many activities organized, and little time to discover the countryside, although Andrew was determined to show his wife the sunflower field before it was time for them to leave.

Marie Claire's daughter was five weeks old, and as her mother gazed down at her sleeping peacefully in her cradle she could only marvel that so much ecstasy had ended in such pain and anguish. Marie Claire listened to the rest of them going on about the comings and goings at the château, but she felt too lethargic to move out of the farmhouse, let alone take the walk to the cottage. In any case she had already gathered that a family from Switzerland were staying there for the celebrations.

Reluctant to ask questions, she was filled with curiosity. How could she ask if Andrew was staying at the château without divulging her interest in him? It was Margot who supplied the information quite unwittingly when Jeanne asked, 'Who is the beautiful blonde woman who came down to the gates with the Vicomtesse yesterday afternoon? Everybody was asking about her.'

'She is married to the Vicomtesse's brother,' Margot answered, flattered that she should be so well informed. 'Thérèse says she needs more waiting on than any of the others. She demands only a certain tea, and she's pregnant, so she doesn't appear with the other guests until the afternoon.'

'Is her husband with her?'

'Yes of course. He is the Vicomte's friend, Thérèse says he's visited the château many times in the past. I remember him coming here, I'm sure it's the same man we supplied with produce last year.'

After they had left the house, Marie Claire felt physically sick. They were wrong of course, it could not be Andrew. The Vicomte had a great many friends who visited the château, and yet somehow in her innermost heart she was desperately afraid. She made herself do things around the house, take an interest in her child, proclaim that she felt well enough to walk a little way, and her mother, relieved that at last she was showing signs of returning to the land of the living, agreed that a walk would do her good.

She elected to go in the afternoon while they were still busy at the farm and before it was time to leave for yet another display of fireworks and country dancing, and her mother asked anxiously. 'Wait a while so that one of us can come with you.'

'No Mama, I won't be long. I'll only go a little way.'

She caught sight of herself in the long mirror on the landing before going downstairs, a painfully thin girl with lacklustre hair and eyes shadowed with pain. There seemed nothing left of that beautiful vibrant girl she had once been, but there was little left in her life to tempt that girl to return.

She walked slowly, stumbling a little over the rough ground that her dancing feet had once skipped along and she made for the tree-lined lane that led to the field she had once loved.

It stretched before her dark brown and furrowed, and tears rose into her eyes and coursed down her cheeks. She skirted the field making for the trees and it was then she heard the sound of voices and the steady clip clop of horses' hooves.

There was only just time for her to crouch behind the trees as a pony and trap drove slowly along the lane. A man jumped down from the driving seat, lifting up his arms to assist the woman on to the path.

She recognized Andrew at once. How could she not have done when she had lived and dreamed him for so many long months? The sun gilded his blonde hair, and the woman smiled up at him before taking his arm to walk with him to the end of the field. She was blonde and beautiful, her dress a confection of lavender silk and, as he smiled down at her, Marie Claire could hardly stop herself from crying out with anguish.

They stood at the end of the field, the man with a frown of surprise on his face, the woman staring at the field expressionless.

It seemed like an age before they turned, and started to walk towards her and she could see that the puzzlement was still on his face and now she could hear their voices.

'I can't understand it,' he was saying. 'I can't believe that they would not sow sunflowers again.'

'Poor Andrew,' the woman said. 'Your beautiful field has gone, but you still have your picture to remind you.'

'I know, but what a pity, I would really like you to have seen them growing, even if it is a little early for flowers.'

'Is that the cottage you stayed in?'

'Yes. I was very comfortable there, André's servants looked after me very well.'

'Did you cook for yourself?'

'Some of the time, there's a farm nearby, they supplied me with the basics.'

'And the girl?'

'Oh, she lived at the farm. She was a nice little thing, she loved the sunflowers. I hope she makes it to Paris and fulfills all her ambitions. She was very confident.'

'How droll. To be so pretty and so boring.'

'Oh, I don't think she was boring, unusual I think, but no, she wasn't boring.'

'I've always found ambitious women boring. They miss so much, darling. Mummy always emphasized that men liked a woman to be pretty, able to hold an intelligent conversation but never to be a blue stocking. Clever women confuse them.'

'Your mother had an answer for everything, Constance.'

'Well yes. We never had much money after Father died so she had to scheme and plan for both of us. I wish you liked her better, darling.'

'I like her well enough.'

'Your father doesn't like her at all.'

'Don't let that worry you, there are not many women he does like.'

'But Mummy's always charming to him, he could make an effort.'

Her voice was plaintive, but at that moment neither Marie Claire nor his wife could see Andrew's face. He was looking at the cottage with a bemused expression on it and his thoughts were far removed from the machinations of his wife's mother. He was thinking of the dusk of a summer's evening, perfumed with the scent of the earth, and the fleeting figure of a girl running lightly across the grass, her black hair streaming in the breeze before she turned at the gate to wave to him. There was laughter on her lips, joy in her green eyes and all the urgent promises of another day.

His reverie ended when his wife said petulantly, 'Andrew, you're not listening to me.'

'Sorry darling, I was thinking it was time we were getting back. Isn't tonight the climax of all these festivities?'

'Yes. I do hope nobody else has decided to go as Lady Hamilton.'

'And I have to wear a patch over one eye and cover up my arm. How can I whirl you round the ballroom with one arm?'

'Have you any idea what Vivienne will be wearing?'

'No, she's been very secretive, probably some woman from the French history books.'

'And your father?'

Andrew laughed. 'He's refusing to dress up so he'll make a brief appearance before retiring for the night.'

'It's a bit hard on your mother.'

'Oh she's accustomed to his vagaries. She'll thoroughly enjoy her role as Catherine Parr without Henry beside her. Wasn't she the queen who outlived him?'

Marie Claire watched them climb into the trap and turn the pony round, then she waited in her hiding place until they were out of sight.

That was the moment that hatred was born in her. The moment when she would cease to be the giver and become the taker.

12

Jules Moreau was in a foul temper. There was work to be done on the farm and his son-in-law had fallen in the barn and broken his leg. He could hear him moaning from inside the house where the doctor was seeing to his leg and his wife was blaming everybody else for the accident.

That meant there would be two pairs of hands less and the harvest was upon them. He would have to take extra help on from the village and preferred to keep the work on the farm strictly on a family level. The girls worked hard, even Marie Claire, although she did it with ill-concealed resentment, but it was hardly his fault that she had to work as a farm hand when she should have been working on something more interesting and lucrative.

Jeanne had had the good sense to present him with a grandson but he was still a baby and needing a lot of attention, and Marie Claire's daughter would be just another woman around the place in the foreseeable future.

He glared at the child sitting with her doll in the farmyard. She was talking to one of her imaginary playmates, and there was nothing in the child's appearance to bring back memories of Marie Claire. The child's hair was like the sun-kissed corn, her eyes an incredible dark blue, that she was a beautiful child hardly registered in his thoughts. Chantal Moreau was a born disaster and had remained one in his mercenary unrelenting heart.

Chantal was wary of her grandfather. In her short life he had never lifted her on his knee or smiled at her, never held her hand while she walked across the cobbled farmyard or given her a toy, but if his heart remained unforgiving so did his daughter's. Marie Claire never spoke to him, never looked at him for reassurance, never asked for his forgiveness or pleaded with him for the love that had gone for ever.

There were times when he looked at her and saw again in her the beauty that had enchanted him. The lustre had returned to her black hair, the hot sun had painted her delicate skin with tints of gold and her eyes were as strangely beautiful as always, but around her warm passionate mouth were set lines of discontent and supressed resentment.

Marie Claire thought she had never been so tired in her entire life. Margot was obsessed with nursing her husband and Jeanne with her baby. She was out in the fields from dawn until sunset when she wearily dragged herself back to the farmhouse and the preparations for the evening meal. Then there was her daughter waiting for her, sometimes fretful after neglect throughout the day and she burned with resentment when she saw how the rest of her family fawned over the new baby and ignored Chantal. Every day was the same and in the years that lay ahead she could see no lightening of the gloom that was now her life.

It was the sight of a nun cycling along the narrow path on her way to the cottage that brought the idea into her mind: an idea that she tossed aside as too ridiculous to contemplate, but once it had taken root it returned again and again to tantalize her.

It was the smallest and most trivial of episodes that finally brought it to fruition. She was carrying a large tureen of potatoes to the dinner table when she stumbled against Marcel's injured leg stretched out across a stool. His cries of anguish brought his wife rushing to his side, the potatoes were scattered across the floor and suddenly everybody was screaming at once. Her father was accusing her of incompetence, her sister of clumsiness and her child and the baby were screaming in unison. With a set expression she cleaned up the floor and, picking up her daughter, carried her upstairs.

She was very hungry after the long day in the field and Chantal too was hungry, but even when her mother came to plead with her to go back to the table she adamant that she would eat later when they had all finished their meal.

Only her mother was left in the kitchen when they finally went downstairs and in silence Marie Claire helped her with the dirty dishes before cooking eggs and potatoes for herself and Chantal.

Her mother looked at her uncertainly. She did not understand Marie Claire these days. Her gentle sunny daughter had gone, to be replaced by a nervous easily provoked woman whose angry eyes and cold severity kept her at a distance. It was no longer a happy household but one plagued by jealousies, condemnation and heavy periods of accusing silences.

After she had put Chantal to bed she wandered disconsolately outside rather then sit with the rest of them in the overcrowded living room.

It was a warm balmy night with a gentle breeze stirring the branches of the poplars. A half moon flitted fitfully through the clouds and the scents of the earth were potent, acrid river smells and damp soil, wood smoke and clover, stocks set against the garden wall and in the midst of it all the idea suddenly came to life and she realized only she could put an end to a life that had become insupportable.

She went back into the house and up to the room she shared with her daughter, then taking out the small suitcase that had once held the books and clothes she needed at the convent she started to pack the clothes from the wardrobe and others from the chest-of-drawers. Only her daughter's clothes were left, and then after she had heard the rest of her family retiring for the night she went downstairs.

She sat down at the kitchen table staring down at the sheet of paper in front of her, thinking it was the hardest letter she had ever been asked to write. She addressed it to her mother, begging her to understand that she could not go on. She thanked her for her love and support but she was leaving the farm in the hope that she could find something better, something that life had once promised her before it was spoiled. She asked her to care for Chantal until she was able to return for her, which she promised would be as soon as she could promise a decent life for both of them. She signed the letter, 'Your ever loving daughter, Marie Claire', then she placed it in an envelope and sealed it.

Leaving it on her mother's breakfast plate, she returned upstairs and, with tears streaming down her face, she kissed her daughter, left the room and closed the door. As she crept down the stairs, her heart beat wildly for fear of making a sound to alert those sleeping upstairs. With a last look around the familiar room, she let herself out of the door and into the night.

It was only when she was sitting outside the station waiting for the first train into Dijon that she faced the enormity of her decision to leave the farm. She had very little money. Her father had not been generous, believing that the food she and Chantal ate were adequate compensation for the work she did at the farm, but she had saved what she could without quite knowing why she was saving it.

The only people she knew in Dijon were the friends she had made at the convent and while they sent her birthday cards and Christmas greetings they could not be expected to provide her with a home. Her only hope was the convent, surely the Reverend Mother would not decline to help her.

The station master stared at her in bleary surprise and she looked away quickly. He was acquainted with her father and when she saw him walking towards her she got up from her seat and sauntered towards the end of the platform. He stared after her perplexed, then, shrugging his shoulders, he went into the office and the breakfast his wife had packed for him. Of course all the village knew about the Moreau girl and her baby, the village had talked about nothing else and it served Jules Moreau right, he'd always been so boastful about the girl, maintaining that she was better than anybody else, prettier, cleverer. Well obviously she was off to Dijon and up to no good. It was none of his business.

The streets of Dijon were coming to life when Marie Claire stepped down from the train and a remembered excitement filled her heart at the sight of city dressed people hurrying along the platform, men in formal suits and women wearing fashionable hats and high-heeled shoes.

She felt dowdy in the dress and coat she had worn as a schoolgirl. The sleeves were too short and the coat an unfashionable length but nobody spared her a second glance as she hurried out of the station and across the city square.

It was early and the boulevards were quiet. It was too early for shop girls to pour into the city's large shops and salons, but newspaper boys clattered along the street and over all came the pealing of bells from the cathedral.

She stood for a long time looking at the façade of the convent before plucking up enough courage to pull the bell.

Several minutes later a stout nun was staring short-sightedly at her and Marie Claire's heart sank when she realized that the nun was unknown to her.

The nun continued to stare, and in a small voice she said hesitantly. 'Please, I would like to see the Reverend Mother.'

'Who are you?' the nun asked.

'My name is Marie Claire Moreau, I was a pupil here.'

The nun's face relaxed somewhat. 'Does the Reverend Mother know that you're coming?'

'No. But I'm sure she'll see me. She will remember me.'

The nun opened the door wider, saying 'Wait inside and I'll see if it is convenient for the Reverend Mother to see you. You may need to make an appointment, she's very busy.'

'Yes I'm sure she is. Will you please tell her it's very important.'

The nun took her into a small side room off the familiar garden and Marie Claire watched her shuffling along the path towards the tall building beyond.

She had said it was important, but would the Reverend Mother think so? She had left her home and her daughter, she had been guilty of so many indiscretions, what would the Reverend Mother think of her behaviour?

99

Why was it taking so long? she agonized. Perhaps the Reverend Mother was refusing to see her, and yet it could only have been minutes, because she heard the convent bell striking the hour, and here she was in Dijon, impatient with time and too anxious for results. The nun was returning, shuffling across the square and narrow paths, smiling now, and holding the door open for her.

Marie Claire's spirits revived as she followed her along the familiar corridor towards the Reverend Mother's door, then she was there, standing in the entrance, smiling her gentle familiar smile and her embrace was warm and tender with the familiar scents of lavender and incense.

'My dear, how good it is to see you. But you haven't brought your daughter.'

Marie Claire shook her head and immediately burst into tears.

Concern showed on the Reverend Mother's face. 'Oh dear, I do hope there's nothing wrong. You're unhappy, my child, come sit here and tell me about it, I am here to help.'

So the words came tumbling out, words filled with resentment and anger, and the story she unravelled was one of loneliness, betrayal and hurt from people she had loved and from whom she had expected something better. Through it all the Reverend Mother could see that from being the idol her parents had made of her, she had become an encumbrance, an outcast, and even their grandchild had become unacceptable. Of the child's father Marie Claire never said a word and the Reverend Mother was quick to realize that he would be the secret she would carry to her grave.

'Why have you come to see me today?' she asked gently. 'I will pray for you Marie Claire, but what else can I do?'

'Please, Reverend Mother, you must help me. I can't go back to the farm, I can't face that life a moment longer.'

'But your daughter? What can you have been thinking of to leave her behind?'

'How could I bring her with me? I have no home for her, I have no work and little money. Here in Dijon I can find work, there must be something I can do. Perhaps I could go into service.'

The Reverend Mother looked at her aghast. This was the girl who had shone like a star in the firmament, the girl who would show all France that a woman could rise to the top, and that the convent of St Agnes had helped to put her there, now she was talking about going into service. She was looking at her hopefully, believing that she only had to ask and everything would happen for her.

'You may stay here at the convent tonight, but I seriously advise you to return home tomorrow and make your peace with your family,' she advised. 'The city can be a hard world for a girl on her own, with little money and the prospect of looking for work.'

'But I can't go home,' the girl cried. 'I've left a letter telling them that as soon as I can care for her I'll go back for Chantal, until then I have to find work. Anything is better than going back there, I'd rather die.'

'I shall ask Sister Emelda to take you to a room in the old part of the convent. Nobody will disturb you there, and I hope you will pray for God's guidance and his forgiveness.'

'Forgiveness, Reverend Mother?'

'For the distress you've caused your parents and your child by coming here.'

Marie Claire stared at her. Had the Reverend Mother not been listening to the anguish of her life since Chantal was born, was everybody in the world innocent except herself?

In response to the bell on her desk a young nun appeared and was despatched to bring Sister Emelda. Her eyes lit up when she saw Marie Claire, but the smile died on her lips when she beheld the girl's pale tearful face and the concern on the Mother Superior's.

'Marie Claire is staying with us tonight, Sister, she will return to the country in the morning. Take her to one of the rooms in the old convent and see that she has everything she needs. You may go into the old chapel to pray and I will see you in the morning before you leave.'

Without a backward glance she followed Sister Emelda out of the room and along the winding passages that led into the old part of the convent. She was handed a candlestick containing a tall white candle which the sister lit before entering the darkness beyond. In the small bare room at the end of the passage she found a narrow single bed, a tiny chest-of-drawers and a wooden chair. Another candle on the drawers was lit, and she watched as Sister Emelda pulled the shutters across the small paned window before she turned to smile at her. 'Bless you, my child,' she said softly. 'Sleep well.'

It was over, the day that had started with such promise, such faith. Tomorrow a nun would accompany her to the station to see that she returned home and in the days and years that lay ahead nothing would change. She would grow old, she would see her daughter grow into a woman, but what sort of a woman with the stigma of illegitimacy surrounding her? She had learned to her cost the narrowness of the environment she lived in, a narrowness devoid of either compassion or understanding.

She did not go into the chapel to pray, instead she lay sleepless on her narrow bed with her resolve to stay in Dijon undiminished.

Sister Emelda came for her early next morning, taking in at once the girl's pale face and air of dejection.

'You'll eat breakfast in the kitchen, Marie Claire,' she said brightly. 'Reverend Mother will see you later.'

Marie Claire didn't speak and the nun said gently, 'I hope you slept well?'

Marie Claire smiled bleakly, 'Yes, thank you, sister.'

'Perhaps you would like to see some of the other sisters who remember you?'

'Perhaps, if there's time.'

'Well, we shall know when you've seen Reverend Mother.'

In the kitchen they served her with bread and fruit and she was told to help herself to milk from the milk churn on the kitchen floor. She heard the convent bell striking eight and almost immediately Sister Emelda was back to take her to the Mother Superior. She made no mention of taking her to meet the other sisters, and was left sitting opposite the Reverend Mother's desk in an empty room.

She could see through the window that the sun was shining and in some strange way it helped to revive her spirits.

She rose to her feet when the Reverend Mother entered the room and stood looking down while the older woman went to take her seat behind her desk. She smiled, 'Good morning, Marie Claire, I hope you slept well.'

Marie Claire decided that honesty was the best policy.

'I didn't sleep, Reverend Mother, I was too worried for sleep.'

'You were worried about your daughter?'

'No, Reverend Mother, whatever my parents think of me they will care for Chantal, I was worried for me, for the immediate future and the rest of my life.'

'My dear child, the rest of your life is in your own hands.'

'I know that, Reverend Mother, I knew that yesterday morning when I left my home. If I stay there my life will be a nothing, my daughter's life too. It has been made plain to me over the last three years that I am no longer a daughter in that house, I am a pair of hands. My father ignores me, my mother is afraid of him. My sister Margot has always been jealous of me but her husband would not be averse to making love to me if I would allow it. My sister Jeanne is content with her husband and children, we get along, but she would not miss me if I wasn't there. This is the life you will be sending me back to and, as I said last night, I would rather die than go back there.'

The Reverend Mother was looking at her sorrowfully. In Marie Claire's face she saw only determination. She could insist that she return home, send a nun to make sure she boarded the country train, but only Marie Claire could make her stay there. She could wash her hands of the whole wretched business, say it was none of her affair and that she had done her best, but her conscience would not let her send this girl away without trying to help her.

She drummed her fingers impatiently on the blotter in front of her, all sorts of possibilities were presenting themselves but she had to be sure that in the end there was something worthwhile for Marie Claire.

Marie Claire was aware of the uncertainties chasing themselves across the expressions on the Mother Superior's face. She had made the Reverend Mother see that she was still resolved to stay in Dijon, that she could not return home but she was puzzled with regard to the help she could offer.

She waited anxiously. The Reverend Mother knew so many institutions in the city. Businessmen of note who sent their daughters to the convent to receive their education, surely among all these would be somebody willing to offer her employment. Fortunately she could not know of the thoughts passing through the Mother Superior's head.

News of Marie Claire's fall from grace had swept through the city like wildfire. The convent's most illustrious pupil, the most popular girl with teachers and students alike to return to the convent after the summer holidays pregnant and refusing to divulge the father of her child.

She was remembering the whisperings in the convent's dormitories, the tittle-tattle amongst the parents, the shocked tones of the mayor's wife as she said it was hard to comprehend that a girl with so much potential and with such a religious background could have ever made such a mistake.

She had looked at the mayoress's prim florid face under it's ridiculous feathered hat and seen little Christian forbearance in its sanctimonious expression. Among people like that there would be prejudice, the desire to teach the girl a lesson that she could not sin and expect to be taken in as though nothing had happened. She could be as hurt in Dijon as she had been in the country, but looking at the girl's calm set face she believed Marie Claire was capable of rising above anything they could throw at her. She had not left the farm defeated, these last few years had made her strong.

'I am going to ask you to remain here at the convent another day,' she said at last. 'It will give me a little time to decide if I can help you. Don't build your hopes too high my child, but I can see that if I don't help you I do not know who will.'

'Oh thank you, Reverend Mother, thank you,' the girl murmured.

She returned to her room in the old convent and said her prayers in the crumbling chapel. She renewed her acquaintance with a group of nuns who had once been her teachers and she talked about her daughter's beauty and asked a multitude of questions about the girls who had once been her friends and were now out in the world.

Life was going to be wonderful again. She would have friends in the city, girls to tell secrets to, parks to walk in and shops to tantalize her with their window displays. One day she would have enough money to do more than gaze in their windows, and she would work again at her studies.

She would never be famous, but there were a thousand and one things she could do. They had taken away her self-esteem, they had not taken away her spirit.

13

It was three days before the Reverend Mother sent for her again and by this time Marie Claire was desperate to know what the future had in store for her.

It was early afternoon when she was taken back to the Reverend Mother's office expecting to find her alone, and unprepared for the sight of a small middle-aged man sitting opposite her, who looked up with interest as she entered the room.

The Reverend Mother smiled. 'This is Monsieur Pouillac, Mademoiselle Moreau, Monsieur,' she said, and introductions having been performed she went on: 'Perhaps you do not remember Monsieur Pouillac's bookshop in Rue Grenelle, but he supplied the convent with books for a great many years.'

'Oh yes, I remember it well. I stood for hours staring through the windows and wishing I could afford to buy many of those rare volumes.'

Gratified, Monsieur Pouillac's smiled, and the Reverend Mother said, 'It is well then. Monsieur Pouillac's bookshop is an institution in this town since it was there in his grandfather's time, unfortunately recently he has suffered a great setback. Madame Pouillac was always there to help him with his accounts and the ordering of new editions, now she has suffered a quite serious stroke and is unable to do anything. He has a nurse living in to assist his wife, but the business is suffering. Do you think you could help him in the shop, Marie Claire, and perhaps shop and run errands for his wife?'

Marie Claire's face lit up with a smile. 'Oh yes, Reverend Mother, I shall enjoy working in the shop, helping in any way I can.'

'Well, for the time being, perhaps in the background. He also has a room on the top floor that you can occupy which will serve your immediate problems of finding somewhere to live.'

'Oh yes, Reverend Mother, that will be wonderful.' She embraced them both with her smile. 'I promise, Monsieur, that I will do everything I can to help both you and Madame Pouillac.'

'Then I suggest when you have collected your things from your room you go along to the shop where Monsieur Pouillac will be waiting for you.'

How her feet danced along the corridors on the way to the dismal little room in the convent. It took her only minutes to pack the tiny valise she had brought with her, and then minutes later she was hurrying away from the convent along the steep cobbled street that led to the sprawling city below.

Rue Grenelle was a street of small shops with leaded bay windows: art shops mostly, filled with pictures and bric-à-brac. A small cafè from which the odour of roasting coffee wafted stood next door to another filled with exquisite pastries, but it was the bookshop with its air of gentility and permanancy to which Marie Claire's steps were drawn. There was only one gentleman in the shop who did not look up when she entered but stood pouring over a thick volume, occasionally removing his spectacles to wipe them before replacing them on his nose.

The doorbell brought Monsieur Pouillac from the back of the shop. He held up the counter so that she could join him before he ushered her through the door into the room behind the shop.

'I'll get my wife's nurse to show you to your room in case my customer needs assistance,' he said. 'When you have unpacked, perhaps you will come down to the shop and if I am at liberty I will introduce you to my wife and familiarize you with the layout of the house.'

She thanked him with a smile, and then knocked on the door of what she thought must be his wife's room and immediately a tall middle-aged woman wearing a stiff white apron and a white cap on her dark hair came out.

'This is my new assistant, Mademoiselle Moreau. Please show her up to her room,' he said briefly.

The woman nodded, and marching ahead she indicated that Marie Claire should follow.

On the second floor, there was a small neat room with a single bed, a small desk and wardrobe, a chest-of-drawers and an easy chair and Marie Claire looked round her with delight.

The nurse said,' My room is next door, but more often than not I sleep in the same room as Madame Pouillac.'

'How is Madame Pouillac?' Marie Claire asked.

'Today she isn't at all well, but every day varies. Would you like coffee?'

'Yes, thank you, that would be very nice.'

'Then I'll see you in the kitchen when you've had time to unpack.'

After she had gone, Marie Claire hugged her arms with joy. She would be happy here, work hard and prove to her employer and the Reverend Mother that their faith in her wasn't wasted.

In the days that followed she came to realize that Monsieur Pouillac's accounts were in a state of hopelessness and she spent long hours sorting them out. She spent little time in the shop since he preferred to work in there himself, but he found her plenty to do. Unwrapping parcels containing books for the various schools in the city as well as those for the convent, delivering books that had been ordered to various people in the city, and shopping for anything he thought his wife might fancy.

It did not take her long to see that the nurse was only concerned with nursing. She did not take kindly to housework or shopping, and it was left to Marie Claire to tidy rooms as well as see to the office work but when her efforts began to take shape Monsieur Pouillac was quick to show his appreciation and to bring in a daily woman to help around the house.

She was happier than she had been for months. She had time in the evenings to read and her quick mind absorbed the knowledge she had been forced to abandon. The autumn days passed and winter took its grip on the city and countryside surrounding it. Now from the façade of Notre Dame she could look out to where Mont Blanc reared its snowy head and as far as she could see the mountains of Switzerland sparkled in silver white.

She was beginning to save a little money every week, but always when Monsieur paid her salary she went out and brought a present for Chantal, a doll or a little dress, and often a gift for her mother of handkerchiefs and scarves. She received no letters from home, it was as if they had already forgotten her, but the parcels were never returned.

She was waiting to be served in the cafè next door to the shop while a large fashionably dressed lady at the counter was trying to make up her mind what she wanted for a small dinner party at her house. She constantly changed her mind, but the assistants smiled good-humouredly, as if they were accustomed to her peculiarities.

Marie Claire looked at her curiously. She felt she had seen her before, but the memory was illusive. The woman had a list in her hand and was busy ticking off the items one by one, she turned at last to smile at Marie Claire saying, 'I'm sorry, I am keeping you waiting, but you will understand this is a very important dinner party. We are entertaining dignitaries from Paris, it is important we show them that Dijon knows how to do things well.'

Marie Claire smiled.

The mayor's wife was enjoying herself hugely. The guests from Paris would be arriving in the morning and with them her sister and her husband. At last she would be able to demonstrate to her sister that life in Dijon was hardly bourgeoise. She would invite the Vicomte de Mirandol and his new wife, the daughter of an English earl no less, oh yes indeed, she would show her sister Claudette and Paul her husband that they knew how to do things in Dijon.

She looked again at the girl waiting to be served. There was something familiar about her but she too was tantalized by uncertainty. She smiled, 'Perhaps you would like to be served while I think about my list,' she said graciously, and, equally gracious, Marie Claire thanked her and stepped up to the counter.

That was the moment when the Abbè Fauriel entered the shop and immediately he was greeted by the mayoress and they stood chatting amicably while the assistant attended to Marie Claire's modest request for bread and pastries.

As she left the shop she smiled at them and bade them good-day and it was only later when the mayoress and the Abbè walked down the street together that the mayor's wife said curiously, 'That girl in the shop, *mon père* I seem to know her. I know I've seen her somewhere.'

'But of course. Marie Claire Moreau, she was at the convent of St Agnes.'

'Moreau? Isn't her father the banker Claude Moreau?'

'Claude Moreau is a bachelor, Madame, her father is a farmer in the vicinity of Mirandol.'

Of course. Now she knew who the girl was and the memory of what she knew about Marie Claire made her lips set in a hard thin line and the Abbè began to regret that he had successfully nudged her memory.

'Wasn't she the girl who had to leave the convent in disgrace because she was pregnant? Such a thing had never happened there before. Wasn't she a very clever girl who dismayed everybody by making such a mess of her life?'

The Abbè remained silent, and Elise Grolan went on, 'Beauty and brains evidently didn't go together in her case,' she said vindictively. 'The child must be about three years old by this time, I wonder if she got married and if they are living in Dijon?'

'That I cannot tell you,' the Abbè replied. 'You'll be looking forward to seeing your sister again.' he added, hoping that she would allow him to change the subject.

She beamed. 'Yes, of course. You will come to our dinner party, Monsieur l' Abbè it is in three days' time and I am hoping the Vicomte de Mirandol and his wife will join us. I met her at the festivities after their marriage, such a beautiful girl and most charming. Do you know this is the fifth time my husband has been asked to be the Mayor of Dijon?'

'Which must tell us how well respected he is in the city,' the Abbè said with a smile.

'Well of course. You and I both know that it is very gratifying to be well thought of by those we try to help.'

They parted at the spot where the mayoress's carriage waited for her and the Abbè walked on alone, wondering idly what Marie Claire Moreau was doing in Dijon. He was a constant visitor to the little street in the shadow of the Church of St Michel, perhaps he would see her again.

Meanwhile Marie Claire was entertaining her employer by telling him about the mayoress and her catering problems, and in the middle of it she remembered Madame Grolan stepping down from the Paris train and smiling up at Andrew as he held the carriage door open for her.

It had all happened a lifetime ago, in another world, a large woman in a flowery hat followed by the tiny figure of the Abbè in his black habit, and the sunlight gilding Andrew's fair head as he bowed courteously over the woman's outstretched hand.

How ridiculous that one brief moment should come back to torment her now, and how ludicrous that such a moment could build up into the hopeless tragedy that came after. That fleeting moment had taken what was left of her childhood, her girlhood and every dream she had ever had. She had never been one to look back with despair but now for the first time in many months she was being made to face the past, and it seemed incongruous that a brief meeting in a small cafè should have made it possible.

Her employer was staring at her curiously. One moment her face had been gay with humour as she mimicked Madame Grolan, now her eyes were sombre with remembered pain. He waited, reluctant to break in on her reverie, then suddenly she collected her thoughts and smiled. 'I have just remembered when I saw her last,' she said. 'I was going home for the summer holidays and she stepped off the Paris train.'

He only knew what little the Reverend Mother had told him about Marie Claire. Her history did not concern him since all he wanted was a willing assistant, and she had been more than that. For the first time in years he could knowledgeably face his bank manager because his books were in order. He could leave her to order supplies and handle them when they arrived, and she would read to his wife, enabling him to saunter out into the city streets for a breath of fresh air.

He would like to have been able to think that she would stay with him for ever but she was worth something better, better pay, a better position, perhaps in some government office where the prospects were far superior than anything he could offer.

There were times when he found her looking sad and reflective, times when he caught the odd tear in her eye, but hastily she would wipe it away and the bright beautiful smile would come and the moment was forgotten.

It was several days later and they were filling one of the bookshelves near the window that the door opened and the Abbè Fauriel entered the shop.

He smiled and bade them good morning, then, while Marie Claire went on with her task Monsieur Pouillac went forward to attend to the Abbè.

The Abbè said that he had merely come to browse because he had time to spare, but he watched as he made his leisurely way around the room, stopping now and again to pick up some volume from a lower shelf, at others teetering on shallow steps to look at volumes placed higher up, then when he reached the kneeling girl he paused to say. 'How are you, my child, are you now living in the city of Dijon?'

Marie Claire looked up with a smile. 'Yes Father.'

'And you work here?'

'Yes Father.'

'And where in the city do you live, my child?'

'I live here at the shop. Monsieur Pouillac gave me work and somewhere to live.'

His eyes twinkled down at her from behind his spectacles. 'You will be happy here, Marie Claire, with so many books to read. You loved books.'

It was several days later that he learned from the Reverend Mother the full story of how Marie Claire came to be working at the bookshop in Rue Grenelle.

Not from his lips would the mayor's wife learn it, however, but the woman was an inveterate gossip, she set herself up as the city's conscience with a superior knowledge of what was right and what was wrong. Not a very forgiving woman to those she believed had transgressed, and her popularity was based on the decency of her husband's standing in the town and her own belief in hobnobbing with those she thought worthy of her attention, the rich, the popular and the high-flyers.

He had seen her at work at many different functions in the city and elsewhere, heard the groans from various groups as she sought to join them and witnessed her endeavours to be the best, have the best and only associate with those she considered to be the best.

Marie Claire was hardly likely to come into contact with Madame Grolan, who was not a great reader and hardly likely to visit the bookshop, but if she saw Marie Claire around the town she would behave like a dog with a bone and never rest until she had learned her recent history and the reason for her living in Dijon.

It was one Sunday morning when Marie Claire left the church of St Michel to walk through the park that she heard her name being called from across the grass and then she saw a young woman running towards her, waving her arms joyfully in the air. Her face lit up with pleasure when she recognized Diane Cladel, one of her friends from her schooldays at the convent.

'Marie Claire,' her friend called out. 'I couldn't believe it was you. It's ages since you sent me a letter.'

The two girls embraced and Marie Claire said softly, 'I know, but so many things happened. Have you written to me at the farm?'

'Many times, but there was never a reply.'

'That is because I'm living here in Dijon.'

'But didn't they send my letters to you?'

She shook her head, and, puzzled, her friend said, 'Why are you here then, are you married, and what about your little girl?'

'I'm not married but I work here. Chantal is with my parents until I've earned enough money to send for her.'

The other girl looked at her sadly. 'Oh Marie Claire, everything that happened was so sad. Why didn't he marry you, whoever he was, was he married already?'

'No, but he is now.'

'Did he know about Chantal?'

'No, I was never able to tell him.'

'There's a little cafè near the lake, let us have coffee and you can tell me all about yourself.'

So while they drank their coffee Marie Claire told her what little she could about the past few years, and Diane said at the end, 'Nobody could believe it, Marie Claire, all that promise, and now this.'

'I know, now tell me about you. I'm sure your life is far more interesting than mine.'

'Well I'm engaged to be married, I'm getting married at the Notre-Dame in six weeks, a banker from Lyon.'

'And you love him?'

'Of course. He's called Henri de Montfortes, the de Montfortes, the big banking family. I think Mother must have invited everybody in Dijon to the wedding, including the Vicomte de Mirandol and his lady. You'll come too, won't you, Marie Claire?'

'Thank you, Diane, but I rather think not. I'm hardly the sort of friend your mother will want to see at your wedding.'

'You're the friend I want to see, Marie Claire. If only I'd known you were in Dijon, I'd have asked you to be one of my bridesmaids, but you will be my guest.'

'I have nothing to wear for such a function.'

'You will have, besides you're so pretty that will be enough.'

Sitting in the deep dark depths of the church Marie Claire was wishing agonizingly that she had not come to her friend's wedding.

She had watched Diane making her entrance on her father's arm and the long procession up to the altar, followed by a retinue of her old school friends, girls she had known in other carefree years. These were the girls she had played with, laughed with, delighted in being one of them. Now she seemed a century older than any of them.

She had not been with them on the day they had collected their diplomas, celebrated their coming of age parties or shared their first shy experiments with love. She would have to endure their curiosity, their pride when they introduced her to their escorts and they would be ill at ease with her, unsure if they should ask about her life and her child.

They received her kindly, and if their parents frequently gave her fleeting glances of doubt tinged with uncertainty, after the wedding itself, she was aware that she was the topic of conversation when small groups had their heads together.

She was relieved to see the Reverend Mother standing chatting to Diane's parents, and immediately the older woman's smile embraced her as she called to her to join them.

'I am so glad that you are here, my dear, it is wonderful for me to see so many of my girls enjoying themselves at this most happy of occasions.'

Turning to Diane's parents, she said, 'Marie Claire is making quite a career for herself at Monsieur Pouillac's bookshop, he speaks most highly of you, Marie Claire, indeed he doesn't know how he ever managed without you.'

Her companions smiled and Diane's mother said, 'I know Madame Pouillac is unwell and the poor man is quite distraught about it, are you looking after the shop for him?'

'I am helping him with the accounts and the ordering of books.'

'I hadn't thought one could make such a career in a bookshop,' then realizing that perhaps her words seemed an accusation she hurried to say, 'I don't really know anything about working in a bookshop, my dear, I'm sure there is a great deal to do and I'm glad you are helping the poor man.'

Diane's parents smiled and moved away and the Reverend Mother, looking down at her, said, 'You are looking very pretty, Marie Claire, the dress brings out the colour in your eyes.'

It was a new dress bought days before in one of the city's modest shops. She had admired the colour and although she was aware of its cheapness when she viewed the creations worn by the other guests, she was unaware that the beauty of her face and figure gave the gown an enchantment it did not otherwise possess.

Nor was she aware that she was being appraised by a great many masculine eyes or that many of the women were resentful of the fact. As she helped herself to food from the buffet table, several men gathered around her, helping her from the dishes and pouring her wine, and across the table her eyes met the eyes of the lady mayoress, small shrewd eyes in her puffed up face.

That she was surprised to see Marie Claire at the wedding was no exaggeration. Anybody who had behaved as Marie Claire had behaved deserved to be ostracized, not fêted as if nothing had happened. She already decided that she would no longer be a customer at Monsieur Pouillac's shop and she would advise her friends to boycott it also. How could the young people of Dijon be expected to know right from wrong when wrong was rewarded.

Marie Claire smiled at her tentatively, but instead of responding she fixed the girl with a cold hard look and turned away. It was the first truly outright snub she had been subjected to and as she turned to greet her friend Diane was aware of the hint of tears in her eyes.

'Is something wrong?' she asked gently.

'It's nothing.'

'It's Madame Grolan, isn't it? She's a poisonous woman but Mother said we had to ask her because her husband is nice and he is the mayor.'

'It doesn't matter, Diane.'

'We're leaving very soon now, Venice and Rome, then we're going to live in Lyon where Henri's business is. You'll come to see us, Marie Claire?'

'Thank you, I would like to.'

'You're saying that to be polite, but I mean it, Marie Claire.'

She was still aware that from across the room Madame Grolan was watching her and that she had gathered around her a crowd of women who were only too willing to listen to her.

Suddenly she wanted to get out of the scented room and into the fresh air and, meeting her friend's concerned gaze, she said hurriedly, 'I must leave now, Diane, I've had such a lovely time but I promised to do some errands for Madame Pouillac on the way back.'

'You should have a better job than that,' Diane persisted, 'I asked my father and he's promised to let me know if anything suitable for you comes up, I'll be in touch.'

'Really, Diane, there's no need, Monsieur Pouillac has been very kind to me and I'm happy there.'

'Marie Claire, you had a brain we all envied, let my father see what he can do.'

Marie Claire smiled tremulously and after embracing her friend she escaped as quickly as she could from the room. Without looking back she ran down the long curving staircase and out into the late afternoon sunshine, then almost immediately she was swallowed up by the crowd on the narrow street surrounding the cathedral and the sense of freedom gave wings to her heels.

14

Elise Grolan pulled hard on the laces of her corsets, aware of the sharp pain round her midriff. She had eaten far too much at the wedding reception that afternoon and ahead of her lay another reception for visiting dignitaries from Strasbourg.

Her physician had warned her on more than one occasion that she must cut down on the rich foods she loved, but it was difficult for a woman in her position when there was one function after another, and she did so love her role in the community.

Her husband had been tetchy all day. Something was worrying him but she had enough to do with her own problems without going too closely into his.

She tried again to pull in her corset, succeeding this time, but the pain intensified and, defeated, she slackened the laces and put the gown she hoped to wear back into the wardrobe. It would have to be the green satin. She's worn it several times before, but these people may not have seen it, in any case she couldn't face a night sitting at the dinner table ignoring the rich food and feeling sick with discomfort.

Her husband put his head round the door enquiring if she was ready.

'I'm having to wear this old thing,' she complained. 'I hope nobody will notice.'

'What's wrong with it?' he said sharply.

'Why nothing, but I did have a new one all ready but I ate too much at the wedding reception. I wish we hadn't gone.'

'We had to go, the Cladels are important people in the city.'

'I was surprised that they had felt it necessary to invite that Moreau girl. She was an absolute disaster at the convent and left it in disgrace. You're not listening to me, Maurice.'

'No, there's no time for conversation, the carriage is waiting for us. I'll wait for you downstairs.'

He left her to finish her toilet and in some annoyance she thought that he was becoming more and more forgetful and thoughtless about important things. It was just as well that she was there to look after him. That secretary he thought so much of was getting too old, it was time he retired.

When she joined him downstairs he was standing at the door staring out into the night, hardly giving her a second glance to say he approved of her attire.

'Really Maurice,' she complained, 'You might at least have the courtesy to see how I look. You've been wrapped up in your own world for days.'

'I have plenty to worry about,' he said testily.

'What have you to worry about? You're a popular man, we're a very popular couple and I run your house and your life most efficiently.'

He frowned. He had no complaints with the way she ran his home, as for his life, he prided himself that she only thought she ran that, in effect the reality was very different.

'I have plenty to worry about,' he said sharply. 'Pierre is leaving me, he's decided to retire and go and live with his brother.'

'And that's the most sensible thing for him to do. He's getting forgetful. Twice last week I had to take him to task over my guest list for the wine tasting.'

'He had more important things to attend to.'

'That isn't the point. If I were you I would replace him with somebody you could rely on for a great many things other than secretarial work.'

'Come along, the carriage has been waiting some time, if there's anything I hate its arriving late for something like this.'

Well he was going to replace Pierre. But he had his own views on the sort of person he wanted.

It was Monsieur Pouillac himself who first mentioned the position to Marie Claire and she stared at him in some dismay asking, 'Haven't you been satisfied with my work, Monsieur?'

'Indeed I have, my dear, very satisfied, but this really isn't a position for you. You can do a lot better for yourself.'

'But I'm very happy here and I have somewhere to live. If I was even considered for the situation you are talking about I would have to find somewhere to live.'

'But that wouldn't be any trouble, you would have a very good salary, far better than anything you could expect to earn working for me.'

'I'm not sure,' she said doubtfully.

'Well, you don't need to do anything immediately, think about it.

The position becomes vacant in about six weeks so you have ample time.'

She thought about it and discounted it, but it was her friend Diane who hurried into the shop one morning, a happy and smiling Diane, evidently in love with her new husband and with life in general.

She talked about her honeymoon and her new home, said she was visiting her parents for a few days, then went on to talk about the position at the City Hall and that it was one Marie Claire should apply for immediately.

'My father will speak for you, Marie Claire, and the Reverend Mother will be only too happy to endorse everything he says.'

'But where would I live?' Marie Claire cried.

'There are apartments all over Dijon, and you would have the money to pay for one. Think about it, Marie Claire, in no time at all you could bring your daughter to live here and send her to school here.'

'Madame Grolan is hardly likely to approve. She makes it plain she doesn't approve of me or like me.'

'Who cares about her? Everybody knows what she's like, besides it has nothing to do with her.'

'She's the lady mayoress.'

'Because he's the mayor, it was him the city elected, not her.'

'Diane, I don't know. I'm happy here, I like the work and I'm putting a little money away for later. I don't want to take something on that I might live to regret.'

'How can you possibly regret something with more money, more prestige and a better future?'

The more Marie Claire thought about it, the more tempting it became. There was no harm done, she supposed. Perhaps the Reverend Mother would speak up for her and Diane's father had given his promise. If the mayor's wife saw for herself that she was seriously trying to make something of her life, surely she would applaud the attempt instead of denouncing it.

She filled in her application form and together with a letter written neatly in her best handwriting posted it, kissing the envelope briefly, then wishing she had it back again.

Every morning for two weeks she waited avidly for the postman, but in the end it was Monsieur Pouillac who placed the envelope on her desk with a smile saying. 'Here it is, Marie Claire, I am as anxious as you are, so please open it at once and tell me what it says.'

He looked over her shoulder as she read the brief request that she attend for an interview at the mayor's office at ten o'clock on Friday morning, bringing her references.

117

How slowly the rest of the week crawled, but promptly at a quarter to nine on Friday morning she joined two women and a man waiting on the steps of the City Hall and Marie Claire's heart sank. The women were elegantly dressed and older than herself. Inside the hall they sat in silence, occasionally looking up with interest whenever somebody entered the room, and promptly at ten o'clock a tall severe looking man opened the glass doors and said. 'You will be called in alphabetical order. When your interview is over you will leave by the far door and you will be notified in a few days' time if you have been successful or not.' Marie Claire was the last to be called.

The mayor sat behind his large mahogany desk accompanied by two other men and she was told by his secretary to sit in the chair opposite. They smiled and bade her good morning, then they scanned her references and smiling, the mayor said, 'These are excellent, Mademoiselle, and Monsieur Pouillac has already endorsed their words in his letter to me.'

They engaged her in conversation in turn, and to his secretary sitting watching the proceedings it seemed that they had already made up their minds. Marie Claire was the youngest applicant but she was also the most beautiful of the women, and if references were anything to go by, well qualified.

One of the applicants had been disdainful, so that in the end it seemed she had been conducting the interview rather than the men involved. She had done herself a great disservice. The man had been useless, but he had rather liked the girl from Lyon. But the fact that Marie Claire lived in Dijon and had been educated in the city was very much in her favour.

It was over at last and she was hurrying through the park towards the narrow streets in the old part of the city. They had been kind, but no doubt they had been equally kind to the others. She had no means of knowing if she had done well, and over and over throughout the evening she relived the interview, remembering their faces, their smiles and their polite farewells.

In the mayor's office the three men put their heads together but the mayor had already made up his mind. He liked the girl so highly recommended by Monsieur Pouillac and the Reverend Mother, as well as his friend Cladel. To be fair to him it wasn't her beauty that had drawn him to her, but rather her air of quiet efficiency and the soft timbre of her voice.

The argument was brief. Marie Claire had impressed them all, and as he walked home through the park the mayor felt happier than he had felt since his faithful secretary had announced his intention to retire.

A complacent woman, Madame Grolan had betrayed hardly any interest in his secretarial problems. She had thought Pierre efficient, and boring, and of course her husband would miss him, he had oiled the wheels of his position for a very long time and Maurice would be looking for such another treasure to replace him.

For the first time in weeks she heard her husband singing as he entered the bedroom.

She decided not to ask any questions but wait until he raised the subject, but when he had not done so by the time they had finished their meal she said coyly. 'Haven't you something to tell me Maurice?'

He raised his eyebrows maddeningly. 'Have I?' he asked absently.

'Well, of course you have. For weeks I've been listening to you going on and on about Pierre leaving, and you haven't had the courtesy to tell me who you have appointed in his place.'

'I'm sorry my dear, I didn't think you were all that interested. You never had much good to say about Pierre.'

'Well of course I'm interested. I'm always interested in the efficiency of your office. Did you take my advice and choose a man?'

'There was only one male applicant, and he wasn't any good. We interviewed three women, two from Dijon and one from Lyon.'

'From Lyon! travelling would be a problem and finding somewhere here to live. I don't suppose you have appointed her.'

'No. When she left we all heaved a sigh of relief. She interviewed us, it was very unladylike.'

'Really. I hope you put her in her place.'

'We made up our mind from the other three and we were all in agreement. We liked the girl and she had excellent references.'

'She lives in Dijon, of course?'

'Of course, but there is a slight problem. She lives in her employer's house so we shall have to find somewhere else for her to live. That shouldn't be a problem, several of our employees live in apartments owned by the city.'

'What was wrong with the other girls who presumably have somewhere to live, either with their families or elsewhere.'

'As I said Elise, this was the girl we preferred.'

Warning bells were sounding in Madame Grolan's head, and sharply she asked, 'Who is this girl, and who employs her?'

'Pouillac, in his bookshop in Rue Grenelle.'

'Marie Claire Moreau.'

'Why yes. I wasn't aware that you knew the girl. How do you know her?'

'I thought all Dijon knew Marie Claire.'

He stared at her in surprise.

'Really Maurice, how obtuse can you be. She's the girl who left the convent in disgrace, pregnant and refusing to say who was responsible. She was supposed to be the pupil to end pupils but she had no more sense than to make a complete mess of her life. The Reverend Mother was astounded and so was everybody else.'

'The Reverend Mother gave her an excellent reference.'

'Well she would, wouldn't she? I don't suppose it would matter for any other position in the town but not for the mayor's office Maurice. If you employ a girl like that it is tantamount to giving free license to every other girl in Dijon to ruin her life and then expect to be rewarded for it.'

'Isn't that a bit hard, Elise?'

'No, it is not. Really Maurice, is it always me who has to protect you from criticism? Your office and the people employed in it should be sacrosanct, anything less than that reflects upon you. Surely you must see that.'

'I don't think the girl has to be forever damned because of one mistake, evidently she has risen above it and aspires to make something of her life.'

'But not at your expense, Maurice. Let her go on working for Pouillac if he thinks so much of her, after all a city bookshop is hardly to be compared with the office of the mayor of the city.'

'Léon Cladel spoke up for her and he is a big friend of mine.'

'Well, his daughter was at the convent with her, she was invited to Diane's wedding, but when I've spoken to Madame Cladel and explained the circumstances I'm sure they'll understand.'

'I'd rather you kept out of it, Elise.'

'Somebody has to watch out for you, Maurice, you're evidently incapable of doing it for yourself. Appoint one of the other girls, you don't need to give any excuses to the Moreau girl, after all the choice was yours.'

The days seemed endless as Marie Claire waited for the letter that she believed would change her life. Every morning Monsieur Pouillac asked her if she had heard anything, and seemed strangely worried when she said she had not.

One morning after she had once again shaken her head in reply to his question, he said. 'I'll try to find out something, surely by this time they must have decided.'

'Really Monsieur Pouillac, I'd rather you didn't, they might get the feeling that I am desperate for the job and I am happy here with you.'

He stared at her sadly for a few moments before saying, 'That is the problem, Marie Claire. I want you to get this position in the mayor's office, I have grown very fond of you and I would like to think you were settled into something good before we move away.'

She stared at him in astonishment.

'Move away!' she exclaimed.

'My wife would like to move nearer her family in Grenoble. She has a brother there and two sisters and she was brought up there. We have heard there is a bookshop for sale near the University and although I am a Dijon man and am happy here, my wife is my first consideration at this time.'

'Of course. When will you go?'

'I shall have no difficulty in selling this shop, for years I have had people wanting to buy it if I should think of selling. My best offer has come from an old friend who has been persistent over the years.'

'Would he be willing to keep me on if I fail to get the job in the mayor's office?'

He shook his head sadly. 'He has two daughters, Marie Claire, he is anxious to buy the shop for them.'

'I see.' She sat down weakly on her chair, but he smiled at her cheerfully. 'Come now,' he said, 'There is no need to look so despondent, of course you will get the position the mayor has to offer, the wheels in government circles drive exceedingly small.'

The letter from the mayor's office arrived two days later and her fingers trembled as she tried to open it while Monsieur Pouillac stood watching expectantly. The letter was polite but terse. It informed her that she had been unsuccessful on this occasion and that another candidate had been chosen.

They stared at each other in dismay. Her mind was busy with her memories of that morning she had sat facing the mayor and his colleagues. Their smiles, their extreme politeness, their geniality in opening the door for her and ushering her out of the room – had all been so false. As the tears filled her eyes, Monsieur Pouillac's thoughts were entirely different. This was not the mayor's doing, but the vindictiveness of his wife.

Men were above this sort of thing, it was women with their spites and their jealousies, their feuds and their shallow spiteful little minds that did this to one another, it was no wonder that they were excluded from so many things predominately male, and where more often than not they caused mayhem if they were allowed in.

He could well imagine Elise Grolan tittle-tattling among her acquaintances, putting in a word here and there to discredit the girl before him, instilling into her husband's mind the belief that he should not reward Marie Claire for her past sins but rather show the people of Dijon that punishment should be her lot.

'Don't worry, my dear,' he said gently, 'There will be something else for you, something better. I will keep my eyes and ears open.'

'There will be nothing for me in Dijon after this,' she said sadly.

'Why do you say that?'

'Because the punishment will go on and on in the minds of people like Madame Grolan.'

Meeting his sympathetic gaze she knew that his thoughts matched her own.

In the few weeks that followed she watched the disintegration of her world. Suitcases standing in the passages, the departure of Madame Pouillac's nurse and the new owner who came with his daughters to view the shop. They were polite to Marie Claire but, although she was willing to help the two young women, neither of them wanted her help, rather than to indicate that she was superfluous. It was on one such afternoon that she decided to get out into the fresh air. It was cold in the park but she was hardly aware of it as she walked towards to lake where two children were feeding bread to the waterfowl.

She stood at the water's edge staring into the water, her thoughts unconcerned with the flurries of snow and the squabbling of the ducks as they vied with each other for the bread.

In less than a week's time she would have no job and no home. Monsieur Pouillac had urged her to return home to her family. 'They will welcome you back, Marie Claire, they love you, they can't go on year after year grieving for the hurt you did to yourself and them. Besides you must think of your daughter. She needs you in her life, go home for her if for nobody else.'

But did Chantal need her? Did she even remember the mother who had walked out of her life and had not seen fit to return to it? By this time she had probably forgotten what her mother looked like.

The waters of the lake were encouraging. She could walk into those deep dark depths and nobody in the city would miss her, and her death would be a punishment for that poisonous woman who she was convinced hated her enough to deprive her of her livelihood. She took a step nearer the water's edge, so close that the water lapped against her shoes, but to the man walking briskly along the path she was already a figure surrounded by despair and a great loneliness.

The mayor of Dijon had disdained to ride in his ceremonial carriage but favoured instead a walk in the park to revive his spirits. The meeting had been overlong and extremely boring, besides he was not looking ahead to the dinner party his wife had planned for them. There would be invitations to admire her choice of dinner gown, the constant visits to the kitchen where she would interfere with everything that was going on until the kitchen staff wouldn't know whether they were coming or going. Then when the guests began to arrive, the effusive flattering of the women, the coy flirtation with the men and the rich food would do little for his digestion.

He stared again at the girl. Was she not aware that the water was lapping over her shoes, then horrified he watched her take a small step forward until the hem of her gown was awash in the lake. With a sharp cry he left the path and hurried across the grass, breaking into a run and calling out at her at the same time, he realized that she was unaware of his cries, unaware of anything outside a terrible need to leave behind a world that she found intolerable.

As she took another step forward he reached out suddenly and dragged her back, she turned to look up into his face. Then with a little moan she sank helplessly into the water. He reached down and pulled her to her feet, then half dragging, half carrying her he moved backwards on to the grass.

15

Elise Grolan was furious. Her dinner guests were almost due and her husband had not as yet returned home. She had sent a servant round to his office but the entire building was closed and in darkness.

The dining table groaned under heavy crystal and china. The aroma of roasting lamb was overpowering from the kitchens and at any minute her guests would begin to arrive. She was wearing a new gown purchased on her last visit to see her sister in Paris, one which her sister envied if her expression had been anything to go by, and her plump fingers were encrusted with the rings she loved.

The doorbell sounded and after another look in the mirror she hurried into the hall in time to welcome the first of her guests, then almost immediately the others were arriving and she was making excuses for the absence of their host.

'I can't think what has detained him,' she exclaimed. 'He's usually so careful to let me know if anything unusual has cropped up and I'm beginning to feel rather anxious.'

Her guests were quick to pacify her while her servants moved among them serving drinks.

The mayor sat back in his carriage on the way back from Monsieur Pouillac's shop. Marie Claire had gone instantly to her bed but the two men had talked together in the shop, hardly disturbed during the course of the afternoon. Monsieur Pouillac had kept nothing back. He spoke of her disappointment at not being offered the position in the mayor's office, of the trauma that now faced her of having to return to a family she had disappointed, a father who no longer loved her, and a young daughter whom she had promised to bring to Dijon to live with her, something that was no longer possible.

The mayor had listened in silence. He had wanted to employ Marie Claire. She had the best credentials, he would have employed her but for his wife, and looking into Pouillac's eyes he knew that the other man was well aware that it was she who made him change his mind.

Before leaving Pouillac's shop he had promised that he would help to find something to keep Marie Claire in Dijon, after all he knew a great many businessmen. Employment in the city hall was not possible because there would be too much talk, but there would be other irons he could put in the fire.

He frowned at the row of carriages outside his house, remembering that his wife had dinner guests and he was late. She would be in a fine old temper and he had very little time to think of a good excuse for being late home. Fortunately he was saved from making an immediate excuse by greetings from his guests, then he was in the dressing room changing into his evening attire.

During the meal that followed he was constantly aware of the sharp glances of his wife from the other end of the table, but he devoted all his attention to the ladies sitting on either side of him and it was only much later after the guests had departed that his wife said, 'Really Maurice, you might have let me know that you intended to be late, didn't you remember that we were having guests for dinner?'

'I had other things on my mind,' he answered her tersely.

'I sent a servant into the city hall but the place was in darkness, where were you?'

'With a business colleague, nothing you would be interested in.'

'All the same it was thoughtless of you, Maurice. Did you know that the Vicomtesse de Mirandol was shopping in Dijon last week with her English sister-in-law?'

'No I didn't know, what of it?'

'Monsieur le Vicomte's mother never shopped in Dijon, she always went to Paris.'

'It isn't something that interests me.'

'Really Maurice, you are getting quite tetchy these days. We should be glad that the Vicomtesse shops locally, it is good for the city.'

He watched her taking off her rings and dropping them one by one into a glass tray on her dressing table. He allowed his mind to drift on to the events of the afternoon, the girl's large tear-filled eyes and the tragedy in her beautiful face, the frozen dampness of her slender form in his arms, and the air of hopeless that had surrounded her. Looking at his wife unclasping the pearl necklace from around her plump throat a feeling of dislike swept over him.

She had been a plump pretty country girl when he had married her. Her father had been a humble watch-mender with two young daughters and a wife who worked in a local bakery. The elder daughter had married a local gendarme who had left Dijon to work in Paris and risen dramatically at the Sûreté of Police, and after that Elise had always been at the back of him urging him to make more of his life.

Politics had set him on the right path and he had tried to be a good public servant without her pushing him. He was aware of his wife's unpopularity in certain sections and he had been quick to cover up for her, the events of the afternoon were making him see that her interference in his life could have had the most tragic consequences. It seemed that fate had made him walk across the park at that particular time so that he was made aware that Marie Claire's death was something he could lay at his wife's feet.

Well Marie Claire had not died, and now he had the task of finding her employment and somewhere to live. He did not intend to fail, and he had no intention of discussing it with his wife.

Within three days he summoned Monsieur Pouillac to his office to inform him that he had secured a position for Marie Claire with his wine merchant, Honn Devroix, where she would take care of his books and learn about good wines and deal with his customers. A small house owned by the Château Mirandol on the outskirts of Dijon would be found for her and two mornings later he took her there in his carriage to look at it.

The house was one of several occupied by people who worked in the Vicomte's vineyards, the Vicomte's agent had given his permission for Marie Claire to live there, and as she walked through the tiny rooms of the stone cottage, her face was alive with joy.

There was a bedroom for Chantal, and she pictured it adorned with pretty floral curtains and bedspread. There would be pictures on the walls, delicate water-colours and the cupboards would be filled with her toys. There was a tiny garden for her to play in, and in the summer they would grow hollyhocks and marigolds under the cottage walls and in the tiny flowerbeds.

Monsieur Pouillac had promised to leave furniture for her since he had far more than they would ever need and she was taken to meet her new employer, a charming middle-aged man whose wife invited them to tea.

As Marie Claire walked out to the carriage, the mayor stayed behind to speak to his friends and she would have been more than surprised if she could have heard their conversation.

'I do not want my wife to hear of this appointment,' the mayor said. 'She never visits your shop and the girl is well out of the city so they are hardly likely to meet.'

Seeing the twinkle in his friend's eyes, he added shortly, 'The girl has an unfortunate story which she will no doubt relate to you one day, my wife is aware of it and you have known Elise almost as long as I have so you know what mischief she is likely to make. She has already caused the girl some distress? I do not want it repeated.'

The husband and wife exchanged glances before assuring the mayor that they understood, then he turned and walked towards his carriage.

Marie Claire was ecstatic. In a very short time she would be able to go home for her daughter. She would go home filled with news of her cottage and her work, the friends she had made and even the mayor's great kindness and perhaps even her father would relent a little and see that his daughter was not a disaster after all.

That night she wrote a long letter to her mother to say that very soon now she would be coming for Chantal and asked that she tell Chantal a little of why she was leaving the farm and where she was going to live.

In the next few days she said a tearful farewell to Monsieur Pouillac and his wife and she quickly became immersed in her new employment to the delight of all concerned.

Chantal Moreau dawdled on her way from school. The other children all lived in the village and they had not made friends with her. The older children were often unkind. They regarded her as something of a curiosity whose mother was talked about by their parents as somebody who was not quite nice, somebody they had hardly known, somebody who thought herself superior and who had disgraced herself and her family.

Egged on by their elders the younger children played among themselves and Chantal told herself she didn't care. Occasionally along the country lane she paused to pick wild flowers, knowing well that Tante Margot would throw them out immediately, saying that the window-ledges already had too many of them.

She stepped back into the grassy verge as a carriage came along the road, and she stared at the occupants curiously, at a fair-haired woman in a large pink hat and a boy about the same age as herself who smiled and waved his hand.

She had seen them several times along the lane, sometimes accompanied by the Vicomtesse. Once she had been with Tante Jeanne who said it was the Vicomtesse and she had spent every day since trying to imagine what it must be like to live in a château surrounded by gardens and with a drawbridge over the moat.

The boy was nice. She supposed it was his mother who was driving the two horses, the woman never looked at her. As she neared the gate leading into the farmyard, Tante Margot came rushing out of the kitchen calling sharply, 'Hurry child, I only have one pair of hands and there are the chickens to feed. Throw those flowers away, we already have too many.'

She pushed them into the grass in the hope that they would live and, feeling sorry that she had plucked them, then she waited until her aunt thrust a large bowl into her hands and pointed towards the hens scratching at the ground in the yard.

Every day was the same. There would be arguments at the supper table, the baby would be crying and her little boy cousin would scream if she attempted to play with his toys.

After she had fed the fowl she was told by her grandmother to wash her hands and face and take her place at the supper table. Her grandfather was already there, ignoring her presence as usual, but Tante Jeanne came to sit beside her, carrying a letter in her hands. She smiled. 'We have a letter from your mother Chantal, she is coming for you very soon now.' she said.

'When, when is she coming?'

'Very soon. You are going to live in Dijon and you will go to school there.'

Tante Margot snapped, 'But not to the convent of St Agnes I'll warrant. It was wasted on your mother, she'll not be wasting it on you.'

'Leave the child alone, Margot,' uncle Marc said. 'You never waste an opportunity, do you. Be thankful the child's going, it's what you've always wanted, isn't it?'

'It will be one mouthful less to feed considering my dear sister's contributed very little.'

'She sent a little money every week, didn't she,' he replied. 'And she was saving up for something better for them in the city.'

'Oh well, you always took her part.'

'Didn't you always fancy her?' Uncle Marcel put in, and immediately Uncle Marc reached out and lifted him by the collar so that they faced each other angrily.

'Sit down both of you,' Grandpère said, 'I'll have no brawling in the house, nor any more talk of Marie Claire. If she comes she comes, I'd like her to be quickly gone.'

Chantal didn't understand. Talk of her mother always brought that look of anger into her grandfather's eyes, and as she lowered her eyes over her plate to thank God for her evening meal she asked herself anxiously how long it would be before her mother came for her.

Now every day after school she wandered down to the station to watch the country train from Dijon disgorging its handful of passengers, and the great Express came roaring through the station without stopping.

She was trying to remember what her mother looked like. She had

128

seen pictures of her put away in a drawer by her grandmother, a very young girl with black hair and a beautiful face wreathed in smiles. They were taken when her mother was only a schoolgirl; perhaps she wouldn't look like that any more, perhaps she wouldn't even remember her.

Once Tante Margot came looking for her at the station, shaking her angrily and saying, 'What are you doing here, there's errands to run and work to be done, you'll see your mother soon enough, when she decides to keep her promise and come for you.'

After that she stayed away from the station except on Saturday morning when there was no school and they were glad she was out of the house amusing herself.

She was sitting on a bank overlooking the station watching people alight from the morning train, mostly villagers who had been up to Dijon to the big market. Some of them looked at her curiously and she was about to turn away when from further down the platform she saw a woman stepping down from the train. She was tall and slender, and she was smartly dressed in a navy-blue skirt and white lawn blouse. She was wearing a navy-blue straw hat on her dark hair and she walked gracefully along the platform carrying a small valise. There was something about her that kept Chantal's eyes riveted on her, and as she left the station yard and started to walk along the path she looked up and their eyes met. In that one brief moment Chantal knew that this was the mother she had been waiting for, and with a little cry she leapt from the bank and into Marie Claire's arms.

'How did you know I was coming today?' Marie Claire asked gently.

'I didn't. I hoped. Every day I hoped.'

Hand in hand they walked along the path, oblivious of those they met on the way, but long before sundown the entire village knew that Marie Claire Moreau had come home.

Her mother welcomed her with tears in her eyes, her father with a long cool stare, Jeanne and Marc with pleasure, Margot and Marcel not at all.

Her employer had given her four days' holiday but she knew she would go back to the city on the first train on Monday morning. There was nothing for her at the farm, there would never be anything for either herself or her daughter.

She was not encouraged to stay. Her mother had always been troubled by her father's moods; now she knew her presence was upsetting the house and there was no forgiveness in his heart.

Chantal helped her to pack her clothes in the valise. There were not many of them and Marie Claire promised that she would soon be able to chose new ones to take their place. Uncle Marc drove them to the station in the trap and as he pulled up, a grand carriage was pulling up next to them and a coachman was assisting a woman to descend, accompanied by a young boy. The boy smiled at Chantal, but the woman swept ahead without a backward glance. At the same moment a woman rode along the path on a chestnut horse, dismounting at the station gate and the servant carrying the luggage went forward to tether the animal to the fence.

Marie Claire and Chantal watched with interest. Marie Claire had seen the blonde woman before when she walked with Andrew across the sunflower field, and as she stared at the boy her eyes grew hostile. He was so like Andrew, fair-haired and commanding, even in one so young, and when they reached the platform she continued to watch them chatting easily together.

They could hear the sound of the train, and the Vicomtesse bent down to embrace the child before she embraced the woman, then the Express train from Switzerland was stopping and the woman and the boy were being assisted into their compartment. They stood at the window of the compartment until the train rounded the bend on the track and then the Vicomtesse mounted her horse and rode away.

Looking up at her mother Chantal couldn't understand why her mother's face suddenly looked so bleak, as if she had been hurt. Of course it must have been Grandfather who had not even said goodbye.

Marie Claire would not allow bitterness to cloud the future she had planned for herself and her daughter, the past was past, she had to get on with living but in her innermost heart she felt the bitterness still there, the pain of rejection, the anguish of giving herself to a man who had thought her of little worth.

Although the cottage was small she knew how to make it homely and attractive. She had good taste in embellishing the furniture Monsieur Pouillac had been so generous with, and she chose her curtains and cushions with care to the limit of money she had available. She made friends with her neighbours although they regarded her as something of a mystery and she debated whether she should call herself Madame or be strictly honest and retain her Mademoiselle status. In the end she decided it should be the latter.

The visit of the Reverend Mother set the seal on her respectability and as they sat in the tiny living room drinking coffee Reverend Mother admired everything she saw but most of all Chantal, who was a pupil at the small village school.

'I hope one day she will come to us at the Abbey,' she said with a smile. 'You will help her Marie Claire, and I can tell that the child has potential.'

'You would take her at the Abbey, Reverend Mother? Even without a scholarship?'

'But she will have her scholarship, Marie Claire, I am convinced of it.'

Marie Claire smiled. It seemed at last that things were going right for her. She had work which interested her: oh, not her high-flung ambitions, but every day she was learning the absorbing knowledge of wines, the best years, the best vintages, the preferences of Monsieur Devroix' customers, and because he was hopeless with figures, more and more he had come to depend upon her. For three years life was good for Marie Claire and Chantal, until that summer's day when she stood with Chantal at the edge of the lake watching the antics of the waterfowl.

She never thought of that afternoon when the waters of the lake had seemed so inviting and she had been on the verge of ending her life. Now everything had changed, and she could laugh with her daughter at the squabbling of the ducks and the sunlight gleaming across the rippling waves.

Elise Grolan, driving in her carriage along the wide central avenue, was intent on the charity meeting she was expecting to chair that afternoon and she was silently rehearsing her opening speech. She looked across towards the lake and the two figures strolling along the banks. The little girl ran on towards a small dog playing in the long grass and the woman turned to watch her. Surely she couldn't be mistaken.

There were many tall slender women in Dijon, but there had always been something about Marie Claire Moreau that had set her apart, an enchanting elegance, a strangely mature grace even as a child, and that shining blue-black hair that lifted gently in the breeze. The child too had a grace, but otherwise they were very different for the child's hair was honey-coloured. She had to be sure, and so she reached out with her parasol to poke the driver saying sharply, 'Stop the carriage right here.'

The driver complied and she sat back to watch the two figures sauntering together now along the margin of the lake. They were walking towards her, and in minutes she was staring into Marie Claire's green eyes and had the satisfaction of seeing the younger woman's face grow pink with embarrassment before she hurried the child on, and she waited in the carriage until they had reached the park gates and the road beyond.

Neither the woman nor the child turned round once, but there was no mistaking her. What was she doing back in Dijon and where was she living? She had every intention of informing Maurice that very

131

evening of all she had seen. She would demand that he find out where the girl was working, indeed some man could have been foolish enough to marry her and give her some semblance of respectability. Maurice had enough irons in the fire to find out all she needed to know, indeed there were women at the meeting who might know.

Maurice Grolan was aware that his wife had been unusually silent over their evening meal. Normally she prattled on about her meetings, what they talked about, who was there, and all that was necessary from him was an occasional grunt. They were at the coffee stage before she said, 'I drove through the park this afternoon and who do you think I saw, that Moreau girl who hoped to be your secretary.'

The mayor's eyes narrowed, but he waited in silence for what was to come.

'I'd have recognized her anywhere, and she had her daughter with her, she looks about seven or eight, a blonde child, the father must have been blond. Do you suppose she's living in Dijon again? I wonder where she's working, the Pouillacs are still in Grenoble.'

Still he remained silent, and in some annoyance she snapped, 'Aren't you interested, Maurice? The nerve of that girl never ceases to amaze me. Most decent girls would wish to return to their families and stay there, not be seen showing themselves in a city as though nothing had happened.'

'I don't think it's any of our business, Elise.'

'If nobody took a stand against women like her the city would be deluged with illegitimate children.'

'So you think it's a good idea to persecute the girl, do you? Your interference has already cost her one position, do you intend to go on time and again acting as judge and jury in something that is none of your business.'

She stared at him open-mouthed.

'Really Maurice, when I interfered with your selection of a secretary it was so that people would not say you were encouraging and rewarding her behaviour. In my position as your wife I feel I have a duty to speak out about people's morals, take a lead in what is right and acceptable in everybody's behaviour.'

'Even if it means making yourself unpopular?'

'I? Unpopular?'

'That's what I said. There are people in this town who resent your high-handed pontificating on what is right and proper. A little Christian charity can often be seen as more helpful than a stream of platitudes.'

She stared at him out of a red angry face, then rising to her feet she said haughtily, 'Nobody could ever accuse me of unChristian behaviour. I am hurt and appalled at your suggestions that I am un-popular and at the stance you are taking about this girl. I shall go to bed, this business has given me a terrible headache. Perhaps when you've had time to think about it you will apologize, Maurice.'

'Don't you intend to finish your coffee?'

Without another word she swept out of the room and, after pouring himself another cup of coffee, he sat back to ponder on what he could do to protect Marie Claire from his wife's crusade against her.

He knew Elise. She would make it her business to find out where Marie Claire was living, where she was working and any other titbit of information that would show the girl up in a bad light. He had to make sure that she did as little damage as possible.

16

Marie Claire sat in front of her fire with an open book on her lap but she was not reading. She had tried to concentrate on the dress she was making for her daughter but that too had been unable to maintain her attention, and now all she could see in the fire's embers was the big disapproving face of the mayor's wife and her small openly hostile eyes.

It was all going to start again. She would threaten her husband to take his custom away from anybody who employed her, she would talk to her friends and they would boycott the shop, and where could she run to this time?

She had thought returning to the farm was an impossibility before, it was doubly so now and what could she tell Chantal who was happy in the city and who was fast making friends?

She had no armour to fight a woman like Madame Grolan, no man to stand besides her and take her part, and unbidden the tears rose into her eyes and slowly fell upon the pages of the open book. She looked up startled at the sound of the door knocker, and stood hesitantly behind the door. She could not imagine who could be visiting her in the dark and in a trembling voice called out, 'Who is there?'

'Open the door please,' a man's voice replied.

'Who are you?'

'Maurice Grolan.'

She stared at the door incredulously, then went forward hurriedly to open the door. He was alone, standing on the threshold with a slight smile on his face, then removing his hat he followed her into the room. He looked round appreciatively. 'This is quite charming,' he said softly. 'You have done well Marie Claire.'

She blushed, then indicated the other chair opposite hers. She asked, 'Can I offer you a glass of wine, or coffee?'

'A glass of wine please, if you will join me.'

She went into the small kitchen and after a few moments came back carrying a small tray on which rested two glasses of red Burgundy. He raised his glass and sniffed the wine appreciatively, then raising his glass he said softly, 'To you my dear. Now please sit down and let us talk.'

Out came the trauma of the afternoon, her fears, her helplessness and he listened without speaking, watching the girl's beautiful face and the expressions that chased themselves across it, and the more she talked the angrier he became with the woman who was his wife.

At last he said, 'You are happy here, Marie Claire?'

'Yes, very happy, and Chantal is happy too. I have to think about my daughter, it is I who have sinned, Chantal is innocent, and what of my sin. Is loving a man desperately a sin, is believing that he loved me a sin, and how long must I go on paying for that sin?'

'There will be no more paying, Marie Claire. My wife will be silenced, I shall see to it.'

'But how is it possible?'

'Trust me, Marie Claire, I have promised, haven't I?'

He had promised but he did not as yet know how much that promise was worth. He visualized the storms ahead, Elise on one of her crusades of righteousness was a formidable adversary, but this girl had been hurt enough, Somehow or other she had to be silenced.

'Now tell me about your daughter,' he said. 'Is she as beautiful as her mother?'

'Oh yes, much more so. She has golden hair and dark blue eyes and people stare at her all the time to think how lovely she is.'

'And how unusual in a land of dark-haired girls.'

Marie Claire blushed.

'She takes after her father then this daughter of yours?' he said gently.

Marie Clare nodded, leaving him wondering where she had met a man with such colouring. He could not remember having seen anybody except at the Vicomte de Mirandol's banquets and memories of them left him wondering about those young confident aristocrats with too much money, and too much time on their hands.

There were many times over the next few weeks when the Mayor of Dijon visited the woman living with her daughter in the tiny cottage on the outskirts of the city, and he came to look forward to those visits when he could peacefully smoke his pipe while he watched her dark head bent over her sewing, listen to her gentle voice speaking on matters that interested her, and he came to see the keen probing mind and the dazzling intellect that had promised so much.

135

He enjoyed the peace on those innocent winter evenings and he was careful not to advertise his presence by using the mayoral carriage.

His wife complained bitterly that he seemed to have more and more meetings in the evening and she began to make enquiries. She was good at probing, innocent questions that evoked answers that infuriated her although she hid her chagrin well.

She told herself that Maurice had never been interested in other women. He had steered clear of any hint of scandal even when those around him had their little affairs and foibles, but now she began to ask questions of those evenings when she dined alone and when she lay in bed waiting for the sound of his key in the lock. She was wise enough to ask no questions. There was another matter that commanded her attention and that was Marie Claire, where was she working and where was she living?

She had seen her several times in and around the city, around the shops and walking in the park, meeting her daughter from school and when her curiosity was sufficiently satisfied she set about the task of destroying Marie Claire's newfound prosperity.

She decided it would not be through her husband, not at her door would he be able to lay the girl's downfall, and surreptitiously she got at her friends and acquaintances. Now Marie Claire's employer was puzzled as one after the other his customers began to desert him, customers who had been loyal to him for a great many years, and seeing his puzzlement Marie Claire's heart sank. It was all happening again, and she was well aware of the identity of her enemy. She decided that her anxieties should not be expressed to the mayor himself, her employer would do that in his own time, but with deep anger in her heart she set about making herself a more charming companion. She cooked delicious meals for them to enjoy, and she dressed in her prettiest clothes. He was old enough to be her father but that did not worry her.

There was no other man in her life and her experience with a younger man had hardly been a happy experience. Maurice Grolan was happier than he had been in years. He thought about his wife with her dictatorial meddling, her large overpowering presence and her strictures on what he should or should not do. Now here was this young woman with her beauty, her softness and her accommodating charm. He was so besotted with her that he failed to see his wife's angry narrowed eyes and her lack of questions should have alarmed him but he merely congratulated himself that she was totally unaware of his ever-increasing visits to Marie Claire.

She believed there was another woman and she racked her brains to think who it could be. She thought about the wives of his friends, her

136

own friends, some of whom were flirtatious and who would be nothing loath to relieve the boredom of their marriages with a light flirtation. That, she complacently told herself, was all that it could ever be.

It was one evening when she was driving home from one of her charity afternoons that she saw her husband stepping into a carriage in one of the small cobbled streets near the cathedral. Why wasn't he using the mayor's carriage, and why was he looking up and down the street with some degree of anxiety? Without further ado she commanded her driver to follow his carriage, and as they left the city centre behind at first there was only puzzlement and then anger when she realized where he was going.

She sat in her carriage while he descended on to the road, then she waited while he walked along the narrow lane lined with cottages. With her face red with resentment she watched him walk up the path of the middle cottage and knock on the door, then clearly she saw the joyous welcome he received from the young woman in her fashionable pale-blue silk gown.

She wanted to go inside the cottage and face them both. She wanted to rake her long fingers along the girl's pretty face, to destroy her beauty for ever, and then to threaten her husband with every dire scandal that would ruin him. Instead she ordered her driver to take her home, and if there was a smirk on his face she wasn't aware of it.

In the days that followed Elise sulked and her husband was unaware of it, she vented her spite on Marie Claire whenever she could and in whichever company she happened to be until those others present asked themselves why this should be, and gradually they began to drift back to the wine merchant who had always pleased them, and wondered carelessly why they had ever left him.

It was one morning when she was shopping in the exclusive part of the city that she came face to face with Marie Claire in the doorway of her favourite shop. The younger woman looked at her calmly, betraying no recognition and as she watched her walking away such a feeling of anger consumed her that she stepped out into the roadway without thinking and immediately became aware of the sound of carriage wheels and the high startled whinnying of a horse. She never knew what hit her, but from all directions people came running and within minutes in the mayor's offices all was consternation as the accident of Madame Grolan was reported to the mayor.

He was by her bedside when she died several hours later, and his face was sad and bleak with memories of the simple country girl he had once loved. What was it that had changed her, turned her into a spiteful harridan, obsessed with power, envious and jealous of her own shadow?

For weeks after his wife's funeral he stayed away from Marie Claire, then he forgot to be remorseful and the sheer loneliness of his life took him back.

There were those in Dijon who were only too anxious to remember her past and thought that he of all people should remember his wife's strictures and leave her alone, but there were others who wished him well, even envied him.

After a respectable interval the marriage of the Mayor of Dijon and his beautiful bride promised to be the event of the season. Marie Claire had wanted a quiet affair, banquets and parties would come later, but the mayor said he owed it to his standing in the town to make no hole and corner ceremony that would open everybody's mouths.

'And what about your family, my dear, surely they will want to come up to the city to see you marry the mayor?'

'Papa was always too busy to do anything. They never took holidays, never visited relations, he attended my sisters' weddings in the morning and attended to his cattle in the afternoon.'

'So you don't intend asking them? Have you told them about the wedding?'

She smiled. 'But of course, and I have told them not to send a wedding present, there is nothing we need.'

Her parents had received news of her wedding with mixed feelings. Jeanne and Marc thought she would make an excellent lady mayoress, and Jeanne had the temerity to say, 'You see Papa, Marie Claire didn't make her way in Paris but she will be the first lady of Dijon.'

Her father scowled. 'And how has she done it? By making herself available to a man old enough to be her father, and while his wife is still warm in her grave.'

Marcel was cynical, Margot envious, and Madame Moreau wished fervently that she could go to the Notre-Dame church in Dijon to see her daughter married, to see the congregation of fashionable people, why even the Vicomte himself and his lady might be there.

On the day of the wedding it seemed that the city of Dijon came to a standstill and the bells pealed out across the city and the surrounding countryside. Marie Claire had never looked more beautiful in a delicate pink crêpe-de-chine gown. In her hair she wore a halo of pink roses and white cyclamen, and there was a proud smile on Monsieur Pouillac's face as he offered her his arm. He had come all the way from Grenoble to attend the wedding, and while the congregation looked on in admiration there were tender knowing smiles for the young girl who followed her mother down the aisle.

Chantal showed all the promise of beauty her mother had shown at the same age. Wearing pale blue silk with white roses in her hair her colouring was a complete contrast to her mother's vibrant beauty and there were those in the church who speculated.

The Vicomtesse de Mirandol was tantalized by the bride's face. Where had she seen it and when? They told her that she was employed by a wine merchant in the city and that an unfortunate incident in her youth had produced the daughter. Vivienne de Mirandol admired the girl's efforts to rise above such a calamity, but later at the reception she watched the girl's laughing face, the grace of her movements and again she was puzzled.

She made herself be especially gracious, inviting the mayor and his new mayoress to the château, enthusing charmingly on the effect a new and beautiful mayoress would have on the life of the city and after kissing Marie Claire graciously on both cheeks and after watching her husband reciprocate the gesture they walked away.

Marie claire watched them go and for the first time in her exiting day a vague feeling of anxiety swept over her. In Vivienne de Mirandol's face she had seen something she thought she had forgotten, something so elusive she felt unsure, but as her eyes followed the Vicomtesse's dazzling figure across the room, memories that were painful refused to go away. Today of all days she had not wanted to feel this bleak awareness of a remembered pain, but there had been something in the slow charm of her smile, the clipped English voice and the intense blue of her eyes.

How long must she remember? How long would the memories hurt? Across the room she found her husband's eyes on her and he smiled. Life would be different now, no man would ever hurt her again and no man would hurt Chantal. She would teach her daughter how to take what she wanted when she wanted it, never to be swayed by love or compassion. No man would ever hurt Chantal as she had been hurt.

Now Marie Claire shopped in the best and most expensive shops in Dijon. They visited Paris and Nice and he found pleasure in indulging every whim as they shopped for silks and satins and furs. There were presents for Chantal too, and he had raised no objections when Marie Claire had asked if she could join the pupils at the convent of St Agnes.

After their short honeymoon they returned to Dijon so that Maurice could take up his duties and she could take up hers as the youngest and most beautiful hostess the city could remember.

Indulgently, he watched her efforts to entertain his guests, and he could hardly believe that this young and vibrant woman was now his wife. If he thought about Elise at all, the comparison was too unkind and he thought about something else quickly so that his memory of her would not be distressing.

He had no illusions about his second marriage. Marie Claire was not in love with him although she did love him as her benefactor and dear friend. In time there would be admirers, other men, some of whom she might love, but for now life was good for him, the future was something else.

As the months passed it seemed to Marie Claire that she had never known another life because nothing of the past came to trouble the present.

The admiration she read in mens' eyes pleased her but she was wary of it. She found she could flirt with the best of them but she gave nobody the chance to read anything in those flirtations in case they might remember the cruel things Elise had said of her.

All Burgundy was bracing itself for the wine festival and Maurice showed her with pride the beautifully embellished invitation they had received to take part in the festivities at the Château Mirandol. Once she had gazed at the château through the trees and wondered what it would be like to ride across the drawbridge in a handsome carriage with a gallant gentleman beside her. It was true he had never resembled Maurice. Her dream escort had been young and handsome, a man who would waltz her round the ballroom, gazing into her eyes with boyish admiration.

They were to stay three nights at the château and she packed with care after asking Maurice what sort of clothes she would need. She found herself remembering the woman she had seen with Andrew, the beautiful blonde woman with the pretty dress and the charming hat, and her heart suddenly missed a beat. Would Andrew and that woman be guests at the château, and in the fashionably dressed mayoress of Dijon would Andrew remember his Sunflower Girl?

She looked along the table at the array of beautifully dressed women and their escorts on that first night and knew she was a match for any one of them. They had been received graciously by the Vicomte and his lady and the man sitting next to her, a high ranking army officer was attentive and flattering.

She didn't know whether to be relieved or disappointed that Andrew was not among the guests and she racked her brains in an effort to think how she could question her hostess about him. She knew he was a friend of the Vicomte, but there was more than that. She remembered the talk in the village at the time of their wedding and the English relatives that had come over from England to attend it.

Before they retired for the night the Vicomtesse asked if any of her guests would like to ride with her in the morning, and meeting Marie Claire's eyes she said, 'Perhaps you would like to ride with me Madame le maire?'

'I am not a very good horsewoman,' Marie Claire answered, 'I have not ridden a horse for many years.'

'Oh, but we can find you a docile mount, and if you have not brought riding clothes, some of mine will fit you. Please say you will come, you will enjoy it.'

'Thank you, I would like to.'

Maurice was pleased, but she said anxiously. 'I shouldn't have agreed to ride with her, she's known to be a good horsewoman and I shall be hopeless, I just know I will.'

'Nonsense my dear. You heard what she said, a docile mount and a riding habit to fit you. She likes you, Marie Claire. It is gratifying to know that.'

Maurice was delighted that she had been singled out for special attention by their hostess. Elise had never merited such discrimination. He watched her ride out with the Vicomtesse on a gentle mare trotting sedately beside the prancing black horse ridden by the other woman.

'We will keep to the lanes,' Vivienne said, 'There is so much farm land around here, we do not want to make ourselves unpopular with the farmers. Do you know this part of the country at all?'

'Yes, I have always lived in Burgundy.'

For some little while they rode in silence, and Marie Claire looked out across her fathers fields towards the farmhouse where she had been born, and her companion strove to restrain her restive horse.

'He would like to gallop,' she said with a little laugh. 'He would have been happier in the grounds of the château, but I was mindful that you said you were an inexperienced horsewoman.'

They rode on and eventually came to a field that had once been filled with sunflowers, now stretching away from them in straight empty furrows.

'My brother came here many years ago to paint,' Vivienne said. 'He painted the picture of a field bright yellow with sunflowers but I have never been able to find it. Any one of these fields could have been the one I suppose, but it is such a pity to have taken them away.'

Marie Claire remained silent and Vivienne mused, 'It was the best thing he ever did. My father was always scathing about his work but that picture he very grudgingly admired.'

'Just a field filled with sunflowers?' Marie Claire ventured.

'No, there was a young girl sitting on a stile looking out across the fields, a girl with long black hair and wearing a pretty dress. A schoolgirl Andrew said, probably one of the farmer's daughters.'

141

'Did he never come back here to paint something else?'

'No. He came back for our wedding but Constance was with him. He had no time for painting.'

'Constance?'

'His wife. He came here to forget her, then unfortunately my eldest brother was killed in India and Andrew was ordered back home to claim his brother's title.'

'It is strange that he came away to forget her and yet he married her,' Marie Claire said. She had to know the answers to questions that had lain dormant for so many years.

'Not so very strange, my dear, if you knew the sort of things that go on in our class-ridden society. Constance loved him for his title; before the title her mother thought him entirely unsuitable.'

'I'm surprised that his pride allowed him to marry her at all if that was the case.'

Vivienne smiled. 'People in love are not always very rational, my dear. My father would have agreed with you, it was a marriage he disapproved of entirely.'

'Are they happy?'

'I shall never know. My father died last year so Andrew is now an earl. They have a son Sebastian and a daughter Grace.'

'Is your sister-in-law very beautiful?'

'A great many people think so. She makes a very engaging countess. I think perhaps we will ride back now. Have you enjoyed yourself?'

'Very much, the horse has behaved beautifully.'

Vivienne smiled. 'You will be good for Maurice, he is a dear man and he dotes on you.'

'I know. He is a very kind man.'

'I hardly knew his first wife, although she did accompany him to the château once or twice. You have a daughter I am told.'

'Yes, Chantal.'

'And where is she while you and Maurice are here?'

'She had permission to stay at the Abbey, and she has made many friends there.'

17

Vivienne asked no more questions and Marie Claire was glad that her restive horse needed all her attention. As they neared the cottage and the great iron gates beyond she was momentarily disconcerted to see Marcel driving his buggy along the road. Their eyes met, but in Marie Claire's eyes there was no sign of recognition, not even when Marcel's surprise turned into a sly sneer.

When he returned to the farm she had no doubt he would embroider on their meeting, but she could only remember his coarse hands caressing her arm when he thought he was unobserved, and his thigh pressing against her as they sat around the supper table.

Her hostess had given her too much to think about: those weeks of tenderness and love which she had cherished from a man who loved another woman, and she knew now that he had never intended to return to her. She had meant nothing to him, and a terrible and remorseless anger was born in her, more terrible than anything she had felt before.

That night the wine flowed freely and in the park the guests gathered to watch the fireworks and rejoice in the fruitfulness of the grape harvest. Vivienne moved among her guests with easy charm, and watching her Marie Claire saw Andrew's smile in her smile, even the turn of her head brought him back to her and with her memories came the desire to wipe that confident smile off her face for ever.

With Maurice she mingled among the other guests. She chatted to aristocrats as if she had known them all her life, and the women were tolerant while the men basked in her smiles. It was the end of the evening when the Vicomte kissed her hand and smiling down at her asked her if she had enjoyed the festival.

This man was Andrew's friend, she told herself, and he was handsome, her hand lingered in his for longer than was necessary and under his regard her beauty blossomed. Superfluous, Maurice drifted away.

He was tired, it had been a long day and only the younger element were still intent on enjoying themselves. The Vicomte was only too willing to entertain his pretty young guest as they sauntered together underneath the trees. Like his father before him he loved beautiful women, he knew how to flatter them, how to charm them with his attentions and he was handsome.

From her place with her friends on the terrace, his mother read the signs well. André was too much like his father, readily flattered, easily swayed. She had been amused by it and ready to play him at his own game; Vivienne was a different matter. Her fine eyes swept over the gatherings below and found Vivienne in the midst of a laughing crowd, complacent and unaware of the two figures strolling across the lawn, totally engrossed in each other.

The Mayor of Dijon was sitting with his cronies on the terrace, stupidly mellow with all the fine wine he had consumed, pleased with his young wife's success at the festival and entirely happy that somewhere she was doubtless enjoying herself.

Catching her daughter-in-law's eyes she smiled, and excusing herself Vivienne left her group to join her on the terrace.

'It has all gone remarkably well,' the older woman said, 'but then it always does.'

'I'm so glad that you came,' Vivienne said, 'especially when you said last year that you wouldn't come again.'

'Oh I say that every year, my dear. This year the people have been particularly charming, that little wife of the mayor is so much more entertaining than his late wife ever was.'

'Yes, Elise Grolan had a reputation for meddling, and particularly spiteful meddling at that.'

Vivienne's eyes surveyed the crowds below them. 'I don't see her,' she said with a little smile. 'His Worship the Mayor seems happy sitting with his friends, I hope his mayoress is not amusing herself too ardently with her many admirers.'

Only with one admirer, the Vicomte's mother thought cynically but was careful to say nothing.

Marie Claire smiled to herself the next morning as she drove with her husband into the city in his brand-new Mayoral carriage. They had said their farewells to their host and hostess and the many others who had been part of the house party at the Château Mirandol but it was her host's last words that were making her smile now.

He had asked her to have dinner with him one evening when he was next in Dijon. She had charmingly thanked him for his invitation but said it might not be possible, but he had waved her protests aside. He knew the mayor was often engaged on civic business and wife was going home to England to attend the christening of her brother's youngest daughter. It was this last statement that made Marie Claire agree to any assignation he might propose.

His wife had done her no harm – in fact she liked her – but her heart was burdened with the hurts and anguish of the past. If she could hurt Vivienne it was aimed at the hurt she wanted to inflict on Andrew, and it would be the beginning.

As she knelt in the confessional box the following Sunday in church she knew the sin of vengeance was one she should confess but she could not. Over and over she told herself that Andrew and anybody close to him deserved to suffer as she had suffered, there was no need to confess any of it, it was justice.

When the Vicomte's invitation did not come immediately she became angry. Of course people like him did not honour their promises so why had she been naïve enough to think he would? Indeed it was early spring when she recognized the coat-of-arms on the envelope addressed to her. Unfortunately Maurice noticed it also and for the first time she had to lie to him.

'Is it from the Vicomtesse?' he asked with a smile.

'Yes, one of her charities she has asked me to help with.'

Maurice smiled well pleased. 'I told you she liked you, dear, I don't recollect that Elise was ever asked to help with anything.'

He departed for his office in high good humour.

The letter was from the Vicomte himself asking her to have dinner with him at the château on the following Wednesday, a day he knew the mayor would be Lyon on civic business. He himself had been expected to be one of the party but had had to decline on the grounds of having more pressing business to attend to. The invitation was followed by expressions of how urgently he was looking forward to being with her, and to please, please say she would come.

That evening Maurice went into great detail about his visit to Lyon and she quickly realized he was expecting her to be visiting Lyon with him. Dismayed she started to make excuses, 'But I have a fitting at the costumiers that morning, dear,' she said anxiously. 'I didn't know ladies were invited and in the afternoon there is the Vicomtesse's charity meeting.'

It was the letter that wiped the frown off the Mayor's face. Of course, the Vicomtesse and her charity were every bit as important as having his wife beside him in Lyon, and it would have been very boring for Marie Claire.

Maurice Grolan made his plans for his visit to Lyon, and his wife replied in the affirmative to the Vicomte's letter. She felt confident that

Maurice would not learn that Vivienne was visiting her family in England and that the charity was a fabrication of his wife's.

Deception leant excitement, excitement which increased as she drove along the familiar lanes of her childhood in the Vicomte's carriage. She had waited for this carriage to bring Andrew back to her but it never came; now she sat in it alone, savouring the rich dark leather and the prancing gait of the two grey horses. An attentive driver had placed a rug over her knees and inside it her hands felt warm and cosy, and if those she passed on the country lanes stared at her curiously, she merely stared back unconcerned. They would not recognize the elegant woman visiting the château as the young Marie Claire who had danced her way along these same lanes on her way from the station at the start of her school holidays.

The Vicomte was at his most charming, attentive to every want, escorting her through the rooms of the château as an honoured guest, and she said nothing of the years she had stood on the outside romanticising on what went on behind the old stone walls and the people who lived there.

She had grown up since those innocent years. She knew that the Vicomte admired her, but he was a man who would admire many women and she was not interested in his attempts at flirtation, only in what she could learn of his wife's family in England.

'I have wondered Monsieur le Vicomte why you married an English lady, were our French ladies not to your liking?' she asked with a smile.

'There were a great many ladies to my liking but I was not looking for marriage at that time. Vivienne was always different.'

'How was she different?'

'We met as children, and there were years in between when we did not meet at all, but we met again at her brother's wedding and she had grown up beautifully. We fell in love, it was as simple as that, and perhaps the time had come for both of us to marry.'

'Didn't her family mind that she married a Frenchman?'

He smiled. 'Obviously there had been no lack of suitors for the hand of an earl's daughter, but none of them had captured her heart. Perhaps it was always mine.'

'And her father approved?' she persisted.

'Her father would have disapproved of the Archangel Gabriel. He disapproved of me and the woman his son married. He was that sort of man.'

'Why did he disapprove of his son's wife?'

'Chérie, I have shown you the château and all its beauties and now you are more interested in my wife's family in England, I had thought

146

this might be a time when you would be a little interested in me.'

'Well of course I am, but I have never been to England, never been anywhere at all, so naturally I would like to know what happens in other cultures and in other lands.'

He laughed, disposed to indulge her.

'Her brother Andrew was my friend. He came here to get over the fact that the woman he loved had decided to marry another. He decided to stay at the cottage rather than enter into the festivities that might be going on here. He wanted to be alone I think, to paint and get over his disappointment. I have no idea how well he was succeeding. He was recalled home because his elder brother was killed in India, that meant of course that Andrew was now the heir to an earldom, and the next I learned about him was that he was to marry. I rather think the lady of his choice had regretted her engagement and Andrew had considerably more to offer her.'

'That is horrible. How can a man be so foolish, surely he must have known why she was marrying him?'

'Not necessarily, my dear. I rather think she had loved him when she agreed to marry somebody else, but she had a very formidable mother and marriages in our exalted circles are not always engineered in Heaven.'

'And have they been happy in their marriage?'

The Vicomte shrugged his shoulders. 'Who can tell. The old man died a few months ago, so Constance is now the Countess of Westmond which I have no doubt has pleased her mother considerably. It is amazing how happiness and ambition can go hand in hand.'

'Do they have children?'

'A son Sebastian and his twin sister Grace, now they have another daughter Alice. My wife has gone home for the christening since she has been invited to be the child's godmother. Now Chérie, have I answered all your questions and is it possible that you can be a little more curious about me?'

'I had not thought that you were inviting my curiosity, Monsieur le Vicomte?'

He threw back his head and laughed. 'No, I shall be curious about you, why someone so young and beautiful was content to marry an old man and spend her young life among all those pompous civic dignitaries?'

'Perhaps because he was a truly kind man, a rarity amongst the men I had known, appearing in my life at a time when I was very vulnerable.'

'But do you never think that a younger man would make your life more exciting, more fulfilled. A younger man who would show you the

147

delights of Paris in the springtime, Nice in the summer sun and Chamonix in the winter snows.'

'Not many men could afford such luxuries and I am content with the more modest comforts an adoring husband can give me.'

'But a younger man who could afford such luxuries as you call them?'

'Where would I meet such a paragon?'

'Perhaps you have already met him, Chérie.'

His eyes looked deeply into hers and there was no disguising his meaning. Although her heart was racing with a strange feeling of triumph she deliberately kept her voice dispassionate.

'These last few days of freedom have lulled you into a false sense of security, Monsieur le Vicomte. Your wife will soon return from England and your life will take up it's pattern.'

He laughed. 'My wife is a very beautiful woman, she will understand my little foibles and she has a great many admirers.'

'It is hardly flattering to be called a foible.'

'By Vivienne, not by me I can assure you.'

His hand was lightly caressing the nape of her neck while the other was drawing her close to him. She looked up at his smiling handsome face and her heart felt strangely stirred. It had been so long since a man like Andrew had made love to her, and here was his friend as well as his sister's husband gazing down at her with dark passionate eyes and then she was clinging to him with a raw urgency she believed she would never feel again for any man.

Tearing herself from his embrace she murmured desperately, 'I should go, it is late.'

'And what will you go home to, an empty house with your husband in Lyon.'

'There will be talk, the servants here, my servants.'

'My servants have been chosen over the centuries for their loyalty and their discretion, your servants will surely think you have been staying with friends.'

'They know I have not gone with Maurice to Lyon.'

'They are not paid to question your actions or where you spend your time, Chérie.'

They had been brought up in different worlds. She would be no more to him than she had been to Andrew, but their affair could hurt Vivienne de Mirandol. Revenge was very sweet and it was only the start.

Two days later Marie Claire returned to her home in Dijon in the late morning in time to receive her husband and listen to his comments on Lyon over the dinner table.

He asked how she had got on with the meeting for the Vicomtesse's charity, and she made some vague remarks that seemed to satisfy him. Only much later did he return to the subject of his absence, 'I've been so busy relating my comings and goings in Lyon, dear, that I haven't even asked what else you found to do in my absence.'

'Oh I visited friends, went to the shops and I had lunch with the Vicomte, I met him unexpectedly in Dijon.'

Maurice smiled. 'I am very pleased that you entertained him. I really think they were quite taken with you, my dear. What did you talk about?'

'About you Maurice and Madame la Vicomtesse. About this and that. I found him very charming. You didn't mind me lunching with him, Maurice?'

'Well of course not. He would never have invited Elise to lunch, men never flirted with Elise, she took her civic duties very seriously and flirting with handsome vicomtes was not one of them.'

'Maurice, I did not flirt with him.'

'Of course not, but he would flirt with you, my dear. He has a lot of his father in him, but you wouldn't remember the old Vicomte de Mirandol.'

Doubtfully she remained silent and Maurice sat back complacently in his easy chair smoking his cigar entirely at peace.

Marie Claire racked her brains and after a long silence Maurice asked, 'What else did you talk about over your luncheon, Chérie?'

'He mentioned the racing at Deauville, he wondered if you would be interested?'

Maurice laughed. 'I'm not a racing man and there are too many calls on my time here, there's no reason why you shouldn't go. Are you interested?'

'I've never been to a race meeting, I don't know anything at all about horses.'

'The Vicomte and his wife would see to it that you enjoyed yourself, and think how envious everybody would be. Quite a feather in your cap, my dear, to be invited to Deauville.'

'I couldn't go without you, Maurice.'

'Well of course you could, and with my full permission. I want you to enjoy yourself. You're a young girl married to an elderly man and there have been a great many times when I have asked myself if I was fair to marry you.'

'Oh Maurice, you are the kindest man I have ever met. I will only go to Deauville if you tell me to go.'

'Then you will go, Marie Claire, and to anything else you are invited to. No doubt Elise's old friends will have a lot to say, but I can very soon tell them to be quiet. I want you to enjoy being Madame le Maire but I also want you to be the free spirit I fell in love with.'

She ran to his side and sank on the floor next to his chair, holding her face against his knee. He trusted her and she had betrayed him, but her betrayal was a thing apart, it belonged to another time and place. To a girl he had never known. Maurice would never know that her betrayal was born out of despair and the overpowering desire to repay hurt with hurt. She had no means of knowing how she was going to accomplish that hurt but she believed that destiny had brought her so far, it would not fail her now.

In the weeks and months that followed Marie Claire's life changed as she became part of the Vicomte de Mirandol's set. Gay and sophisticated, the beautiful people on whom fortune and money had smiled, aristocratic people who knew how to enjoy themselves at the racetracks, at regattas on the south coast and at the ski resorts in winter.

Maurice saw to it that his wife had the right clothes for the occasion, that the young gallants who came to the house for her and acted as her escorts had the right credentials and there were so many of them, charming, attentive but always deferential. Maurice was not aware that their deference was not for the mayor's wife, but for the Vicomte's mistress.

In Dijon Maurice's friends were often appalled at his complacency, but they were quick to defend him and his wife. Others kept a stony silence, while their wives, mostly the friends of Elise, chatted over their coffee cups and their comments on the young lady mayoress were hardly flattering.

Of course the Vicomte would tire of her, didn't they always? And all their sympathy was for his aristocratic young wife, an Englishwoman, who could hardly be expected to understand the more relaxed attitudes of the French aristocracy.

They learnt nothing from Vivienne de Mirandol's cool smiling face. She treated Marie Claire with easy charm, but at arm's length. Never again was she invited to ride with Vivienne along the quiet country lanes that surrounded the château and sometimes when their eyes met Marie Claire was discomfitted by the haughty severity in Vivienne de Mirandol's blue gaze.

Vivienne was unhappy. She loved André and now all her father's scathing comments came to trouble her. She could hear his voice on her wedding morning as he walked down the long curving staircase with her on their way to the church.

'You're not thinking straight, my girl, he'll have other women just like his father before him, and if that's how you want to live your life you're not the daughter I thought you were.'

Blinded by love she had been a fool. She could have taken her pick from a dozen suitors but it had always been André's remembered face she had seen in the background. Now he was running true to type and it did no good that his mother gave her the benefit of her advice by saying, 'My dear, it really doesn't mean anything, he is flattered by her youth, and she is of course very pretty, but you are his wife and will remain so. Play him at his own game – it always brought his father to heel, and André is a lot like his father.'

'There is nobody I am in the least interested in,' Vivienne said shortly.

'Then pretend an interest, he won't know the difference.'

'I'm not very good at pretending.'

'Then, my dear, you are just going to have to sit it out. He hasn't fallen out of love with you, Vivienne, this little dalliance will pass, be patient.'

'And there will be others no doubt,' Vivienne snapped.

'And they will mean no more than this does. Men often get bored with women who make themselves too available.'

How she wished her father was alive with his scathing wit and his cynical eyes which would merely confirm that he had told her what would happen.

Her mother would weep for her, and Andrew, well Andrew had enough troubles on his mind with his interfering mother-in-law and his wife's wants which were unending.

Book Two

Chantal

18

The nuns congregated on the steps of the convent of St Agnes on a warm late July morning, watching the girls depart for their holidays. It was always the same, and the Reverend Mother looking back over the years reflected on the years since she had come to the convent as a young novice.

The convent had changed hardly at all. True, there had been added more stained-glass windows in the chapel, gifts from the Vicomte de Mirandol who was ever generous, and there were new beds in the dormitories, but the essential building had hardly changed at all. Only the girls were different: more sophisticated, more confident, less innocent.

Every year she told herself that it was a different world, old values were changing, but then women like herself had been saying this for centuries, deploring a lost youth and hiding their fears that the years would bring other changes they might feel unable to cope with.

As ever the girls walked with the utmost decorum towards the gates, their laughter hidden, their chattering restrained until the gates closed behind them, and even as she stared after them she was aware that a new and imposing carriage was sweeping towards the convent from the city and with a wry smile she realized it was coming to collect Chantal Moreau, the Mayor of Dijon's step-daughter.

She could see Chantal walking with a group of her friends and in the girl's easy grace she recognized the grace that had been her mother's and she frowned a little.

Chantal had been a popular pupil at the convent, she was pretty, not perhaps as clever as her mother had been, but she had an enchanting serenity that had evaded Marie Claire.

There were many people who believed that the Reverend Mother was an unworldly woman who knew very little about the pressures of life in the outside world. Those people would have been surprised how much she knew about that world and the people in it, and it was reflection on that world that troubled her now and how it might affect Chantal.

Dijon had taken to its heart the Mayor's beautiful young wife and Elise Grolan's friends had been silenced as she had gone about her duties with charm and graciousness. Her husband evidently adored her and as the years passed it became easy to forget what had gone before.

Girls could be cruel and she had watched, and ordered her nuns to watch for any sign that they were being spiteful with Chantal, but Chantal had gathered around herself a bevy of friends who were both loyal and generous-hearted. The few girls whose mothers had been Elise's friends kept their thoughts to themselves, but under the surface it was all there, just waiting for new scandals to set it in motion. This last year had not been good for Chantal.

At first there had been murmurings, then sly giggles in corners, then open antipathy. Marie Claire's past was resurrected in hostile groups, then the new scandal of her association with the Vicomte de Mirandol.

She knew that in the city itself there were groups of men, egged on by their wives, who talked about deposing the mayor in favour of a younger man, saying he was too old, had been in office too long, reluctant to accuse his wife, but there were others who had an eye on the benefits the city derived from the Vicomte. Morality and prejudice were at war with expediency and enrichment.

She had hoped to be able to speak to Marie Claire about her activities but Marie Claire had kept well away from the convent and she could not bear to think about the home that Chantal was returning to. The mayor was unused to children or young people since he had never had children of his own and, although he was undoubtedly very fond of his wife, he would have little real interest in her child. That was why she had been a boarder at the convent since her mother's marriage. Marie Claire had deemed it was unfair to burden her new husband, at his time of life with a child who was not his own.

The carriage had stopped and Chantal was inviting a group of her friends to ride with her. She could hear their laughter now, and she watched another group standing with their heads together staring after them.

One after another the girls left the carriage, laughingly making promises to meet during the summer holidays, issuing invitations to their respective homes, and after the last one had left Chantal sat back in her seat with a contented smile.

She would have been less complacent if she could have heard her two friends discussing her after they had left her.

Camille Valois had been her friend from their very first day together at the convent. The daughter of the Vicomte de Mirandol's estate manager, she was well aware of what the community were saying about her father's employer and his mistress, and Annette Dupois whose father was a high-up civil servant in the city was also aware of the undercurrents surrounding her friend.

They walked along, absorbed in their conversation.

'How awful it's going to be if she finds out about her mother and the Vicomte,' Camille was saying. 'She adores her mother. She would be devastated.'

'Well, she'll have to know sooner or later. Do you suppose we should have told her, at least she'd have been prepared?'

'I can't tell her, she would hate us both if she heard it from us.'

'Oh well, she's sure to tell us if she hears anything herself, she must have wondered what they were all whispering about, they made it very obvious.'

A maidservant opened the door to let Chantal into the mayor's house and immediately servants went out to bring in her luggage. She looked around with interest, thinking that the house was very grand, particularly set against her memories of her grandfather's farmhouse in the country.

She went to stare at a large portrait of her mother set at the head of the first flight of stairs. She knew that her mother was beautiful, but this was the portrait of a serene fashionable woman in a dark-blue ball gown, a woman wearing jewels in her ears and round her throat, one long white hand holding a fan, the other resting lightly along the balustrade, one dainty foot emerging from the hem of her gown. Chantal smiled. How many girls at the convent could boast a mother as lovely as hers?

The portrait was new. Her stepfather's first wife's portrait had once stood in its place, a rather large lady with a big highly coloured face wearing a cream silk gown emblazoned with her mayoress's chain of office. She felt strangely pleased that her mother had not elected to wear it.

There were flowers in the hall and in the large living room, but she stood hesitantly, wishing there had been somebody to welcome her. She knew the mayor was always busy and probably her mother was also, but the silence of the empty rooms was disturbing.

After a brief tap on the door a servant entered, saying with a smile, 'Your room's ready for you and a servant has unpacked your cases, Mademoiselle. Lunch has been left out for you in the small dining room.'

'Is my mother out?'

'Yes, Mademoiselle. She and the mayor have gone to the Château de Mirandol to a garden party.'

'Do you know when they'll be back?'

'Early this evening, I'm sure.'

What would she do all afternoon in this town house with its pompous adherence to civic pride: the coats-of-arms of Dijon and other cities, and other regions, the coldness of the tiled hall in sharp contrast to the rich red carpet in the centre of the shallow flights of stairs.

The small dining room felt cosier and the lunch left out for her was more than adequate, although she had to admit that she was hungry. She had been too excited to eat much breakfast and in any case the fare at the convent was hardly luxurious.

Here was deliciously poached salmon and salad and a bowl of fruit, an array of cheeses of every description, and a silver coffee pot with rich brown sugar and a jug of cream. There were pastries too, and Chantal forgot her misgivings in the pleasure she found in the lunch laid out on the table overlooking long sweeping lawns and chestnut trees.

There was nothing for Chantal to do. She had thoughts of visiting the city streets to look in the shop windows but she had to be there for when her mother returned, so, instead, she sat on the windowseat in the salon looking out across the gardens and the civic buildings behind them.

A small chill wind had arisen and the roses stirred, shedding their velvet petals on the short green grass while above the clouds gathered and a light shower of rain swept across the gardens.

The house had never known children or young girls on the threshold of life. The books in the library were dull tomes concerned with laws and civic grandeur. There were one or two novels that did not interest her and there were no games to play. Her stepfather had promised to teach her how to play chess, but he had never seemed to find the time to do so, now she began to think nostalgically of the farm. She had never felt one of them, never been made to feel one of them, but there had been the animals. The dogs had been her friends, and the kittens and their mother she had adored. Even Cassie, the old horse her grandfather rode around the fields, was a friend. Here in the mayor's house there were no animals.

She strolled out into the hall and looked up again at the portrait of her mother. She thought about her conversations with her friends that morning. They had been speaking delightedly of where they would be going with their parents during the holidays and what they would be doing. When they asked her to tell them her plans, she had nothing to say, only that it would depend on her stepfather's commitments.

It was late in the afternoon when she heard the sound of voices and laughter from the front of the house and she rushed into the hall to stare through the windows. Her mother and stepfather were standing on the pavement waving to some other people who were driving away and then they were walking towards the house, arm in arm, wreathed in smiles.

A servant came from the back of the hall, hurrying to open the door, pulling down the hem of his black jacket, reassuring himself that he was both neat and tidy, then Marie Claire was there and Chantal was rushing forward with outstretched arms to fling herself into her mother's embrace. Her stepfather patted her head affectionately and with a smile he said, 'I declare you are getting taller every time I see you. Did the carriage pick you up on time?'

'Yes thank you.'

She had never felt able to call him Uncle Maurice, and her mother had never asked her to think of him as her father. She preferred simply to answer his questions politely and he saw nothing amiss in this.

'And did you like the new carriage?' he asked proudly.

'Oh yes, very much. I wished the horses lived here.'

'They are happy in the stables and will no doubt be used again and again for some function or other. Doesn't your mother look very pretty?'

She stepped back and stared at her mother's attire and Marie Claire did a little pirouette for her benefit.

She was wearing a gown in pale peach lace, a gown whose skirt swept down to the floor in folds of shining lace, and on her dark head was a large hat in peach chiffon adorned with two sweeping ostrich feathers in pale cream.

Chantal's eyes shone with delight. 'Oh, Mother, you look so beautiful, there cannot have been anybody at the garden party as beautiful as you.'

Marie Claire laughed, and once again the mayor patted the girl's head, well pleased with her praise.

Taking hold of Chantal's hand, Marie Claire said, 'Come up to my room with me, darling. I'm going to change into something less pretentious and Maurice has work to do in his study, so we won't get in his way. While I'm changing, you shall tell me about the Reverend Mother and the other nuns. I expect they are still exactly the same.'

While her mother changed into a blue velvet tea gown Chantel sat on the edge of her bed chatting. Occasionally her mother smiled or uttered the odd word, but she seemed more concerned with seeing that her maid put away her finery to her entire satisfaction.

'Did you eat all your lunch?' she asked. 'I'm so sorry we couldn't be here when you arrived, darling, but it was very important that we went to the Vicomte's garden party. I'll tell you all about it over tea if you like.'

'Oh yes, Mother, I do like. Have you really been in the gardens of that beautiful château?'

'And not only the gardens, darling, into the château itself.'

Chantal's eyes grew wide with wonder. 'Is it very beautiful, as beautiful as the gardens, and does the Vicomte speak to you and to Maurice as though you were really his friends.'

'But of course, we are his friends. His name is André.'

'And his wife, she is your friend too?'

'Of course. Her name is Vivienne and she is English.'

'I saw her once, she's very beautiful. She used to ride her big black horse across the fields. I wished I could ride like that.'

'Well one day you will Chantal, I promise you.'

Her mother's eyes had suddenly grown serious, locked in hers with a promise she could not understand, but in the next moment she was laughing again, taking Chantal's hand to walk with her down the stairs.

'Maurice has to go out this evening,' she said softly, 'but you and I will spend it together. I will try to make it up to you that I was out when you came home.'

'Mother, it doesn't matter, not now when you are home.'

They had tea together in the salon and Marie Claire looked at her daughter and thought that she was growing up beautifully. There would be no clandestine affairs for Chantal; she would be able to hold her own in any company, choose from an array of aristocratic gentlemen, become the sort of woman any man would be proud to make his wife. Chantal would have been amazed if she could have seen into her mother's mind at that moment, but she was too occupied by the array of delicious pastries on the silver tray in front of her. Marie Claire looked on, serenely complacent.

Her love affair with the Vicomte de Mirandol had taught Marie Claire a great deal. He was amused at her preoccupation with his wife's family in England and when he remarked on it she merely said, 'But I want to know about other cultures and other countries, André. One day I must ask Maurice to take me to England.'

'Why particularly to England?' he had asked.

'Well not just England of course, to Spain and Italy, oh everywhere.'

She had learned for instance that Andrew's eldest daughter would finish her education in Switzerland, that she would become a débutante

160

and curtsey before the new English King and his Queen at a great ball, and then there would be a great many other balls and other functions so that she could meet all the eligible young aristocratic gentlemen, searching for the right kind of wife.

There was nothing in France to equal these proceedings, but she had already decided that Chantal would be a part of those functions. Oh not perhaps the curtseying to their Majesties, but the parties and balls that followed. At this moment in time she had absolutely no idea how she was to accomplish this for her daughter, but she knew with the utmost certainty that she would.

André had already informed her that his wife's family would be visiting them for the wine festival and her heart missed a beat. She knew they would be invited guests, but she wasn't ready to meet Andrew. Perhaps he would not recognize the girl Marie Claire in the sophisticated mayoress of the City of Dijon, but it was a chance she was not prepared to take.

Unknowingly it was the Vicomte's mother who had solved her problem.

The dowager Vicomtesse thought the Wine Festival had become a bit of a bore and had stated her intention of staying away from it.

André had argued against it. 'I would like you to come this year, Mother,' he said firmly. 'Vivienne's brother and his wife and children are coming and it would be ungracious if you stayed away.'

'Andrew would understand, there was an occasion when he stayed away on the pretext of getting over an unhappy love affair.'

'Which was happily resolved, Mother, and now I would like you to be here to meet him.'

'Your father had considerably more imagination than you have André about entertaining our guests at the wine festival,' the Vicomtesse de Mirandol said provocatively.

'What sort of imagination?'

'Well it's the same every year now. Endless dinners with the same people talking about the same things. Now and again we get a fresh face like that delectable little wife of the mayor with whom you seem to be spending so much of your time, but on the whole I seem to spend my time listening to pompous old men talking about their good works while they try to inveigle me into one dubious charity after another.'

André laughed. 'And what did my father have in mind that relieved the boredom for you?'

'We had a Masked Ball. He would choose a period of French history and we would be expected to dress adequately for the occasion.'

'An occasion that would hardly appeal to a great many of my

guests. Besides it would be too expensive for some of them. You also said that my father was too extravagant for his own good. It made him very unpopular with his tenants.'

'His tenants were never invited.'

'That's what I mean, Mother. Have you forgotten that in less enlightened times we would have been sent to the guillotine for less.'

'I haven't forgotten, but we do need now and again to put a little spice back in our lives. I want a Masked Ball, André, it could be the very last I shall attend, I'm getting old.'

'You'll never get old, Mother, I refuse to believe it.'

'Well indulge me a little, André. Let me have my Masked Ball, Louis XIV the Sun King, Pompadour and the Du Barry, silks and satins and powdered wigs. Even the children could dress up and the château lends itself to such an event. It would be a journey into the past, to more gracious days, and I could think about your father and think of all those women he subjected me to over the years.'

'I would have thought you wanted to forget about those, Mother.'

'On the contrary. It amuses me to think about them, after all your father is no more and I am left here to think about them. I have a feeling sometimes that he isn't very pleased about that.'

'Very well. You shall have your Masked Ball. Do we take our masks off at twelve o'clock to the astonishment of everybody.'

'I always thought it was more fun to keep them on, we never quite knew who had been in the conservatory with who and speculation was almost as much fun as the ball itself.'

Marie Claire had thought it was a wonderful idea.

'What will you wear?' The Vicomte had asked.

'I'm not sure. There will be so many Marie Antoinettes and Madame de Pompadours. There were so many interesting people at the court of Louis XIV. What do you suppose your English guests will wear?'

'Oh something entirely British. Something to make we French seem pale and flighty, even though we have a air that they can never quite attain.'

Marie Claire laughed. 'And his wife?'

'Oh, Constance will do us proud. She's beautiful and aristocratic. Nothing less than a queen will do for Constance, but whose queen I can't imagine. Certainly not one who would supersede her by innumerable mistresses.'

'Is that what kings did, André? I always believed a mistress was merely some very available woman, someone to dally with until the next one came along. How can it be otherwise?'

He looked down at her, his expression inscrutable.

She waited but he did not answer her. How could it be otherwise? Their love affair might last a few years, but it was not a permanent thing, she was not a woman he would leave his wife for, and yet he was not prepared to think about the ending. They were still young, she was still beautiful, and if in the end there was only friendship left, wasn't that the way a great many marriages ended? Wasn't that what she had with Maurice?

In the second week of Chantal's school holidays she went with her mother and Maurice to Trouville. For Chantal it was an enchanting time; the first time she had seen the sea. She discovered mile after mile of golden sand, high rocky cliffs and shell pools.

Maurice spent much of his time at the gaming tables in the Casino and her mother sat on the sun terrace under a large umbrella, looking entirely enchanting. She was always surrounded by a group of admiring young men who set themselves out to entertain her, and during the second week the Vicomte de Mirandol arrived in the company of his mother.

After that the young men drifted away. Relieved of his duty of looking after her, Maurice stayed longer at the gaming tables and Chantal rarely saw her mother.

One evening as she watched her mother getting dressed for dinner she asked, 'Why hasn't the Vicomtesse come to Trouville, doesn't she mind that he is here with his mother?'

'Well, it is really very nice of him to bring his mother and no doubt Vivienne is visiting her family in England.'

'Doesn't Maurice mind that you are always with him?'

'Chérie I am not always with him. He spends a great deal of time with his mother and Maurice is fond of gambling.'

The Vicomte's mother was rather more searching.

'Now I know why you decided to accompany me to Trouville, it had nothing to do with your happy memories of the place or your wish to be kind to me. You knew that woman was coming.'

'I knew, but you are wrong about the other things. I did wish to come with you and I did wish to renew my acquaintance with the town.'

'You never liked Trouville. Like your father you preferred Nice.'

'I don't much care for Burgundy in August and Vivienne has gone off to England.'

'Who's the young girl I've seen with the mayor's wife?'

'Her daughter, I believe.'

His mother raised her eyes and André was quick to say, 'Not my daughter, Mother, I assure you.'

'And not the mayor's daughter I'll be bound.'

'I only know that she is a pupil at the Abbey of St Agnes and I've not asked questions.'

'There may come a day when she will break hearts like her mother must have done. There's a resemblance but their colouring is different. Who do you suppose fathered the child?'

'I've no idea.'

'Somebody blond and probably a gentleman. The child has an air. Indulge me, André, ask a few discreet questions.'

'No Mother, not even for you. If there was a scandal Marie Claire has successfully lived it down, I have no intentions whatever of bringing it to life.'

19

Her holidays were behind her. Chantal sat with her mother in the mayoral carriage as they drove back to the convent. She had so much to tell her friends, the sun and the sea, the sound of ballroom music in the evenings when she sat by her bedroom window after watching her mother waltzing for her benefit around the room.

Her mother had looked so beautiful, the most beautiful woman in the hotel, and she had ridden her first pony, and driven along the promenade in the Vicomte's carriage with her mother and the Vicomte, aware that from the café's along the boulevards people were smiling and staring at them.

Maurice too had been kind. He had bought her a riding habit which her mother said was a great extravagance when she hadn't got a pony of her own, but the Vicomte had said that could easily be remedied since there were ponies to spare at the Château de Mirandol.

Back in the anonymity of her school uniform, the silks and voiles of the last few weeks put away in numerous drawers it seemed that those weeks had passed as if in a dream, and as the carriage stopped in front of the great iron gates she could look along the road and see other girls arriving. She waved excitedly. Most of them were with parents, and turning back to where her mother sat smiling in the carriage, she said anxiously, 'You are coming with me, Mother, it is the first day?'

'But you're not a new pupil, dear, is it expected of me? My mother never came to Dijon.'

Chantal was saved from answering by the sight of Sister Emelda bearing down on them from the path surrounding the convent. There was no mistaking the fact that she wished to speak to her mother and Marie Claire leaned forward, smiling graciously.

'How nice to see you, Sister Emelda,' she said. 'You haven't changed at all.'

'Please come in, Madame, there are refreshments and some of

Chantal's work is on display. Did you not get our invitation?'

'Why no, but we have been in Trouville and there was so much mail waiting for us on our return. Somehow or other it must have been missed.'

'Then do please come into the abbey. The Reverend Mother and the parents of the girls will expect it.'

Marie Claire obliged, but she was not enthusiastic. She had seen the groups of women exchanging glances, walking with their heads together, and she had seen it all before. It seemed as she walked with her daughter into the convent, that Elise Grolan's shadow was directly behind her.

She spent the next hour enthusing about the pictures and drawings on display, the written essays she could pick up and read, and she noted that Chantal's had been highly recommended. The nuns she had known greeted her with smiles as did some of the mothers, but there were others who looked away, their looks of disapproval most evident.

How soon before she could make an excuse to leave, what excuse would be acceptable, and even as she sipped her tea, her heart missed a beat at the sight of the Reverend Mother bearing down on her, and she felt like a child again, a little anxious, unprepared with an acceptable excuse for the unprepossessing candour she read in the older woman's eyes.

'I would like to speak to you in my study, what I have to say will not take long, but I think we should talk. Please come with me now,' the Reverend Mother said, and without waiting for a reply walked on towards her study, and Marie Claire hurriedly placed her tea cup in its saucer and followed after her.

Behind her back she was oblivious of the knowing smiles of a great many of the women present, but Chantal watched thoughtfully. Of course her mother was the lady mayoress, it was only natural that the Reverend Mother would wish to speak to her alone. Why then had her mother looked so reluctant, and why had the Reverend Mother appeared so stern and unsmiling?

Suddenly her appetite seemed to have left her as she watched her friends helping themselves from the plates piled high with pastries.

The Reverend Mother eyed her one-time pupil with some exasperation and she quite purposely did not ask her visitor to sit down. Marie Claire on the other hand showed no sign of discomforture. Her stance was graceful, and showed no signs of the resentment she was feeling. The Reverend Mother had no right to treat her like an erring schoolgirl, that time had long gone.

The Reverend Mother decided to attack, there was no point in evading the issue.

'You might think I have no right to speak to you like this,' she began, 'but I am mindful that you were once one of my pupils, a very competent pupil, and you have chosen to place your daughter in my care. But I am hearing rumours about your private life that I do not like and I do not like what they might do to Chantal.'

The intensity of Marie Claire's defiant gaze increased but she remained silent and the Reverend Mother said in a gentler voice, 'I would like you to tell me if the rumours are true.'

'What are the rumours, Reverend Mother?'

'That you have become the mistress of the Vicomte de Mirandol, that you are seen everywhere together and if your husband is flattered by the attention you are receiving I very much doubt if the vicomte's wife will be quite so accommodating.'

'There is no danger to the vicomte's marriage, if that is what you mean.'

'No, that is not what I mean. My life has not been so sheltered that I do not know the sort of things that go on, particularly in high places. Your husband is an elderly man, the vicomte's wife is young and very much in love with her husband. Besides, there is your daughter to consider. Have you not thought what this tittle-tattle might do to her?'

'I'm not sure what you mean?'

'She has made friends here, and she is happy, but the whisperings will increase. Girls can be extremely cruel to each other, particularly cruel to a girl who is pretty, whose parents are wealthy and respectable in the town, and if one of them errs against society the whisperings will go on and intensify. Chantal will be aware of them, then she will be hurt and miserable and in the end she will blame you for what they are doing to her.'

'What I do with my life is my business, it has nothing to do with anybody.'

'But you are wrong – it does affect your daughter. And think of the vicomtesse and think of your husband. There has already been more than enough scandal in your life, Marie Claire, have you forgotten so soon?'

'No, I have not forgotten. I don't want to hurt the vicomtesse or Maurice, but everything I do is for Chantal. I can't explain why, but only Chantal is important.'

'Then I do not understand you, Marie Claire.'

For a long moment they stared into each other's eyes, then shaking her head sadly the Reverend Mother said, 'There does not seem anything more to say, I have done my best. When your daughter comes to you unhappy and miserable because of the accusations levelled against you, I hope that you will remember that I have warned you.'

Marie Claire walked back to the refreshment room where Chantal was waiting for her, anxious to know why the Reverend Mother had wanted to speak to her.

'Was it about me, Mama, is she displeased with me, am I not doing well with my lessons?'

'Of course dear, you are doing very well. We talked like old friends, that is all.'

Marie Claire was well aware of the hostile glances from many of the women as well as the gushing politeness of many of the others. She had too many enemies. During the evening she had to talk seriously to Maurice about Chantal's future.

The opportunity came over dinner when he was relaxed and benign over his glass of Cognac.

'Maurice, have you not thought that Chantal should have your name. We have been married several years and she's very fond of you, a daughter with a name unlike mine only raises too many suppositions.'

'I hadn't really thought of it, Chérie.'

'Well, I think you should. I would prefer her to be Chantal Grolan rather than Chantal Moreau. My father has forgotten her existence and mine. You are the one she is fond of. I'm sure she never gives my parents a second thought.'

'She has had twelve years to become accustomed to her name, will she not find it rather ridiculous to change it now?'

'Well of course not, besides I want her to be able to say that the mayor of Dijon is her father. It doesn't matter whilst she is still at the convent, but later when she is finishing her education somewhere else.'

'What is all this about finishing her education elsewhere?'

'The Vicomte has told me that all aristocratic English children finish their education in Switzerland. If he and his wife have children it will be so for them.'

'I am not an English aristocrat, Marie Claire, and neither are you.'

'But you are the mayor of Dijon which is a position of some standing I think.'

'And one which I could lose at any time. It is not a position for life. The Vicomte will always be a vicomte, it was a title he was born with, mine is a title I acquired. I doubt if I would ever have the means to send your daughter to school in Switzerland.'

Marie Claire pouted prettily. 'I have been extravagant Maurice, often spent money foolishly. I will economise for Chantal.'

'My dear girl, you have just spent a small fortune on your gown for the Masked Ball in October. Some Russian duchess at the court of the French king, isn't it?'

'Then I'll change it. I'll go as a French peasant like the ones who hammered on the gates of Versailles before the revolution.'

'I won't have my wife going to the ball as a French peasant.'

'You mean you will require your wife to uphold your position but your daughter's education is relatively unimportant?'

'She's receiving a first-class education at the convent.'

'But Switzerland would give her something else Maurice, an air, a polish, the sort of polish that will attract the right sort of young man.'

'Somebody like Mirandol, is that what you think?'

'No, somebody quite different to André. He's not the sort of husband I would want for Chantal.'

'You surprise me, Marie Claire. Particularly when you're so fond of him yourself.'

'I like him. I'm not in love with him. He tells me things I need to know. He brings Chantal's future into perspective.'

He stared at her curiously. 'I'm not sure what you mean by that, my dear.'

'And I can't properly explain it to you. It has nothing to do with us, Maurice, but it has a great deal to do with the girl you once saved from a watery grave in the park that winter's afternoon. I'm happy with you, Maurice, you are the most wonderful generous person in my life, but there is much of my life that haunts me, even now when I have found happiness with you. So much misery that has to be accounted for.'

'Then I would advise you to forget it. Bitterness nursed too long becomes destructive.'

She smiled. 'That is what I would expect you to say because you are a good kind man who has never had anything to forgive. I am not proud of my thirst for vengeance but it is too powerful to be ignored.'

They came from far and wide to the Vicomte's Masked Ball and the villagers from around the château lined up early in the afternoon to watch the guests arriving. These were the people who were staying overnight there but it was the people who came in the evening who delighted them the most.

High-stepping lords and ladies in silks and satins, buckled shoes and powdered wigs. Their jewels glittered in the night and their carriages filled the narrow lanes around the château.

The attire of a great many of the vicomte's guests gave rise to much merriment. Satins stretched too tightly over ample bosoms, elderly dowagers tottering on too high heels and wigs flopping and bouncing on heads never designed for them.

A ripple of interest swept through the crowds around the gate at the sight of the Mayor of Dijon in the robes of a cardinal, accompanied by his beautiful wife who gazed at them haughtily through her lorgnette before she acknowledged their presence with a warm dimpled smile.

How Marie Claire would have shone at the court of Louis XIV in her pale parchment satin gown heavily embroidered with crystal beads and the gems sparkling in her white powdered wig.

She eyed the ballroom over the embroidered fan, her jade green eyes searching among the guests for the man she had not seen since that day long ago when he left after promising to return. There were so many tall distinguished men in the fashions of headier days. André looked particularly handsome in the clothes of one of his ancestors whose picture hung on the walls of the château.

Vivienne's mask could not disguise her dark lively eyes, and meeting Marie Claire's cool green gaze she inclined her head in acknowledgement. After that Marie Claire watched her progress around the room with interest and presently she was rewarded by seeing her in conversation with a tall slender woman in an elaborate gown accompanied by a young girl. Her heart began to race when almost immediately they were joined by a tall man in rich ruby brocade and a boy dressed in white satin so that the two children stood out like a pair of porcelain figures. Andrew's twin children Marie Claire thought, and she moved nearer, after assuring herself that Maurice was being engaged in conversation by a group of men of his own age.

She stood close to them staring across the ballroom, but from where she stood she could hear their voices, English voices, and the sound of Andrew's laughter brought back all the enchantment she had found in the sunflower field and in the cottage with the leaping flames lighting up the white walls. His laughter had been for her, now it was for others, but as she turned to circle the room he turned also and for a brief moment their eyes met.

Had he no memories of her unusual jade green eyes, when she remembered his English blue ones so poignantly? She strolled across the ballroom and on looking back she saw that Vivienne was in earnest conversation with her relatives. Andrew's wife stared directly into her eyes and she was glad of the mask covering her face.

If their masks had been removed, would she have read accusation in the other woman's long cool stare? Andrew was staring at her now, and she could read behind his mask, the righteous anger that he was looking at a woman who had caused his sister grief. At that moment she longed to tear his mask away, remove her own so that he could really look at her.

Oh Andrew, she thought miserably, it was never André, it was always only you. It is you who took away my childhood, you who

170

turned me into a harlot, you who brought the spirit of vengeance into my life.

As she watched him walk away with an arm around the shoulders of his children she thought savagely, 'I have not done with you yet, Andrew. I have accomplished much but there has to be more.'

She did not know how she could make Andrew pay for the past, but she would not fail now, and later as they danced one of the old dances of France they came face to face again. Unsmiling they stared at each other, and he was the first to look away.

She found Maurice sitting alone in the conservatory while the rest of the party were taking off their masks, and their squeals of recognition could clearly be heard. Maurice was not feeling well. He blamed it on the Champagne, on the sultry heat of the rooms, of the noise of music and laughter, on the fact that he had probably overeaten.

His wife's relief that she need not take of her mask was overwhelming and long before the ball had settled into normality they were on their way home.

Next morning Maurice was full of contrition in case he had spoiled his wife's evening, but she was quick to reassure him that she had found the ball boring and rather silly.

On the morning after the ball, the vicomte faced his brother-in-law over the breakfast table and Andrew remarked rather tetchily, 'I didn't get the opportunity to see your lady friend without her mask, in fact I didn't see her at all after midnight. Was she entertaining one of your rivals in some other part of the château?'

'On the contrary,' André said evenly. 'She was on her way home. Apparently her husband was unwell.'

'You're a fool,' Andrew persisted.

'And you, my friend, are being sanctimonious. One of these days you will stand back and look at your predictable marriage which was undoubtedly engineered by your wife's ambitious clever mother.'

Andrew scowled, but unperturbed the vicomte went on, 'Oh I know you fancied yourself desperately in love, unfortunately no other woman came along to tempt you when she was most needed.'

'There is nothing wrong with my marriage to Constance,' Andrew said staunchly.

'Well, of course not. The marriage goes her way, the way her mother dictates. If you were less indolent, my friend, you would not be so complacent.'

'There has been no other woman since I married Constance, I have never needed another woman.'

He did not miss the cynical raising of his friend's eyebrows and for the first time in many years he found himself remembering Marie

Claire Moreau. A beautiful child with hair the colour of a raven's wing and eyes as green as the jade figurines on the mantelpiece. He remembered her sitting looking out across the field of bold yellow flowers etched against a summer sky and he remembered her dancing besides him as they explored the city of Dijon.

Marie Claire had been a tantalizing diversion, as heady as his favourite wine. He was not proud of seducing her, but she had been more than a willing partner; it never entered his head for a single moment that she had loved him.

The vicomte was watching the differing expressions on his friend's face and he found them curious. He had always found his friend predictable, an unimaginative Englishman with a love of blood sports and horses: a friend he could rely on implicitly, but not one he could interest in more dubious pleasures. Now he found that same friend plagued with memories that were searching and alien.

His wife took her place at the breakfast table and immediately the talk became general, the ball, the costumes, the guests.

'The Grolans left early,' Vivienne remarked coolly.

'Yes, the mayor was not feeling well.'

'He came as a cardinal I believe, but who was his wife supposed to be?'

'Just some beauty at the court of Louis XIV.'

'Well, I can assure you Andrew, that my husband's little friend is indeed a beauty, it is a pity you did not get to see her face,' she remarked acidly.

'No doubt I shall see her again on some other occasion,' Andrew answered dryly.

'I take it Constance is not joining us for breakfast.' the vicomte said.

'No. Constance eats very little breakfast, and invariably in her room. The children were up early and walking with me in the gardens.'

It was time he and Vivienne had children, the vicomte pondered. There had to be somebody to hand the family name on to and as his eyes met his wife's she knew the thoughts coursing through his mind.

She was prepared to give him children, but she was not prepared to be treated like a brood mare. When his affair with Marie Claire and any other woman was over then she would consider children but not before.

20

Marie Claire had a great deal to feel complacent about over the next three years. Her husband was returned to office with an increased majority although with her usual honesty she had to admit that she contributed nothing to his popularity.

The men admired her and flattered her, the women were less ecstatic. The whisperings continued and intensified but the Vicomte de Mirandol's involvement with the city intensified and the money he poured into every civic scheme was thanks to her.

She had become adept at posing questions regarding André's wife's family in England and learned that Andrew's elder daughter was to become a pupil at a fashionable finishing school in the Bernese Oberland district of Switzerland and within days she had engineered Maurice into taking a short break in Interlaken so that they could assess the school. The outcome was that Chantal was enrolled as a pupil and on their way home Maurice was strangely silent.

He was in effect a very worried man. He was not a wealthy man, simply comfortably well off, but school fees of this magnitude and the clothes she would be expected to equip herself with he believed were completely out of his range.

His wife sat beside him entirely happy, adoring him for what he was doing for Chantal. He had never discussed the state of his finances with her. He would take out a loan, he had good friends in the city who would advise him, perhaps even the vicomte himself.

The vicomte was vaguely amused. It had always puzzled him why Marie Claire had been so obsessed with Vivienne's English relatives. What did she hope to achieve by having her daughter installed at the same school as Andrew's daughter? Chantal was hardly likely to figure largely in the annals of the British aristocracy.

The Vicomte too was troubled. Vivienne had none of his mother's tolerance. His mother had been indulgent with his father's frailties, not so Vivienne who had gone off to England at the beginning of the season and remained there. She had embarked on a merry-go-round that never stopped, Ascot and Goodwood, sailing regattas, May balls, and weekends in stately homes.

Marie Claire Grolan had had a long reign as the other woman in his life but there was a new star on the horizon in the shape of a promising young ballerina he had met in Copenhagen. She had proved to be a very pleasant diversion on a particularly boring business trip, but he had taken it no further, not when his wife was proving difficult.

At the beginning of August he decided to visit his brother-in-law's house to bring his wife home.

Vivienne received him coolly, Andrew was hardly welcoming and Constance was too wrapped up in playing the lady of the manor at every local fête that she largely forgot his existence.

Andrew informed him shortly that he was a bloody fool to risk losing his wife for some little light of love and Vivienne would have no difficulty in replacing him if he continued to play around. With a wry smile André said, 'Surely Vivienne knows that is all it is. I love her. I've come to take her home.'

'And I think she will go home when she's good and ready,' her brother retorted.

Indeed it was the end of November when Vivienne decided she would return to the château, and in Dijon speculation rose as to whether this was not the end to his involvement with the mayor's wife. They considered it a certainty when Vivienne gave birth to a son the following May.

There followed a garden party at the château to celebrate the birth of Armand de Mirandol and in the evening the fireworks that followed could be seen for miles.

Vivienne received Marie Claire and the mayor graciously. They duly admired the baby and stayed to watch the fireworks but on the way home they were unusually silent. They both knew that the Vicomte's involvement with Marie Claire, the mayor and many of his interests in the city of Dijon had come to an end.

Marie Claire had bought an expensive new gown for the event at the château, the first new gown she had bought for some time. The women in Dijon talked among themselves that their mayoress's wardrobe was more restrained. Most of her apparel had been worn before on many occasions. Always a beautiful woman, she wore her dark hair taken back from her face in a demure chignon. Her bone structure was so exquisite she had no problems with the plainness of her hairstyle, and there were rumours that she had sold much of her jewellery.

She had sold it to a jeweller in a small village just over the Swiss border and the money she obtained for it went towards Chantal's education. She was aware that Maurice was a worried man. He was repaying the loan he had taken out, and they were living frugally, but she agonized over the long silences and the look of utter dejection she surprised frequently on his face.

He became forgetful, he missed meetings and had constantly to be reminded of matters that had always received his most urgent attention.

It came as no surprise to Maurice that he was deposed at the next local election in favour of a much younger man and to the older citizens of Dijon it seemed that a legend had gone from their midst.

For Marie Claire it was a disaster. They had to leave their comfortable beautiful home overlooking the park and leave also the sumptuous furnishings. For the first time they were house-hunting and it was not the luxurious houses in the select part of the city that interested them. Instead they purchased a very modest stone house several miles out of Dijon and were immensely grateful for the odds and ends of furniture the previous occupant had been willing to leave behind.

Maurice was bored. He had enjoyed being in the centre of things, now he was discovering that he had never had time for hobbies. His garden had always been cared for by others and he viewed the wilderness surrounding their new house with dismay.

Marie Claire worked happily in the garden, uprooting weeds that had been there for centuries, lopping overgrown trees, clearing paths hidden by moss and weeds of all descriptions. The few visitors who called went back with stories of a neglected garden, damp walls and worm-infected furniture.

Marie Claire was not a farmer's daughter for nothing. She shopped at the local markets for curtain material and cushions. She scrubbed faded carpets and rugs, and in the evenings she taught Maurice how to play cribbage and prayed that the storms of winter would be over quickly and that spring would bring a change in their fortunes.

Dutifully Chantal wrote every week, newsy letters about her new friends, where they came from and the sort of things she was studying at Madame Lafayette's school in the mountains of Switzerland.

She was learning music and painting. Dancing and ski-ing. Skating and horseriding. Most of the girls were English, although there was one girl whose father was an Indian Rajah. She wrote about the daughters of dukes and earls, and she was popular because she could help them with their French lessons and their conversations with tutors, ski instructors and in various establishments in Interlaken.

These letters were a godsend to Marie Claire, who read them eagerly to Maurice in the evenings and she would watch him nod his head and smile at her enthusiasm.

What would Chantal think about their reduced circumstances? She had envisaged inviting Chantal's friends to her home in Dijon, she would entertain Andrew's daughter, witness the blossoming friendship between the two girls, wait eagerly for that moment when Chantal would tell her she was to be a guest at the Earl of Westmond's stately home.

She had no doubt that that invitation would still arrive, she had not come so far to have it fail now. What happened afterwards would be out of her hands, it would depend on Chantal. One thing she was sure of. Chantal would go to England with an open mind. She would tell her nothing about her father or his family in case her antagonism came to light, she would simply tell her that her father had been an English nobleman and leave it at that. If Chantal asked questions she would simply say that her father had died before he had had the chance to come back for them.

She did not miss the charity meetings and civic occasions but Maurice missed them, and she often watched him sitting in their small garden gazing pensively before him, more concerned with his memories than the view of the countryside.

He received an invitation to the Mayor's Dinner in late September but said immediately that he would not go. It was some distance into the city and they no longer had a carriage to take him there.

Marie Claire was insistent that he should attend. 'You always enjoyed them so,' she persisted. 'Surely somebody would come for you and bring you home, after all they must remember all the years of service you gave to Dijon and its citizens.'

'People soon forget,' he answered sadly.

'Maurice, you are being defeatist. For my sake, you must go, otherwise people will blame me for keeping you away.'

So Maurice swallowed his pride and asked if there was somebody who could collect him on the night of the dinner, and was delighted to receive a letter from the mayor himself saying the mayoral carriage would call for him in the late afternoon and he was invited to stay the night at the mayor's house which had once been his home.

Old friends and colleagues received him in a most friendly manner and he sat next to the new mayor at the dinner table. Wine flowed freely, and after listening to the speeches he was encouraged to make one himself. He demurred saying that he was now a country gentleman with nothing exciting to tell them. Day followed day, each one exactly the same, with only his garden to think about, but they would have none of it. In the end he stood up and for several minutes entertained them with his memories and small humorous anecdotes from his years of office.

'And what of the future?' one member of his audience called out.

'Only the past is important,' Maurice answered. 'The future is concerned with our daughter. The future is for the young.'

There was warm applause and he sat with the new mayor in his little morning room drinking wine until the sky became tinged with the first rosy light of morning.

He slept late and ate a solitary breakfast before the mayor returned to say he would take him back to his home late that afternoon. He sat at the window staring out across the park, the park he had once thought of as his own.

The beech trees in the park were already turning golden and there were dry leaves scampering along the path and across the lawns. There were children in the park, bowling their hoops along the paths, dancing with their skipping ropes in the afternoon sunshine. He decided he wanted to be out of the house and into the park. There was life there, rabbits jumping across the lawns, bird song in the trees and people. Young boys and girls on their way home from school, babies pushed along in perambulators by nannies, deep in conversation with others of their kind.

It was a warm autumn day. He did not need his coat but he took his walking stick and as he strolled towards the boating lake he was greeted with a great many smiles from people who recognized him. He sat on a wooden seat overlooking the water and he watched children feeding the ducks that splashed and squabbled there.

He had been greedy the evening before at the civic dinner. He had missed the rich exciting banquets of former years because now their food was often frugal, grown in their own gardens and Marie Claire was careful of her expenditure when she shopped in the village store.

At the banquet he had eaten freely of the rich food. The venison and truffles, the pastries and gateaux. Now he was paying for it.

There was a dull ache around his midriff, interspersed with sudden sharp pain which seemed to reach right down to his elbows. A feeling of nausea swept over him, and then as quickly as it had come the pain subsided and he vowed that he would eat nothing else that day.

He thought about the afternoon he had rescued Marie Claire, and he could remember vividly the anguish in her eyes as she had sunk on to his feet in the water of the lake.

He remembered her sitting in his office on the day she hoped to find work there, a young beautiful girl with hope in her eyes and a smile on her lips, and the despair that followed, and he remembered Elise with her sharp tongue and moments of spite.

177

Elise had been a good wife. Loyal, dutiful and caring, but he had had few illusions about her. She had been greedy, ambitious and something of a trouble-causer, but she would have had nothing good to say about Marie Claire who had been extravagant, unfaithful and flighty.

The pain was returning. He sat back against the wooden seat waiting for it to go away.

A small chill wind had arisen and the sun had left the sky when one of the gardeners walked along the path sweeping up the leaves. They were coming down more frequently now. Soon the lawns and paths would be covered with them, he would hear them crunching underneath his shoes and the gates would be closing early to keep out the visitors.

The paths were empty, only one man sat on the form overlooking the lake. He appeared to be asleep and his walking stick had fallen on to the ground where it lay at his feet. He walked towards him and it was only when he was close that he saw that the sleeping man was the old Mayor of Dijon.

He smiled. Mayor Grolan had been a good man, approachable, always ready with a word of greeting, even if Madame Grolan, his first wife, had been imperious and never a woman to recognize a lowly parks keeper.

He smiled to himself. Serve her right that he had replaced her with a girl young enough to be his daughter. His smile faded. There was something not quite right in the way the old mayor was leaning against his seat, and he went forward to touch him saying, 'Mr Mayor, it's getting cold, time to go back.'

As his hand touched Maurice's shoulder, he fell sideways and the gardener gave a little cry as he looked into his wide sightless eyes and felt the cold clamminess of his fingers. Maurice Grolan was dead.

Marie Claire stoked up the fire and warmed up the kettle for the third time. She had expected her husband home long before this and the day had changed from bright sunlight to a cold showering sky and the distant roll of thunder.

Every sound sent her hurrying to the door to stare out at the blackness of the night. Maurice would surely not stay another night in the city without letting her know, and yet when a man was with old friends who knows what he might do.

The room felt cosy as the firelight fell on pieces of china and copper, on the bowl of red geraniums on the table. She wished she had something to do. Never fond of embroidery, she had been the clever academic one, a little scornful of things she called womens' pursuits. Even the making of the cushion covers and curtains had been a chore, but now she was unable to concentrate on the book she had left open on the table.

Her heart lifted suddenly when she heard the sound of men's voices, then footsteps along the path outside and an urgent knocking on the door.

Three men stood on the threshold and she instantly recognized the new mayor and two of Maurice's friends. Of her husband there was no sign but the expression on their faces made her suddenly afraid. She held the door open wider and they followed her into the house.

She received their news calmly, and they could not have known of the sudden fear in her heart or the desperate feeling of loss. Maurice had been her father, her friend, her benefactor. She had loved him with a deep and abiding respect, but it had never been the love of a woman for her lover.

They were kind. They promised her the civic funeral he deserved, and when it was over she returned to her empty stone cottage and a terrible loneliness.

The city and the citizens of Dijon had done their best to honour the memory of the mayor who had seemed a permanency. Indeed there were people in the city who could hardly remember having had another mayor until recently and had believed Maurice Grolan to be in the nature of a king with a hereditary title that went on and on, like the Vicomte de Mirandol himself.

Marie Claire had never concerned herself with her husband's finances. She was aware that they had taken a turn for the worse since he had been deposed or they would not be living in obscurity and he would not have objected to Chantal's removal from the convent to the school in Switzerland. She did not know about his loan from the bank, and now she was being urged to repay it as quickly as possible.

She was amazed that he had left very little money and she was forced to think back to the carriages, her wardrobe filled with expensive clothes, their expensive holidays and the dinners and parties she had invited all and sundry to. She was alone in the world with little money, owing a substantial sum and her daughter's school fees to find.

She could not ask Andrew to pay for his daughter's education but she could approach his brother-in-law.

André opened her letter at the breakfast table several days later and for several moments he sat staring down at it, until his wife asked, 'Is something wrong? Who's the letter from?'

'Madame Grolan.'

Vivienne raised her eyebrows. 'Really André, her husband is hardly laid in his grave and she's seeking attention from you, what does she want?'

'She's asking to see me.'

'To start it all up again, now that her husband is dead. If.you and she get together again André, I shall leave you and take our son with me. I will not have it.'

'Her letter is businesslike. It is hardly the letter of a woman wishing to renew a love affair. Here, read it for yourself.'

He passed over the letter and after reading it she said, 'Then she is asking for money, it can only be that. Hasn't she had enough from you?'

'I should tell you, Vivienne, that Marie Claire never accepted money, jewellery or expensive gifts from me. My father's mistresses took things from the château, pictures, ornaments, furniture. Marie Claire would only accept a birthday present or a Christmas gift, none of them particularly valuable. Another woman would have asked for much more.'

'Several of them have.'

He smiled. 'That is why I think I should see her. I love you Vivienne, I liked Marie Claire, she had an honesty about her, a childlike assumption that life ought to play fair and a strange sadness that it had not.'

'When you say you liked her, does that mean that you do not like me?'

'Of course I like you, Chérie, but you have never had to fight for anything in your life, everything came to you package wrapped in expensive wrapping paper – life, love, a home, money, everything you ever desired was yours for the asking. You never knew that Maurice Grolan stopped his wife from drowning herself in the lake in Dijon, because life was too much for her, because she was losing her home, her job and she could not support her child.'

'She did very well for herself. She captured the mayor and lived like a queen. Even her daughter is now at a finishing school in Switzerland I believe, so you might say Marie Claire has succeeded in feathering her nest.'

'With a man who adored her.'

'And whom she cheated on unmercifully.'

'Nevertheless Vivienne, I still think I should go to see her. Would you turn your back on a friend in need? Would you walk away from somebody who might need your help?'

'You must do as you think fit, André, but I warn you, if she worms her way into your affections again, I shall return to England and Armand will go with me.'

He smiled, his slow lazy smile saying, 'Your are always most beautiful when you are forceful, Vivienne. I never saw your father in Andrew, I see him constantly in you.'

180

'Is that supposed to be a condemnation?'

'Not at all. I always had the utmost respect for him, but I would never have dared antagonize him. I shall never dare antagonize you.'

'But you have André, constantly. Andrew and my father warned me that you would be exactly like your father and you have proved them right. I hated it when they said I told you so.'

'My father and I were alike in many ways, but there were certain differences. My parents were told when they were little more than children that one day they should marry, it was a duty, and they were singularly alike. My mother loved her days of freedom as much as my father did. I married you because I love you, our marriage was never in danger from me, only from you.'

'Because I minded so much?'

'Exactly.'

'Go see your Marie Claire, André, but I shall want to know all that transpires, and how much money she is asking you for.'

21

The Vicomte de Mirandol wrote to Marie Claire advising her of the precise date and time when he would call upon her, and when she opened the door to him his first and rather uncharitable thoughts were that she had dressed for the part and adopted the role she would play.

She was very pale with her dark hair tied back from her face, and she was wearing deepest black mourning and no jewellery. She smiled, opening the door a little wider as she invited him inside.

He looked round the small room with interest. It was cosy, with a fire glowing bright red in the grate, but although it was homely there was nothing in it to remind him that he was in the home of the woman who had once lived in great style as the lady mayoress of Dijon.

He was reminded that most of their possessions had belonged to the city and to the large house they had left behind them. There were several nice pieces of porcelain that Maurice had liked and purchased for himself, and the glow from the flames fell on brightly polished brass and copper.

Marie Claire indicated that he should sit on one side of the fireplace while she sat on the other. In spite of her sombre attire and her plain hairstyle there was enchantment in her smile. It was a fact that Marie Claire would never be a plain woman however much she tried to disguise her beauty.

He had made up his mind that she would be the one to break the silence, even so the loud ticking of the clock and the sound of the cinders falling on to the hearth unsettled him.

'Will you have a coffee?' she asked softly. 'I have brandy if you would prefer it.'

'Coffee, thank you.'

'Then please excuse me, it will not take long.'

He heard her in the kitchen busying herself with crockery and he looked again round the room. What had prompted Maurice Grolan to live out of the city in this small stone house? He had always assumed he was well placed financially, but this was hardly the abode of a man with private means.

Marie Claire came in carrying a tray laid out with cups and saucers and a jug of coffee, laying it on top of the table and pouring the coffee without looking at him. Passing him a cup she said evenly, 'There is cream and sugar if you prefer it.'

'I prefer it black, thank you.'

She took her cup of coffee back to her seat and this time when their eyes met he became instantly aware of the tears rolling unchecked down her cheeks and that her lips were trembling.

This was not an act, there was genuine grief here and something else, something approaching fear.

'How can I help you, Marie Claire?' he asked gently.

'It is kind of you to come, André, I didn't want to ask you, I hoped to handle Maurice's death on my own but things are happening that I do not understand. Maurice never talked about his money, never discussed anything with me, but now men are calling to see me to ask for money. The bank has written to me saying there are bills that have not been paid, payments that have fallen behind. I don't understand any of it, why didn't he tell me he owed money in the city?'

'Have you got the letters to hand?'

'Yes, they are all here. Please tell me what I should do about them, tell me if it is true that we owe them this money?'

She pushed a pile of letters across the table and one by one he took them up and read them. Maurice Grolin had taken out a substantial loan and had been making regular payments to the bank. After his death no further payments had been made and now the demands were coming in, as well as demands for the money he owed on his purchase of the house.

She watched feverishly as he laid the letters back on the table one by one, her eyes willing him to tell her that they were not true.

Gently he explained the true facts to her, seeing incredulity turn to despair and he sat watching her sobbing helplessly, crying, 'What shall I do, what shall I do?'

'If the money is not paid the house will be sold over your head Marie Claire, they have a right to do that, and I am at a loss to understand why he needed to raise this loan.'

She looked at him pitiously. 'It's all my fault, it must be. We lived beyond our means, always doing something, going somewhere, always somewhere expensive, and then I asked for Chantal to go to that school in Switzerland. Maurice told me it was too expensive, that we couldn't afford it but I never let him alone. I did it for Chantal.'

183

'I thought your daughter was adequately taken care of at St Agnes' convent, why Switzerland? I found that most unusual and unnecessary, why Switzerland, for heaven's sake.'

'She was unhappy at the convent, there was too much talk, about me, about us. Even the Reverend Mother lectured me. I listened to you talking about the finishing schools English girls attended and I thought Chantal should be given her chance. She is pretty and clever, she had a terrible start in life and I owed her so much.'

'But Chantal is French. Her future will in no way resemble the future of the English girls you speak of.'

'I thought it would be good for her.'

'Do you know why those girls go to Switzerland to finish their education? They are not necessarily academically bright, they go to learn a little French, to skate and ski, to add a continental lustre that might tempt the right aristocrat at the débutante balls that will follow, but in the main the lustre is false and brittle. You should never have asked your husband to finance such a venture.'

She hung her head low and remained silent, and gradually the indignation left him.

'This money will have to be repaid, Marie Claire,' he said adamantly.

'They can have everything I have and if they take it all it will not be enough. How can I tell Chantal that she will have to leave Switzerland?'

'How old is your daughter?'

'Seventeen.'

'So she has at least another year in Switzerland. I will lend you the money to pay off your loan and I will pay for what is left of your daughter's education, is that what you expected me to say?'

She stared at him wide-eyed, at first unable to believe what he was saying, then with a little cry she ran to his side and kneeling on the floor besides his chair she laid her head against his knees. 'Oh André,' she cried. 'You are the dearest kindest friend I have ever had. I shall love you for ever for what you are doing today.'

He smiled. 'No, Marie Claire, you won't love me. You never loved me, and I never loved you. I desired you. We gave each other joy, amusement and a certain audacious danger as heady as wine, now with this money it's over for both of us.'

She watched as he wrote out a cheque, then when he handed it to her she took it with a feeling of deep shame. 'Does this mean that you have paid for my services, André, like you pay your other servants?'

He shook his head. 'If you had been in the habit of taking from me,

184

Marie Claire, I doubt that you would have seen me this morning. You haven't looked at the cheque.'

She looked at it and her eyes opened wide. 'But it's too much. I haven't asked for this amount.'

'I know, but you will need to live when your bills have been paid.'

'I'll find work André, I'll pay you back, every penny, I swear it.'

'I don't want you to pay me back. I am still curious, Marie Claire, why all those questions about my English relatives, the schools for their children, why was it so necessary for Chantal to emulate them?'

'I was always a daydreamer, always wanting to do something else, be someone else. I wanted Chantal to be different too. I thought she would be invited to visit England, meet one of their English aristocrats perhaps. I have been a very silly woman.'

He smiled down at her, then taking her hand in his he raised it to his lips and kissed it.

'I fear so, Marie Claire,' he said softly. 'Tis au revoir.'

She stood at the door watching him walk down the path and remained there until the sound of his horses' hooves had died away.

Her secret was still safe.

How much of the afternoon's events would he tell his wife, but more urgent, what would she do with her life now? She could not live here outside the city in obscure gentility, no job, no real friends, no going back ever, but Chantal was safe, and hadn't something always happened to restore her battered courage?

That night she wrote a long cheerful letter to Chantal. They had wept together at Maurice's funeral and Chantal had left her to go back to Switzerland with tears in her eyes. She had not known that her daughter had cared so much for Maurice, that he had been the bulwark in Chantal's life just as he had been in hers. Dear Maurice with his fatherly gentleness, his pride that late in life he had captured the regard of a young wife and her child.

The next morning Marie Claire went into the city to settle her debts. If the bank manager was surprised he received her with urbane civility and she treated him with equal aplomb. Although she was wearing mourning she had chosen to wear an attractive black hat and the veil hiding her face gave her the courage to eat lunch in one of the city's more fashionable restaurants.

She had removed her veil but paid no heed to the people lunching around her, and after she had eaten she walked out into the city streets and sauntered along the boulevards and into the older part of the city where she had once worked. It was on one of those streets that she saw the vacant shop window and the 'For Sale' sign hanging behind the glass door. Madame Foularde was selling her millinery shop, and she thought back on the numerous hats she had purchased there, expensive hats for expensive occasions.

The longer she stared in the empty window the more enticing the idea became. André had given her a substantial sum of money. She had paid her bills and he had said she would need to live on what was left, but living wasn't enough. She could stay in her old stone cottage and stagnate, that was what she might have done if she'd been old, but she wasn't old. She was young and why couldn't she work to make her money grow?

Without a second's thought she tried the door, surprised when the latch yielded to her fingers.

The shelves were empty, only the long mirrors were ranged around the room and the stands on which the hats had been modelled. There was no sound from behind the door at the back of the shop and her spirits sank a little. Surely they wouldn't have forgotten to lock the door, and yet Madame Foularde could hardly be expected to linger on in her empty premises waiting for a buyer. The shop had had a certain appeal even though it was in an unfashionable part of the city, and Madame Foulard's clientèle had had its supply of older, more lucrative customers.

With a sinking heart she knocked on the door leading to the room behind, then she knocked a little harder, and her heart lifted when she heard someone call out, 'I am here, you will wait.'

It had been a woman's voice and she waited where she could stare out through the window at the citizens of Dijon going about their business. At last the door opened and Madame Foularde was standing staring at her in some surprise, wearing a dust cap on her bright red hair, and carrying a brush and dustpan in her hands.

'Madame Grolan,' she exclaimed. 'I though you had left Dijon, but you can see the shop is for sale.'

'Yes I know. I read the sign in the window. Why are you leaving?'

'To marry a widower in Lyons, a very rich widower whose wife used to buy all her hats from me. I have been on my own too long, ever since my husband died, and I am very tired of being a shopkeeper, particularly when nobody wants to pay my prices any more. Were you looking for a hat Madame?'

'No. I'm interested in your shop. How much are you asking for it?'

Madame Foularde's eyes narrowed, and in a matter-of-fact voice she said, 'So they have not been without foundation the stories I've been hearing.'

'What stories are those, Madame?'

'That Maurice Grolan was not a rich man, that you were living in reduced circumstances so that your daughter could go to a very expensive school in Interlaken. I am not a gossip, I listened to them but took no part. After all I have known most of my customers for a great many years, I was accustomed to the sort of gossip that interested them. You're having to find work then?'

'I have money. I simply want to invest it in a business that would find me something to do. I'm too young to sit back and dream about the past.'

'But you'll marry again, a woman as pretty as you.'

'I've no plans to marry, my husband died very recently, besides I don't want to marry again. I want to look after myself and work for myself.'

'Very laudable, my dear, but in any shop goodwill is a great advantage, have you friends you can rely on?'

'Oh surely I have. My husband served this city very well and I helped him, surely they will remember that.'

'Some of them will, but there are others, Elise Grolan's old friends, and your life with Maurice Grolan did not endure without its share of scandal.'

'You mean the Vicomte de Mirandol?'

Madame Foularde did not answer and after a while Marie Claire said, 'I want to try. Tell me how much you are wanting for the shop and I will speak to my bank manager in the morning.'

'Perhaps if you were to speak to the Vicomte.'

'Like I said I will speak to my bank manager. I will call again after I have seen him. Will you be here, Madame?'

'Why yes. I'm trying to leave everything in good order and I have some paperwork to see to. If you are going to see the bank manager you will need some figures from me. You know without my telling you that the shop was exclusive but this is an old part of the city and there are a great many new shops in the city centre that have taken trade from me. I have kept my old clients, but I cannot say if they would be your clients Madame.'

'You are not very encouraging?'

'No. I am a poor shop seller. I should be telling you that the shop is famous, that they come from all over France, even from Paris to buy my millinery but you know that would not be true.'

'No. I have seen this shop going down for some time and I thought it was a pity. I always loved your hats, I bought a great many from you.'

'That is why I'm being honest with you now. I always liked you Madame. You had a warm heart, your feet seemed to dance through life oblivious of its pitfalls, and when it didn't play fair you bounced back, even if your methods did not always earn you respect. If you buy my little shop I wish you well in it. Do you know anything about the millinery trade?'

'Not a thing. I am clever with my fingers and I have style. In recent years we could not afford your hats but I was able to alter my old ones so that nobody ever knew they had not been bought that morning. In the time left to you, will you help me?'

Madame Foularde smiled. 'You can depend on it, Madame, and I will advertise the fact that you are to be the new owner of my shop. They will come at first out of curiosity. Make your hats so beautiful they will find them irresistible.'

Marie Claire laughed. Her excitement stayed with her all the way home, and that night as she sat in front of the fire it was easy to dream of the success she would make of the boutique she would call simply 'Marie Claire.'

The bank manager was cautious, extremely doubtful, but nothing and nobody could have discouraged her. He wished her well with a handshake and a stern look that spoke volumes. After she had gone he returned to his chair and sat for several moments gazing down at the papers she had left with him.

The Vicomte de Mirandol had been more than generous but there would be no more funds from that quarter. He had little faith in the future of the milliner's shop but Marie Claire was young and a beautiful woman. Some man would come along, perhaps some man with too much money and too little sense and in the meantime it would give her something to do, something to keep her out of mischief.

Madame Foularde was as good as her word. Together they dusted and polished the long mirrors and those over the drawers. She moved her furniture into the living room behind the shop and into the big bedroom over it and Madame Foularde found her boxes of hats made out of buckram and rolls of satin and chiffon. There were boxes filled with chiffon roses and daisies, feathers and paste ornaments and Marie Claire knew that this was how she would spend her evenings, fashioning hats exclusive to Marie Claire's salon and not to be found anywhere else in Dijon.

She had her own hats that would serve as copies, and she decided she would alter some of these if it became necessary.

'I shall put only one hat in the window,' she said to Madame Foularde, 'a beautiful hat, side by side with a bowl filled with flowers and I shall search for a beautiful head to place it on. I saw one this morning at the warehouse, a haughty aristocratic face, but even the plainest women in Dijon will think they can do it justice.'

Her enthusiasm was something to wonder at, Madame Foularde

thought. It would be too terrible if nobody came to buy, too awful if nobody even came to look in the window.

On the morning Madame Foularde left for Lyon she, Marie Claire pressed a porcelain figurine in to her hands as a wedding present. It was a pretty thing, something Maurice had bought for her many years before when she admired it. There were tears in the older woman's eyes when she received it and she offered up a silent prayer for the woman who gave it to her.

The hat was in its place on the model's head in the centre of the window side by side with a bowl filled with roses, and the days passed and the petals dropped on to the carpet, but if people came to stare at the creation nobody came into the shop to buy.

She sat alone waiting for the doorbell to ring and the days passed. Other hats took the place of the first one and the flowers changed from roses to autumn leaves and still nobody came into the shop, and despair took the place of anticipation.

The shop had been open over three weeks when she heard the sound of the bell tinkling and, hardly daring to hope, she opened the door only a few inches believing that it had been her imagination.

A woman was standing in the shop gazing around her curiously, a tall beautifully dressed woman, and opening the door wider she turned to close it behind her. The woman turned her head, and she found herself staring into the Vicomtesse de Mirandol's dark-blue eyes.

She put out a hand to grip the counter, aware of the rich red blood colouring her cheeks and that her heart was thumping alarmingly. Vivienne showed no such discomfort.

'I saw the name,' she said. 'I was visiting the book shop, I do not often come into this part of the city except to visit the church of St Michael.'

Marie Claire remained silent, she could not at that moment have trusted her voice to reply.

'It is quiet in the street today,' the Vicomtesse said gently.

'It is quite most days, Milady.'

'Trade is not good then?'

'No, it's terrible. I had such hopes, they don't even come to look.'

'Perhaps, it's early days yet. Did you make the hat in the window?'

'I decorated it. I have had it in the window and out of it for days. This morning I decided to try again. It is a beautiful hat.'

'It is a very beautiful hat. I would like to try it on.'

Marie Claire's eyes flew open, but she hurried to get the hat out of the window and stood while the Vicomtesse sat before the mirror removing her hat and reaching out her hand to take the one she wished to try.

Their eyes met in the mirror and the Vicomtesse smiled. The hat did her more than justice, swathed in black chiffon and adorned with black osprey feathers it was a hat for a grand occasion, and only that morning Marie Claire had thought she was wrong to display hats of this calibre and should confine herself to more mundane ones.

'I'm going to London at the end of the week,' the Vicomtesse said easily. 'It is a sad occasion but people will expect me to look the part of a fashionable French woman and my sister-in-law needs some keeping up with.'

'Oh I am sorry, is it a death in the family?'

'Yes. My grandmother. She is well over ninety. She's had a very good innings so it is not too distressing.'

'Innings?'

The Vicomtesse laughed. 'A cricket term my dear, one you wouldn't be familiar with.

'I shall take the hat, and in the summer we are going to Ascot and Goodwood, I shall need others. If you like you can place a note in your window to say that you are under the patronage of the Vicomtesse de Mirandol.'

Marie Claire burst into tears.

'Oh Milady, you are so kind and I do not deserve it. Why are you being so kind to me?'

Vivienne de Mirandol smiled. 'The more successful you are, my dear, the less likely you are to seek unfortunate consolation. I would not have been so charitable several years ago, but something of the sang-froid I have found in France must have rubbed off. Now do put this hat in a beautiful box with your name on it so that everybody who sees me will be curious to see what others you have.'

She left the shop with a bright smile, and Marie Claire stood in the doorway watching her walk blithely down the street.

Both men and women stared after her, and there were groups of women with their heads together staring up the street towards the shop so Marie Claire went inside to find another creation to place in the window.

22

Marie Claire had another visitor to her shop later in the afternoon. She went forward smiling to meet the tall darkly clad woman who entered her shop, shyly, almost diffidently, but when the woman turned round after closing the door she came face to face with her sister Jeanne.

For a long moment they stared at each other then with a little cry Marie Claire went forward to embrace her.

'Jeanne, how wonderful,' she cried. 'How did you know I was here?'

'I didn't. I saw the Vicomtesse walking down the road carrying your hat box and then I saw the shop with your name over it. I didn't really know it was your shop. I came to stare though the window and I saw you inside. I know that your husband died, I thought about you often and wondered where you might be living.'

'But none of you ever wrote to me, Jeanne.'

'I know. It was difficult. Papa was so terribly bitter, he never asked for you, never forgave you. I told him he should be proud of you, married to the Mayor of Dijon, and Marcel told us you were visitors at the château. It didn't make any difference to his anger with you.'

'What did he say?'

'Does it really matter now, after all you survived without help from any of us.'

'Did he never think I might have called to see you when I was so close?'

'He said the daughter he knew was destined to make her own way in life without selling herself to some man or other. I didn't agree with him, I thought he was hard and cruel and I often told him so, it didn't make any difference, and now he's dead.'

'Papa is dead!'

'Yes, in the winter. He caught a bad chill which turned to pneumonia. He was a very difficult patient, he wore Mama out.'

'He never asked for me, not even then?'

'No. He carried his bitterness to the grave.'

'And what's happening to the farm, I hope he left it to Marc.'

'Yes. After all Marc deserved it, and now Marcel hardly does a day's work on the place and Margot has all my father's rancour. Marcel has other women, she knows about them but refuses to admit it, and the entire house is plagued by angry scenes.'

'I remember Papa when he was kind and gentle, it seems to me that everything that has happened to you is all my fault, I changed Papa and he changed in a way that made it miserable for all of you.'

'Well, you're not responsible for Marcel, and now that Papa has gone perhaps you will visit us one day Marie Claire.'

'I can't face seeing the farm again, but you are very welcome to visit me and bring Mama with you.'

'She would like to see your little shop. It doesn't seem very busy.'

'Well it is new. The vicomtesse bought an expensive hat and she has said she will buy others. With her patronage people will come.'

'They were saying things about you and the vicomte in the village, now perhaps I can tell them that it is his wife who is your friend, not the vicomte.'

'They are both my friends, Jeanne.'

'It was Marcel who brought home the gossip from the village. He delighted in bringing up any tittle-tattle about you, knowing very well that it upset our mother and angered our father.'

'I can imagine. And now we'll have something to eat and you shall tell me about your children and all the other things that have happened to you. I'll pull down the blind and close the shop for the day.'

'But your customers?'

'If there are any they will come back. I suppose you are going home on the train?'

'Yes, but we must talk, it's been so long, Marie Claire, and I did miss you.'

In the days that followed Jeanne's visit the shop prospered.

Diane Cladel and her mother were among her first customers. Diane came with ready smiles, enthusing rapturously on the pretty hats and encouraging her mother to buy recklessly.

'But I have spent so much,' her mother complained. 'When am I going to wear hats like these?'

'In Paris, Mother, when you go to see Aunt Marie and she will be pea green with envy and want to know how you could buy such models in Dijon.'

'And what will your husband say about your spending such a vast amount of money on something so frivolous?' her mother asked doubtfully.

'Pierre likes to see me looking fashionable. He'll be delighted.'

'I shall tell everybody I know to buy their hats from you,' Diane said on parting. 'You'll see, your little shop is going to be a great success.'

The customers came in twos and threes, hesitantly, at first out of curiosity and to look, then the more monied among them started to buy. By the end of two years she had repaid the small amount of money she had borrowed from the bank and was starting to make more.

The vicomtesse came often. Hats for Ascot and Goodwood, race meetings in Paris and Deauville and others for her garden parties and soirées. The ladies of Dijon liked to be in her shop when the vicomtesse was choosing hats, so that they could study her style and talk among themselves about her attitude towards Marie Claire.

Marie Claire told her customers about her daughter's delight in her school in Switzerland, oblivious of their raised eyebrows and unconcerned about their thoughts on the matter. She lived for Chantal's letters filled with stories about her new friends and how they were coping with French lessons and other ventures.

The girls from aristocratic English families were a source of amusement to Chantal. They did not take to their lessons because none of them would ever be expected to have to earn a living. They were happiest learning to play tennis, skate and ride, and in the evenings they would gather in giggling groups to chatter about the appeal of their ski instructor, the tennis coach and the art master. Most of them were in love with one or another of these handsome young men, changing their allegiance from day to day with lighthearted abandon.

They talked of the aristocratic possibilities of the young men at home, who might or might not be on the marriage menu when they came out, and the sort of balls and parties they could be expected to attend as débutantes. It was a world new and alien to Chantal Grolan and when they asked what particular aristocratic family she came from in France she had to say simply that her stepfather had been the mayor of Dijon.

They howled with laughter, and Charlotte Vane-Dronsfield remarked sympathetically, 'But of course, darling, you had that awful revolution, didn't you, didn't they dispose of all your noble families in that? I suppose they were replaced by mayors and such like.'

Chantal was quick to say, 'My mother is friends with the Vicomte de Mirandol and his family, they get invitations to all their parties.'

'How lovely. Aren't they relatives of the Earl of Westmonds's daughter, Grace, she'll be coming here next year?'

They made friends with Chantal, she was pretty, far cleverer than any of them and she spoke French. She helped them with their homework and was disinterested in any of the young men they professed undying love for.

Her letters amused her mother, particularly the one about Grace who was expected to join them next year. Chantal had thought this item of gossip might interest her mother simply because she was related to the Mirandols. Her mother was interested in the English aristocracy for some reason or another, her mother had a great many interests, perhaps they had something to do with the fact that she had been Dijon's mayoress.

After the summer holidays she found that Monsieur Devoix, the music master, had retired and a new music master had taken his place. He was an Austrian, Herr Deiter Steinberg from Vienna. He was tall and blond and handsome and the girls *en masse* fell in love with him.

Herr Steinberg brought a new dimension into the lives of the girls. Chantal listened eagerly to her friends' stories of a flighty King Edward happily released from his mother's inflexible rules on morality, and his string of mistresses were discussed freely.

'How do you know all this?' she asked in some amazement.

'Darling, everybody knows. I listen to my parents talking, everybody in London is talking about it.'

Another of the girls had said meaningly, 'Of course the French have always been unconcerned about such goings on, but the British were always far more circumspect.'

Madame Lafayette was anxious to instill decorum and seemliness into her girls. She was well aware that they chattered and giggled together about the things that were happening to influential members of their society, and she was quick to condemn such goings on.

That the girls flirted outrageously with their coaches annoyed her and they were given strict instructions not to presume on these flirtations. Herr Steinberg had not been her choice even though he was the most qualified. He was too good looking, too charming and he brought with him all the lush glamour of Vienna, his tantalizing knowledge of the court of the Hapsburgs, the waltzes of Strauss and the haunting melodies from the operettas.

Herr Steinberg basked in the admiration of the English girls, but he was intrigued by Chantal with her French savoir-faire. The English girls were the daughters of aristocrats but it was Chantal who had the keener mind, the greater aptitude for learning, the more mature concept of life. The English girls had enjoyed an uncomplicated childhood and girlhood, Chantal Grolan had memories of more difficult days.

Madame Lafayette wished she had employed the services of an older man who would have inspired her girls with the tragic music of Chopin or Beethoven rather than the lilting headiness of Johann Strauss. She had been foolish enough to be swayed by the pleadings from her assistants who had all succumbed to the charms of Herr Steinberg without a second's thought for the gullibility of her young pupils.

Herr Steinberg was not only a brilliant musician, he was also an expert on the ski slopes and a graceful performer in the ballroom. He could speak French, English and German fluently and had an aristocratic background even though it was faintly remote. His father had been an officer in the Emperor's Guard and his mother's family were barons from the Tyrol.

In Madame's presence the young man was always circumspect, but when she was absent he showed his liking for Chantal Grolan quite forcefully, much to the delight of the English girls who teased her unmercifully.

Lady Marcia Charlesworth felt sure that he would ask her to marry him before she left the school, and her friend Lady Sarah Charmers said she ought to be choosing her bridesmaids and deciding what they should wear.

Chantal was bemused. She was dreaming of what it would be like to be married to the handsome young Austrian. How would she cope in being a music master's wife and no doubt living in some small chalet on the mountain slopes while he walked up to the school every morning with his violin?

During the Christmas holidays her mother did not miss the long silences, the expression of dreaming anticipation in her daughter's eyes, and her sudden lapses of memory.

Her own memories were brought vividly to life. She remembered those breathless moments when she had run along the country lanes in anticipation of her meeting with Andrew, the wild enchanting embraces, the ridiculous assumption that nothing would ever change.

She longed to ask questions but refrained, hoping that Chantal would tell her all she needed to know, but the days passed and nothing was said. It was the day before Chantal was due to return to Switzerland that Marie Claire found her sitting in her bedroom staring absently out of the window, her bed strewn with articles she needed to take back to school. There was a look of dreamy reflection on her daughter's face and perhaps more sharply than she had intended she said, 'Chantal, what is the matter with you? I've hardly had a word out of you all day and you haven't finished your packing.'

The girl leapt to her feet and turned towards her bed, but her face was flushed with embarrassment and she set about folding garments and placing them into the suitcase. She was aware of her mother's curiosity and after a few moments' silence Marie Claire persisted, 'What is wrong, darling, are you sorry to be returning to school?'

'Oh no Mother, I love it there.'

'There was a time when we could talk, tell each other secrets, laugh together, but not during these last few weeks when you have been secretive and unlike yourself.'

Chantal turned to look at her, and the next moment she was kneeling on the floor beside her mother's chair and the words came rushing out with passionate abandon.

'Oh Mother, I have wanted so much to tell you but I wasn't sure how you would receive it. I have fallen in love with the most wonderful man, he's everything you would want him to be, handsome, talented, charming, and I know he loves me.'

Totally astounded, Marie Claire was able to prompt her. 'Has he told you that he loves you?'

'No, but it's very difficult. He will though when I leave in the summer, nothing will stand in his way then.'

'But who is he, this young man who is so wonderful and is unable to tell you now?'

'He is Austrian, Herr Deiter Steinberg. He comes from Vienna, he's our music master at school.'

Marie Claire stared down at her daughter's fair head resting against her knee with her thoughts in turmoil.

How safe that school in Switzerland had seemed, peopled with English girls from titled families. Never for a moment had she visualized handsome music masters and other such distractions and this was not why she had insisted on sending Chantal to Madame Lafayette's.

The school had been a means to an end, a means of introducing her daughter to the daughters of people Andrew would know, would call his friend, a means of ensuring that Chantal would have the same opportunities as she would have had, if he had honored his obligations. Now this handsome young Austrian had come along to thwart her and it could not be allowed.

Carefully choosing her words she said, 'My dear, you're far too young to fall in love with the first handsome young man you meet. There will be many other handsome young men before you really fall in love.'

'You fell in love when you were younger than me, when you were my age you had me.'

'I know, darling, and surely you remember how cruelly my father treated me and that I had to leave you with them so that I could earn

196

enough money to care for you. For your sake, I married Maurice who was a good kind man even when he was old enough to be my father, and Chantal, there were so many other things I did for you that you don't know anything about.'

'I know about the Vicomte de Mirandol. They taunted me about him at the convent and I thought that was why you took me away. Marie Gasparde said the Reverend Mother had chastized you, are you telling me that you had an affair with the vicomte for me?'

'Oh Chantal, that sounds so terribly crude. There are so many things you don't know, so many times when I have thought I couldn't go on because I didn't have any money, any family, and because people were being unkind. Maurice paid for you to go to Switzerland and had to borrow money to do so, and then when he died I had to throw myself on André's mercy. I am not asking you to repay me for any of this, only to make the best of your life, and falling in love with a music master straight out of the schoolroom is not the answer.'

'Doesn't it matter that I love him?'

'Of course it matters, but before you really decide that this is the solitary passion of a lifetime you should live a little. Travel, meet other men, give yourself some space. As the years pass and you realize you are still in love with this young man then we shall need to talk again.'

'Are you saying that he will be still in Switzerland waiting for me to grow up?'

'He will if he really loves you.'

'Oh Mother, you don't really believe that.'

'How old is this man, Chantal?'

'I'm not sure, twenty-five perhaps, perhaps more, I'm not sure.'

'And you are seventeen. He's the first man in your life, you will not be the first woman in his.'

'How do you know that?'

'I do know a little about men, my dear.'

'There has been nobody, I'm sure of it. Music has been his life, besides even if there have been others it is me he loves now.'

'Chantal, I am asking you to be completely sure of your feelings and you can only do that by measuring this young man against others you could meet. What had you thought to do with your life if you spend it with him?'

'I shall work hard at my studies, perhaps one day Madame Lafayette will take me on as a teacher, that way we could find somewhere in Switzerland to live and work at the school together.'

'Have you discussed it with him?'

'No. It is too soon.'

'Because you are unsure. There is no certainty in your life about anything, no certainty that Madame Lafayette will offer you work, no certainty that you can set up house together, no real certainty that that is what he wants, and even if it all falls into place it will not do so immediately. Like I said before, my dear, you are too young and I know what it is like to dream about impossibilities. I loved a man I thought loved me, I thought he would come back to me and that we would have a life together, it didn't happen and I don't want that sort of disaster for you Chantal.'

'Because it didn't happen for you, you don't want it to happen for me.'

Sighing sadly Marie Claire rose to her feet. 'I want what I have always wanted for you, Chantal, the best, and I am unconvinced that this man is the best thing for you. Until you are of age I am responsible for you and I cannot give my consent to anything that I think will be bad for you. Learn from my mistakes, darling, and trust me.'

She stood on the station platform the next morning watching the train for Switzerland pull away and Chantal sat in her corner seat tight-lipped and unsmiling. There had been long silences between them on the morning she left. Her daughter's face had been frozen into anger as she sat at the breakfast table and in the end Marie Claire had given up trying to involve her in any sort of conversation.

She was not unsympathetic, she had long and vivid memories of the girl she had been, but disaster had shaped the sort of woman she had become and nothing Chantal said would have shaken her now.

As she unlocked the door of her shop two women standing across the road watched and before she had taken off her coat they had entered the shop. The taller women seemed strangely familiar as she stood in the centre of the shop looking round her curiously, and the older woman was busy scrutinizing a large black hat on one of the model heads.

She spoke to her companion in English and then Marie Claire saw with sickening certainty that the tall blonde woman was Andrew's wife.

'What do you think of this one, Constance, a little too flamboyant perhaps?'

'You will need to try it on, Mother.'

'But is it suitable for a funeral? I'm not looking for a garden party creation!'

'If you think it's too ornate, look around for something else, I suppose you have other models in black?' she said addressing Marie Claire with direct condescension.

'Of course.'

Her tone had been superior and decidedly cool and Marie Claire was well aware that Constance was aware that she was addressing the

198

one-time mistress of her brother-in-law. She could afford to be supercilious with such a person.

She produced several black hats, most of them beautifully made, one or two less ornate than the one in the woman's hand.

'Perhaps this one would be more suitable for a funeral,' she said handing a plain felt hat to her, its only adornment a spray of osprey feathers.

Her customer tried it on, turning this way and that to look at herself in the mirror, watched by her daughter.

'What do you think?' she asked finally.

'It's very nice, Mother. I'm sure you could have bought one very similar in London.'

'I've looked in London. I've liked the hats Vivienne's been wearing recently. They've been different, very chic, very French.'

'I didn't think it was so important to be chic at a funeral, Mother.'

'We're talking about Uncle Guy's funeral, Constance, not anybody's funeral.'

'Well then, it's very nice, I should buy that one.'

'What about you?'

'Perhaps I'll try that one,' she said pointing to the one on the model.

'Well really,' her mother protested. 'If it was too ornate for me it surely will be for you.'

'I didn't say I wanted it for the funeral, Mother, there will be other occasions.'

The hat sat on her blond head with sophisticated elegance, and well pleased with it she said, 'I'll have this one, and the other of course.'

The Countess of Westmond paid for both hats and they watched while Marie Claire packed them into hat boxes before she went to open the door for them to depart.

They passed her with the briefest inclination of their heads and she stood in the shop doorway watching them walk down the street.

The visit of the woman she felt she should hate had left her numb. What was there in that cold haughty woman that Andrew had found so that he had forgotten her as quickly as a summer storm?

23

They came back with excited stories of what was in store for them at the end of their two years in Switzerland, and the scandal they had overheard during their holidays.

Chantal sat at the window staring out at the snow-covered peaks, listening to the laughter and the whispered innuendos.

The new girls who had joined them sat together listening respectfully to the girls who were already to leave Switzerland, and as Chantal looked across the room at them, one of them smiled. Chantal had noticed her earlier, a pretty blonde-haired girl with a warm gentle smile and a beautiful porcelain complexion.

Amanda Wentworth called out to her, 'Mummy is going to invite you to my coming-out ball, Chantal, you'll love it, there will be so much to do you'll stay in England for months.'

Chantal smiled, and Louise Stedman said coyly, 'Can you actually ask Chantal without asking her Austrian pianist to accompany her?'

'Well, of course,' Amanda retorted. 'The ball will be crawling with handsome British aristocrats. Chantal will be able to have her pick.'

'I hope not,' said another. 'Isn't that why we shall be there.'

Chantal wasn't interested in their festivities. She had seen Herr Steinberg walking in the gardens, and passing the window he looked towards her and smiled. There was so much charm in his smile, she could feel her heart fluttering like a wild thing and behind her came the laughter and the teasing voices of her friends.

'My parents would be horrified if I even suggested that I was in love with a music teacher,' Louise said caustically. 'I would have to elope with him and hope they'd forgive me.'

Without answering any of them she picked up her needlepoint and started to work on it. The blonde girl who had smiled at her rose to her feet and came to sit beside her. Chantal looked up and smiled, 'You're new here, aren't you?' she said. 'When did you arrive?'

'Two days ago. Mother and Granny brought me so I was here all on my own until the rest of you arrived.'

'Why did you come so early?'

'They were going on to stay with Aunt Vivienne and Uncle André near Dijon for a few days. They'll be going home for the season.'

'Do they always have to do that?'

'Well no, but Granny is very circumspect. She would hate to be out of England at such a time. You're French, aren't you?'

'Yes, my name is Chantal Grolan.'

'My name is Grace Martindale.'

'Lady Grace?'

The girl blushed. 'Yes, I'm afraid so.'

Chantal laughed. 'All my friends have titles, it's something we French have learned to live without, although we do have our smattering of titled people.'

'Leftovers from the Revolution?'

'Something like that. Do you live in London?'

'We have a town house in London but our real home is in Buckinghamshire. We also have a house in Bath, have you ever been there?'

'I've never been to England.'

'Really. But you will go when you leave school, your friends will invite you. You'll have a wonderful time in the season.'

'The season?'

'Yes. All the balls and parties, the garden parties and regattas, the race meetings. I can't wait until I'm old enough to take part in all that.'

'Do you have to be a débutante before you can go to these places?'

'Not really. I've been to Ranelagh and to Cowes for regattas but I'm too young for the balls, one has to be a deb to enjoy those.'

'I see.'

'What part of France do you come from?'

'The city of Dijon.'

'I've been there. I was taken to look at the cathedral, it's very grand. My aunt and uncle live near Dijon at the Château de Mirandol. You probably know it.'

'Yes.'

'Do you know my relatives?'

'No. I think my mother does.'

'I'm here for a year, that's all. My father didn't want to send me here, he said it was archaic and something quite unnecessary but Granny insisted.'

'Granny insisted?'

'Well yes. She and Mummy between them talked him round, he said he couldn't fight both of them. Actually I wanted to come, I wanted to see Switzerland and Mummy said a finishing school gives a girl so much more panache, whatever that is.'

Chantal liked her. She had a warmth about her that she found charming and when she asked how old she was, she was surprised to learn that she was only a year younger than herself. In many ways she seemed so very much younger and when she said as much to Maria Garvey, she merely said, 'Oh well, she's had a very sheltered life, her mother is a bit of a snob actually, and her grandmother is a positive social climber. At least that's what my mother has always said.'

'Does she have to be a social climber, isn't Grace's father an earl?'

'Yes he is, but the grandmother had to do a bit of social climbing to get him. I expect that's what she meant.'

Their teachers saw that the girls were adequately informed about everything that was happening in England; the wearisome boredom of politics, the exploits of British servicemen in trouble spots throughout the world and the ever-increasing scandals of King Edward VII.

Madame Lafayette described his succession of mistresses as very available women and later in the common room Chantal asked curiously, 'What does she mean by "very available women"?'

'Well, you know mistresses,' Louise answered. 'Mummy says they are flattered by his attention and they make themselves available. After all he was told who he had to marry and although Princess Alexandra is very nice and very beautiful she might not have been his choice.'

'Why does she put up with it?' another girl asked.

'Because she's a royal princess and knows it has always happened. After all she might not have wanted to marry him, but it is her duty.'

Chantal thought miserably that that was how they would describe her mother, an available woman, and her antagonism towards her increased.

Louise Stedman was probably the most sophisticated of her friends. With an American mother and a father who was a diplomat, and both of them widely travelled, she seemed to know a lot about most things. Now airing her knowledge she said, 'Kings and queens have always done it, it's natural. They're told who they have to marry, they're not going to be told who they can fall in love with.'

'And not only kings and queens,' another girl said feelingly.

'I suppose you are thinking about your father,' Louise said.

'Well yes. It's all so awful at home these days, there is poor Mummy in Yorkshire and that awful woman is everywhere in London where father has to be.'

'My aunt and uncle are very much in love,' Grace said softly, 'but I used to listen to my parents talking. They didn't know I was listening but they said Uncle André had a mistress. How could he if he really loved Aunt Vivienne?'

Chantal felt the warm blood colouring her face and once again an aching antipathy towards her mother.

Her mother's letters began to worry her. She was relying on Chantal to be sensible, not to encourage her music teacher because nothing could come of it, and if matters were getting really serious then it could quite easily lose him his position. Marie Claire would have no hesitation in asking for his removal on the grounds that her daughter was infatuated and he had overstepped his position by encouraging her.

Some of the girls were curious about her background. When they chattered on and on about their stately homes, their exclusive town houses and extensive parklands, she kept silent about her mother's modest milliner's shop in a quiet corner of Dijon. It was all very difficult when Grace suggested that they should meet during school holidays when she would be staying with her relatives so close to Dijon.

'I'm not really sure where I shall be,' Chantal prevaricated. 'We may be going to the country to stay with relatives, or perhaps to the sea. Nothing has been planned.'

'But you must come to the château, Aunt Vivienne would love me to have friends there.'

Chantal smiled but promised nothing.

Grace did not give up so easily. On the day before their departure for the Christmas holidays she waited for Chantal as they walked through the garden on their way back from skating practice.

'Will you be in Dijon over Christmas?' she asked with a warm smile.

'I don't really know until I get home. Why, aren't you going home to England with the others for Christmas?'

'This year my family are coming here. There will be all sorts of festivities at Mirandol and my brother Sebastian is coming with one of his friends. He's my twin.'

'Don't you have any other brothers or sisters?'

'I have a sister. Alice. She's much younger than me.'

'There will be so much entertainment at the château I can't really think you will need anybody else there.'

'My mother is always going on and on about the sort of friends I should cultivate, girls in our station of life, girls who would include me in all their activities when schooldays are over.'

'Then why are you so anxious to ask me?'

'Because you are much cleverer than any of them and because you are French. She wants me to speak French like my aunt does, but Aunt

Vivienne is married to a Frenchman so it's easy for her. Having a French girl as a friend would please her I think.'

Privately Chantal didn't think it would please her at all. When Grace told her family that she had met Chantal Grolan and had invited her to the château they would be appalled, and would not hesitate to tell her that neither she nor her mother would be welcome. And what of the months to come? Grace would tell them all about the milliner's shop and as much as she could learn about her mother's past.

Grace was looking at her curiously. 'If you're not going away for Christmas, will you come to the château, Chantal?'

'I can't tell you what I shall be doing, Grace. It is kind of you to ask me but I am sure my mother will have made plans.'

After that Grace did not press the matter, but the two girls travelled to Dijon on the train together and although Grace offered to take Chantal to her home in the carriage that was waiting for her at the station, Chantal said, 'There is no need, my mother will be coming for me.'

They walked together along the platform surrounded by crowds of people and when they reached the station's entrance a groom stepped forward to take Grace's luggage and she asked, 'Can you see your mother Chantal? Are you sure we cannot drive you home?'

'Quite sure, my mother will be here.'

She watched them drive away while she stood hesitantly on the pavement in the cold wind, chilled by a fine flurry of snow.

Her mother would not come to the station to meet her, she would be unable to leave her shop, so there was nothing for it except to take a hansom cab or walk. She picked up her case and started to walk in the direction of the cathedral.

Lamps along the street shined eerily through the dusk and shop windows were alight; it was different as she neared the narrow streets leading to the cathedral, historical medieval streets that spoke of darker days in a more dangerous Burgundy, and she walked in the centre of the lane distrusting the dark corners and winding alleyways.

The lights in her mother's shop shone cheerily through the gloom but by this time the flurry of snow had changed into great descending flakes and for a moment she stood on the footpath shaking it from her coat and the soft felt hat covering her hair, then she stepped forward to open the door.

There were several customers in the shop who turned round when she entered and her mother came forward to embrace her.

'Darling, you're so wet,' her mother said. 'I hadn't realized it was snowing, why didn't you take a cab?'

'The queue was too long, Mother. I would probably still have been there.'

'Oh well, change into something warm and make yourself a cup of coffee. There are pastries in the kitchen and we'll have something really nice later on for dinner. This is my daughter, Chantal, ladies, home from school.'

The women in the shop smiled at her but went on trying on their hats.

The room behind the shop was warm and cheerful. A bright fire burned in the grate, shedding its glow on a bowl of dark gold and red chrysanthemums and a table already laid with china, silver and glassware. The room's entire appearance was so festive Marie Claire gazed at it in some surprise until she noticed that the table was laid for three.

They were to have a guest and she could not think who it would be.

Lying on her bed was a soft red woollen skirt and a red shawl to wear over a pale cream blouse and on them a note wishing her a Happy Christmas and with love from Mother.

Marie Claire had left them out in the hope that her daughter would wear them for their evening meal, and as Chantal gazed into the long mirror in her bedroom she knew the rich ruby red lit up her face and made a perfect foil for her pale golden hair. She had always wished she had had her mother's colouring, always admired her dark shining hair and jade green eyes but her mother had always assured her that such colouring in France was not unusual while her own colouring most certainly was.

After unpacking her suitcase and putting her things away she went downstairs to the kitchen and started to make coffee. She hoped her mother would close the shop early, but of course it would depend on how many customers came into it.

From the shop she could hear the sound of their voices and laughter, the ringing of the tinkling bell above the door when customers came and went, and after what seemed an age silence. She heard the turning of the key in the lock and the sound of her mother tidying up and she went into the shop to see if she could help.

'I've almost finished, Chérie,' her mother said smiling. 'Business has been brisk this afternoon, I've never had so many people in the shop at one time before.'

'I'm glad. So the shop is doing well now?'

'Well yes, very well, but it's hard work, Chantal. When I'm not in the shop, I'm visiting the markets looking for something new. We're closing for three days at Christmas but you can help me when we're open.'

'Couldn't you take on an assistant?'

'I could, but something else has arisen, we have to talk about it.'

'Another shop, Mother?'

'No darling, another life, another place.'

Marie Claire would tell her no more, saying it would keep until later.

Bustling into the kitchen her mother called out, 'We're dining at eight, Chantal, you can help me in the kitchen but everything is prepared, I got up very early this morning to see to things before I opened the shop.'

'Who is joining us for dinner?' Chantal asked curiously, and was instantly aware of her mother's blushing face and her quick attention to the kitchen stove.

'I'm going to change now, Chantal, I'll tell you all about it when I come down.'

'Is it Aunt Jeanne?'

'Why no, of course it isn't Aunt Jeanne, she wouldn't dream of leaving her family at Christmastime.'

'I thought she might be visiting just for one day.'

'Make me a cup of coffee, darling, I'll be down directly.'

Several possibilities leapt to Chantal's mind. Surely not the vicomte when his château would be crowded with English visitors. Perhaps one of her mother's schoolfriends, but they were all married and only one extra place had been set. Even stranger possibilities came into mind, the Reverend Mother perhaps, now in a more forgiving frame of mind with her mother's affair over and a new Marie Claire working hard to make a success of her shop. Even the Abbé Fauriel came to mind simply because he always greeted them kindly with merry twinkling eyes and a friendly smile.

Her mother looked totally enchanting in a jade green dress that she had not seen before and as Marie Claire gave a little twirl for her inspection she said, 'You look beautiful, Mother, is the dress new?'

'Yes, the first I have bought for over two years, I've been wearing up my old ones. I couldn't resist this, your father always said I should wear jade it was the colour of my eyes.'

'My father?'

'Yes.' Why had she suddenly felt compelled to mention Andrew after all these years? Was that really the reason she had bought it, a strange intrusive memory that she had spent so long trying to forget.

'I never ever hear you speak of my father,' Chantal persisted. 'Whenever I asked about him you always changed the subject. You never wanted to talk about him. You said he was dead, you didn't want to talk about the dead.'

'Nor do I.'

'You just did, Mother. You have no idea how many times I have wanted to talk about him.'

'But not tonight, darling. Tonight we are celebrating the beginning of Christmas and we have a visitor. We must make him feel very welcome.'

'Who is the visitor, do I know him?'

'No. You have never met him. His name is Henri Devroix and for a while I worked for him in the wine trade. Both Henri and his wife were very kind to me at a time when kindness was in short supply. Unhappily Madame Devroix died last year and people should not be alone at this time of year.'

'Did he come to tell you that his wife had died?'

'No. I met him quite by accident in the city one morning and he told me then. He was very sad and lonely and one evening he invited me to the theatre, this little dinner party is my way of saying thank you. Now we must get on with the meal, Chantal, I think everything is ready but he will be here in a few moments.'

Indeed she had hardly had time to return to the kitchen when they heard the knocker on the shop door and Marie Claire said, 'I'll let him in Chantal, just take a quick look around the kitchen to see if everything is ready.'

She stole a quick look in the mirror, patted her hair before going into the shop to admit her dinner guest.

Chantal went into the kitchen from where she could hear the sound of their voices and their laughter and then her mother was at the door saying 'Come along darling, our guest has arrived and I want to introduce you.'

Henri Devroix stood in the living room, a tall slim man with dark hair peppered with silver. He had a charming smile and he was good looking.

Chantal went forward to meet him and hastily he laid the many parcels he was holding on a chair so that he could take her hand.

He smiled, 'I have heard a great deal about you,' he said, 'and now let me present you with the Christmas presents I have brought.'

He had been more than generous. There were several bottles of good Burgundy as well as a bottle of champagne. There was a large box of expensive chocolates and from his pocket he extricated two gaily wrapped parcels which he gave to each of them.

'Keep them until Christmas Day,' he said, 'I just hope you like what I have chosen.'

Marie Claire had learned her lessons well when she held the position of mayor's lady. She knew how to make entertaining conversation and the meal she had provided was cooked to perfection. Chantal did not miss the way Monsieur Devroix basked in her mother's smiles and set himself out to be pleasant and charming. That he admired her mother was evident, and her mother too was aware of it. A kindly man, he included Chantal in their conversation, showing a keen interest in her studies in Switzerland and what she intended to do with her life when she finished there.

'I don't want Chantal to be in any hurry to do anything but enjoy life,' Marie Claire said gaily. 'My little shop is doing very well and she has so many English friends in Switzerland. I am hoping they will invite her to spend some time in England, those girls will be going home to a great many festivities.'

'And is that what you want, Chantal?' he asked gently.

Chantal smiled and Marie Claire was quick to say, 'I've told her everything I know about the débutante balls and all the other wonderful things the young girls from aristocratic families have waiting for them. Will you be staying on in Dijon at Christmas, Henri?'

'No. I am visiting my sister in Lyon. I might feel rather out of things, my sister has a large family and to a man without children it can be rather too much. Will you and your daughter be going to the country?'

'No. I have sent presents for the children but like your sisters the house will be crowded and because it is a farm the work never stops. No Chantal and I will stay here, we shall go to church in the morning, open our presents and indulge ourselves on your chocolates. Christmas Day will soon pass.'

The evening passed charmingly. Monsieur Devroix departed in a flurry of good wishes and it was only later when Chantal lay in bed listening to the sounds of horses and carriages rumbling through the city streets and the peal of bells from the cathedral and the church of St Michel that she reached the conviction that very soon perhaps her life might be changing yet again. Nothing her mother did would surprise her.

24

Spring came shyly to the Bernese Oberland. Now the mountain, slopes were painted by golden sunlight and snowdrops and tiny hyacinths carpeted the fields. The winter visitors were going home with the melting snow and soon the summer visitors would appear.

The girls were going home for the Easter holidays, taking a great many things with them since when they returned it would only be for a few months until they left Madame Lafayette's for ever.

Chantal's fleeting friendship with Grace had not continued. They were pleasant with each other but that was all and Chantal knew that Grace must have heard that the French friend was the daughter of a woman who had at one time been André de Mirandol's mistress.

Grace was a nice girl. She kept the information she had received secret from her friends, after all none of it was Chantal's fault, and surely it was as much Uncle André's fault as Chantal's mother.

Just two weeks before the Easter holidays Chantal received a letter from her mother in which Marie Claire informed her that Monsieur Devroix had asked her to marry him and she had accepted his proposal. She could imagine her mother writing that letter, a smile on her lovely face, perhaps a little troubled, but with a confidence that Chantal would understand and all would be well.

Things will be so much better for us now, Chantal, her mother wrote happily. Henri has bought a small château near Bordeaux, oh nothing as grand as the Château de Mirandol but quite charming none the less. It is on a hillside overlooking the river Gironde and with views of the sea. Henri has spent all his adult life thinking about the wines of Burgundy, now he is happily looking forward to working among the vineyards that produce the Claret and wines of Bordeaux, and, darling, you will be able to bring your English friends to visit. You could never have invited them to my little milliner's shop in Dijon. Henri is taking me to America for Easter, imagine it darling, your mother in America when she has rarely even been to Paris.

Chantal was not surprised by her mother's news but she kept it to herself. She did not want to visit the homes of her friends in England, and when Madame Lafayette sent for her only a few days after receiving her mother's letter she was glad she had kept things to herself.

Madame Lafayette was smiling and holding a letter in her hand.

'I have just heard from your mother, Mademoiselle Chantal, and she tells me that she is getting married and they are going to live in Bordeaux. I am delighted for her, but we have the problem of where you should spend your Easter holidays. Have you made any plans?'

'No, Madame.'

'I am sure if any of your friends became aware of your news they would be only too happy to invite you to their homes. Would you like that Chantal?'

'Is there an alternative, Madame?'

'I could invite you to stay here, not to do lessons, but to enjoy the countryside. Interlaken is a nice town, and there is the city of Berne that you could visit. Your mother has enclosed with her letter a generous sum of money so that you can indulge yourself a little.'

'Oh yes, Madame, that is what I would like to do. I can go to England later, when I have finished here, but I love Switzerland, it will be heavenly to see more if it.'

So it was settled, the next thing was to inform Herr Steinberg that she would not be going to Dijon for Easter and the opportunity came at the end of the next lesson.

She stayed behind after the others had left on the pretext of putting the room in order and Dieter Steinberg smiled his thanks across the room. On her way out she asked shyly if he was going home to Vienna for Easter, and smiling he said 'No, I hope to see more of Switzerland, if I go home I shall be unable to work on music I am composing, if I stay here I can work in the morning and explore the area in the afternoon.'

'That is exactly what I am going to do,' she said with a bright smile.

'You are not going home then?'

'No. My mother is remarrying and going to America for a holiday. I am staying here, Madame Lafayette suggested it, and I too wish to explore Switzerland.'

'Perhaps we shall meet in the village then and if we are discreet explore it together.'

'Oh yes Herr Steinberg, that would be lovely.'

She danced along the corridor with a singing heart. It was all falling into place. In four months she would leave the school for ever, her mother would be so engrossed with her new marriage and her pretty château that she would be glad not to have her daughter loitering around the place. Indeed by that time she might even be glad to have her daughter off her hands permenantly.

That Chantal had elected to stay on at the school troubled Marie Claire. Why hadn't she gone to England with one of her friends, and where was the Austrian music master intending to spend the Easter holidays? She had hoped to depart for America without a cloud in the sky and already she was wishing her honeymoon in America was over and she was back in France where at least she would be able to insist on obedience from her daughter.

Chantal sent her mother a long affectionate letter wishing her and Henri every happiness in the years ahead, assuring her mother of her love, and then duty done she conveniently placed her and her new husband at the back of her mind.

With Dieter she sailed the deep blue lakes and walked through the enchanting meadows. They took impossible ski lifts up the mountain slopes where the only sounds were from round the necks of peacefully grazing cattle. Chantal forgot everything and everybody except that she was wildly passionately in love and when he looked at her across his glass with blue eyes alight with passion nothing else in the world mattered.

They behaved with the utmost discretion. They met well out of sight of the village and from the places were Madame Lafayette and any of her assistants or friends were likely to be congregating.

He told her about the sonata he was composing and his eyes shone with enthusiasm and hope that one day it would be played by some great orchestra.

'Does that mean that you will leave the school, that you will stop teaching music?' she asked hopefully.

'Teaching music is only a beginning, I don't want it to be for always. One day I want to compose great music, conduct great orchestras and you shall have the place of honour at my first concert.'

'But when, how soon will that be?' she cried impatiently.

'Soon I hope. I am frustrated working as a music master, teaching girls how to play some instrument that they are not remotely interested in but which they regard as merely a social asset. The world is filled with people with real talent, why should my talent be wasted on girls who will play only for amusement?'

She sensed his frustration, the frustration of a talented man having to listen to the inept floundering of incompetent performers.

'You must be very frustrated with me,' she said sadly, 'I wish I was musical. I love music but I'm not good at it much to my mother's annoyance. My mother would love me to be brilliant at everything.'

'You have a very pretty voice,' he said gently.

'And that is all it is. Are you very bored with me?'

'No, Chérie, I am enchanted with you. If I found you boring I would not be here.'

She wanted him to love her, she wanted to be a part of his dreams but if she would have thrown discretion to the winds Deiter Steinburg was made of sterner stuff. To him Chantal was one of his pupils. He lumped them altogether, the daughters of rich parents, to be regarded with caution in case they were threats to his future.

He knew little about Chantal Grolan's background, but quite obviously she must be part of a wealthy family or she wouldn't be at the school. He had heard the girls giggling in the common room about their feelings for the men who coached them in various pursuits. None of them knew anything about love, only about flirtation, but he had always sensed that Chantal was different, more mature, less giddy. He know if he made love to her she would respond but common sense held him back until the afternoon it rained heavily and they ran laughing to his modest lodgings outside the village.

The house was empty. He know his landlady had gone away to her daughters for three days and he had been quick to assure her that he was quite capable of looking after himself.

They dried their clothes in front of the fire while Marie Claire sat wrapped in a warm woollen robe he had found in his landlady's cupboard.

He made a meal for them and after they had cleared away he sat at the piano and played. The shadows lengthened and occasionally the room was lit with flashes of lightning and thunder reverberated in the surrounding mountains.

She stood behind him allowing her arm to cirle his shoulders and when he looked up she smiled, lowering her body on to the seat beside him moving naturally into his arms, holding up her face for the kiss that was inevitable.

He was aware of the urgency of her love-making but something old and sane held him back, something that only came with years and when he gently put her away from him she stared after him with amazed distraught eyes. He did not love her, he had never loved her, she had to go, she would never see him again, and with a little plaintive cry she leapt to her feet and ran towards the door. He went after her, clutching her hand, entreating her to turn and with anguish in her voice she cried, 'You don't love me, I must go. What can you think of me?'

He held her firmly, willing her to look at him and there was a sternness in his handsome face she had to obey.

'Chantal,' he said firmly. 'Do you know what happens to young music masters who disobey the rules of their employment by making love to their pupils? They are dismissed in disgrace and their career if it is not over is interrupted.

'I am a man with a beautiful girl in his arms and I so desperately want to make love to you but I am not a fool. One day I want to be more than a mere music master but this is not the way.'

'Nobody need know,' she whispered desperately.

'How many misguided young men have said that I wonder and don't you think I don't know what will happen in a few months' time. You will all leave here and laugh about the poor fool who thought he could become something permanent in your life.'

'But I love you Dieter, I'm not like the others.'

'I know that, but you come from a family who could afford to give you this sort of education, they would not be pleased for you to sacrifice it on your music master. Think, Liebchen, your parents would be horrified.'

'I have no parents, at least there is only my mother.'

'And I am not what your mother would want for you.'

He watched the doubts and uncertainties trouble her beautiful face and he knew that he had spoken nothing but the truth. He drew her gently into the circle of his arms and with his chin resting lightly on her hair he said softly, 'One day Chantal, there could be something for us, but the time isn't now. You have to grow up and I have to make something of my life. There may come a time when we can meet, a time when we have achieved our ambitions and when there are no barriers conventions have placed around us, will you try to understand, Chantal?'

'If you really loved me nothing else would matter.'

'And you, my darling, only confirm that you do not think beyond the here and the now, it is amazing what a few years can do to your reasoning.'

'They are all coming back the day after tomorrow, shall we not be able to meet like this again?'

'It is better so. Think of all those eligible young men you will meet in the months ahead, if there is any truth in what I have been hearing from your friends.'

'What do I care about them?'

'Nothing at the moment, but you will.'

He reached out his hand and brushed away the tears on her cheeks, and his smile brought a tremulous smile to her lips.

'That is better,' he said laughing. 'And now it seems the rain has finished and it is time for you to return to the school. Do they never ask how you have spent your day?'

'Yes. I tell them I have been to the mountains, on the lake, around the shops. I haven't told them any lies.'

'Of course not, but you have not said who you have been with.'

'No.'

'Love should not have to be a secret, Liebchen, it should walk proudly before the world. Does that not prove my theory, I think it does?'

He walked back with her along the straggling village street and up the short hill towards the school gates where Madame Thevenet caught up with them, much to Chantal's annoyance. Dieter bowed and it was only when they were inside the school that Madame Thevenet said sharply, 'When did you meet Herr Steinberg? You know it is forbidden to spend time with male instructors?'

'I met him in the village when I was walking home. We sheltered out of the rain and he was kind enough to offer to walk back with me.'

The teacher favoured her with a long hard look and Chantal's eyes met it in all innocence. That was how it would have been, she reflected on reaching her room. Lies and more lies and always the danger of being discovered. And if they had been discovered, her mother's anger and her determination to have him dismissed.

Her mother and new stepfather met her as she stepped off the train in Bordeaux. The day before she had said a tearful farewell to the girls who had been her friends, received a perfunctory smile from Grace and her friends and the usual lecture from Madame Lafayette.

She was hurt and angry that Dieter Steinburg had already left for Vienna. He had said his farewells the day before and had perhaps held her hand for slightly longer than was absolutely necessary. This had been the only intimation that she was special, except for the warmth of his smile which the other girls had commented upon and teased her throughout the evening.

She had left them with their promises to write, that invitations would follow thick and fast ringing in her ears, and then had come the long lonely journey across France to her new home.

Marie Claire embraced her warmly, and then her stepfather came forward rather shyly with outstretched hands. They loaded her luggage into the waiting carraige, and then they were driving through the city streets and out along the banks of the river and Marie Claire was saying, 'You'll love the château, darling, you'll see it on the hillside very soon and all the terraces lined with vineyards.'

The countryside was enchanting with the blue Gironde winding peacefully, alive with river craft. Her stepfather drove without entering into their conversation, but Marie Claire was prattling on with inconsequential gaiety.

'Darling, I'm so looking forward to hearing all about your plans. You've been invited to England of course. Which one of your friends has invited you?'

'Several of them Mother.'

'How about that Martindale girl, didn't you say you were friendly with her?'

'Not really, Mother, she was a year younger than me.'

'I know that, dear, but surely that didn't matter.'

'She wasn't in my year, besides, she was related to the Mirandols.'

She wished she hadn't said that. She was aware of her mother's swift intake of breath, and what had happened in her mother's past was her own affair. She was sure Henri Devroix would know nothing about the Vicomte de Mirandol beyond the fact that he was important in the Dijon area.

For a moment Marie Claire's face was bleak, and Chantal reached out to take her hand, squeezing it gently. Marie Claire's face cleared.

'Before you start on that round of enjoyment, darling, you must get to know Bordeaux and the countryside of the Medoc. We can visit Biarritz and you will see the Pyrenées and beyond them Spain. Oh darling, there is so much here for you and your friends, and you will invite them here, won't you, we are just as proud of our château as the Mirandols were of theirs. Of course it isn't so grand, but we love it.'

Without its turrets and battlements the château was simply a beautiful country house built from warm stone and with a rural charm more welcoming than the vastness of Mirandol.

From her bedroom window she could look out across the vineyards to the gentle meandering river and the Bay of Biscay beyond and for the first time in her life she was aware of a strange and delicious contentment.

There had been so many changes, so many comings and goings, so many times when she had not dared to hope that this time it would be for ever.

To Chantal Burgundy had always seemed stern and echoing with the turbulence of France's history, but Bordeaux possessed a mild frivolity in keeping with the distinctive quality of its wines.

Her stepfather was a gentle, kindly man who adored her mother and Marie Claire blossomed under his regard. Maurice had adored her too, but it had always been the rather pompous adoration of a father for a daughter rather than a man for his wife. Now Marie Claire became more beautiful, gayer, more enchanting, as she urged her daughter to invite her friends to meet her.

Chantal was not to know that, in spite of her mother's contentment, the old punishing ambitions were still there and would continue to be there until the compelling reason for them had been assuaged. That she was relying on her daughter to make an end to the years of waiting was both her atonement and her vengeance. That either of these desires might harm Chantal was something she never thought of.

It was Marie Claire who watched the post arriving every morning for those letters from England, urging her daughter to issue invitations of her own. Finally Chantal was forced to say, 'Mother, they are débutantes in England. This is their year and there will be so many things for them to do. I listened to them talking, balls and race meetings, regattas and a host of other things, they won't want to leave England at this time, they'd be missing so much.'

'But don't you think they will want to travel and see other countries?'

'Yes, of course, but they have all the time in the world to do that. This time they want to be in England, other countries will come later.'

If this was the time to be in England, this was where Marie Claire wanted her daughter to be. This was where she would meet a man like Andrew, a man who would want to marry her, and if she stole one of Grace's suitors so much the better.

With this aim in mind, she set about seeing that Chantal had a wardrobe filled with beautiful gowns, riding habits, garden party dresses and less formal wear, and there would be no milliner's shop in the background; instead, there would be the château Marguerite and the fields of vineyards, the enchanting French countryside and the French sophistication of Chantal's parents.

Marie Claire dreamed on without knowing that her daughter was still pining for a handsome young Austrian who had proved to be more honourable than she had given him credit for.

The invitation came in October to visit the Mayfair home of the parents of Lady Amanda Stedman. The invitation was formal but with it came a letter from Amanda urging her to accept. Darling Chantal, she wrote, we have so many wonderful things lined up for us you'll love it. Do come.

Marie Claire and Henri accompanied her to Paris and saw he embark on the boat train for Calais. Her last sight of her mother was a frantically waving figure in pale grey and Arctic fox, standing with Henri on the platform, her smile warm and encouraging, the smile of a woman well pleased with events and totally unaware that her daughter would have preferred to be in some tiny chalet in the Bernese Oberland with Dieter Steinberg.

25

Amanda's parents – the Earl and Countess of Sutton – received Chantal graciously. They fully approved of their only daughter's choice of a friend, a girl who was polished, well spoken and elegant. She would tone Amanda down, insert the right sort of influence on a too exuberant girl with her love for obvious fortune-hunters when she should have been looking for more serious-minded suitors.

By the end of the first few days she had met up with all her old schoolfriends and had been informed that she was to go on from Amanda's parents' home to others equally impressive.

Chantal was bewildered by balls and tea parties where ambitious mothers seem to take charge. Amanda giggled about it. 'Oh Chantal, it's really quite hilarious, the mothers are at each other's throats about us, they are forgetting that we girls are all very good friends.'

'But will you continue to be good friends when your families are so obviously jealous of which débutante is getting the most attention?'

'Perhaps not,' Amanda had to agree. 'This is the year we have to look around to see what is on offer, and choose very wisely, but I don't want to get married just yet, I just want to have some fun.'

'But if you don't get married, what of the future?'

'Well, I suppose next year I'll be old-hat and the new girls will be coming out. Grace's grandmother is already eyeing the field. You really don't understand it, do you, Chantal?'

'It all seems rather vulgar, like a cattle market.'

Amanda laughed. 'It's very proper and genteel. The girls will all look stunning in virginal white and the young men will be discreet and gallant.'

'And when they are not being gallant, they will estimate who has the most money, who comes from the noblest family and whether or not she would be a suitable replacement for mother at some distant time.'

'Replacement for mother?' Amanda asked doubtfully.

'The next Countess or Duchess, Amanda.'

'Well, it is important, Chantal. Not to you perhaps, the French have very few aristocrats left, but we never had a revolution. In England the aristocracy is very flourishing.'

Chantal smiled. She was very fond of Amanda who she was quite sure would be led like a lamb to the slaughter. She thought Amanda was a thoroughly nice girl, always ready to see the best in people, but totally at sea in the cut and thrust world of débutantes.

Amanda's mother confided in Chantal that she was rather worried about her daughter.

'Amanda is such a sweet girl,' she said gently. 'Even as a child she allowed her brothers and her friends to put on her unmercifully and now that she's grown up she can't see for the life of her when she's being manipulated. You will look after her, won't you Chantal, you are so much more sophisticated and worldly.'

Chantal wondered idly if insecurity bred sophistication. She didn't think so. Her insecurity had made her fearful, of her grandfather, of her bad-tempered aunt and her lecherous husband, and then followed the apprehension and doubts about what her mother would do next.

All these things had made her more worldly than the privileged girls who had their futures mapped out for them from the cradle to the grave, but the sophistication had come from something within herself.

Letters from her mother encouraged her to make the most of her opportunities, but the opportunities leant more to girls established on the social scene and not to a beautiful French girl of unknown credentials.

She was never short of dance partners, there was always a crowd of admiring young men around her wherever she went, and she smiled inwardly at their attempts to discover where in France her parents lived and if they lived in some sort of style.

Their interest quickened when she informed them that her stepfather owned a château near Bordeaux, that he owned extensive vineyards, but he was untitled. While titled girls were still on the menu she was not a contender.

She stayed on in England, moving from one house to the next as a guest of one or another of her schoolfriends and during this time she went to their balls, to their garden parties and race meetings, to their regattas and their Polo matches.

It was at Ascot that she saw the Vicomtesse de Mirandol with her husband and a group of other people and the sight of the two of them together brought home miserably the part her mother had played in the Vicomte's life.

She was not one of them, she would never be one of them, and with these thoughts in her mind she halted her stay in England and went home to France.

Marie Claire was indignant. She did not understand a daughter who returned home when she had been surrounded by so much wealth and promise. Nor did Chantal inform her mother what had prompted her return.

She had no plans to return to England. Instead she roamed the enchanting fields around the château, sailed her stepfather's boat on the river. She talked to the fishermen while they worked at their nets, chatted to the men and women who worked in the vineyards, and got to know her stepfather. She found him a gentle man, fond of reading and pottering around his garden while his wife entertained her new friends to tea parties and coffee mornings in her drawing room.

Playing the lady of the manor was very much to Marie Claire's liking but Chantal knew that it was born out of earlier times when she was burdened with adversity. Her mother never talked about the past: it was as though every new chapter of her life was in itself complete, an end to the old, and welcome for the new. She was happy with her adoring husband, happy in her beautiful home, and only anxious that Chantal should have a glowing and secure future.

While Marie Claire lectured her, Chantal sat and listened, smiling wryly at some of her mother's more bizarre ambitions, until Marie Claire was forced to say. 'Chantal, you listen to me and you smile, but is any of this making sense to you?'

'Yes, Mother. You want me to marry a rich successful man and be somebody, while I just want to be myself.'

'But you can be yourself. Think of all the things you could do, the places you could go to, the people you could help, but to do it you need a rich man behind you. You will still be you. Do you really think that money and position has changed me? It has only made me more confident.'

Had she ever really known the real Marie Claire, she wondered. The Marie Claire who had given herself to a man who went away to die? Had she ever really known the young girl who was shy and tender, warm and trusting. She had only ever known Marie Claire the woman, always reaching out for something better, something often unobtainable.

'You will go back to England, Chantal. I do so want you to keep in touch with your friends,' her mother argued.

'But I am French, Mother. Why should you always be urging me to go to England? I'll go back one day if somebody invites me. Most of my friends are now engaged and will be getting married. Perhaps one day one of them will remember me.'

'You could invite one or two of them here?'

'But not just now Mother. I'm sure they are happier where they are.'

So the year passed and another spring came round and it was then she received an invitation from Amanda Wentworth – her old friend had married the fourteenth Baron Wentworth in March.

'You see,' her mother said smiling fondly, 'Amanda hasn't forgotten you, she has her own home and wants you to meet her new husband. This time, Chantal, don't be in such a hurry to run away.'

Amanda's husband proved to be a short stocky young man with a genial smile and a robust sense of humour. he was not at all the sort of young man she would have expected Amanda to marry, not Amanda who always enthused over young men who were tall, dark and handsome with smouldering good looks and athletic capabilities.

'Well,' Amanda cried when they were on their own, 'What do you think of William?'

'I like him, he's very nice.'

'But not what you expected,' Amanda persisted.

'I didn't dare to speculate, not about any of you.'

'Oh, I know we were always giggling and going on about the sort of men we wanted to marry, but we had to come down to earth sometime. The sort of men we drooled over at school we found in gamekeepers and waiters, tennis coaches and young subalterns without a bean. Reality is very different.'

'You are surely not telling me that there are not a host of handsome young aristocrats?'

'Of course not, but they were not around at the time and William was very attentive. Mummy and Daddy are delighted, they both like him enormously and he's fun to be with, and not at all stuffy like some of them might have been.'

It was hardly the passionate love story Amanda had dreamed of, but there was no doubt that she was happy, and as the days passed Chantal came to like William more and more. He introduced her into the breeding of bloodstock, they argued over the chess board and at the Bridge table, and they laughed a lot, so that she was very undecided when she received an invitation to spend some time with the Earl and Countess of Darvish. She had always known that Louise Stedman would marry well, but her husband did not appeal to Chantal as Amanda's had done.

He was a tall slim man who looked entirely elegant, with a bored supercilious expression and very little conversation. He was totally absorbed in his stately home, his priceless antiques and his prize Irish wolfhounds. He expected his wife to dress well, entertain well and bother him as little as possible, which suited Louise very well.

She had an array of blue-blooded young men to dance with, ride with and visit the theatre with, none of whom had any money. It did not take Chantal long to realize that she had been invited to provide Louise with irreproachable alibis on where they spent their time and with whom.

Chantal thought her friend was sailing too close to the wind, but Louise, totally unrepentant, said if she rode through the estate like Lady Godiva Nigel would not notice.

English royalty intrigued her. The King and Queen were stately gracious figures. The queen was very beautiful, the king was stout and smiling, amused by the stream of pretty women hanging on to his arm and on to his words, watched tolerantly by a wife who did not seem concerned or even remotely antagonistic.

She wrote long letters to her mother telling her all the things that would enchant her, the balls attended by royalty, the race meetings where they curtsied respectfully when royalty passed by, but to all her letters her mother seemed totally obsessed with the Earl and Countess of Westmond, and Chantal believed that this was because they were related to the Mirandols.

Indeed rather than British royalty, her mother seemed more concerned with the field of sunflowers that Henri had sown on the slopes above the river.

I do love them, her mother wrote. They remind me of the sunflowers in the field near our farm, I wept for days when Papa pulled them up to make way for turnips.

Chantal had never known of the sunflowers and found it strange that her mother had never mentioned them before, but then there were so may things that her mother had kept to herself.

Why had she never talked about her father, how he met his death, who he had been? There were times when she looked at herself in the mirror, at her blonde tresses and dark blue eyes, wishing fervently that she had her mother's vivid colouring which was decidedly more in keeping with a woman from France.

She wrote to her mother that Grace was this year's Débutante of the year, and that society expected a great deal from her.

She really is very pretty, Mother. Indeed some of my friends say I have a look of her, but I'm sure that isn't true. We are going to a ball at the Earl of Westmond's country home next week, and because I am a guest of the Countess of Darvish she has asked if they can take me with them.

I expect Grace will be surprised to see me there.

221

Marie Claire read her daughter's letter again and again before she sat back in her chair clutching it to her breast. This was what it had all been for, all the long years of pushing and striving. There had been many times when she hadn't been sure what her aims were, but now she knew, it had been for this, for her daughter to be present in her father's house, side by side with the children of his marriage, not as an outsider but as a guest who could look them proudly in the eye.

It was an occasion worthy of the Countess of Westmond's expertise. The elegant ballroom was filled with the bluest blood in the land as her husband escorted his daughter down the shallow staircase to be met with bows and smiles from those waiting to receive her, and Grace looked enchanting in a swirl of white lace, her blonde hair adorned with a spray of white gardenias, her pretty face rosy with blushes.

It was Grace who opened the ball with her father, dancing alone for several minutes before they were joined with others. Chantal stood with her friends at the edge of the ballroom until a young man in uniform invited her to dance.

He was tall, handsome and curious. 'I say, you're new here, aren't you? At least, I haven't seen you before.'

'I am a visitor to the home of Lord and Lady Darvish.'

'Really. But you've been here for the season?'

'I've been to some of the functions. I was at school with Lady Darvish and with Grace.'

'School?'

'In Switzerland.'

'You're not English?'

'No, I'm French.'

'How jolly. I hope we are going to see a lot more of you.'

Chantal smiled. They were all of a pattern, these young men, they were either in some regiment or other, or doing things in the city. Some of them were titled, most of them were upper class, but they all talked about the same sort of things, hunting, fishing, long country weekends and the season.

As soon as the dance was over she was claimed by another man and then her friends smiled complacently. Chantal was having a good time, they could conveniently forget their need to entertain her.

There was a hum of conversation when two young men entered the ballroom and immediately the interest of the Martindales was focused on them from where they sat together at the head of the ballroom.

The two young men stood surveying the scene for several moments before they crossed the floor to pay their respects to their host and hostess, then they were greeting Lady Grace.

Louise Darvish murmured to Chantal, 'The Duke of Tarleton and his younger brother, the catch of the season.'

'They are both very handsome,' Chantal whispered.

'And rich, and with the most beautiful stately home in Shropshire.'

Chantal was intrigued. Lady Constance's mother was positively glowing with pride and the Earl stood beside his daughter looking on proudly.

At that moment two other people entered the ballroom and Chantal felt a sudden quickening of her heart as the Vicomte and Vicomtesse de Mirandol crossed the floor to be greeted by the family.

'Don't you know them?' Louise murmured.

'My mother knows them.'

At the moment the orchestra started to play a waltz and the Duke was inviting Lady Grace to dance. Chantal was totally absorbed with the interest of the Martindale family, the gratification, the confidence, and as she looked at the family group chatting delightedly together, her eyes looked into the eyes of a young man staring fixedly at her. In the next moment he was striding across the hall to ask her to dance.

He smiled down at her and she was immediately struck by his likeness to Lady Grace and his smile deepened. 'If you are thinking what I believe you are thinking, perhaps I should tell you that Grace is my twin sister.'

Brother and sister both had the same blonde hair and startling blue eyes. The beauty of the girl was reflected in the sterner handsome features of the man and for the rest of the evening they danced together and fell in love.

Later that night in her bedroom at the Darvish's house Chantal could not believe that in those few hours her entire life seemed to have changed. Now she found herself looking forward to the weeks ahead, to accepting the invitations to stay with old friends, to drown in the pleasures of race meetings and long country weekends.

He had told her his name was Sebastian and that he was hoping for a commission in a Lancer regiment where his uncle was a lieutenant colonel.

'Does that mean that you will be serving in India?' she had asked.

'Yes. My father's older brother lost his life there in a cholera epidemic. My father's younger brother is out there still.'

'And you are looking forward to it?'

'Very much. Wouldn't you like to see India, the Taj Mahal, the Red Fort, Nepal and Kashmir?'

'Perhaps they mean more to you. I'm French, I've never thought much about India.'

'But you should, it's fascinating, the jewel in the British Crown.'

She laughed. 'I promise to read about India whenever I have the time.'

But time was in short supply in the weeks that followed. With Sebastian she discovered the England she had only read about and not the frothy England her friends had chattered about in their bedrooms in Switzerland.

Sebastian showed her London where they watched the Changing of the Guards in a sudden shower of rain and laughed like happy children as they ran for shelter. She discovered flowers she never heard of in the gardens of Kew and learned of dark deeds in the dark corridors of the Tower.

They stood just before dawn on Westminster Bridge and Sebastian quoted lines from Wordsworth, and Chantal believed him that earth had not anything to show more fair. London before dawn: the smell of damp grass in the empty park with long deserted streets with only the occasional cab clopping along in search of late night revellers.

During the long weekends they went to the country and discovered the beautiful lakes of Cumberland, the dark haunting peaks of Derbyshire and Yorkshire and Sebastian took her to Cambridge where she was introduced to the playing fields at sunset, surrounded by tall elms, the grass emerald green.

They went to the evening service in the chapel at King's and stood enchanted in the quadrangle of Clare, and Sebastian filled her heart and her mind with the history of the land he loved and Chantal listened to his voice, and learned.

Neither of them were aware that they were discussed day after day and night after night in the drawing room of Sebastian's father's house.

'But who is this girl Sebastian is so enamoured with?' Constance demanded sharply. 'She isn't English. All we have been able to discover is that she's friends with Louise Darvish and some others. Apparently she was at school in Switzerland with them. You must know her Grace?'

Grace looked across the table into her aunt's eyes and looked quickly away.

'Do you know her Vivienne?' Constance asked.

'I met her once as a child, I have not seen her since.'

'But who is she?'

'I knew her mother. Ask André, he'll be able to tell you better than I.'

André was at the buffet calmly helping himself to breakfast, nor did he respond to his wife's suggestion.

His silence was sufficient to inform Constance and everybody present who Chantal's mother was and they were remembering the woman they had last seen in her satin gown, her face covered by the black velvet mask edged with diamanté in the ballroom of Mirandol.

'Whatever happened to that woman?' Constance asked sharply.

'She opened a milliner's shop in Dijon and did rather well I think. Indeed you and your mother were customers. She remarried, a widower, and they now live in Bordeaux. Some man from her past perhaps.'

'A man she once worked for in Dijon,' André interrupted, and across the table his wife's eyes met his and hers were the first to look away.

After a few moments Vivienne said, 'André is protective about Marie Claire, apparently she was the one mistress who didn't hold out her greedy little hands for jewellery that should have been mine.'

'I would never have insulted you by giving you the jewellery I gave to others,' André said lightly. 'I was always careful about the authenticity and value of the jewellery I presented to you, mon chérie.'

Both Andrew and his mother-in-law were finding the conversation distasteful. A mistress was hardly the sort of conversation an English family wished to hear about over the breakfast table, and his wife sensing his mood said, 'What is to be done about the girl? Sebastian is obviously infatuated and it can't go on.'

'He'll be off to India soon,' Andrew said. 'That should put an end to the friendship.'

His sister regarded him with a certain cynicism. 'Leaving home doesn't necessarily end an infatuation, Andrew. Out of sight isn't necessarily out of mind, it sometimes helps to make the heart grow fonder.'

Andrew ignored her and went on calmly eating his breakfast. Vivienne had always had a capacity to be scathing, she had all his father's truculence when it suited her.

26

It was Louise, over the dinner table one evening, who informed Chantal that the whisperings had started. 'I hope you're not in love with him,' she said. 'His parents will never agree to his marrying outside the British aristocracy?'

'His aunt did,' was Chantal's reply.

'To a French aristocrat, darling. Can you match the Vicomte's credentials?'

'No, I only know we love each other. Don't you think that will be enough?'

Louise looked at her pityingly. 'Darling, of course not. They're pushing Grace as hard as they can, they're absolutely desperate to have a duchess in the family, they'll want the best for their son and heir.'

'And who do they consider to be the best?'

'Grandmother Fallon will already have compiled a list and presented it to her daughter. You won't be on it, darling.'

'But they don't know me, they don't know anything about me, I think it's disgraceful that they can ignore my existence without having met me,' Chantal said indignantly.

'Grace knew you at school, she will have told them all they need to know.'

And more besides, thought Chantal.

Her mother had told her a great many times that everything she had done had been for her, now it seemed that what she had done would only count against her.

Sebastian too was undergoing a great many scenes with his parents on his friendship with the beautiful French girl, and he couldn't understand it. Chantal was charming and lovely, she had all the social graces the other girls had and he didn't need to marry for money. He knew his father was counting the days before his commission came through with the inevitable departure for India, which hopefully would put an end to this unfortunate liaison.

Vivienne de Mirandol had little liking for her sister-in-law and even less for her mother, but her memories of the hurt Marie Claire had done her had never gone away. There had been other women in her husband's life, and she knew now how little any of them had mattered, but somehow or other Marie Claire had been different, not because she had meant more to André but because in some strange way she had always found Marie Claire to be something of an enigma.

A woman with an illegitimate child surrounded by adversity. A very beautiful woman other women had been afraid of, even her beauty had been a condemnation, and yet Marie Claire had survived in one way or another. She had used men as stepping stones, she had used her beauty and her brains as women had done throughout history, and her ambitions for her daughter had always been paramount.

In Marie Claire's eyes the life of a housewife was not for Chantal. By fair means or foul she had placed her daughter in that school in the Bernese Oberland where the English aristocracy sent their daughters, and it had all seemed totally incongruous. Why? Chantal Grolan was not English, she was not an aristocrat and her stepfather had not been a very rich man. Why hadn't Marie Claire been content to allow her daughter a decent education at the convent, and eventually marry some decent young Frenchman with a good business sense.

Her brother was content to ask few questions and ever hopeful that matters would end; not so his wife who constantly asked questions about the girl's mother and the girl herself, until in the end Vivienne had said, 'The more you antagonize Sebastian by asking questions, the more you push him into her arms.' Wasn't this exactly what her father had done with Andrew, and if Andrew would be honest he would be aware of it.

Chantal was afraid of all the furore over her friendship with Sebastian. She was well aware that wherever they went they were the main topic of conversation and there was a great deal of interest in her antecedents.

It was therefore with something like relief that she bade him a tearful farewell when he left for India, in spite of his promises to write and return to England on his first leave.

'I want you to meet my mother, darling. I want to be with you and nothing and nobody is going to prevent us being together.'

Those had been his parting words, and Chantal, went home to Bordeaux in the belief that he may believe in those words now, but in the weeks and months to come they would be forgotten.

She had decided she would tell her mother nothing about Sebastian.

227

Her mother would be full of hope, full of encouragement that all would be well, and she preferred to suffer silently than be bolstered by hopes that were overwhelmed by impossibilities.

Instead they talked about the homes of her friends, the balls and the parties and Marie Claire asked eventually, 'But didn't you say you were going to a ball at the Earl of Westmond's house. You haven't said a word about it.'

'I went to so many balls Mother and met such a variety of people. Why is the Westmond ball so very special?'

'Well only because I feel I know them, through the Mirandols you know.'

'The Vicomte and his wife were there, she looked very beautiful as she always does, and Grace was so lovely. I believe she is destined to be a duchess.'

'And what about you, darling, which of those rich young aristocrats singled you out?'

'I always had enough partners and enough escorts, Mother.'

'Well of course darling. But who specially?'

'Nobody specially.'

Marie Claire had to be content with that, but she was anxious to say, 'You'll go back surely, Chantal, your friends will invite you I know.'

Instead of going back to England however, they learned that King Edward was dead. Instead of the balls and other festivities there would be long weeks of Court mourning and Chantal received long impassioned letters from her friends lamenting over the enforced inactivity.

'London is absolutely dead.' Louise wrote dismally.

Everybody has gone to ground in their country mansions and I for one am hating it. Nigel is happier here than in London. He's spending all day and every day roaming round the estate and there is simply nothing and nobody to relieve the gloom and doom.

As soon as we get back to normal you really must come to stay with us. All the celebrations for Grace's engagement have had to be shelved but no doubt we'll have them later on. It would be nice if Sebastian could get leave, I'm sure he'll do his best. Some of the girls are pea green with envy that a French girl could come over and snaffle one of our handsomest and most eligible bachelors.

Chantal did not show Louise's letter to her mother. Quite deliberately she had not told her mother anything about Sebastian because she knew that immediately her mother would be making plans to invite the family to Bordeaux, and it was all too previous.

There were too many hurdles to overcome and she was not at all sure that it would happen. She had met the grandmother who had barely acknowledged her existence. His father had been courteous, his mother decidedly condescending and even Grace had seemed ill at ease in her presence.

Grace was happy in her engagement, very much in love with her handsome duke and reluctant to have anything interfere with that happiness. Consequently the feelings her brother had for Chantal were something she didn't even want to think about at this particular time. Indeed to the entire Martindale family, unfortunate as the king's death was, it could not have come at a more opportune moment as far as they were concerned.

As for Marie Claire, she inwardly seethed with annoyance that her daughter was proving to be unco-operative and telling her very little. She could not believe that Chantal, with her beauty, her style and her intelligence had failed to capture the attention of some English aristocrat, but more than that, it had to be somebody within Andrew's circle, even some man his daughter wanted for herself.

The fact that Chantal had told her mother that Andrew's daughter was expected to announce her engagement to a duke was an anathema to her. Chantal had wasted her time in England, wasted all she had tried to do for her and between Chantal and her mother there were long silences, both distant and brooding and Chantal knew they arose from her mother's disappointment in her.

Her friends wrote to her but whilst Britain still mourned the death of her king there was little for them to impart.

'While England is so dead why don't you invite one or another of your friends to visit you here,' Marie Claire suggested. 'After all, the château is very pretty, as is the countryside. I don't suppose any of them know this area of France, so many of them only go to Paris.'

To placate her mother Chantal decided to invite Amanda and her husband. She had no great hopes that they would come and was therefore agreeably surprised when Amanda wrote to say she would visit them on her own because her husband was exceedingly busy on the estate.

During the next few days Marie Claire worked endlessly to make the château as pretty and welcoming as she could, and on the morning of Amanda's arrival she drove the pony and trap to the station to await with Chantal the arrival of her friend.

Amanda came with a mountain of luggage containing numerous presents for them all, and Marie Claire charmed her with her welcoming smile and her efforts to make her comfortable. While Chantal sat on her bed in the pretty bedroom overlooking the river, Amanda started to unpack her suitcases and, smiling, Chantal said, 'We live very simply here in Bordeaux, Amanda, when do you hope to wear all the clothes you have brought?'

'Well, I didn't really know, and one has to be prepared.'

Amanda spoke soulfully about the lack of excitement in London. 'Everybody is simply dying for the mourning period to be over, then you must come over to us, Chantal. There will be Grace's wedding to celebrate. Everybody who is anybody will be invited, including members of the royal family, and already the invitations are piling up for a great many functions. Will Sebastian be coming home for his sister's wedding?'

'I'm not sure.'

'But surely he has said something. He writes often I hope.'

'Yes he does, Amanda, I haven't said anything to my mother about Sebastian. I thought it was too soon.'

'But why ever not? She'll be so thrilled and you are in love with him.'

'You know there are a lot a problems to overcome and I don't want to worry my mother at this time. Please, Amanda, I'd really rather we didn't talk about Sebastian in front of my mother.'

'Well of course not, but I really can't understand why. Surely his family will come round.'

'Perhaps not. There are a great many things you don't know and I can't speak of them. Promise me, Amanda.'

'Well of course, if that's what you want.'

The days passed pleasantly. Amanda fell in love with the Bordelais. With the busy assortment of craft on the Gironde and the mile upon mile of vineyards that lined its banks. They explored the Dordogne and enjoyed a long weekend in Biarritz.

Chantal knew her friend would return home to England with happy memories and delighted stories to tell of her mother's charm and beauty, her stepfather's kindness and the beauty of their home. She had revelled in the history of the Médoc and Aquitaine and on the morning she left she said, 'I've so loved being here, Chantal. I was terribly ignorant about anywhere except Paris, you must have thought us awful duffers at Madame's school with all our silly chatter about the season, the men we expected to meet and our attempts to speak your language must have given you hysterics.'

'Well, of course, I didn't think anything of the kind, after all I didn't know anything about England or British history. Oh I knew all about your wars with Napoleon and the fracas in Quebec but it's all in the past isn't it. I was happy with you in England, I found you all very kind and I found Sebastian.'

'When are you going to tell your mother?'

Chantal merely smiled, and Amanda had to be satisfied with that.

Marie Claire was delighted that her daughter's friend's visit had gone so well. Chantal would tell her all she needed to know one day, and at any rate she never mentioned her Austrian music teacher so it would appear he had been relegated to the past and forgotten.

Chantal had not forgotten him. Those moments in that tiny chalet in Interlaken came often in her quiet moments and a sense of embarrassment filled her. Dieter had not loved her, he had been very wary of her infatuation and had been only too anxious to leave the school without saying goodbye.

She could not reconcile the love she felt for Sebastian with what she had felt for Dieter.

With Sebastian it was saner, calmer, a melding of souls and understanding and not the awesome passion she had experienced with Dieter. Is this what love is really meant to be, she asked herself: gentle, calm and logical, is it enough, or shall I feel cheated that passion can be so restrained, leaving only tenderness and the shadows of regret?

Amanda had spoken of Dieter briefly, saying, 'I often think of him and if he ever went back to the school. You had an awful crush on him Chantal, but then most of us did, he was so handsome and talented.'

She would never see him again. She was never likely to go to Vienna and he would never come to Bordeaux. She wished him well with his sonata but the world was full of musicians who had great ambitions for their concertos and sonatas. Dieter was no different from the rest.

Louise Darvish invited her back. Louise had always been controversial. She loved scandal and if she could have it close to home without actually being involved in it herself she was going to love it. After all, it was not for the Martindales to tell her who or who not she could receive in her home and Chantal was a friend.

Her husband made no objection. If Louise was entertained the less demands she made on himself, and he had to admit he rather liked the French girl, she was unobtrusive and intelligent.

Marie Claire urged her daughter to accept Louise's invitation and Chantal hoped fervently that her friend had issued the invitation because Sebastian would be home.

Louise presented her with a list of activities. 'Everybody has been asking if you were coming back,' she said gaily. 'You will certainly illuminate the weeks ahead, nothing is happening these days, the new débutantes are a pretty ordinary lot, not nearly as lively as we were.'

Nothing had changed except that Sebastian was not around, and the celebration of his sister's engagement to the Duke of Tarleton was a forgone conclusion.

'This is something new,' Louise exclaimed as she opened her

morning mail. 'We are invited to a cocktail party at Amanda Wentworth's prior to an orchestral concert at the Albert Hall. Some composer and his new symphony. I never thought Amanda was much for culture of this nature.'

'People change,' Chantal murmured gently.

Louise was not listening, instead she was scanning the printed invitation with her utmost attention, turning at last with gleaming eyes to say, 'Dieter Steinberg is playing his new concerto, Chantal. There can't possibly be two Dieter Steinbergs. Is it possible it can be our old music master?'

Chantal stared at her. 'He told me he was composing a sonata, do you really think it could be Dieter?'

'Surely not.' Louise said confidently. 'I should think it's a common enough name in Austria and Germany. I would think your Dieter is back at the school in Switzerland coping with duffers like me. Don't you agree Chantal?'

There was no need for Chantal to answer her because by this time she was opening other envelopes containing other invitations.

'We can't go to them all,' Louise said. 'We have to be selective and choose those we want to go to and those we want to avoid.'

'Isn't it very rude to decline an invitation?'

'Not at all. We can't be expected to take up all of them, nobody does. I'll have to ask Nigel of course, he hates the balls and usually retires to the Bridge room, and garden parties as far as he's concerned are entirely out. I'm not even sure he'll be interested in the orchestral concert.'

Chantal was curious. 'I think we ought to go to that one,' she said evenly. 'It would be rather nice to know if Herr Steinberg's ambitions have been realized.'

'And of course you did have a terrible crush on him, Chantal,' Louise added wryly.

'No more than the ones you had on various male instructors,' Chantal argued.

Louise smiled. 'Oh very well then. I'll speak to Nigel, and accept the ones I think we should go to, and I'll insist on the concert. If he refuses to escort us I know a dozen men who will.'

The threat of the dozen young men persuaded Nigel to be their escort. He was proud of his lively pretty young wife, he had witnessed the young gallants who clustered around her and he enjoyed having two sought-after women on his arm. He couldn't understand why Constance Martindale was so much against Chantal as a bride for their only son, but then her mother was probably behind it.

London was coming to life again and although the new king was a far different sort of man from his father at least he and his queen were observing the traditions historically observed by the British Court.

Gone were the stream of mistresses, the eccentricities of a monarch obsessed with the sort of enjoyment Victoria had frowned upon, and in its place were George and Mary, two respectable reserved people determined to do their best in a world of changing values.

From her place in the huge hall Chantal witnessed their arrival to hear the new concerto played by Herr Dieter Steinberg in the newly built Albert Hall. Darker and smaller than his larger than life father the King stood stiffly to attention with the vast audience while the National Anthem was played, and beside him stood his queen, stiff-backed, tall and imposing, glistening with jewellery from the diamond tiara on her head to the row upon row of gems around her throat.

The audience took their seats after the king had acknowledged their greeting, and on the platform the orchestra was looking expectantly at their conductor. Sitting beside her, Louise whispered, 'Aren't you a little bit excited Chantal, suppose it is our Herr Steinberg?'

Chantal didn't answer, the moment was too tense, her memories too recent.

The orchestra started with Beethoven's pastoral symphony and Nigel murmured, 'I suppose it's going to be an evening of German music,' and his wife hissed. 'Herr Dieter is Austrian, isn't there a difference?' then giving Chantal a long-suffering sigh sat back in her seat to enjoy the music.

The conductor acknowledged the audience's applause before introducing the composer of their next work. Louise leaned forward expectantly and Chantal felt at that moment she could hardly breathe as the tall handsome young man came forward to acknowledge the applause.

'It is Herr Steinberg, Chantal, don't you see. It really is.'

He smiled, and Chantal remembered his smile, and as he took his place at the piano her heart and her mind was filled with melody and memories of that tiny room in the chalet with the window boxes filled with geraniums and the distant sound of cow bells.

Her thoughts were all of that room with its piano and its simplicity. She was remembering his voice filled with restraint and a sanity she hadn't wanted to hear, and as she watched his fingers lovingly lingering on the melody that had been his life she thought of him trying to instil the music he loved into the hearts and minds of a bevy of young girls who had little talent and no ambition to pursue it.

She thought about him rushing from the school to spend the long evenings in that tiny room composing music. What a vain silly little girl he must have thought her, and yet there had been a tenderness in his eyes, a desire he had been unable to hide.

Shaken out of her reverie she was aware of the applause and that people were standing up to acknowledge the man who stood smiling, bowing in acknowledgement of their applause. They were reluctant to let him go, and Louise whispered, 'We have to speak to him after the concert Chantal, we can't let him go without telling him that we heard him play.'

'We can't go Louise, there will be too many people,' Chantal whispered.

'We've probably known him longer than any of them. Anyway, we knew him when he was nobody. I'm going to speak to him and you're coming with me.'

Nigel's protestations were swept aside at the end of the concert and while people were still applauding Louise was pushing her way along the seats with smiling apologies.

He stood surrounded by people, a little bemused, and as they stood within the doorway he looked across the room and their eyes met. For a moment it seemed to Chantal that time stood still: he stood quite motionless with a half smile on his face, at first incredulous, then welcoming and Louise was dragging her forward until she stood looking up at him, and he raised her hand to his lips.

He greeted then both, and while Chantal remained silent Louise was chattering exuberantly, flattering him with her smiles, totally unaware of his stillness.

27

'How could you bear it?' Louise was saying. 'Teaching music to us. None of us were talented, none of us really enjoyed it, we were counting the minutes before we could get out on to the snow?'

He smiled. 'It is amazing what people will do to earn enough money to do something else, Lady Louise.' he said.

'Where will you go from here?' she asked him.

'To Vienna. I have already played for the emperor and he has asked for a repetition. Then to Paris and Budapest and Moscow.'

'How absolutely marvellous, so many wonderful places, and my husband refuses to set foot out of England.'

'So you are married, Miss Louise?'

'Yes, during my coming-out year. I'm the Countess Darvish, that is my husband standing near the door and looking thoroughly bored by it all.'

'Then perhaps you should return to him. Everybody is not fascinated by music.'

'Nigel gets bored by a great many things. He's happiest in the country with his horses and his dogs. Don't worry, he'll wait for us. Chantal's been staying with us for a few weeks now, of course London was all frightfully boring after the old king died, the Court mourning you know, but thank goodness it is coming to life. I don't suppose it will be quite the same, the new king is very circumspect.'

'And are you happy in England?' he asked Chantal.

'Yes, I love it.'

'Well, of course you love it, darling,' Louise put in coyly. 'Why shouldn't you with every bachelor within miles dancing attention.'

'That isn't quite true, Louise,' Chantal said firmly.

'Well, there is one very eligible bachelor who would be dancing attention if he wasn't pining away in the Indian Army.'

Dieter's eyes continued to smile, but behind that smile was a sudden reserve that Chantal was aware of, but not Louise.

'A viscount, no less,' Louise was saying gaily, 'the only son of the Earl of Westmond, one of the season's most sought after men and Chantal snaffled him from under the noses of a dozen débutantes.'

'And when will you marry?' Dieter asked her evenly.

'I don't even know when I shall see him again, and we are not engaged,' Chantal said. 'Louise is exaggerating.'

'Well, of course I'm not exaggerating, didn't you go up to London with him so that he could show you the sights, and doesn't all London know that you were together at every function before he went away?' Louise said indignantly.

'India is an awfully long way away.'

'Well of course it is, and Delhi is bursting at the seams with young women looking for eligible young officers, but he deluges her with letters; that means something in my book.'

'May I wish you both every happiness,' Dieter said with a bow, 'and now I am afraid I must speak to all these people who have waited so long.'

'Heavens yes,' said Louise, 'we have been monopolizing you, Herr Steinberg.'

She held out her hand which he raised to his lips and then he held Chantal's hand briefly before he smiled and walked away.

Unsettled by the meeting Chantal was unable to sleep. She stood for a long time looking down from her window at the empty square lit fitfully by gas lamps. A small wind rustled gently through the trees that edged the square and in the distance came the occasional sound of traffic. Chantal wondered if somewhere in this vast city Dieter was thinking of her, but then why should he? He was a successful man, the new idol on the musical scene and he would perhaps smile at her schoolgirl infatuation and how quickly it had faded when something more substantial took its place.

Closing the curtains she returned to the room but still sleep eluded her.

She was thinking about Sebastian with his tender charm and the feeling that she had known him always, the meeting of soul to soul that she had not felt with Dieter. With Dieter it had been a passion, a torturing desire that had given her no peace and as she analyzed her feelings it seemed to Chantal that with Sebastian it must be love, with Dieter it had been foolish infatuation. And still she was unsure and the morning found her heavy eyed and weary from lack of sleep.

She stayed with Louise for several weeks before she was invited to stay with Amanda who had given birth to her first child, a son, and she joined with her friend and her husband in their delight at the baby's birth.

Her mother's letters were filled with delight at her decision to stay in England. Marie Claire waited impatiently for the letter that would tell her that her daughter had found an English aristocrat she wished to marry and couldn't understand why it never happened.

She spent money lavishly on hats and gowns which she sent to Chantal affirming that French fashions were streets ahead of anything she could buy in London, even when Chantal remonstrated with her that she did not need such expensive gifts.

Chantal knew what her mother was about, and as she unwrapped yet another parcel Amanda said feelingly, 'They're all so beautiful Chantal, they must have cost the earth.'

'My mother is very good with her fingers,' Chantal said dryly.

'These were never made by your mother.'

'She was always good with hats.'

'Possibly, but these hats are perfect for Ascot. Stay for Ascot, Chantal, wear the pale pink and that gorgeous hat with the chiffon roses.'

'Ascot is tempting, Amanda. I've heard of it but never been there.'

'Then that's settled, you'll stay.'

It was in the Royal enclosure at Ascot that Chantal came face to face with the Vicomtesse de Mirandol and the Vicomtesse inclined her head graciously and smiled.

Vivienne de Mirandol had watched Chantal strolling with her friends across the lawns at Ascot, beautiful in pale rose, her exquisite hat a froth of chiffon roses covering her dark blonde hair. She was very beautiful this daughter of Marie Claire, and she could well understand why she was always surrounded by a group of admiring young men.

Chantal Grolan was different, not simply that she was French, but she had an air about her, an intelligence and enchanting grace, and this was the young woman her nephew wished to marry.

André had told her she must not interfere, enough of them were interfering without her, but she did not want Sebastian to marry the French girl. André believed that she had forgotten about Marie Claire, that she held no grudges, but he was wrong. André had been amused, even light-hearted, about many of the women in his life, but he had never been light-hearted about Marie Claire. He had never been able to laugh about her, discuss her at length or treat her with the same triviality he reserved for others.

Vivienne had known some of the others. Pretty fashionable women who were flattered by her husband's attentions, their hot greedy little hands only too ready to accept the jewels he indolently lavished on them, knowing that he would tire of them quickly so that it was essential to take what was on offer while the affair lasted.

There had been an unusual integrity about Marie Claire, but she was unsure if it was in her daughter. She was here in England with the friends she had made in Switzerland, here with her intelligence and her beauty, here, Vivienne felt sure, with the object of finding a titled rich man to marry her. She agreed with her sister-in-law that it should not be Sebastian, but Sebastian had been as besotted with her as once his father had been besotted with Constance, and father and son were very much alike.

Her father had never liked or agreed with Constance's mother, but in this they would have been as one.

Her brother would announce the engagement of his daughter to the Duke of Tarleton any day now and then there would follow the ball, and all the other festivities she as a débutante had hated.

Grace was in love, walking on air, revelling in every moment of what life had to offer and a future of similar advantages. If Sebastian came home for his sister's ball or her wedding he would insist that Chantal Grolan be present, and she thought dismally of all the problems that lay ahead.

She looked across the lawn and saw André in the company of two young women, both of them looking up at him with coy admiration. André always looked so elegant at functions of this nature, today in his formal morning attire with his grey top hat sitting elegantly at an angle, his binoculars slung casually over his shoulder he seemed hardly to have changed from the enchantingly elegant young man she had fallen in love with one summer in Trouville.

He smiled across at her, a smile that completely excluded the two women commanding his attention, and then with a smile and murmured word he left them to walk across the lawn to his wife.

'You're looking very pensive, my dear.' he said gently.

'I was watching that girl, she seems to spend more time in England than she spends in France.'

'Not surprisingly, Vivienne, she has friends here. They evidently enjoy her company.'

She bit her lip nervously, and André said feelingly, 'Stop worrying about something that doesn't really concern you, chérie.'

'Sebastian concerns me André.'

'She could make him an excellent wife.'

'And she could make him a diabolical one. Her mother has been something of an adventuress and nobody knows who her father was, probably some yokel from one of the villages.'

André didn't answer, but looking across at the girl's slender figure and enchanting grace he could not think that any yokel had fathered such a girl.

Catching their eyes upon her, Chantal felt sure they were discussing her and she felt a sudden desperate urge to go home, to leave these people who were not her people, and this scene that was far removed from the life she had known. If Sebastian really loved her he would find her wherever she was, and, if he didn't, then it had all been a dream.

'A penny for your thoughts,' a laughing young man said staring down into her eyes.

'I doubt if they are worth that,' she replied smiling.

How easy it was to laugh and flirt with them, they expected nothing else and they were all of a pattern, these young men who followed the fleshpots, as anxious to be seen and heard as the girls who had flitted hopefully throughout the Season.

Some of them came from titled families, some of them had money, others were hangers-on, but they had all been well educated, knew how to dress and how to talk, how to dance and ride, and how to keep an eye open for the main chance.

She was an enigma to them. That she was French lent her some sort of glamour that was alien, but they asked innumerable questions about her family background while here friends informed all and sundry that her father owned vineyards in the region of Bordeaux and that they lived in an old château.

Chantal smiled to herself. Most of these young men would be visualizing a château as grand and ancient as the Mirandol, not one recently built and as modest as the Château Marguerite.

Chantal told them nothing, but they looked at her gowns and her millinery and thought that they could only have come from a monied family, and parents who spoiled her and gave her everything she wanted.

There was a class-consciousness about England that she had never felt in France. These young gods who strolled across the lawns of Ascot in 1911 seemed so sure of themselves, their empire and a world that would be left unchanged for posterity and she marvelled at the arrogance of it.

Amanda opened her invitation to Grace's engagement ball with delighted anticipation, passing it across the table for Chantal to look at.

'I told Grace you were staying with us so surely she'll send your invitation here. I wonder if Sebastian will get leave. It'll be the highlight of the season.'

'He hasn't actually been out there very long,' Chantal felt obliged to point out.

'Well no, but his uncle is somebody very high up in the Indian Army – I'm sure all the relatives they have will be there.'

'I shall probably be back in France when this event takes place,' Chantal said airily. Indeed she was determined to be back in France because she felt certain there would be no invitation for her.

She had reckoned without Louise who encountered Grace when they both arrived at the same moment to stare in a shop window of New Bond Street's newest dress salon.

The two girls smiled at each other and embraced warmly.

'Thank you for your invitation,' Louise said. 'Nigel and I are looking forward to it tremendously.'

'I'm so glad.'

'I expect we shall know everybody, Chantal is staying with Amanda Wentworth at the moment. Is your brother likely to get leave?'

'We're not sure.'

'It would be lovely if he could. So nice for Chantal.'

By this time Louise realized Grace was looking decidedly uncomfortable, and some devilment within her prompted her to continue.

'How do your parents feel about two weddings in the family?'

'They haven't discussed it, at least not with me.'

'Well it's very much on the cards, I'm sure. There they all were setting their caps at Sebastian, and Chantal came along to steal him from under their very noses.'

Grace's smile was a shade fragile, nor did it reach her eyes.

'Oh well,' Louise said airily. 'I expect Chantal will be going home to France in the meantime, but I'll have her stay with us for the ball so you can send her invitation to us. I know her home is in Bordeaux but I've never been there. Amanda went and had a simply lovely time.'

'I didn't know Amanda had been there.' Grace said in some surprise.

'Oh, some little while ago. She said her parents were absolutely charming and most welcoming.'

Grace smiled again, that doubtful wistful smile, and then after a brief embrace, Louise said, 'I must go. Do you intend to go inside the shop. Diana Lostock had her wedding dress made up here, it was quite beautiful but I expect you have already seen to all that?'

'Well yes. Goodbye Louise, remember me to Nigel.'

Later that evening over dinner Louise said to her husband, 'I don't think Grace's parents have any intention of inviting Chantal, it would serve them right if Sebastian came home and found out what they're about. It's her mother and grandmother of course.'

Nigel was unconcerned, and faced with his indifference she said sharply, 'They've found a duke for their daughter for heaven's sake, what are they expecting to find for Sebastian?'

'You really are reading too much into this, old girl. You don't really know what they think about Chantal and I'd advise you to keep out of it.'

'Chantal happens to be my friend, and I am not your old girl. Surely you don't expect me to stand by and see her slighted by the Martindales.'

Nigel viewed his wife's face with cynical amusement. Louise was not in the least troubled by a slight to Chantal, but she was decidedly put out that she might be missing a very intriguing situation that would hopefully keep her and her friends entertained for weeks.

Women are the very devil, in a man's world a situation like this would never have arisen.

Meanwhile over dinner at the Martindales' London home Grace was raising the point of Chantal's invitation with her parents.

'I really don't see how we can not invite her, Mummy,' she said anxiously. 'If she is staying with any of the people who're coming to the ball we can't exclude her.'

'Nor can we risk giving her any encouragement,' her mother said sharply.

'But if Sebastian comes home, he'll be furious if she's left out,' Grace persisted.

'It's highly unlikely he'll get leave so soon,' her father said calmly. 'It will either be leave for your engagement ball or leave for your wedding. I don't think he can expect both.'

'Not even with Uncle Daniel pulling the strings?'

'Not even then.'

'I suppose Daniel and his family will want to stay with us,' Constance said somewhat irritably. 'I'm still in shock at the fact that he wanted to marry that woman.'

'I'm still in shock that he married at all,' Andrew said feelingly.

'I liked her,' Grace put in staunchly. 'She was very amusing and there was nothing at all snobbish about Aunt Jean.'

'She had nothing to be snobbish about,' her mother said sharply. 'For a girl who spent most of her young life in some chorus or other to find herself suddenly elevated to being married to the son of an earl who is also a high ranking officer in the Indian Army must be very satisfying indeed. If she was to give herself airs people would be more inclined to remember her background.'

'You sound so awfully snobbish, Mother, just like Granny.'

Her father smiled across the table at her. He had been married to Constance for a great many years and he had married her because he believed himself in love with her. Totally infatuated and against all the better judgement of his father, disenchantment had come slowly and painfully over the years.

She was still a very beautiful woman in what his father had always called a chocolate-box fashion. She was still completely under the thumb of her dominant mother and hardly had a thought in her head that her mother hadn't put there.

He hated those long weeks when her mother descended on them, and looked forward longingly for the weeks Constance spent time abroad with her mother, either cruising or in some expensive fashionable hotel in the South of France. He grumbled about the expense but he put up with it because in their absence he could potter around his estate, ride across the downs and pursue any other activity he enjoyed and which his wife did not.

He saw his younger brother rarely, since Daniel had elected to stay in the Indian Army, but he had been amazed when Daniel decided at the age of forty to marry an actress from some London revue. Jean was a handsome woman, she had a lively sense of humour and if people were taken aback by her, they invariably liked her. She had produced a son during the first year of their marriage and even when his wife and mother-in-law frowned upon her he had to admit that he rather enjoyed her company.

Of course they would be staying with him, Daniel had no home in England, and would expect nothing less than hospitality from the only relatives he had.

He had to admit the prospect gave him a certain satisfaction. Jean was a worthy opponent of his mother-in-law and on several occasions the older woman had lost out to Jean's mischievous humour.

He was not surprised by the antagonism his family showed towards the girl his son had fallen in love with. For one thing she was foreign, for another she was not of noble birth, and nobody seemed to know very much about her origins. All these inconsequences could have been put on one side if she had not been the daughter of the woman who had been André de Mirandol's mistress.

That affair had been over a long time and no doubt replaced by several others, but it had been that liaison which had caused his sister considerable pain.

The girl had beauty and great style. That she was intelligent he had no doubt and his daughter had admitted a grudging admiration for her. At the same time they were both very young, but when had infatuation been surmounted by wisdom?

His wife said that it was evident the girl's mother had set her sights on a British aristocrat for her daughter, hence the school in Switzerland where she would meet British girls only too anxious to invite her to their homes.

His mother-in-law said she was obviously a fortune-hunter; his sister and her husband had been rather less forthcoming.

The eventual outcome was that Grace said Chantal should receive an invitation to he engagement ball. Sebastian would not be home for it and therefore no anticipation would be aroused by her presence.

In the end it proved that all their worries had been unfounded when Chantal graciously declined their invitation on the grounds that she would be in France on the evening of the ball.

28

In the event Chantal's absence raised almost as much speculation at the ball as her presence would have caused.

It was a glittering occasion with nobody feeling more satisfaction than Lady Grace's maternal grandmother. Geraldine Fallon had reached her ultimate goal, a granddaughter destined to marry a duke, with relatives within the royal family itself, and in every step of the way she had played her part.

Now as she sat with her daughter surveying the scene, the smile of self-satisfied exultation was evident on her handsome features. She had done her best, and her next hurdle would undoubtedly be her grandson Sebastian.

The French girl was out of the question and he must be made to see it. With an earl as his father and a duke as his brother-in-law how could he possibly expect to bring an unknown French girl into the family circle? People had a nasty habit of searching for hidden scandals, so no doubt somebody somewhere would quickly discover that her mother had been something of an adventuress.

She frowned at the noise of laughter from the adjoining table. The Hon. Mrs Martindale was regaling those around her with one of her humorous and probably risqué stories while her husband looked on complacently. Why did people like the woman, she was too earthy by half and as usual her bodice showed too much flash. And whatever prompted her to dye her hair in that quite indescribable colour?

Jean Martindale was well aware of her disapproval. The woman was a pain, a snob of the first water and she had little liking for her sister-in-law who sat besides her mother with the same haughty expression on her face. As she looked away her eyes met the eyes of Vivienne de Mirandol and she smiled to herself. She had little in common with Vivienne but she was rather fond of André, he flirted so charmingly.

It would not be a long engagement, Jean reflected, and then would follow the society wedding and Sebastian had hinted that he would be asking some girl to marry him, some French girl, but when she had asked if she might meet her she had been told she would not be at the ball.

Even if Sebastian couldn't be there, there was surely no need to exclude the girl he was in love with, Jean thought, but then there had been a great many times when she had been excluded from their functions and Daniel had felt obliged to cover for them.

She liked Sebastian, he talked to her as a friend and told her things she doubted he would tell his mother. The poor boy could hardly be unaware of the hurdles that lay ahead.

Dancing with her brother, Vivienne said, 'I see that Chantal Grolan is not here, surely she was invited?'

'Apparently she is home in France and unable to attend.'

'I see. And she was not persuaded?'

'Why should she be? If people decline an invitation they don't expect to be encouraged to change their mind.'

'But she will be invited to the wedding, won't Sebastian be home for that?'

'We very much hope so.'

'And Chantal?'

'Why are you so persistent when you have so little liking for her mother?'

'I haven't seen her mother for some time, she no longer lives in Dijon.'

'So that makes it right for the girl to be accepted.'

'I'm merely looking around at a bevy of British beauties and wondering why none of them appealed to Sebastian.'

'I don't know. Perhaps he discovered something different in the French girl.'

Silently Vivienne agreed with him. Chantal had something else, an indefinable glamour that set her apart.

'How long before the wedding?' she asked.

'About three months. They are hoping to go to America for their honeymoon, sometime in April, I believe.'

'Why don't you come to us for a few weeks, we never seem to see you on your own these days, and I know Constance and her mother go to Provence in the springtime.'

'I'll think about it, Vivienne.'

There was an impatient frown on Marie Claire's face as she watched her daughter strolling nonchalantly across the lawn. She had said so little about her stay in England, she had had to ask questions and the replies when they came were not what she wanted to hear.

Yes, she had enjoyed everything and her friends had been so kind. Ascot was marvellous, as were the operas and concerts, and no, there was nobody special.

As for Chantal, she could not say why she did not want to discuss Sebastian with her mother. When she thought about becoming Sebastian's wife it seemed too remote, something that she could not believe in and yet his letters were warm and loving and they came often.

She did not tell Marie Claire about Grace's engagement ball, because she knew her mother would never understand why she had not elected to attend. Her mother was so wrapped up in the Martindale family and she could only think it was because they were related to the Mirandols. When she talked about the other people she had met, her mother was disinterested, so in the end she ceased to speak of them at all, and that this omission added to her mother's frustration she was well aware of.

'Who writes to you from India?' her mother demanded one morning as she watched her opening the envelope.

'A young Englishman serving in the Indian Army.'

'I doubt if you would be happy living in some hot country, Chantal, I hope you are not seriously interested in this young man.'

Chantal merely smiled. If she had said the letter had come from Sebastian Martindale it might well have been another matter.

'Surely your friends have young men in aristocratic circles? you worry me, Chantal, first you fall in love with your music master and now there is this young man far away in India.'

'There is no need for you to worry, Mama, I am quite happy.'

'No doubt, but where is it all leading to? The young music teacher in Switzerland will no doubt be enchanting some other naïve girl by this time – it is all part of growing up, and English women are brought up to be empire-builders in some far flung outpost,you have not been reared in that mould.'

When Chantal did not answer her mother persisted, 'When do you intend to return to England?'

'One day perhaps, Mother. I am sure one or another of my friends will invite me, I thought you would enjoy having me here.'

'Oh I do, it's wonderful having you here, but this is not Paris Chantal. Nothing very exciting happens here. true we have the wine festival but one festival is very much like another and I haven't seen anything very interesting in the young men who appear. Now if we were in Paris it would be different, there would be the opera and the racing, the café society and the boulevards . . .'

'And perhaps some young French aristocrat,' Chantal said smiling.

'In France they are unimportant, in England they are somebody.'

She was tempted to tell her mother that Dieter Steinberg was no longer a humble music teacher in the Bernese Oberland but a young man of consequence with the world at his feet. Her mother might be impressed in a small way, but it would not alter her burning desire for her daughter to marry the right British aristocrat.

In some perverse way she did not want to gratify this wish of her mother's. Marriage to Sebastian would be everything she longed for but she could not bear to see the look of triumph on her mother's beautiful face.

In her innermost heart she believed that Martindales would not let it happen. Ranged against her were Sebastian's family but more than all of them was Vivienne de Mirandol, the woman her mother had wronged.

That her mother showed little interest in visiting England herself surprised her, particularly when Henri had often suggested it. She did not know that even after all these years Marie Claire could not bear to think of Andrew happy in his own environment with his family around him. In her heart he was still the man who had taken away her girlhood, the despoiler of every dream she had ever had.

It seemed to Marie Claire that with every passing day her anger against Andrew only increased. She would never be able to punish him personally. By this time he had no doubt forgotten her existence, but if she could place her daughter in the home of some man as important as himself, as admired as his own wife and daughter, something would have been salvaged from the ruin of her early life.

There had been nobody in her life to tell her she was wrong. Instead, it seemed that everybody had only conspired to push her into an abyss of bitterness, a burning desire for retribution: her father's anger, her wretched existence under his roof, and Elise Grolan's spite. Marie Claire had closed her eyes to the good things and the kind people in her life, and in it all Chantal had been the weapon she would use to redeem those lost years. Andrew had been her lover, now he was her obsession.

Neither of the men she had married had been able to obliterate Andrew from her memory or remove the desire for vengeance. Maurice had been a father figure, kind, generous, a rock to lean on, and Henri too was somebody who had restored stability and it was wonderful to be adored. She had never felt able to talk to either of them about her past, it had always been something she had shut away as something private, something belonging to her and only her.

Only André de Mirandol had tried to discover why there had been such a deep-seated feeling of pain behind the beautiful eyes that smiled so serenely and bravely on a world that was new to her, but he had never discovered the inner self around which she had wrapped a citadel of despair.

Now, just when retribution was in sight Chantal was playing unfairly with her insecurities.

Chantal received long ecstatic letters from her English friends about the ball to celebrate Grace's engagement. Louise in particular left nothing out, the splendour of the occasion, the beauty of the women's dresses, the gathering of eligible young bachelors of noble birth. With all her caustic wit she enlarged on the gratification of Grace's grandmother which to the older guests was reminiscent of her display of triumph when years before her daughter had married the Earl of Westmond's son and heir.

'People were asking why you were not present.' Louise pointed out, 'and why Sebastian hadn't got leave when his aunt and uncle were there. Apparently it was the engagement ball or the wedding, and Sebastian opted for the wedding. That is one function you will have to attend since all society is talking about you and Sebastian.'

Louise also informed her that she intended to shop in Paris for her gown for the occasion of Grace's wedding. 'I don't want Nigel with me.' she wrote, 'men are hopeless around the shops so perhaps you could be in Paris and we could spend some time together.'

She would enjoy spending time in Paris with Louise and this was the only portion of Louise's letter that she imparted to her mother.

'But of course you must go to Paris,' Marie Claire enthused. 'I might even come with you.'

Dismayed, Chantal said, 'But Mother, wouldn't you be terribly bored with the two of us, Louise will want to be here, there and everywhere.'

'I would leave you two girls to get on with it, but we could dine together, perhaps go to the theatre or to some concert or other. I can never get Henri to Paris, he's happier here among his vineyards.'

'Well, of course, Louise could change her mind about Paris, one never really knew with Louise.'

'Wouldn't you like to ask her to spend some time here, Amanda was very happy with us?'

Chantal did not want Louise in Bordeaux. All she would talk about was the Martindale ball and her mother would be dismayed that she had declined her invitation. There would be questions. Her mother would make her disappointment plain and on her mother's face would be that hurt and angry look she had seen on so many occasions.

In the end Marie Claire was prevented from accompanying her to Paris because Henri had a stomach disorder and was unwell for several days, and so, on a wet dismal day at the beginning of February

248

Chantal set off alone for the capital and the several days she would spend with her friend in an exclusive, expensive hotel of Louise's choice.

Louise was waiting for her in the ornate resident's lounge of the hotel, 'This is my treat, Chantal.' she said. 'You can imagine Nigel has grumbled that I need to come to Paris at all but I've been so looking forward to it. People are talking about your gowns, how exquisite you always look, how different, so I thought it was time I tried to be different too. I've got a list of all the salons I need to go to and you can advise me on what suits me.'

'But you always look stylish, Louise, I look the way I am because I'm French, you are English so why don't you want to look English?'

'I don't mind looking English. I just want something different for Grace's wedding, and Paris is surely the best place to find it.'

In the days that followed she sat with Louise in one exclusive fashion house after another, watching a stream of elegant mannequins parade before them while Louise made her selection. Not content with selecting a gown for the occasion of Grace's wedding day, she chose others, evening gowns and garden party creations and Louise giggled wickedly, 'Nigel will be furious,' she said acidly, 'He's really quite frugal you know, he can spend as much money as he likes on horses and the stables, but I've had to be very careful about my spending money. Anyway I got a fair-sized cheque from my father and Nigel will have to foot the rest. Aren't you going to buy anything for yourself Chantal, how about the blue dress I saw you looking at, that would be perfect for the wedding?'

'You forget that I don't have a husband to pay my dress bills,' Chantal said with a smile. 'I agree the gown is beautiful, but I'm not even sure if I shall be at the wedding.'

'But of course you will. Sebastian will see to that.'

It was the last day of Louise's visit and they were walking together in the narrow streets of Montmarte with the majestic white-domed basilica of the Sacré-Couer rising behind them that Louise suddenly clutched her arm, exclaiming excitedly, 'Chantal, over there, the man standing in the square, watching the children on the carousel.'

Chantal followed her pointing finger and her heart was immediately filled with great confusion. Dieter Steinberg stood on the pavement leaning on his stick, a smile on his lips as he watched the children clambering on the carousel, but before she could say anything Louise was striding across the square, her hands outstretched in welcome and he was waiting with Louise for her to join them.

'How strange that we should be meeting like this, first in London and now in Paris. Who would have thought it when you were our

249

teacher and we were your somewhat unwilling pupils. What are you doing in Paris Herr Steinberg?' Louise trilled.

'I have been in Paris two weeks, Concert engagements.'

'Oh I wish we'd known, we would have come to them, wouldn't we Chantal? Unfortunately I'm going home to England this afternoon.'

He smiled politely. 'Are you both returning to England?'

'No, Chantal is going home in the morning. What a marvellous idea Chantal, you could go to Her Steinberg's concert this evening.'

'That won't be possible, I'm afraid,' he said, 'I gave my last performance last night, I am leaving for America in the morning.'

'Oh, what a pity,' Louise said. 'You really are becoming very famous.'

He smiled but offered no comment, and Louise, irrepressible as always, said, 'Do please have tea with us, we could talk about Madame Lafayette's school and the fun we had there, and then I shall have to leave for Boulogne.'

'You prefer the night sailing?' he enquired.

'Gracious yes. I hate early rising and I prefer to have dinner and a berth for the night. Perhaps we'd better take a cab to the hotel, the time seems to have gone so quickly.'

Afternoon tea was a pleasant affair with Louise doing most of the talking and completely unaware that both her companions seemed unduly reserved. It was only after she had left them to collect her luggage that he said, 'You have said very little about your activities Chantal, or your plans for the future.'

'I have been with my mother in Bordeaux for several weeks now, life is slower there but very pleasant.'

'I do not know Bordeaux at all. But your friend seems very sure that you will be returning to England soon.'

'I'm not sure.'

'Not even to be with the young man your friends told me about?'

'What did they tell you about Sebastian?'

'That he is a highly eligible, handsome and very much in love with you. It would be nice for him if it was reciprocated. Didn't I tell you that life would change for both of us Chantal?'

'Yes. Your life has changed more than mine though.'

'Why do you say that.'

'Because you have come a long way from being a music master in a girl's school in Switzerland. Now you are famous, your dreams came true, I'm not very sure where my dreams are leading me.'

'To an assured future with the sort of man that crowd's of young girls pray for. They came to Switzerland to prepare for it, to put the polish on all that had gone before. A great many of them have achieved what was planned for them, you will be no different Chantal.'

'You thought I was like them, that we were all of a pattern?'

'Yes, that is what I thought.'

It didn't matter now what he had thought then. Chantal reasoned that it was Sebastian who loved her who was offering her marriage and everything that went with it, but when she looked into Dieter Steinberg's eyes she knew that she still desired him. She wanted Sebastian to come back into her life to reassure her that he was reality and the rest frangible, but her heart was a treacherous thing with its vain longings and unreal desires.

'Have dinner with me this evening,' Dieter was saying, 'when your friend has gone you will be alone in Paris and there is a new charming little restaurant on the Left Bank which I am particularly fond of.'

When she did not immediately accept his invitation, he said, 'The restaurant is owned by a fellow countryman of mine. If you have never had Viennese food you will enjoy it.'

'Thank you, I shall look forward to it.'

'I will call for you here in your hotel at eight o'clock. The restaurant is completely informal.'

Dieter had reserved a table situated in a small alcove and, as they took their places, Chantal looked around the room with delighted interest. There were red and white check tablecloths on the tables, the men were drinking their beer from steins and the waiters wore white silk shirts with wide sleeves and velvet trousers under the red cumberbands.

In a corner of the room a man was playing soft haunting waltz music on a zither and leaning across the table Dieter said. 'The music is of old Vienna but you will hear waltz music and gypsy music also.'

'Don't you care for French music?' she asked.

'Oh yes, indeed I do. I find French music plaintive, haunting and very beautiful, you should know Liebchen that I love all music, it is my life.'

'What has fame meant to you most of all, Dieter?'

'When I climbed the mountain slopes in Switzerland and strolled through the villages I was a young man with very little money. The salary I earned at the school covered the bare essentials for living. I could have brought you coffee and strudel but very little else. Now I can buy you jewels and entertain you royally, but it is all too late, is it not?'

Chantal blushed and looked down at the tablecloth, and after a few moments, Dieter said lightly, 'That young music teacher in Switzerland did not flirt with you, he was too afraid, for his job, for his dignity, and you so desperately wanted me to flirt with you, Chantal.'

She looked up quickly. 'No,' she disclaimed, 'I never wanted you to flirt with me, I wanted you to be honest with me.'

'And I was honest with you, very honest.'

'But tonight you are flirting with me.'

'Perhaps, perhaps not.'

At that moment a waiter appeared at their table and Dieter spent the next few minutes advising her on the delights of Viennese food and wine, and on the dais a gypsy band played czardas music and a man and a girl in colourful costumes came to dance with much clapping of hands and stamping of feet.

'This music really comes from Hungary,' Dieter explained to her, 'but Hungary is our neighbour, part of our empire, you will soon hear the music of Vienna.'

'Oh I love waltzes,' Chantal said happily. 'Our dancing teacher told us that waltzes were born in the heart.'

'And he was right. Tell me, Chantal, did you ever fall in love with your dancing teacher or that tall muscular young Swiss who taught you to enjoy yourselves on the mountain slopes?'

'No, I never did, but there were a great many of the girls who believed they were in love with them.'

'And all no doubt happily married to genteel young Englishmen with money, a title and further expectations.'

'You are laughing at me.'

'A little perhaps, life had a pattern did it not, and everything else was coincidental.'

29

The atmosphere in the drawing room of the Earl of Westmond's London home was decidedly frosty. Lady Grace was in tears, her mother, taking her cue from Grace's grandmother was more angry than tearful, and Andrew surveyed his family with exasperation.

His mother-in-law as usual had the most to say.

'This is Grace's wedding,' she said adamantly 'and she should be the one to say who she invited to her wedding.'

Grace looked at her nervously. 'I would like to invite Chantal, I liked her at school and it would please Sebastian,' she said.

'We are not in the business of pleasing Sebastian,' her grandmother snapped. 'It is over a year since he saw this girl, he can't possibly be in love with her, he is merely infatuated. You should not allow him to have any hand in dictating who or who should not be invited to Grace's wedding.'

Andrew referred to his son's letter.

'He has said quite plainly that if she is not invited he will not attend himself. It is his intention to ask the French girl to marry him.'

'You can forbid it,' said Mrs Fallon.

'The boy is over twenty-one, he can do what he likes.'

'Not if it means incurring your displeasure. You can cut his allowance, threaten him with all sorts of dire consequences.'

'I remember that my father threatened me with a great many dire consequences but it didn't stop me marrying your daughter,' he said testily.

'It's all going to be so awful,' Grace sobbed. 'Can't we invite Chantal and sort everything out later. Why is everybody punishing Chantal for what her mother did to Aunt Vivienne, it was all over long ago.'

'And should never have taken place,' her mother said firmly.

'Well, it had nothing to do with Chantal.'

'And where will she stay? Sebastian will want her to stay at Blaire and I think that would be too previous. Surely one or another of her friends will have her to stay with them.'

'We are putting no feelers out about where the girl can stay.' Andrew said adamantly. 'She will be invited to stay at Blaire for one or two weeks before the wedding, that will give us all time to get to know her before Sebastian arrives home, and we will be gracious to her, as my family were gracious to you Constance.'

'Your father was never gracious to me,' his mother-in-law snapped. 'He was invariably tetchy and made me feel like an interloper in my daughter's house.'

Andrew didn't answer. It was true his father had never liked her but understandably. She had spent too much time in their house, dictating policy, interfering with the children, lording it over his servants. He would make up his own mind about the French girl. His sister and her husband would be with them and Vivienne would assess the girl, perhaps even find a little forgiveness for her mother's short-comings if the daughter was worthy.

Geraldine Fallon had to be content with that, and silently thought to herself that there was a lot of his father in Andrew. At such times she had to go warily and although she was looking forward to queening it at the wedding she was not looking forward to the few weeks at Blaire before the event.

The Vicomte de Mirandol would be politely charming as only Frenchmen knew how to be, but his wife would be as distant as her father had always been, and what affect would the daughter of André's one-time mistress have on the gathering? She would not be able to watch Sebastian's infatuation for the girl and there would be people coming and going, all no doubt only too eager to discuss every aspect of what they had seen at Blaire.

Chantal stared at the invitation in her hands with some dismay. Her friends had told her they had received theirs weeks before and she had not expected one. She knew this was Sebastian's doing and the prospect of spending several weeks with his family held little joy for her. They would be receiving her with bad grace, and he would not be there to make her feel welcome, nevertheless her refusal would hurt him

When she thought about Sebastian it was sometimes difficult to remember his face, the charm of his smile, the tenderness in his eyes. They had become elusive, those memories of their time together in Oxford and London, and too many times it was Dieter's face that haunted her quiet moments, leaving too many misgivings.

She was glad her mother was out when the invitation arrived. Her mother would glory in the culmination of all her scheming, and the more she thought about it the surer she became that her mother must not know. She would tell Marie Claire that she was going to England to stay with friends, that she would go to a wedding of another friend while there, but she would not say which friend.

She could not bear to think of her mother's questions, and her delight that it was the Martindales with whom she would be staying. If she and Sebastian were destined to become one, that would be the time to tell her mother.

Marie Claire accepted her news without comment, pleased that once more she would be a part of British society, and concerned that she had the right clothes for every occasion the British held dear.

Henri was indulgent. He admired his beautiful step-daughter and enjoyed seeing her wearing pretty clothes. He was gratified at the admiration his wife and Chantal were subjected to at every function they attended and enjoyed spending money on them. In his estimation it was not wasted, Marie Claire charmed his customers as well as his tenants, and in recent weeks Chantal had done likewise.

Chantal had been informed that she should go to the London House and they would all journey up to Blaire early the following week.

Grace had not wanted to marry in London, preferring the cathedral whose soaring spires she had known all her life from the windows at Blaire. On the afternoon of Chantal's arrival they were all gathered in the London drawing room and as Vivienne looked around she thought they would present a formidable gathering to the girl they were waiting for.

Constance and her mother sat together on the Chesterfield opposite the fire and Vivienne was wishing her niece had elected to marry in the summer rather than in April when the days could be blustery and chill.

Andrew sat with his newspaper. She knew that her brother was fully aware of the tension in the room, while André sat in front of a small table playing patience. In a few days Sebastian would be arriving at Blaire in the company of his aunt and uncle, now all on their way home from India, and then would follow the speculation and the machinations of Constance's mother.

Vivienne had tried unsuccessfully to analyze her own feelings on the suitability of Chantal as a wife for Sebastian. She had only spoken one or two words to the girl. That she was pretty was evident, that she was cultured and stylish was obvious, but always in the background were those early days of her marriage when she discovered that André and Marie Claire were embroiled in an affair.

Always too was the feeling that he had liked her. Men had affairs with women they did not like, could never have married, even disliked. It had nothing to do with passion or even lust and none of the other women in André's life had given her the slightest anxiety, but Marie Claire had been different, and there was no reason why she should make things easy for her daughter, she had no right to expect it.

There was a discreet knock at the door and a maidservant announced, 'Mademoiselle Grolan has arrived, my lord.'

Andrew laid his paper aside, looked around the room at the rest of them, then went out into the hall to receive his guest.

He had seen her on several occasions here and there on the social scene with various friends she had made in Switzerland and he had seen his son dancing with her and becoming more and more fascinated.

She stood in the centre of the hall, a tall slender girl, exquisitely dressed and with a mature sophistication that seemed to come naturally to most Frenchwomen. He smiled and took her hand in a friendly gesture, at the same time marvelling that she looked remarkably English with her fair complexion, honey gold hair and dark blue eyes. Indeed her colouring was very much like his daughter's.

'I trust you have had a pleasant journey?' he said with a smile.

'Yes thank you. The sea was rough but I didn't mind, I enjoy sailing.'

'I've crossed the Channel in a good few March gales, it can be very unpleasant. The maid will take your outdoor clothing, we are all gathered in the drawing room.'

He waited while the maid took her clothes, then he led the way to the drawing room and all Chantal was conscious of were a sea of faces, haughty unsmiling faces until Grace came forward and kissed her cheek.

She smiled, and Grace said gently, 'Your are looking well Chantal, I have been looking forward to your coming. Come and meet Mother and Granny.'

Constance Martindale extended her long slim hand but did not squeeze her fingers, and beside her the older woman merely inclined her head without extending her hand.

'I trust you have had a good journey,' Constance said formally.

'Yes thank you.'

'This is my aunt Vivienne,' Grace said, 'the Vicomtesse de Mirandol and Uncle André her husband.'

André gallantly raised her hand to his lips and Vivienne smiled. The girl was everything an ambitious mother had hoped to achieve, why couldn't she take her at her face value, why must she always think about Marie Claire?

Andrew frowned at his wife who immediately said, 'I'm sure you would like some refreshment, we will have tea,' and rising from her seat she went to the fireplace to pull the bell rope. It was answered almost immediately by a servant and instructions for afternoon tea were given.

Chantal was invited to sit where they could all look at her, and in those first few minutes she was wishing she might be anywhere in the world except this London drawing room with the people who were chilling her to the bone.

Grace was the only one making any effort to put her at her ease.

'Sebastian is on his way home, but he won't be here until two days before the wedding. They were in Calcutta and of course the boat sailed from Bombay,' she said with a little smile, and Chantal merely asked, 'They?'

'Why yes, Uncle Daniel and Aunt Jean. They came to my engagement party and we all thought they couldn't possibly come over for the wedding, but they've managed it.'

'How nice.'

'We're all to go to Blaire the day after tomorrow. My fiancé will be joining us for a few days at the beginning of next week.'

Chantal smiled. How could she possibly swallow the piece of Madeira cake on her plate without choking? Why had she come, why had they invited her when their welcome had been so lacking in warmth?

'I think you should show our guest her room after tea,' Lady Constance was saying, 'You may like to rest a little after your journey, we dine at eight, Grace will show you the dining room.'

'Thank you Lady Constance.'

As she followed Grace up the shallow curving staircase she saw that lights were burning brightly in the hall and Grace said wistfully, 'I do hope we have better weather than this for the wedding, but it had to be April, everything is organized for our honeymoon in America.'

'There are a few weeks for the weather to change.'

'Of course. Mummy thinks I should have got married in London, it is so much more convenient for the wedding guests, but I love the cathedral, it's the place I've always worshipped in and if the guests want to come they shouldn't mind putting up at the inns and hotels in the area.'

'I'm sure they won't.'

'You'll know a great many people, all the girls we knew at school are coming, most of them are married now of course.'

By this time they had reached the large room on the first floor that was to be hers for two nights. It was beautiful in shades of pale turquoise and peach with its *en suite* bathroom and massive mirrored wardrobes.

She saw immediately that a maid had unpacked the small suitcase leaving the larger one on a shelf in the corner of the room and Grace said 'Marie will have unpacked, Chantal, I expect the larger case is for clothes you wish to take to Blaire?'

'Yes, that's right.'

Grace went to stand at the window and after a few moments Chantal followed her. The London square below was awash with rain and the gas lamps had already been lit, shedding an eerie glow on darkly clad figures hurrying through the gloom with lights streaming out occasionally from some open door.

'This is London with a vengeance,' Grace said almost contritely. 'It would only have been worse in a pea-souper, they occur mostly in November. They're so eerie, with the hooting of river boats and police whistles. That's how I remembered London during those two years I spent in Switzerland. The memory made me very homesick. Were you ever homesick Chantal?'

'Many times, and wondering what I was doing there.'

'You mean among a group of English girls, did you find us very strange?'

'Different perhaps.'

'It must be wonderful to speak another language with such ease.'

'The sea is a far more formidable frontier than our man-made ones, perhaps that is why we feel compelled to learn the language of our neighbours. I never really thought much about it, learning English seemed so natural to me.'

'Are you looking forward to seeing Sebastian, it seems such a long time since you met? Does he write often?'

'Yes he does.'

When she did not say more Grace said hurriedly, 'I'll leave you to rest before dinner. We do usually change, but not into anything too dressy.'

'Thank you Grace, and thank you for being so kind.'

Grace paused at the door, her face thoughtful, 'We're not a very demonstrative family and Granny has always interfered. Occasionally she and Daddy have words and she doesn't come for a while. She always comes back. Mummy's her only child and they are very close.'

Chantal smiled, and after a moment Grace left her to run quickly down the stairs.

They would be discussing her now, Chantal thought, telling each other that she was unremarkable so why couldn't Sebastian have fallen in love with a girl from his own sphere of life?

Stretching in front of her were a few weeks at the Martindales country seat, in a countryside she was unfamiliar with, in a stately home that was a show place for lesser English people to marvel at.

She was remembering that little girl who had stared entranced through the iron railings of the ornamental gate set before Mirandol, gazing enraptured at the medieval turrets and tall chimneys, the beauty of the formal gardens and the sweeping parklands with their memories of feudal past that still haunted the hills and valleys of Burgundy. In Burgundy there had been much that had been reminiscent of old Spain, even though it had been annexed to France as long ago as 1482, and other feudal memories of the days when it was ruled by the dukes of Burgundy. She doubted if those people downstairs knew anything about the region she was born in, unless it was the Vicomte whose ancestry was more noble than her own.

Constance and her mother were visiting people they knew in the area of Blaire while André had gone riding with the two girls and Grace's fiancé.

Vivienne was loving it. It was wonderful to be sauntering through the graceful rooms of her family home, remembering her father slumped in his favourite chair in front of a log fire, his black spaniel at his feet, a glass of rum toddy at his elbow.

Younger sons and daughters might be brought up in surroundings like this, they might love them deeply and remember them lovingly, but only the eldest son could ever really regard them as home. Andrew had never thought that one day he would be Earl of Westmond, and Vivienne had always known that in her life Blaire was only a stepping stone, but now as she looked up at pictures and ornaments she had known in her childhood, at the faces of long dead Martindales and more recent acquisitions of the present earl and his family her heart was plagued by nostalgia.

There was a huge painting of Constance at the head of the stairs, elegant in her white satin gown, wearing her tiara on silvery, gold hair that gave her porcelain face a strangely Nordic beauty. In one slender hand a long-stemmed red rose trailed against the sheen of her gown and as Vivienne moved up the stairs it seemed her blue eyes followed her. One day Chantal's painting would hang on these walls, but in all honesty she had to admit her beauty would not disgrace them.

From somewhere above she heard a door close and realized it was probably Andrew who had not elected to go with the others. She paused on the staircase and waited for him to come running lightly to join her.

'I'm loving looking over the old place,' she said smiling. 'I always loved it, far more than you or the other two.'

'I didn't see any point in loving it too much,' Andrew said. 'It was never going to be mine.'

'And now it is. I suppose Charlotte will be here in a few days and the girls. How have they grown up? I'm ashamed to say I haven't kept in touch except for weddings and funerals.'

'Well, they've both married well, one of them to Johnny Graham. the other to Alistair McDonald, an Irish peer and a Scottish peer with extensive estates and well blessed with money. Neither of their husbands likes the social whirl and the girls seem happy enough.'

'I thought Charlotte might have remarried?'

'I never thought so. She disappeared from the social scene to spend most of her time in the mists of Scotland, I think she's been happy enough.'

'Oh well, we shall soon be meeting again, no doubt we'll have much to talk about. I wonder what she thinks of Daniel's wife.'

Andrew laughed. 'Well the two women are very different, they couldn't be more so, actually the more I see of Jean the more I like her, she doesn't suffer fools gladly.'

'She's not at all the sort of woman I thought Daniel would marry, but she's been good for him, knocked that effeminacy out of him and they're obviously happy.'

'Perhaps Daniel was never effeminate, he never had a chance with Father, he was always so scathing if we didn't like the things he liked and Daniel was pretty brave to go his own way.'

'He was pretty scathing about your painting Andrew.'

'I know.'

'Do you do any now? I remember how you sat in the garden painting the trees and flower beds, and how you loved to go to Burgundy to paint around the château. Why don't you come to see us on your own and paint some more.'

'One gets out of it, and there are so many other calls on my time now.'

'That painting you did in Burgundy was beautiful, Andrew, even Father had to admit it was better than anything you'd done before.'

'It was the best thing I ever did.'

'Then why did you hide it away?'

'It's in my study, I didn't think it could compare with the old masters and Constance agreed with me.'

'Well, she would, wouldn't she. That painting was good, Andrew. You should have hung it in the drawing room where people could see it. How many people see it in your study?'

'Well I see it. Sometimes I stand and look at it and think how good it was. I wonder why that field of sunflowers was ever abandoned for the growing of turnips and cabbages.'

'Cabbages are food for growing children, Andrew. Come along, show me your picture again, let me see if I still think it's beautiful.'

30

Andrew was still using the study his father had had, a small room carpeted in crimson with long crimson curtains at the windows and furnished simply with a mahogany desk, a large comfortable chair and one or two others of no remarkable craftsmanship. The walls were white and apart from one or two sporting prints the only ornamentation was the picture above the fireplace.

Vivienne stood below it and her immediate thoughts were, why did Andrew ever stop painting when he had this sort of talent. The clumsy elaborate flowers came to life in the painting as they stretched out in a golden pattern towards the softly muted hills. Her eyes shifted to the figure of the girl with her raven hair a halo about her face, her blue dress floating in the breeze.

By the time she had married André, the sunflower field had long gone but where was the girl? She moved closer to the picture and her eyes narrowed. The girl was little more than a child but there was something tantalizingly familiar in the wide-spaced green eyes and the exquisite contours of her face. She was suddenly shaken out of her reverie by Andrew asking, 'Do you still think it's the best thing I ever did?'

'Yes, oh yes I do. Tell me, did you manufacture the girl or did she actually exist?'

'Well of course, I couldn't dream up somebody like that, however much I tried.'

'Where did you meet such a beauty around the fields of Mirandol, and who is she?'

'She was just a girl I found sitting on the grass looking out across the sunflower field. I stared at her for a long time thinking that the field would be nothing without her, but I didn't want to startle her by suggesting that I should paint her.'

'But who was she?'

'A local farmer's daughter. The strange thing was that I met her on the train from Dijon. I was going to the château, she was going home from school for the summer holiday.'

'She was that young?'

'Yes. She talked about her ambitions, she so badly wanted to excel in her studies and I gathered her family were very proud of her, she had ambitions to go to the Sorbonne.'

'And did she?'

'I don't know. I never went back to Mirandol, at least not for many years and I have never seen her again.'

'But in those weeks of summer when she sat for you to paint, how well did your friendship develop, Andrew?'

He laughed. 'I told you she was a schoolgirl, Vivienne.'

'A very beautiful and mature schoolgirl. What was her name?'

'Her name. Gracious, it was all so long ago, I don't think I ever knew her last name.'

'You don't have to tell me her last name, I don't want to know.'

'Her name was Marie Claire.'

He did not see that her hand was clenched tightly against the mantelpiece and that her knuckles were white with the strain.

'Was she very much in love with you, Andrew?'

'What makes you think she was in love with me at all?' he answered defensively.

'Oh Andrew, do you think that I have forgotten what it is like to be sixteen and in love for the first time. Here was an unsophisticated country girl and a mature attractive man, the situation was bristling with desire. You had to be aware of it and it was a challenge most men would have responded to. I was sixteen when I first fell in love with André, believe me I know about the torment, the ecstatic joy and the despair.'

He was remembering now, evident by the expressions that chased themselves across his face. The potency of those long summer days were alive in his memory and she did not need to ask again if they had been lovers in the fields around Mirandol or in that tiny cottage in the midst of the sheltering trees.

'I never went back there,' Andrew said ruefully. 'I came home and you know the rest.'

'But you must have thought of her often, particularly when you look at that picture.'

'Yes of course. I think about her in Paris, happy and successful, but by this time she's married and with a family, indeed I hope so.'

She was remembering all she had heard about Marie Claire, the spite and the scandal, but she had been a survivor and in some strange elusive way she had been determined to make Andrew pay for his desertion.

She sat down weakly on a chair and Andrew stared at her curiously, 'You've gone very pale Vivienne. Is something wrong?'

'Just one of my headaches,' she said. 'I'll go to my room and rest a little before they all come back. I'm sure you have a great many things to do.'

'Sure you're all right?'

'Of course, don't fuss Andrew.'

She was far from all right. She knew now why Chantal Grolan was so like Grace that they could have been sisters, and why she had found in Sebastian a sympathy and understanding rarely found immediately.

In ten days' time Sebastian would be arriving in England, hoping to be reunited with the girl he loved, but Chantal must not be here, she had to be told that Andrew was her father, that she would never be able to marry Sebastian, but the telling was her responsibility and hers alone.

It would also have to be her secret for as long as she lived. Not even André would know why Marie Claire had cultivated her friendship and André's love, and why, in the end, Chantal had to take her place in the same environment as the children born to him by his wife.

She lay on her bed with her thoughts in chaos. How would she tell her, and when? It had to be soon, soon enough for Chantal to make an excuse to leave? Marie Claire had thought to bring only joy into her daughter's life but she had succeeded in bringing great tragedy and despair.

Vivienne slept badly, tossing and turning until the morning light invaded her room and she rose and went to the long windows overlooking the vast parklands. The morning sun was still only a promise in the eastern sky and it was too soon for the deer to retreat into the hills behind the house. She loved Mirandol, she was enchanted by its stone turrets and graceful bridges but the view she was looking at now was one she would remember all her life. It was part of her childhood, part of all the enchanting days of being a Martindale, admired, cosseted and independent, even when that same independence covered a vulnerability whenever André de Mirandol was mentioned.

After breakfast she would talk to Chantal. She would take her into Andrew's study and show her the picture and she would watch the uncertainty and disillusionment give way to defeat.

While the rest of them at a hearty breakfast Vivienne toyed with hers until her brother said, 'Are you sure you are over your bad headache Vivienne, you don't seem to have much of an appetite?'

'I'm saving myself for all the high living that has to come,' she said lightly.

'Heavens yes,' his wife said, 'I don't want to put on weight, it's so hard to get rid of. Mother and I are going over to Aunt Edith's this morning so we won't be in for lunch. We're trying to persuade her not to attend the wedding, after all she is over ninety and needs far too much looking after.'

'Well, I shan't have time to look after her,' Mrs Fallon said meaningly. 'I know she's the only great aunt in the family but there comes a time to be aware of one's limitations I'm sure.'

Andrew merely favoured her with a wry smile, but Grace said quickly, 'I love Great Aunt Edith, Granny, she should be at my wedding.'

'Well, we'll see how she is,' her grandmother said. 'If she's too doddery we have to plead with her to be sensible.'

After breakfast they all went their separate ways, Constance and her mother to Aunt Edith's, Andrew to the office of his estate manager and André and Grace elected to ride after she had seen her fiancé depart for his home in Shropshire. They would not meet again until their wedding day and as she waved him goodbye from the terrace Chantal said gently,

'He's nice, Grace. You must be very happy.'

'Oh yes I am, he is nice and you too must be happy. Sebastian will soon be home.'

Watching them from the drawing-room window Vivienne was hoping Grace had other things to do than chat to Chantal, and was relieved when André left the house to walk to the stables and Grace elected to go with him. Chantal turned towards the house and Vivienne went out of the room to meet her.

'I don't suppose anybody has invited you to look around the place,' she said smiling.

'No, but I'd love to if you have time to show me.'

So they wandered from room to room and through the conservatories. They explored the vast library and the music room and ballroom. They strolled along the corridors looking at pictures and portraits until Vivienne said casually, 'My brother loved painting, he went often to Mirandol when he was young to paint the scenery around the château.'

'Are any of his paintings on the walls here?' Chantal asked curiously.

'Not in this part of the house. My father wasn't at all sure that Andrew had any talent, but he did one very beautiful picture that hangs in his study – of a sunflower field near the château. I'll show you if you like.'

'Oh yes, I'd love to see it. I don't remember any sunflowers near the château. My grandfather had a farm there, but I left when I was very young and we never went back.'

'For some reason or other the sunflowers were never grown again after my brother painted them. Here is the study, see what you think of it.'

The pale morning sunlight illuminated the room, falling on the picture so that it came alive in colours of green and gold, throwing up the figure of the girl in sharp relief. Chantal stood below it, staring up with intense concentration and Vivienne was only aware of the stillness, the illusion that they were on the verge of something momentous, and when at last Chantal turned to face her, she was aware of the pallor of her face and the searching intensity of her gaze.

'Did you know that the girl in the picture was my mother?' she asked in a small voice.

'I suspected it. My brother brought me in here yesterday to look at the picture. I wasn't sure at first, I asked my brother for her name, but this morning I am sure. The girl is your mother?'

'Yes. She never told me about the picture. Did she know your brother very well?'

'I believe so, Chantal. Your mother was sixteen years old when they met. She was on holiday from school and they spent the summer holiday in the fields around the château, he painting his pictures, your mother as his model. He tells me this is the best one, the one he was most proud of.'

'He never went back to Mirandol?'

'Oh yes, many times after he was married to Constance.'

The girl's eyes were filled with questions and already Vivienne was hating her role in it all. Chantal had to be told, there was no future for her in Sebastian's life, and in a voice little above a whisper she said, 'You are very like Grace, Chantal, did nobody every remark on it?'

The girl nodded without speaking, and Vivienne went on 'Hate him if you must, my dear, but I can tell you he never knew about you, like so many men he never thought beyond the moment and your mother never told him.'

'She told me my father was dead.'

'Perhaps she preferred to think of him like that.'

'Why couldn't she just forget about him, why did she have to go on year after year thinking of ways to punish him? She will never be able to do that, I'm the one she has punished, I'm the one she has hurt, and Sebastian? What harm did he ever do her?'

'Chantal, I don't think your mother ever intended you to fall in love with Andrew's son, I simply think she wanted you to be somebody in

265

your own right, on a level with his legitimate children and without any help from him. That it has all backfired is your misfortune, but it was never planned that way, I am sure of it.'

'I can't meet Sebastian now, I have to get away before he comes home, but what shall I tell him, what shall I say to everybody?'

'You could tell him your mother is ill, that you have been recalled home.'

'And he would come looking for me. A man would look for the girl he was in love with, that excuse would never be enough.'

'Then you intend to tell him the truth. Think, Chantal, what the truth would do to him and to his family.'

Chantal stared at her for several minutes before she whispered, 'You're glad about this, because my mother hurt you. You don't really care about me.'

'Of course I care about you. I'll admit that at first I thought your mother had been paid back for what she did to me but not any more. Now I'm ashamed of those thoughts. I am sorry Chantal, but I cannot advise you. If you want to punish your father for what he did all those years ago, the decision lies in your hands, but you have to think that by punishing Andrew you punish Sebastian. What is more important to you, revenge or some other way?'

'Any other way would hurt Sebastian.'

'I know. But he would only be hurt once, by losing you. If you seek revenge, he will be hurt twice, he will lose you and he will blame his father for everything. You have a little time to think about it before he comes home.'

The more Chantal thought about it the more hopeless it seemed. There was only one certainty, she had to leave Blaire before Sebastian came home. Where she went after that was a problem she hardly dared contemplate.

She was not ready to face her mother. On her part there would be anger and accusation and she could not bear to see her mother's face filled with remorse and shame. Where else could she go, and she would need money so it was essential for her to find work. Those girls who had attended Madame Lafayette's school so light-heartedly had never had such a mundane thing as work on their minds and whenever she had discussed a job with her mother, Marie Claire had merely tossed it airily aside. She had been so confident that there would be better things than work in store for her daughter.

She was not looking forward to meeting the family over dinner that evening, but she need not have worried. Aunt Charlotte had arrived during the afternoon and after introducing Chantal as a schoolfriend of Grace's and a friend of Sebastian's, she was left to listen to the con-

266

versation and to Charlotte's distaste for railway travel and the British weather.

'I'm surprised you don't spend more time in London,' Mrs Fallon said tartly, 'those dark lonely lochs always make me feel so miserable, what on earth do you do with your time?'

'I never liked London when my husband was alive and on leave, without a man beside you it is impossible,' Charlotte retorted.

'Well, there is no man beside me and I adore London. I love the theatres and the shops, I love being in the centre of things. I couldn't bear to think I had to live anywhere else.'

Across the table Andrew met his daughter's eyes and smiled. That smile of tenderness was like the twisting of a knife in Chantal's heart.

'Do you spend much time with your daughters?' Andrew enquired politely.

'Well yes. Of course I see Emily frequently since we live within twelve miles of each other. Three times a year I take the night ferry from Stranraer and my son-in-law meets me at the boat but of course I never see Esme. I can't think why she had to marry a Canadian and go off to Ottawa.'

'You could visit,' Andrew suggested with a little smile. 'Ottawa is a most beautiful and civilized city.'

'If they wish to visit me they will be made welcome, I have absolutely no desire to visit them.'

Vivienne was bored by the conversation. She had never particularly liked Charlotte or Constance, and her thoughts now were all on Chantal who sat at the table pale-faced and unhappy. She had toyed with her food throughout dinner and thanks to the conversation from the new arrival it had gone unnoticed by the rest of them.

André too watched Chantal's absorption with the piece of French pastry on her plate and by this time Grace too was curious about her lack of appetite.

'You've hardly eaten anything, Chantal,' she whispered. 'Aren't you feeling well?'

Chantal looked up with a start. 'I have a headache and I'm not very hungry. I hope they won't mind if I go to my room immediately after dinner.'

'Well of course not. Aunt Charlotte does go on a bit and Granny always goads her. They don't get on at all.'

Chantal managed a feeble smile and Grace went on airily, 'We're to have a rehearsal at the church tomorrow, my four bridesmaids are coming here and two of their brothers will stand in for the bridegroom and his best man, both of them are to be ushers with Sebastian when he gets here. Will you be coming to the church, Chantal?'

'I'll see if I feel well enough, but I do have letters to write. Would you mind very much if I didn't come?'

'Of course not. The parents and Granny are coming but I don't suppose either Aunt Vivienne or Uncle André will be there. Just think about it, in a very short time now I shall be a married woman on my way to America.'

'Why did you choose America, Grace?'

'Well it's the ship really. I've never been on anything larger than the steamboat from Dover to Calais and here I shall be sailing on the most wonderful ship ever to have been built. You'll think it's absolutely heavenly to be sailing out to India on the *Empress of India*, but next to the *Titanic* she's like a cockleshell.'

Chantal merely smiled, and Grace said quickly, 'You must get Sebastian to take you on the *Titanic* one day, Chantal. Of course it won't be her maiden voyage but it will be very exciting nevertheless.'

Sitting at the head of the table Andrew felt overwhelmed by women's chatter. André and Vivienne chatted together, completely disinterested in anything the others had to say. Charlotte and his mother-in-law were hardly congenial. Grace was chatting to the French girl who seemed a little pale and had taken no part in the general conversation, but who could blame her. He wondered idly what she thought about the family she expected to join. At that moment Chantal looked across and their eyes locked. He inclined his head courteously, but Chantal's expression did not change but remained aloof and faintly hostile. Disconcerted momentarily Andrew looked away and from the other end of the table he found his sister gazing at him with an expression he could not read.

There were too many undercurrents around the dinner table and Andrew disliked undercurrents. He remembered them from his youth: his father's intolerance and his mother's anxieties, his sister's amusement with the trivialities that had troubled him, but why should he be troubled tonight? In a few days his daughter would marry most advantageously, the man most parents would have wished their daughters might marry. He only had to look into his wife's self-satisfied eyes to know how gratified she was by the events, he supposed the only fly in the ointment was Sebastian's choice of a bride but he had to admit the girl was beautiful and charming. She was also intelligent and with a sophistication that left many other young women of her age standing.

The women were rising to go into the drawing room and he nodded across the table to André to indicate that they should go with them. As they crossed the hall he noticed that Chantal stood chatting to his sister and it was several minutes later when Vivienne came into the drawing room alone.

'Chantal has asked to be excused,' she said addressing him. 'She has a headache and has gone to her room.'

'I noticed she only picked at her dinner,' Mrs Fallon said.

'She won't be coming down again this evening,' Vivienne said before going to sit next to her husband a little away from the others.

André whispered, 'Is everything all right Vivienne?'

'Yes, she is going to write Sebastian a letter and give it to me to hand to him in the morning.'

'So she intends to leave Blaire?'

'Yes. There wasn't much time to talk. We'll talk tomorrow when the others are at the church.'

'What a mess it is,' André complained.

She had not intended to tell André but she had reckoned without his astuteness. Now he gazed down at her with sympathetic anxiety.

'What a mess it is,' he said again, gently.

'Yes. A mess that my brother conveniently forgot and one that you were totally unaware of even when it was all happening within sight and sound of the château.'

André shrugged his shoulders, the habit of her French husband when he was nonplussed.

31

Chantal stood at the window of her room watching a number of motor-cars disappearing along the long drive towards the gates. It was a chill misty morning and minutes before she had seen the group of excited young people come laughing out of the house, followed by their elders all clad warmly against the early morning chill.

She had slept very badly and long into the night had sat at the small ornamental desk in her room composing her note to Sebastian. It would have been easy to be truthful but Sebastian must never know the truth. Consequently she had to lie, or at least make an excuse that would make sure he did not try to find her.

Reading the letter through again, she was aware of its cruelty, but it was a cruelty designed to kill any feeling he might have for her, and any hope that they had a future together.

She had packed her suitcase early and before it was properly light, now all that was needed was to get away quickly before the others returned and after she had spoken to Vivienne.

The older woman was waiting for her in the library, and her face too was pale as though she had lain awake for much of the night. Chantal was disconcerted to see that André was with his wife, standing gazing through the window, turning to acknowledge her presence with a swift smile.

As she handed the sealed envelope to Vivienne her hand trembled and Vivienne said, 'Have you been kind, Chantal?'

'Kindness would not have been appropriate in this instance.'

'But you have not told him the truth?'

'No. I have lied twice, by not telling him the truth and by telling him the wrong reason for my leaving.'

'What reason have you given then?'

'I have told him that I have had second thoughts, that I am not the sort of woman who could ever live as a serving soldier's wife in India.

A British woman could do it, but I am French, I do not have his dedication to India or the British Empire. I have quoted the usual platitudes, that I feel sure he will find a woman more worthy of his love and that I hope he will forget me quickly as I shall try to forget him.'

'You are right Chantal, it is cruel, but suppose he goes to Bordeaux looking for you.'

'I have told him that I am not going home, that I am staying in Paris. Paris is a large city, he will not look for me there.'

By this time André had joined his wife and looking down at Chantal asked, 'And where do you intend to go if you are not going home Chantal?'

'I have to find work. That school in Switzerland gave me polish and sophistication but not perhaps the qualifications that might help me find work.'

He reached inside the breast pocket of his suit and brought out a white envelope.

'I have written this letter to an old friend of mine in Paris Chantal. He has a great pull with a good many expensive fashion houses. When he sees you I am sure he will be convinced that you have a future in that world. My letter is previous but I thought this would be your reaction.'

She took the envelope and stared down at it, then she whispered with a tremble in her voice, 'You are very kind, Monsieur le Vicomte.'

'I wish I could have been more kind Chantal. Now, if you will allow me, I will drive you into Gloucester, so that you can catch the train for London. Have you sufficient money?'

'Yes of course, my mother insisted that it was adequate.'

'You are sure?'

'Yes.'

She did not hold out her hand, nor did she embrace Vivienne de Mirandol. They stood for a moment exchanging a long anguished look, then Chantal crossed to the door which André held open for her. They walked in silence along the corridor leading into the hall where several of the house servants were busy at their household tasks. If they were surprised to see the Vicomte de Mirandol escorting the young Frenchwoman to his car they did not show it.

Conversation was minimal on the drive into Gloucester but when they discovered they had an hour to wait for the train André suggested they went into the buffet to pass the time.

'Thank you for driving me here,' Chantal said. 'I'm sure you would prefer to return to the house.'

'There is no hurry, Chantal, and this is an unhappy time for you. I prefer to remain here until your train arrives,' André said gallantly.

He escorted her to a table at the end of the room and where the tables around them were unoccupied. He brought coffee to the table and two small glasses of brandy, saying with a smile, 'The brandy will warm you up, station platforms are notoriously unwelcoming.'

She was trembling, whether with cold or emotion he could not decide, but after a few minutes he said, 'You will take my letter to my friend in Paris, Chantal. You cannot afford to be too proud and he will give you all the help he can.'

'What can I say if he asks what experience I have had?'

'You will tell him the truth, but Philippe is not a fool, he will see your potential and I have cautioned him to be understanding and careful.'

'Careful?'

'Why yes. It is a great bewildering world out there, Chérie, and you are relatively untried. He will know what I mean when I ask him to be careful. I hope you will write to your mother so that she will know you are well and happy.'

'I don't want my mother to come looking for me in Paris. One day when I have put all this behind me I will be able to look at her without blame, but the time is not yet.'

'Do not make your mother suffer longer than necessary, Chantal. You are blaming her because she did not tell you the truth but allowed you to walk blindly into a situation that has brought you great unhappiness, but be a little charitable. How old are you, twenty, twenty-one, think about your mother who was sixteen, a schoolgirl, little more than a child and desperately in love with a man for the first time in her life, a man who was older, more worldly and sophisticated than the little country girl he found happiness with in the summer sunshine.'

'The happiness he found with my mother did not prevent him marrying somebody else.'

'No. It is unfortunate that that somebody else was a woman he had believed he was in love with for a great many years.'

'You knew he was in love with her?'

'Yes. His father was being difficult, and she had got engaged to somebody else.'

'Why didn't she marry him then?'

André smiled cynically. 'Andrew inherited his brother's title and that persuaded her I think.'

She glared angrily across the table at him. 'It's horrible the way titles matter. It's like a cattle market, it's the same in France, Frenchmen marry for expediency and then they look around for a mistress.'

'So young and so disenchanted. What a pity that you learnt the flippancy of life before you believed in its integrity.'

272

'You never loved my mother,' she accused him.

'You are wrong, Chérie. I did love your mother, she was enchanting and beautiful, but I also loved my wife, I still do. Men, being what they are, are capable of loving a great many women, but only one woman has the power to light a lamp in his soul.'

'And that was not my mother where you were concerned?'

'Alas no.'

'And your wife will no doubt be delighted that the events of these last few days have paid my mother back.'

'When she hands Sebastian your letter, Chantal, there will be no delight in her heart, only a terrible sadness I think.'

Tears filled her beautiful eyes and rolled slowly down her cheeks. André reached out across the table and covered her hand with his and smiling at her gently he said, 'Time to go I think,' and as they passed through the room a great many eyes were trained upon them, and speculation was rife as to why there should be tears in the eyes of a young woman for a man old enough to be her father.

A cold wind tore at the scarf covering her hat, as she stood at the ship's rail on the rough crossing from Dover to Calais. She waited until the lights of England had faded into the darkness and then all around her was the white foam and tossing waves, the creaking noise of a ship being buffeted by the elements, and turning away she returned to the passengers' lounge and the weary acceptance of people anticipating a rough crossing.

She was not short of money but she did not know how long that money had to last until she found work. Consequently she booked into a small Pension where the desk clerk eyed her curiously, thinking it strange for a girl so expensively dressed to be seeking accommodation in so modest an establishment, and all on her own.

While she ate her breakfast consisting of coffee, warm freshly baked baps and black cherry jam she thought about Blaire and the family sitting down to breakfast.

They would be talking about her departure. Grace would no doubt be tearful that anything so terrible for Sebastian should happen just before her wedding, and the rest of the family would undoubtedly feel the utmost relief and try hard not to show it.

It would not dampen their appetites, and as she looked down at her modest breakfast she remembered the side table with its array of china, silver and dishes piled high with eggs and bacon, sausages, and kippers, the sort of breakfast the English loved and missed terribly during their sojourn in foreign parts.

André's friend Philippe's establishment lay in a fashionable part of Paris near the Opera and she approached it with something like fear as she beheld its imposing façade and the big man dressed in uniform standing on the steps under the covered entrance. He showed no surprise at being confronted by a beautifully dressed young woman and was quick to open the heavy doors for her with something like a flourish.

A marble hall lay in front of her leading to a shallow marble staircase edged by a gilt balustrade. She stood for a moment surrounded by a perfumed silence, then taking her courage in both hands she strode towards the staircase and started to ascend it.

At the top lay another hall with several mahogany doors, all of them closed, and while she hesitated as to which one she should enter, one of them opened and a young man came out, immaculately dressed and carrying a leather attaché case. When he smiled at her she asked tentatively, 'I am looking for Monsieur Philippe Grimalde, can you direct me?'

'But of course, the last door in the corridor to your left is his Reception Room.'

She thanked him and made her way across the hall and along the corridor, aware now that she could hear voices behind those closed doors and occasionally the ringing of a telephone.

The room she entered was not large but it was furnished in French period style and behind a white and gold desk sat a young woman who was speaking on the telephone so that Chantal stood in front of the desk looking round her with interest.

She could not but be aware of the girl's telephone conversation spoken in a gentle and faintly condescending voice.

'I'm sorry, Madame, but Monsieur Philippe is engaged all afternoon, it would be advisable to make an appointment.'

For a minute or two there was silence and she could hear the voice at the other end of the telephone arguing noisily while the girl merely smiled and raised her eyebrows in Chantal's direction.

The conversation was inconclusive, the receptionist insisted on an appointment, Madame was annoyed and they both heard the receiver at the other end of the line being replaced with angry firmness.

The receptionist smiled, and Chantal handed the envelope across the desk.

'Monsieur Philippe does not see anybody without an appointment,' the receptionist said after turning the envelope round. 'I can give him your letter and perhaps make an appointment.'

'I would really like to see him this morning if he is available.'

'Is this letter from you?'

'No, it is a letter of introduction from the Vicomte André de Mirandol who I believe is Monsieur Philippe's friend.'

The girl's attitude became rather less condescending.

'Well, it is rather unusual, but I will give Monsieur Philippe your letter. Please sit down and wait.'

Chantal's thoughts were none too happy. Suppose Monsieur Philippe was too busy to see her, suppose he thought his friend should not trespass upon their friendship by sending an unknown woman to see him, suppose he had nothing to offer if he did see her?

The girl returned and sat at her desk with a brief smile, and Chantal continued to wait. She wanted to ask questions but refrained in case she appeared too eager, and after a while the receptionist said, 'Monsieur Philippe has people with him. As soon as they have gone no doubt he will send for you.'

'Thank you,' Chantal said with a smile.

How slowly time passed. From the boulevard below she could hear the rumble of traffic and from somewhere across the hall the sound of doors being opened and closed. After a few minutes there were footsteps outside the room and the door opened to admit a man of considerable presence. He was very tall and slender with silver hair and tanned aquiline features. His eyes were sharp, piercing and assessing, but when he smiled there was so much charm in his smile she found herself immediately responding to it.

He held out his hand and when she placed hers in it he lifted it to his lips and kissed it.

'You will come with me into my office Mademoiselle. My friend André has asked me to help you. First we will talk.'

His office was large and luxuriously appointed and he indicated that she should take the chair opposite his large walnut desk, while he went to sit behind it, eyeing her with a gentle smile, designed to put her at her ease.

He looked again at André's letter, then he said evenly, 'Monsieur le Vicomte tells me you were at school with his niece, a school well known to me in the Bernese Oberland, frequented mainly by the daughters of British aristocrats who never come to me in search of work. He tells me your parents live in Bordeaux but you are anxious to work in Paris, that I can understand. Whilst Bordeaux is very beautiful it is in Paris where life begins. Perhaps you will tell me what you have in mind Mademoiselle?'

'I have no experience Monsieur, but my mother has subsidized me long enough, I need to find work. Monsieur le Vicomte thought you might be able to help.'

'In the world of fashion I presume?'

'I have no idea. I have had a good education and I am not stupid. I do not know anything about your business interest Monsieur.'

'They are many and varied. Stand up, my dear, and take off your hat, let me see your face and the way you walk across the room.'

For a few seconds she stared at him disconcertedly then she obliged by placing her hat on her chair and walking several times across the room.

She was indeed a beautiful girl and she had style and grace, all she needed was the confidence to appear before the discerning eyes of rich, spoilt women discussing her clothes as if the girl they covered was little more than a wax doll.

If they looked at her at all it would be with envy, because they were too old, too fat and too jaded. Did she have the self-assurance to ignore their hard malicious eyes while the younger women handled the material of the clothes she was wearing, oblivious of the girl.

His friend Anton Mordant would like this girl. He designed the most elegant clothes in Paris, for women who could afford to buy only the best, rich elegant women with rich successful men behind them, husbands or lovers.

His models were envied by women and coveted by men, and when they were not modelling they worked as hostesses to visiting ambassadors and aristocrats from many lands.

A few of the girls had married the men who escorted them, others had been content to be their mistresses and made sure that while the liaison lasted they were adequately repaid with jewels and money. What sort of girl was the one who stood looking at him with doubtful anxiety in her dark blue eyes?

'I have a friend, Mademoiselle, Anton Mordant, ah I can see that you have heard of him.'

'Yes, I thought everybody in France knew of Monsieur Mordant.'

'Some of your English friends were his clients perhaps?'

'Yes, as well as their relatives.'

'Of course. I will take you to meet him, I can only tell you that you are the sort of girl he likes from what I have seen of his other models. I can tell you now that it will not all be glamour, there will be long hours of hard work, standing around until you feel you cannot stand another moment, believe me it is not all the glamour of wearing exquisite gowns, the perfumed interior of the salons, but if you are what Anton is looking for would you be willing to work for him.'

'Yes, oh yes, I would love to work for him.'

Her smile was so warm, her anticipation so enthralled he decided to say no more about the dedication she would need, that was something she would have to discover for herself.

With a smile he said, 'We will have lunch, Mademoiselle, and you shall tell me more about events that has brought you to Paris, and how well you know Monsieur le Vicomte.'

276

Throughout their interview he had speculated on why his friend André de Mirandol should be taking such a keen interest in Chantal Grolan. The girl was beautiful and polished, she had a sophistication beyond her years, put there no doubt by that expensive finishing school and perhaps an ambitious mother.

André was partial to a pretty face in spite of the fact that he was married to a beautiful woman with whom he was still in love. This girl had the potential to marry well, of course she was very young, but if she learned quickly there was no end to the possibilities.

Over lunch he entertained her with stories of the world of fashion, the men who designed, the girls who modelled and the clientèle who came to buy.

When he deposited her later in the afternoon at her hotel she realized that she had learned very little about Philippe Grimalde, the man.

It was unimportant. Tomorrow he would take her to meet Anton Mordant and she would do her best. All night she practised walking about the room with a book on her head, keeping her balance, smiling into the mirror. She draped chiffon scarves around her neck and trailed them along the floor, she gracefully divested herself of coats and hats and stood poised with an aloof smile on her face as she had seen models performing in less salubrious salons than Monsieur Mordant's.

She was excited about the days ahead, but not too excited that she did not remember that the day after tomorrow would be Grace's wedding. She spared a thought for the activities she thought would be going on at Blaire and for those she had known there.

Would Sebastian be devastated, or would he be hating her for what she had done? Would they be consoling him by telling him that he had a lucky escape, that Chantal Grolan was hardly the wife who would have helped further his career in the Indian Army, and that he should now look around for an English wife who would know what a serving officer's life was all about.

She stood at the side of the room for what seemed an eternity the next morning while all around her there was activity. Anton Mordant rushed about with a worried air while beside her Philippe merely smiled at the beautiful models, most of them in a state of undress.

'Is it always like this?' Chantal whispered.

'Not always Mademoiselle, but in three days he opens his latest fashions and it is essential that everything is perfect. He knows we are here. This morning he is putting on a performance for our benefit.'

Indeed it was much later when Anton Mordant joined them, looking Chantal over with a practised eye, entirely charming, wholly theatrical so that she began to feel like an exhibit in a glass case. At last he said with a beaming smile, 'Ah yes but you are enchanting Mademoiselle, you know how to dress, how to smile. You will learn how to look bored and supercilious, it seems that is expected of my girls, it is my gowns that make them and my gowns that will make you, never forget it Mademoiselle. Where are you living in Paris?'

'I have a small Pension on the left bank.'

'You will need a better address than that if you are working for me. You have an income apart from what I shall pay you I suppose?'

'No Monsieur, I have not.'

'Then we shall have to think of something. In the morning I shall decide where you will live and if you are suitable without training for my show.'

With a careless pat on her arm it seemed the interview was over and looking up at Philippe in some dismay Chantal asked, 'Is that all, am I to stay here or are we free to leave?'

'He will see you in the morning, but if I were you I would stay here for a while, get the feel of the place, the activity, meet some of the girls and Madame.'

'Madame?'

'Madame who looks after his models, oils the wheels of his exhibitions and sees that all aspects of his Salon run smoothly. She is something of a martinet but she is efficient. Do your best, play your part and I think you will find she is fair and might well be a good friend to you.'

'I will try, Monsieur Grimalde. I am very grateful for the help you have been able to give me.'

He smiled, raised her hand to his lips and with a little bow said, 'I shall watch your career with interest Mademoiselle, au revoir.'

She watched him go with something akin to dismay. He had played his part as André had asked him to do and now she was alone without her mother or any of her friends in a city she hardly knew. It was a daunting prospect but she would not let it defeat her.

32

It was Madame who set out the details of her employment at the Salon, Madame who set about assessing her suitability by having her walk endlessly across the room, instructing her to pose when requested, and, if she was dissatisfied, thought nothing of moving her legs and arms, her head and shoulders until she got the desired effect.

It was Madame who instructed that she be draped with different materials to assess the colours that suited her best, the hats that most became her and the sort of heels on her shoes, and Madame who introduced her to Celeste with a view to their sharing an apartment.

By mid-afternoon she was so weary she felt she could not walk another step or adopt another pose, and Celeste smiled when she finally flopped down on the nearest available chair, accepting the cup of tea she proffered gratefully.

'You are lucky that I have room for you in my apartment,' she said. 'Bernice left when she married her Arabian sheik.'

'Shall I be able to afford it?' Chantal asked doubtfully.

'It is important we have a good address. We get an allowance from the Salon and most of us get subsidized.'

'Subsidized?'

'Why yes. We are entertained and we entertain, but don't worry, most of the men merely wish to be seen with a presentable girl. They do not regard us as anything less than upper-class models whom Monsieur Mordant is kind enough to loan out on social occasions. Play your cards right and you could be invited to embassy dinners, the theatre and any other social occasion. If you have any trouble with any of the men, you will tell Madame and you will not be expected to see him again.'

'Will I be able to move into your apartment this evening?'

'Of course. Collect your things from the Pension and here is my address. It is a pleasant boulevard only a little distance from here, I shall expect you later.'

She had scribbled the address on a small piece of paper and Chantal thanked her warmly before putting it into her purse.

She sat drinking her tea while Celeste sauntered away to join a group of girls chatting on the other side of the room.

They were all very much of a pattern these girls, tall, wasp-waisted and cool patrician faces expertly made up and catching sight of herself in a mirror opposite she could well believe that she would soon begin to look like them.

There was something slightly different about Celeste. It was the golden tinge of her complexion, her dark slanting eyes and the full provocative mouth that made her feel she might not be entirely French. Later that evening she was to learn that her father had been a Tunisian sailor who had left her mother when Celeste was only six years old to return to this native land.

Celeste told her story without bitterness. She spoke of remembered poverty and hardship in a city where she was little more than a street urchin and Chantal found that the humour in her story was more touching that the harshness of her childhood.

'You don't need to feel sorry for me,' Celeste said with a smile. 'It made me strong, like a tiger when there is something to fight for. I don't suppose you can understand any of this, your childhood was privileged.'

'One day I will tell you about my childhood,' Chantal said briefly.

Celeste raised her eyebrows. 'So, there is something to tell. I wonder how long you will stay here? I have lost four room-mates, they have all left to marry, men they have met working for the salon.'

'What kind of men were they?'

'One an Arabian sheik. Remarkably handsome but who knows if it will last. Different culture, different ideals. He will probably have other wives. Two of them married Russian diplomats and one married an American. I rather think only the last one will survive.'

'Isn't that rather cynical?'

'Yes of course. You will come to understand the need for cynicism Chantal. Have you friends in Paris?'

'No, none.'

'Where is your home?'

'My mother lives in Bordeaux with my stepfather, the rest of my family live in Burgundy.'

'But you must have friends of your own age?'

'I have friends in England, girls I was at school with. One of them is getting married tomorrow.'

'Why aren't you going to her wedding?'

'Like I said, one day I will tell you so much more. They are sailing to America on the *Titanic* for their honeymoon.'

'How strange, Martine and her American are going home on the *Titanic*. That is one voyage I would love to be taking. You will be thinking of your friend tomorrow.'

'Yes. I do hope it is a beautiful day and that they will be very happy.'

It was the first thing she thought of when she awoke the next morning, and as they walked the short distance to the Salon, she was delighted that the sun was shining and that there was the feeling of spring on the city streets. At the corner of the boulevard there were barrows piled high with masses of flowers and there were even people braving the early spring sunshine to sit at the pavement carés.

For the first time since she had left England she felt happy. She revelled in the feel of Paris, the trees sprouting into new life, the elegance and zest of those she encountered on the street and she was also aware that passers-by and those sitting at their tables eyed them appreciatively, two beautiful girls on an April morning, in love with life and all it had to offer.

The girls treated their new fashionable clothes with blasé unconcern, they had seen it all before, they were gowns for other women to buy and it was their job to persuade and cajole those women by their professionalism.

As Chantal stood immovable as a statue while designers draped rolls of material around her and started to cut with dedicated skill, Grace was walking down the aisle of Gloucester cathedral on the arms of her father.

The great church was crowded with aristocrats, powerful political figures and lesser members of the Royal family. Behind Grace and her father walked two satin-glad pageboys and four bridesmaids, the daughters of elevated families Grace had known for most of her life.

Those present were generous in their thoughts, the beauty of the bride, the elegance of her mother and the gratification of her grandmother. If they found any flaw at all it was in the bleak expression on the face of the bride's brother and several of those present had already remarked on the absence of the French girl he had wanted to marry.

Sebastian had read Chantal's note with disbelief, remembering the happiness they had shared in those few days they had spent together. He could not believe that that warm generous girl had penned those cold final words before going out of his life for ever.

His aunt had been kind, explaining that Chantal had left with tears in her eyes and regret in her heart, but nothing she had said had rung true. Now all he wanted was for this charade to be over so that he could return to India and hopefully forget her.

That his family had been relieved by her action he had little doubt, particularly his grandmother who had thought it a most unsuitable match and had repeatedly said so.

Later in the day he stood with a crowd of people in the gardens of Blaire waiting for Grace and her husband to join them. Their car was waiting to take them to Salisbury for the first night of their honeymoon and then in the morning to Southampton where they would board the *Titanic* for her maiden voyage.

Grace threw her arms around her brother's neck whispering softly, 'She really did love you Sebastian, she just didn't think it would work. One has to admire her honesty.'

Sebastian wished his sister happiness but refrained from commenting. He stood in miserable contemplation while the rest of them surged around her car, their good wishes ringing in his ears.

Andrew stood with his wife waving his daughter and her new husband goodbye. He would miss her, she had always been his girl, always kind, always sunny, but it was his son's misery that disturbed him now. Could they have done more to make Chantal welcome, or had they by their apathy made her feel unacceptable?'

He looked at his mother-in-law's face, filled with gratification that there was now a duchess in the family and a feeling of distaste swept over him. Watching him from across the terrace his sister read accurately the thoughts in his mind.

At that moment she longed to tell him it was all his fault, all the long years of worthlessness Marie Claire had faced, her desire that her daughter should have the same advantages as his legitimate children.

In Bordeaux Marie Claire read her daughter's letter yet again, her expression sombre. The letter simply told her that she was living in Paris, that she had found a job in which she was very happy and that she had also found friends in Paris and somewhere to live. She said she did not want her mother to look for her and she gave no address: that was the point that hurt Marie Claire the most, but she did say that she would write again when she had any news.

What had happened to make her leave England where she was accepted by the people Marie Claire had wanted her to cultivate? Where were her old friends in all this and what sort of work was she doing? Chantal had not been educated for work, she had been educated to marry well, some rich nobleman, preferably an Englishman.

Henri was little comfort to her. He believed she worried too much about her daughter who was old enough to know what she wanted. Paris would be good for Chantal, she would meet interesting people and have an interesting future.

'How do we know that?' Marie Claire had persisted. 'We don't know what she's doing. Paris is filled with dissolute people who prey on young innocent women. She might at least have told me what sort of work she is doing and where?'

'Give her time, Chérie, no doubt she will in her next letter.'

The French papers were filled with news of the new liner which had set sail from Southampton. She was photographed in all her glory sailing majestically down the Solent surrounded by an armada of small tugs and other vessels. There were flags waving and bands playing and her decks were crowded with people waiving enthusiastically to those below, the whole scene one of joyful anticipation.

Chantal thought about Grace and her new husband, in love, and enjoying themselves, looking forward with enthusiasm to their first visit to the new world.

As she walked with Celeste along the city streets on their way to the Salon on an April morning bright with the promise of spring they were surprised to find groups of people standing at street corners anxiously scanning newspapers or sitting at tables shaking their heads in disbelief at something they had just read.

Concerned Chantal whispered, 'Something is wrong Chantal, I can smell it, disbelief, fear, I don't know, but something dreadful has happened.' She hurried over to one of the tables where three men sat gazing at their newspapers.

'What has happened?' she asked.

They looked up at her with stunned incredulity. 'It is the *Titanic* Mademoiselle, she has sunk during the night. Not much is known, it is too soon. Later we shall all know.'

'Celeste and Chantal stared at each other in horror. All Chantal's thoughts in that first moment were for Grace and her husband, then she thought about those happy people setting sail in a moment of history and pride in the sailing of a ship they had proudly proclaimed to be unsinkable.

All day news was coming in, at first garbled and unsure until later the true extent of the tragedy was known.

They were encouraged that the ship had not sunk but was being towed into New York with no lives lost, but then came the real version, that four days out on her maiden voyage the *Titanic* had struck an iceberg on a cold clear night with a sea as calm as glass.

The great ship had struck the iceberg at twenty minutes to twelve on a night ablaze with stars, a night of incredible clarity and at twenty minutes after two on that April night the *Titanic* sank.

Lists of survivors were appearing, stories of heroism and tragedies: children torn from their parents' arms, lovers separated, husbands and

283

wives who had spent many years together separated for ever, and through it all the simple acceptance that nothing more could have been done. The great ship sank and the band played on.

Neither Grace nor her duke appeared in the list of survivors nor did the name of Martine and her American husband. Four young people in love had embarked on what they believed to be a lifetime together. In England questions were being asked in high places when entire families had either been wiped out or were mourning those members who had. And in America too those people who had been waiting for her arrival in happy expectation of greeting friends and relatives who were sailing on her waited in vain.

In Bordeaux Marie Claire stared down at the newspaper before her. It was full of news of the *Titanic*. As her eyes ran down the list of those who had perished she read an item about a couple of their honeymoon. The bride had been Grace Martindale, daughter of the Earl of Westmond. Neither she nor her husband had survived. Her father must be Andrew! She wept for him. There had been so many times when she had told herself that she hated him, so many times when she asked God to punish him, but not like this, never like this.

Chantal's memories were more recent and she thought miserably of them sitting around the dinner table on that last night she had spent with them. A normal English family with a wedding to look forward to, Mrs Fallon's satisfaction and Charlotte's irritation with her, Andrew's pride when he looked at his daughter and Vivienne's eyes tinged with sadness when they met her own.

In spite of everything she could for the first time think of Andrew as her father and she ached for the sadness he was feeling, and for the first time since she left Blaire she felt the need to see her mother.

She was still hurting, still blaming her mother for not telling her the truth, still agonizing over what she had done to Sebastian but she was remembering André de Mirandol's words to her before she boarded the train for London.

Now she could weep over the young Marie Claire with her dreams lying shattered behind her and her future a bleak and barren waste. She could respect her courage and resolve that life would not defeat her, and she had used whatever stepping stones she had been able to find to ensure her survival and Chantal's future.

As the weeks passed she longed for a few days when she might go home to Bordeaux but there was always something more pressing at the Salon. She was coming into her own. Her face was on the pages of fashionable journals and magazines and as she posed trailing expensive furs behind her, she was well aware of the admiration of the men who accompanied their expensively clad female companions. As she stood poised before them she knew how to tilt her head, how to use her eyes, and read the desire in theirs.

It was Madame who informed her that Monsieur Mordant wished to see her one afternoon in his office, advising her to be punctual and looking her best.

Celeste smiled when she informed her over lunch, saying, 'What do you suppose he wants, I hope I haven't given him reason to find fault with me?'

Celeste smiled. 'Well of course not, if that were the case Madame would not have been so charming.'

When she still looked doubtful Celeste said, 'It is probably some visiting dignitary to the city, some man he wishes you to entertain for the evening.'

Chantal looked at her anxiously and with a smile Celeste said, 'Don't worry, Monsieur Mordant requires the utmost respect for his models from the men he allows to escort them.'

Anton Mordant eyed his newest recruit. He was delighted with her, she was beautiful and graceful and she had worked hard and learned well. Even Madame, who was if anything more critical than himself as a woman assessing other women, had had nothing but praise for Chantal Grolan.

Even in her own clothes, ready for the walk home, she had an air of sophistication and breeding that other women might envy.

He smiled. 'Sit down Mademoiselle, there in the light so that I can look at you. Are you happy with us, is it all you expected it to be?'

'Yes Monsieur, I am enjoying the work.'

'Even that behind the scenes which is far from glamorous?'

'Even that.'

'We had a very distinguished lady at the fashion show the day before yesterday, perhaps you saw her?'

'I thought all Monsieur's clients were distinguished, I was not aware of a special one.'

Not displeased with her comment he smiled. 'This lady is the Grand Duchess Maria Petrova, the widow of Grand Duke Igor, a cousin of the Tsar. She is now living in Paris since her husband died and has been a client of mine for some years. Her brother Count Sergei Drovski is visiting Paris for several days next week as an ambassador from the Imperial Russian Court and as it is his first visit to Paris she is wishing to entertain him well. She has asked if you will allow him to escort you during his visit. Count Drovski has spent some time at the Russian Embassy in London, so you can tell him of your sightseeing there. I will speak to you nearer the time and perform the necessary introductions.'

'Shall I have the clothes necessary for the grand occasion, Monsieur?'

'We will see that you have, and the furs as well as the jewels. Count Drovski will have no occasion to complain that his companion was inadequate.'

Later in the evening when she told Celeste about her interview with Anton, Celeste said, 'I have seen the Grand Duchess here, she spends a great deal of money on clothes and furs and she is very much the grande dame. She entertains members of the Tsar's family here in Paris whenever they visit France, it could be quite an experience for you.'

'You remind me of my mother,' Chantal said with a little smile.

'Your mother!'

'Yes. My mother's family had no money, all my mother had was her beauty and her brains and she made them work for her, you have done the same Celeste. You have come an awfully long way from that little street urchin you said you were.'

Celeste laughed. 'Well of course, one either sinks or swims, I was determined to swim.'

The summons came for Chantal several days later and as she knocked at the door of his office she was aware of voices from inside the room and a woman's laughter.

There were three people in the office with Anton Mordant. A woman seated next to Anton's desk and another woman standing behind her, as well as a middle-aged gentleman standing near the window. Anton performed the introductions and she curtsied as she had been told to do by Madame.

The Grand Duchess was a middle-aged woman with a beautiful patrician face. She wore a dark-blue hat decorated with osprey feathers on her silver hair, and over her dark-blue dress was draped a dark sable stole.

Her companion was introduced as Baroness Marinskaya, the grand duchess's lady-in-waiting.

The gentleman then came forward to click his heels and bow, then after introducing him as Count Drovski he politely raised her hand to his lips.

Chantal judged him to be a man in his middle forties, tall and distinguished with sculptured dark hair greying at the temples and a neat imperial beard. He was wearing a formal lounge suite and murmured the conventional greeting of 'Enchanté, Mademoiselle'.

'Tonight, we are going to the Opera for a performance of *La Belle Hélène*', the Grand Duchess said. 'And the next evening to a concert at Versailles in aid of some charity the Tzar has set his heart on. We would like you to accompany us to both these events.' She smiled, looking at Chantal and demanding an answer.

'Thank you, your Highness, I shall be happy to.'

'The concert is one I am particularly looking forward to. Dieter Steinberg is a great favourite of mine, he will be playing Rachmaninov, Borodin and Rimsky-Korsakov, I hope you like Russian music Mademoiselle.'

'Yes indeed.'

'That is good then. A car will call for you at your home at precisely seven o'clock, it will bring you to my house, where there will be dinner before the performance.

Chantal curtsied, the man bowed and the two women swept out of the room with brief smiles.

Chantal looked at Anton who smiled and appeared well pleased with the events of the afternoon.

33

Anton himself chose her gown and her furs as well as the jewels she would wear on the night of the Grand Duchess's dinner.

The gown was heavy cream satin. 'Virginal,' Anton twittered as he circled round her where she stood in the centre of the room surrounded by the rest of them.

The long heavy folds of the skirt swept from a narrow waist. There was no ornamentation on the gown, and the low neckline showed off her throat and edged her shoulders.

Anton stood back to view the finished result, saying finally to Madame. 'The gown is right but she should have jewels, diamonds I think, or pearls. No pearls are too bland, diamonds will sparkle, has the jeweller arrived?'

'Yes, he is waiting in your office.'

'Then he must come in here and we will see what he has brought with him.'

Two armed gendarmes came in with the jeweller, a short plump man beaming geniality and anxious to open his box for inspection. It was Anton who selected the jewellery. A tiara flashing with diamonds but not too ostentatious as to vie with anything her hostess might be wearing. A diamond necklace and long diamond earrings, then still not satisfied Anton said, 'Yes yes, it is good, but there should be something else. Bring me the fan, that is what is missing.'

An assistant brought a flowing ostrich feather fan and Chantal was instructed to hold it fully opened against her gown. Satisfied at last Anton beamed. 'Perfect,' he said. 'Her Highness will be enchanted and so will her company. Now I will leave you in the hands of Madame so that she can instruct you on what will be expected of you.'

Bemused by the morning's events Chantal looked at Madame doubtfully, and quick to reassure her Madame said, 'You will need less instruction than a great many of the girls we have prepared for similar engagements. You have received an excellent education and mixed with aristocrats, not Russian perhaps, but they are much the same everywhere.

'You will speak only when you are spoken to. You will not offer your opinions on anything unless they are asked for and you will smile and be charming, a fitting escort for the Count. You have nothing to worry about, the Grand Duchess is very charming and extremely gracious, the people she invites to her house are certain to be similar. Do you have any questions Mademoiselle?'

'It would seem my education is irrelevant, Madame, if I am not expected to have opinions or enter into their conversation.'

Madame frowned. 'It will no doubt come in useful if you are invited to participate,' she said shortly. 'Now take off your finery and your jewels and Marie will pack them carefully for you to take home. A taxi has been ordered and I suggest you rest a little this afternoon so that you will be ready for this evening.'

The evening ahead was not worrying her so much as the one the following day at Versailles when Dieter would be performing. Seeing her in such exalted company would convince him she felt sure that she had taken the long downward path to perdition. Somehow or other she had to convince him that it was not so.

The Grand Duchess expressed her approval of her appearance and the Count bowed over her hand with the utmost admiration in his expression.

Chantal smiled, and as introductions were performed to a great many guests she began to think that her smile was permanently fixed. For the large part of the dinner little was addressed directly to her, so that by the end of the meal she felt isolated, until the Count said, 'How bored you must be by all this Mademoiselle, please understand that most of these people are rather self centred.

'I understand Count Drovski.'

'And you will forgive our discourtesy?'

'Of course.'

He smiled, and for the rest of the meal she listened to the hum of conversation and speculated about the man sitting beside her. If he were married, where he lived, what were his interests. It seemed so strange to be a companion to somebody she knew so little about.

He was most presentable in his formal evening dress with the dark blue ribbon with its gold ornamentation across his chest. Several of the men were wearing similar orders in different colours as well as several of the women.

She was the youngest person sitting at the huge dining table sparkling with silver and crystal and she realized that they were accepting her for what she was, Count Drovski's companion for the evening, and not a woman he knew well.

The rest of the evening passed in something of a haze. When they reached the opera house they were shown immediately into their box and she was aware of countless eyes turned upon them. Only eight of them had gone to the opera and, leaning forward, the Grand Duchess said with a smile, 'You will enjoy this part of the evening far better than what has gone before Mademoiselle. You have been very patient with us.'

Chantal smiled, and besides her Count Drovski helped her to remove her ermine cape with the utmost courtesy.

The performance enchanted her and for the first time that evening she felt she could relax and absorb the beauty of the singing, the lilt of the music and the glamour of the occasion.

Count Drovski accompanied her in the car taking her back to her apartment, sitting in the back beside her in the dark anonymity of the car he remained silently aloof while she could enjoy the enchantment of Paris under a moonlit sky. On arrival, the chauffeur opened the car door, and Count Drovski walked with her to her door, kissing her hand and thanking her for her company. Then with a smile he said, 'I look forward to tomorrow Mademoiselle.'

Celeste was waiting up for her and later as they sat over cups of steaming coffee Chantal told her about the evening she had spent with the Russian Count.

'It seemed so awful to be sitting there like a doll while there were so many things I wanted to ask, about Russia, about his life, about why they were here in Paris. All night they only spoke to each other about people I don't know, it was such a relief to go to the Opera.'

'Don't I know it. I've been on so many evenings like that, at the end of them I used to wonder why my escort needed a companion. Monsieur Anton has sorted out what you will wear at Versaille, nothing quite so virginal, a little more exotic I understand.'

Chantal's heart sank. A Russian Count and something exotic, that was all she needed to convince Dieter that she was no better than she should be. There was no doubt about it she had to find him and talk to him soon, he should not be allowed to form conclusions that didn't exist.

In the event she loved the gown Anton had chosen for her. Dark blue satin and sapphires, sable and gardenias. As they drove from Paris to Versailles, Count Drovski murmured. 'You look enchanting Mademoiselle, there will be no more beautiful woman at the Palace of Versailles, I am indeed fortunate to have so enchanting a companion.'

It seemed the Grand Duchess knew everybody. Foreign dignitaries from many countries, royalty and ambassadors, and Chantal walked behind her aware of their smiles of admiration and curiosity.

They sat in a beautiful ornate room on gilt chairs and sofas and on the dais in front of them stood a concert grand piano and Chantal was wishing they were sitting somewhere not quite so prominent.

There was enthusiastic applause for Dieter as he came forward to bow before his audience, looking remarkably handsome. His eyes swept briefly over his audience, pausing only momentarily in Chantal's direction, then with another smile he went to take his seat at the piano.

How beautifully he played. How could that talent ever have been wasted on a bevy of schoolgirls and how disheartened he must have felt at their inadequate performances and giggling incompetence.

As the Russian melodies washed over her she found herself remembering that tiny room of Dieter's overlooking the snow-capped peaks with its old shabby piano. She had so desperately wanted him to make love to her but he had been too wise, too adult, too concerned with his future and a determination that nothing and nobody should interfere with it.

A feeling of deep shame washed over her. Was that how her mother had behaved with Andrew? But Andrew had not had a future to think of, his future had already been assured, he had simply loved her mother for the few weeks it had lasted then gone on his way.

She was brought out of her reverie by the applause around her and Dieter was bowing on the platform and they were moving into another room for refreshments before the second half of his performance.

She looked at him across the room where he stood chatting to a group of people, charming and smiling before he moved on to other groups all eager to speak to him and praise his performance.

Beside her the Grand Duchess was saying, 'I must speak to Herr Steinberg. I believe he is returning to Vienna in a few days to perform before the Emperor.'

He was there at last, she was graciously introduced by the Grand Duchess as 'Mademoiselle Grolan my brother's companion'.

Dieter smiled, he bowed without taking her hand, and she was sickeningly aware of the desperate fluttering of her heart and that he would notice her anxiety.

She listened to the conversation between Dieter and the Grand Duchess, and only once Dieter said, 'Are you enjoying the music, Mademoiselle?'

'Very much. I have always enjoyed your music, Herr Dieter,' she replied and was rewarded by seeing his eyes kindle with a strange amusement.

The second half of the performance was as wonderful as the first.

Chantal knew that she would never hear Rachmaninov's melodies played without the ache of tears in her eyes and the shadows of regret in her heart.

She was glad of the drive into Paris at the end of the evening, and as Count Drovski bowed over her hand on parting he said gallantly, 'Thank you Mademoiselle for your charming companionship, be kind enough to accept this small token in recognition of my gratitude.'

She stared down at the velvet box he had placed in her hands, but already he was walking back to the car, and without another word had entered it and was being driven away.

She looked down at the box curiously, bemused that the Count should have felt he needed to present her with a gift at all. Letting herself into the apartment she ran swiftly upstairs. Celeste would no doubt be in bed by this time unless she was embarked on a similar assignation but the room was in darkness and there was no sound except the distant sound of traffic from the street below.

She went into her bedroom and hurried to light the gas lamp above the mantelpiece, then curiously she opened the velvet box and gasped with delight at the sheen of jewels in the bracelet nesting against the satin lining. It was a beautiful thing composed of gold and glittering with diamonds and even when she admired it she wished he had not given it to her. She did not want a reward of this nature. Men gave such things to their mistresses for services rendered, she did not know if she would ever meet Count Drovski again but she hoped he would not think his gift guaranteed more than she was prepared to give.

She had liked him. He had been charming and courteous, but all the things she had learned from her mother came to worry her. Her mother's rise to prominence in Dijon with her marriage to Maurice, then there had been André and always the long lectures on the cultivation of the British nobility.

She was about to put the box in her drawer when the door opened and Celeste stood in the doorway fully dressed and smiling at the box in her hands.

'A parting gift,' she said. 'Let me see it.'

Chantal stared down at the bracelet, curving it over her wrist and holding out her arm so that it sparkled and gleamed in the gaslight.

'I shouldn't tell Madame about this Chantal. She'll think she had more right to it than you. I've got very wise to her over the years, I only tell her what I want her to know.'

'Do most of the men give presents to the girls?'

'Some. Men like your Russian Count perhaps. If Madame asks if he has given you anything say, 'Of course not, why should he, wasn't the opera and the concert at Versailles enough.'

'But she could ask the Grand Duchess. I don't want to lie to her.'

'I doubt if your Count has informed the Grand Duchess, and besides she's hardly likely to discuss it with Madame.'

'I didn't want a gift, I wish he hadn't given it to me.'

'Don't be silly. It is gifts like this that make us independent, help us to be somebody, without these we are simply mannequins destined to wear clothes only other women can afford to buy, and these clothes of yours that you have worn for the last two evenings will go back tomorrow, and hopefully Monsieur Anton will be approached during the next few weeks by a great many of the women who saw you in them asking for something similar.'

'But they didn't know who I was, where I came from. The Grand Duchess merely introduced me as her brother's companion.'

'But Monsieur Anton will have very discreetly spread it around that you are one of his models. He obliged the Grand Duchess and her brother, but always with an eye on the main chance. Believe what your friend Celeste is telling you, Chantal, and you will not go far wrong.'

For the first time she noticed that Celeste was wearing her street clothes, casual and somewhat unfashionable, and curiously she asked, 'Where have you been Celeste? It's very late but you're hardly dressed for the grand occasion?'

Celeste laughed. 'No, Chérie, now and again I feel the urge to go back to my roots, the back streets of Paris, the seedy cafés and brothels. I know people there, I can still talk to them, laugh with them, suffer with them. They are my roots Chantal, I'll never truly escape from them. What are your roots I wonder, the ones you will always remember?'

Chantal smiled wryly but didn't answer and after shrugging her shoulders Celeste left her alone.

For a long time she sat up in bed hugging her knees, but her thoughts were not on Count Drovski or the luxurious surroundings of the last two evenings.

She was thinking about her roots, remembering the farm near Dijon and the long empty hours when she had waited at the country station for her mother to step off the train. It seemed to Chantal that whenever she had felt she had put down roots her mother had come along to dig them up.

She had loved the convent, felt a sense of security within its ancient walls but her mother had taken her away to send her to Switzerland and those two years had been transient and unfulfilled.

It had always been her mother's life that had affected her own, her marriage to Maurice, her affair with André and now her marriage to Henri and removal to Bordeaux. For the first time in her life she was standing on her own two feet without her mother waiting in the wings to tell her they were moving on.

She loved her mother, she thought she was the most beautiful human being in her life, but she could never go back to live in her shadow, whatever the future had in store, she had to face it alone.

A cab arrived in the morning to take the two girls and Chantal's borrowed clothes back to the Salon, and almost before she had taken off her outdoor clothing Madame was there asking if everything had gone according to plan during the evenings with the Count.

'Yes, thank you Madame,' she answered truthfully.

'I hope he has shown his gratitude adequately Mademoiselle,' she said pointedly.

'Oh yes Madame, he thanked me most graciously for my companionship. I found him very kind, after all there was little for me to do except look pretty and fashionable.'

She was aware of Madame's hard cold stare which she met with all the innocence she could muster.

'Bravo,' Celeste hissed.

All morning she was aware of Madame's eyes on her, and it was only when Anton came into the salon and said, 'The Grand Duchess has thanked me for your performance with her guests Mademoiselle. I have no doubt that she will wish you to accompany her brother whenever he is in Paris again.'

Chantal merely smiled, and Madame said testily, 'One would have expected a little present Monsieur, from either the Grand Duchess or the Count.'

'Perhaps next time,' Anton said absently. 'After all, it was only two evenings, very memorable evenings according to Her Highness. She is a great admirer of Herr Steinberg.'

His words reminded her forcibly that she had to find Dieter before he left for Vienna. She did not owe him an explanation, but she had to dispel any thoughts in his mind that she was little more than a courtesan. That she was still the schoolgirl who had adored him even if he was the darling of music lovers the world over.

Where was Dieter living in Paris and where did he spend his time? He was not a lover of large ornate hotels, so probably had found a smaller less pretentious establishment, but he could be anywhere. Paris was a large city. He could spend Sunday sailing along the Seine as many Parisians did, he could visit the Louvre or the cathedral, there were so many places, too many places, but she had once heard him say that he loved Paris from the steps of the Sacré-Coeur and the narrow streets of Monmartre where he could watch the artists and see the life that strolled and loitered there.

294

Tomorrow was Sunday, she would go to church and visit Montmartre, if she did not find him there what else could she do?'

Spring in Paris, how magical the phrase! How magical the fact, and Paris in May when blossoms weighed down every tree and the sun shone out of a sky as blue and cloudless as an Alpine lake. People were in holiday mood, smiling and glorying in the warmth of the sun and the camaraderie in pavement cafés and along the boulevards.

After the morning service in the great white church on its hill overlooking the city she stood for a while at the top of the steps looking out across the panorama of domes and steeples, at the river winding its way under bridges of exquisite symmetry in a city that seemed made for lovers.

At last she turned and made her way towards the maze of streets that was Montmartre. In the squares artists were already at their easels but she spared them only a cursory glance as her eyes scanned the distant pavements and different groups of people.

For what seemed an eternity she wandered along the pavements where smiling men touched their hats and women stared at her curiously and the longer she wandered the deeper her heart sank. It was mid-afternoon and there had been no sign of Dieter. A small fourpiece band had set up their music stands in one of the squares, and they were playing the gentle melancholy music of France. It was a melody that brought the tears to her eyes and in a haze she became suddenly aware of three people standing listening to the music, a woman and two men, and as one of them bent his head to speak to the woman her heart raced suddenly. It was Dieter.

She moved towards him, then within feet of him stopped. Suppose the woman was with him, what would she say?

They were applauding the musicians, giving freely, when one of them passed around his hat, and then blessedly the other man and the woman moved away after shaking Dieter's hand and bidding him goodbye. At that moment over the hand of the woman he looked up and saw her and as his companions left him he moved towards her with a smile.

'Chantal,' he exclaimed. 'How nice to see you. Are you alone?'

'Quite alone Dieter. I hoped I might find you here.'

He raised his eyebrows in some surprise, and hurriedly she said, 'I want to explain. I was anxious that you wouldn't think all sorts of things that were untrue.'

'My dear Chantal, you do not need to explain anything to me, why indeed should you?'

There was a silence between them and for the first time he was aware of her confusion and that her eyes were shadowed with tears.

Immediately he showed concern, taking her arm and saying softly, 'There is a little café in the corner there, we will drink an apéritif and talk.'

He looked impatiently at the tables crowded with people, none of them intent on moving, and he suggested that they walk back to the church where they might find a quiet corner where they could talk.

As they approached a small rustic seat an elderly man and woman rose to walk away, and Dieter drew her towards it. With a smile he said, 'I think we are fortunate Chantal. We will sit here and you shall tell me why you felt we should talk and why I find you looking sad.'

'Oh Dieter, I have so much to tell you,' she murmured.

'And here was I thinking you were a young lady with a world at her feet and all the world to live for.'

She shook her head sadly and he waited for the tears to stop and the tale to begin.

34

As he listened to her voice, occasionally interspersed with sobs he began to discover the real Chantal. He had always felt that she was not like the other girls at the school, always there had been about her a wariness, a sense of withdrawal; when they talked about their futures she had remained strangely silent about her own.

Now she was trying hard not to blame her mother but the blame was there, in every gesture, every inflexion in her voice, and through it all he could feel only an acute pity for the woman who had wanted the world for her daughter and refused to let go of the past.

'None of them wanted me for Sebastian,' she said mournfully, 'but in the end it didn't really matter did it, and they will never know the truth.'

'Did you love him very much?' he asked cautiously.

'Right from that first moment, I felt close to him, we thought about things in the same way, liked the same people, enjoyed the same places. I don't think I was ever in love with him. I loved him in a different way.'

'Perhaps you never really experienced love,' he said gently.

She looked at him out of eyes swimming with tears but the look said it all and in a rush of words she said, 'Oh I know you never loved me, I was just one of your pupils with a crush, but I was so miserable when you left Switzerland without saying goodbye and, then, when I saw you in London it all came back to me, even when there was Sebastian.

'I shouldn't be telling you all this, I'm embarrassing you and honestly Dieter I don't mind your not loving me, I only wanted you to know why I was living in Paris and where I was working. I didn't want you to think that I was seriously involved with that man you saw me with the other night.'

He didn't answer her. What had he thought? That the man was far

297

too old for her, that she had found her niche in an aristocratic world, that she would never really know the joy and pity of love.

Struggling to bring her thoughts back to normality she said, 'You are going to Vienna soon, the Grand Duchess said, will you remain there?'

'I have engagements in Vienna and it is my home. I love Vienna, I shall meet old friends there and members of my family.'

'I never thought of you with a family.'

'It has dwindled considerably, now I only have my grandmother and female cousins. I have kept my apartment there and performing for the Emperor will be a grand occasion.'

'Oh yes, I'm sure it will. I love the music of Vienna, the waltzes and those beautiful operettas. Tell me, do all the men wear uniform and all the women tiaras?'

He laughed. 'No Leibchen, only on grand occasions, but there is always music in Vienna, in the coffee houses and taverns, in the Prater gardens and ballrooms. One day you should go to Vienna.'

She nodded mutely, and Dieter asked quickly, 'Tell me a little of your work. How did you find work with Anton Mordant? It is known as the most exclusive dress salon in Paris.'

'André helped me. Vicomte de Mirandol, Sebastian's uncle by marriage. A long time ago he and my mother were lovers.'

'I see.'

'He was kind. He gave me a letter to give to a friend of his who was also a friend of Monsieur Anton.'

'And when he saw you, how could he resist you, I do see Chantal.'

'I was told that it was part of my work as one of his mannequins to act as a companion to visiting dignitaries, even royalty. It is all very circumspect, I do not have to speak, not unless I am spoken to that is, I must not express opinions. The fact that I have been educated is unimportant, I am simply an expensive beautifully dressed doll for the occasion, that is all.'

He sensed her bitterness, and behind it all the overpowering blame for her mother. She was not ready to forgive yet, the hurt was too new.

'I would like to have invited you to eat dinner with me Chantal, but I have received an invitation to dine with an old friend of my mother's, perhaps we can dine together when I return from Vienna?'

'Oh yes, I shall look forward to that Dieter. How long will you be away?'

'I'm not sure. I have an engagement here in Paris at the end of January, then I am going to America. It is strange, is it not, but I was asked to play for the passengers on the maiden voyage of the *Titanic*, I had too many engagements elsewhere at that time, but promised to play for them on some future occasion. Now that great ship is no more, there will be no music in her ballroom ever again.'

'No, it was terrible. I think about it again and again, Grace Martindale was so pretty and so much in love, it was terrible that they should both be lost when the *Titanic* went down.'

'I am surprised that Grace was not saved.'

'I do not think she would leave him behind. Why did it happen? They said she was unsinkable?'

'And that I think was one of the problems. Not enough lifeboats, they were so sure, it brings the fact of our mortality very near.'

As they walked down the hill through the streets of Montmartre the crowds were still there, watching the artists and the musicians, and the air of gaiety was undiminished.

They found an open carriage at the bottom of the hill and Chantal said with a bright smile, 'Oh I do so love the carriages, the pace is so much slower and one sees so much more.'

He smiled at her childlike delight as she sat back with dancing eyes surveying a city in love with life. He was glad that she seemed to have put her sadness behind her if only for a little while, and when he left her at the door of her apartment he said, 'When I return to Paris, Liebchen, I will find you, either here or at the Salon.'

He lifted her hand to his lips, then returning to the carriage he was driven away. She stood where he had left her wanting desperately to believe him. Had he just said he would find her to make her feel less unhappy or had he really meant it? His engagement to perform in Paris seemed a lifetime away.

Monsieur Anton was busy with his autumn fashions. It was the season of velvets and furs, rich dark brocades and shimmering satins. Summer roses had given way to chrysanthemums and the perfume in the opulent salons became heavier and more potent.

The shorter days brought with them sleet and rain and there were days when they arrived at the Salon before it was light and they went home in the dark.

It was the season of balls and opera, of organ-grinders and roasting chestnuts and there were a great many functions where the girls were expected to look beautiful on the arms of visiting dignitaries.

Count Drovski did not return to Paris but his sister was present at most of the occasions where Chantal accompanied other high-ranking visitors.

On the whole the men were gracious and charming, the women condescending, and there were a great many times when she returned home frustrated and angry at having to listen in silence to remarks she considered unjust and even scandalous.

299

While she vented her anger in front of Celeste, the other girl merely laughed.

'There's something to be said for a lack of education,' she said. 'It's much easier to be able to smile in the right places without thinking too much about what is being said.'

They were encouraged at the end of their parade to mingle with the clientèle; it gave them an opportunity to look more closely at the cut of a gown and its material, and it was on one such occasion when Chantal found herself staring into the eyes of the Vicomtesse de Mirandol.

Vivienne had watched the fashion show with interest. Over the years she had bought a great many clothes from Anton Mordant but it was the sight of Chantal in a black velvet gown edged with sable that had made her stay longer than she normally did. As Chantal circled the room she made her way towards her.

The girls moved around like automatons, allowing themselves to be touched and prodded, twirling when asked to twirl, walk when asked to walk, and sit when asked to sit. André had told his wife that Philippe had told him Chantal was working at the Mordant Salon and although she was not looking for a new creation she had gone hoping to see Chantal.

'Let us go to the edge of the room so that we can talk,' she said. 'How are you Chantal?'

'Very well, thank you Madame la Vicomtesse.'

'How very formal.'

'Monsieur expects us to be formal with his clients.'

'He could also be affronted if you were churlish with one of his clients who knew you before you went to work for him.'

Chantal had the grace to look contrite. 'I'm sorry Madame, I should be grateful to you of all people.'

Vivienne looked at her uncertainly. Grateful was the wrong word. She had been duty-bound to destroy any hopes the girl ever had of becoming a Martindale, but gratitude had never been the prize.

'Are you happy here?' she asked gently.

'Yes. I have friends here and I enjoy the work, most of it at least.'

'Ah yes, I know something of the sort of work Monsieur Mordant asks of his girls, but I hope you have encountered nothing sinister, Chantal.'

'Nothing at all.'

'Have you seen your mother?'

'No. I have not been home to Bordeaux.'

'But you will be going home for Christmas?'

'No.'

300

'You are blaming your mother for everything?'

'Only for not telling me the truth. I can't face my mother yet, I can't bear to see the hurt and recrimination in her face, and the disappointment that my work is not what she planned for me.'

'I am sure she thought she was doing her best. Your mother too had been bitterly hurt, Chantal. You haven't asked about how your father is taking the death of his daughter and son-in-law?'

Her eyes opened wide at the word father. She had never known a father, she did not want one now.

'Can you imagine what it is like in that family? The house is a desert, their lives are in torment. Andrew loved Grace, she was the beautiful spark in his life. Oh he loved Sebastian, but Sebastian was always too independent. Grace adored her father. Alice is her mother's favourite.'

'It was terrible. I can't put it into words how I felt about Grace and the sinking of that beautiful ship.'

'There are a great many homes in England and America that will never be the same again, in other countries too I expect, but America and England bore the brunt of it. They will have to rebuild their lives, they have to, but it's going to take a long long time.'

'And Sebastian?'

'Sebastian was hurt and miserable. He returned to India within twenty-four hours after the wedding and he writes to his parents, but he hasn't been back to England.'

'And you wonder why I blame my mother? If she had told me the truth I would have grown up with it, accepted it. Sebastian and I would never have met and I would never have had any need to meet my father, as you call him.'

Vivienne shook her head sadly. 'Don't wait too long before you go home, Chantal.'

At that moment Monsieur Anton joined them, smiling and effusive. 'Has Madame la Comtesse made up her mind?' he enquired confidently.

'Yes. I think I shall have this one. I love the sable on the black velvet. Unfortunately I do not have Mademoiselle's colouring.'

'But the Comtesse has beautiful colouring. You still have your English complexion which goes so beautifully with dark hair. It is the clarity of the complexion that makes black look so wonderful. Sallow women should never wear black, for them the jewel colours and the gleam of gold. Black is not funereal when a beautiful woman is wearing it.'

'I hope you get commission on any gown you help to sell,' Vivienne murmured.

Chantal merely smiled. 'I'll take it off now so that we can have it packed for you to take home.'

'Have it sent to my hotel, Chantal, The Ritz, I shall be there for a few days, and there will probably be an occasion to wear it.'

They smiled at each other, before Chantal left her.

The meeting with Vivienne had unsettled her, she wanted to get out of the gown and into her own clothing, then out into the chill November wind. She looked round for Celeste but saw that she was still walking up and down before two older women, neither of whom would do justice to the wild silk crimson gown which fitted Celeste like a sheath.

Cars and carriages were stopping outside the ornate portals of the Salon to pick up the clientèle. In spite of the icy rain cheerful farewells were being called and there was much kissing and embracing going on. Chantal bent her head against the wind, glad of the scarf covering her hat, and the umbrella which was in danger of being turned inside out.

By the time Celeste arrived home Chantal had made sandwiches and coffee and they sat in front of the fire chatting about the events of the afternoon.

'Did either of those women buy the dress?' Chantal asked curiously.

'It had to be let out for the smaller woman and the colour did nothing for her. Of course it really was far too young for her. Did you sell the black?'

'Yes. The Vicomtesse de Mirandol bought it.'

'Is she young enough to do it justice?'

'She's as old as my mother but she's still something of a beauty. She'll do it justice.'

'Why don't you invite your mother to stay, she'd love the shows and we can purchase clothes at a reduced price when they're available.'

'I might invite her one day. It's a long way from Bordeaux.'

Celeste looked at her oddly. 'The distance is in your heart Chérie, Bordeaux is only a train journey away.'

'I know.'

'Why don't you go home for Christmas, the city can be a lonely place then?'

'But you'll be here; won't you?'

'I've had an invitation to spend Christmas in St Moritz. Some man I've known a long time. I can't tell you his name, only that he's French and works at the embassy, pretty high up. He's married and she's an invalid. I've asked Monsieur Anton if I can take a few extra days and he's agreed, after all he was responsible for introducing us in the first place.'

'Are you fond of him, Celeste?'

'We get on. If his wife died tomorrow he wouldn't ask me to marry him, he'd look around for somebody more intellectual, but when people see him with me they know it's just a fling.'

She saw the pain in Chantal's eyes and she grinned, 'They'd never think that about you, Chérie, you're marrying material.'

'I was thinking about my mother.'

'Your mother married twice, two very exemplarary men, you shouldn't think things like that about your mother.'

'This afternoon I heard a woman speak to me about my father, I was shocked. I've always believed my father was dead, I wish he was dead, it would be easier.'

'You're carrying too many crosses, Chantal. I never knew my father, he was always somewhere at sea and when he came back he never took much notice of me. I was glad when he went away for good. I've learned to take every day as it comes. My friend will treat me royally and he is generous with money. If I wasn't such a fool with it I could put some of it away for a rainy day.'

'But you never will,' Chantal said with a smile.

'I doubt it. When the rainy day comes I'll look around for a man who isn't looking for somebody like you. Somebody from the old days perhaps.'

Marie Claire held her daughter's letter in her hands and stared at it with a bleak expression in her eyes. Chantal was not coming home for Christmas. She was spending it in Paris where there were parties and theatres and she said nothing about her escorts or her job.

She hoped her mother and Henri would have a wonderful Christmas and perhaps one of these days she would be able to come home. Again there was no address and Marie Claire despaired.

What sort of bohemian existence was her daughter living so that she felt unable to give her address? It could well be some brothel in the back streets of Paris, and her anger mounted when she thought about Maurice bankrupting himself to give Chantal an education.

Where were all her rich English friends, what kind of work could she do? She hadn't educated her to be a shop assistant, shop assistants were decent hard-working girls who lived with their parents and went home for Christmas.

She had a group of friends who couldn't understand a daughter who never visited, so that she had constantly to make excuses for her. She invented weekends in English country houses, summer cruises on private yachts and now more and more she was becoming aware of the sceptical glances exchanged between her friends.

Henri comforted her to the best of his ability, but he felt annoyed with Chantal. How dare she hurt her mother in this way, if he had known where she was he could have written to her, insisting she come home.

He admired his pretty wife. He admired her taste and the way she had turned an old crumbling château into a real home that was constantly admired. Marie Claire never spoke of Chantal's father and he asked no questions. She wrote often to her sister Jeanne and sent money for presents for the rest of them. She brought warm thick woollens for her mother who must be very old, and bottles of brandy to keep out the winter cold.

'One day I must make an effort and go and see mother,' she would say, but it was always forgotten and he judged that her memories of the farm were far from happy, and that she was still smarting from things that had happened there.

One day perhaps, she would be able to talk to him about the past but he asked no questions. All in good time, he thought.

35

Christmas in Vienna had always been the highlight of Dieter Steinberg's young life. He had loved the festive atmosphere of the Prater as the great wheel in which he and friends were sitting paused at its summit to allow them views over the glittering city.

Now the Christmas days of 1912 were as he had always remembered them, except that he was no longer the young boy staring through windows into lighted rooms beyond, where there were festivities and music. Now he was the musician who played before the Emperor Franz Josef and his court, fêted and acclaimed, and every house was open to him and every echelon in society was his to enjoy.

He thought back on the years of struggle, the tiny rooms and tuneless pianos, even to his childhood where his parents were faded aristocracy and where there was never any money. It was his talent alone that had brought him fame and his life stretched in front of him filled with excitement.

America beckoned. At the end of April he hoped to set sail on the *Ile de France* for New York where he would play his latest concerto for the President and engagements that would keep him busy for months. Indeed he had been unable to make plans in Europe because he was uncertain when he would be able to return.

It was his quiet moments which concerned him most, it was then he could not get Chantal Grolan out of his mind. She was in his thoughts and his dreams, her hair like sun-kissed corn and her dark blue eyes that could shine with excitement or grow stormy with despair. He had promised to see her on his return to Paris, but did he really want her in his life at this particular time? There were times when he still thought about her as one of those giggling condescending girls who had descended upon Madame Lafayette's school in the Bernese Oberland.

Those silly young girls had flirted with him, giggled about him in the same way they had giggled about their ski instructor or their tennis coach. It was only Chantal who had not been so silly.

Christmas had not been a happy experience for Chantal. The other girls had friends to visit, families to go to or some man they thought of as special.

She had watched Celeste packing her suitcase with clothes appropriate for St Moritz before departing with her friend in a flurry of snow. Celeste had eyed her doubtfully on the doorstep before saying, 'You should go home Chantal, Paris is a lonely city when one is all on one's own.'

She wanted to go home, but she was not yet ready to face the questions her mother would ask. The girls were allowed to buy articles of clothing at a greatly reduced price at this time; they were clothes that had not been purchased by Monsieur's clients for varying reasons, and Chantal selected a long silk shawl shimmering in colours of jade and peach which she knew her mother would love. With it she penned an affectionate note and a great many untruths on the many festivities she expected to attend in the capital.

By the time Christmas Day came to an end she was of the opinion that Paris was the loneliest city in the world. She had mingled with the crowds and felt alone, even in Notre Dame when families were worshipping together before they hurried home to their particular festivities.

She ate a solitary dinner and sat reading until she felt she couldn't stand it a moment longer, so she went to bed. Even then she was aware of traffic and laughter, singing and music from a group of musicians outside in the square and she promised herself that in the spring she would go home.

She thought a great many times about Dieter in Vienna. She had her own ideas about Vienna, a city of waltzes and glamour, a city where Dieter could be waltzing the night away with a girl he knew well, perhaps even a girl he could have serious thoughts about.

The girls at the Salon had said New Year was the time they looked forward to most, when Monsieur Anton expected them to accept invitations wherever they came from, because Paris would be filled with exciting people looking for a good time, guests of the rich and famous who were anxious to make their visits memorable.

On the day before, Monsieur Anton issued his instructions. Most of the girls already knew the men they were expected to accompany, but Chantal was his new girl and on the way to his office she began to hope that it was Drovski who was visiting Paris. Her hopes were immediately dashed however when he seemed at first reluctant to talk, looking at Madame expectantly for help which she too seemed hesitant in giving.

Chantal looked at them cautiously, not liking their diffidence. Making up his mind at last Monsieur Anton said, 'You know the Grand Duchess Marie Mademoiselle, you know that she was delighted with the exemplary way you fitted in with her party on the occasion of her brother's visit here, she has now asked if you will join her party again tomorrow evening at her residence here in Paris.'

'Will Count Drovski be my companion?' she asked.

'Well no. He is not visiting Paris at this time, the gentleman is Count Alexandr Petronov, another relative of the Grand Duchess but rather more distant I think.'

'Are you acquainted with the Count, Monsieur? You seemed hesitant, you and Madame?'

'The Count is young, handsome and has the reputation of being something of a playboy. That need not concern you, Mademoiselle, the occasion is for one evening only, and you would be doing the Grand Duchess a great favour. You will meet a great many interesting people, the sort of people she likes to surround herself with, and there will be entertainment I have no doubt. Just be your usual charming and delightful self.'

It was too contrived. Both Monsieur Anton and Madame had been uncertain and as soon as possible she asked the other girls if they knew the Russian Count, immediately aware of their exchanged glances, some filled with amusement, others with alarm.

By the end of the afternoon she had learned that at least six of the girls had acted as companion to Count Alexandr at some time or another. They were reluctant to talk about the experience. Yes, he was very handsome, most presentable, exceedingly rich, but although the Count had been a constant visitor to Paris, none of the girls had accompanied him a second time.

Madame informed her that the Grand Duchess would send a car for her at seven o'clock, and Jeanette said feelingly, 'At least you won't have to put up with him if she's sending a car for you. Just make sure she provides transport for your journey home, alone.'

When Chantal stared at her doubtfully, she smiled, 'The Grand Duchess is aware that he's something of a Casanova. I'm sure she won't subject you to anything devious.'

With an airy smile Jeanette moved away and she could get nothing more out of any of them. She was dreading New Year's Eve.

The girls were given the dresses they were expected to wear and the accessories to go with them. Chantal quickly realized her gown was far more expensive than the others, the jewellery more ostentatious and when she stared at them doubtfully, one of the girls whispered, 'Don't worry, you'll earn every penny.'

'What do you mean?' she asked sharply.

'Oh, simply that he'll expect you to look beautiful, flirt a little, smile in all the right places, even when you don't understand his appalling French and his hands are everywhere.'

Chantal stared at her in alarm. 'Have you ever been asked to be his companion?'

The girl smiled and moved away.

Later in the afternoon she repeated the conversation to Madame who snapped sharply, 'Who told you all this? She should have known better! The girls know they are not expected to talk about any of their escorts.'

'I think it only fair that I should be warned if the Count is a libertine. How shall I handle him?'

'The Grand Duchess would not expect you to accompany a man who was less than a gentleman. Again I ask you who discussed him with you?'

'I can't tell you, Madame. I think perhaps she was right to warn me.'

The car came for her promptly on New Year's Eve and she was relieved that she sat alone in the back. It was too early for revellers on the city's streets, but there was an air of expectancy in the glowing city. Lamps gleamed on boulevard café tables, vying with the street lamps and illuminated buildings. Chantal loved Paris in the sunlight but Paris in the winter when moonlight and starlight came into its own, shining down on a city that vied with the beauty of the midnight-blue sky filled her with a deep and exciting nostalgia.

The Grand Duchess stood at the head of the stairs to receive her guests and Chantal followed a line of them waiting to greet her. The men bowed, the women curtsied and as she raised her head she was aware of the Grand Duchess smiling and holding out a hand to beckon forward a man leaning nonchalantly on the banister rail as he chatted to two women guests.

Introductions were performed and Chantal gazed upwards into the piercing dark eyes of a tall man, staring down at her appreciatively.

His face was thin, saturnine in its expression and the thin line of his mouth was edged with a dark moustache, and although his lips smiled his eyes remained strangely cold.

He had kissed her hand on introduction, now he merely indicated that they should walk together into the Salon, and people were making way for them to walk the length of the room where they sat in isolation on one of the gilt settees.

'You are all the Grand Duchess said you would be, Mademoiselle,' he said in a strange guttural French, while his hand closed around hers in a tight grip.

How she longed to join one of the groups stationed around them, but they were not invited, and she was becoming increasingly aware of his arm drawing her closer to him and his hot breath as he kissed her bare shoulders. She edged away, and his thin lips curved in a smile. 'I am sorry you had to travel here alone, it will give me great pleasure to escort you home.'

'There is no need, Monsieur le Comte, I would not expect you to leave the Grand Duchess's guests on my account.'

'Her guests are unimportant, they are not my guests. You on the other hand, Mademoiselle, are my guest.'

'There are a great many people here,' she said as a way of starting a conversation.

He shrugged his shoulders. 'My kinswoman surrounds herself with people, most of them Russians who prefer to live here, and mostly people Russia can gladly live without. Then of course there are the others.'

'The others?'

'Why yes. The remnants of foreign royalty who flock to Paris when their own countries throw them out, as well as the musicians and artists she patronizes.'

'Many of whom are very famous and accomplished,' she couldn't stop herself saying.

'Well of course. The Grand Duchess is only concerned with the successful people of this world. You will find some of them here tonight, guests she can call upon to entertain the rest of us.'

There was so much mockery in his voice she was tempted to ask him why he was here if he thought so little of his hostess's guests. The Grand Duchess was entering the room now, moving graciously from one group to the next and Chantal's heart suddenly missed a beat when she saw that Dieter stood at the end of the room chatting to a group of people. He looked so incredibly handsome in his formal evening dress with the glow from the chandeliers falling on his smooth blond hair. He had not seen her and suddenly wanted to run away and hide. She did not want him to see her with this man whose careless hand was playing with the tendrils of her hair, whose face was too close to her own.

She was glad when dinner was announced and they could move forward into the dining room to take their places at the long glittering table. They had been placed near the head of the table and she was glad that Dieter was placed at the other end, where a pretty girl was showing every sign that she was delighted with the arrangement.

As they moved towards their places, the Grand Duchess said, 'I have invited Herr Steinberg, who I hope will play for us later on. This will be his decision of course. I have invited him because I find him charming and something of an asset to any dinner party.'

The people around them talked about music, the opera and the Christmas festivities, but all the time Chantal was aware of the knees pressing against hers, and the hand sliding up and down her thigh, so that she could feel the heat of it on the delicate silk of her gown.

The thin superior-looking woman sitting across from them was well aware of what was going on and when Chantal met her haughty stare she longed to leap to her feet with accusation in her eyes.

She was glad she was not expected to make conversation, glad that she could edge away from him and, when she deliberately pushed his hand away, he lowered his head and whispered, 'You will be sorry for that, Mademoiselle.'

She was afraid. He was the nightmare she had feared when Monsieur Anton had told her he would expect her to be nice to visiting dignitaries. Was this the night that would see her running home to Bordeaux? Was this the man who would make her afraid of her own shadow?

Suppose she appealed to the Grand Duchess? Would she look at her with lofty disdain, because she was too immature to handle him, and what of Dieter? His eyes would say it all, that she was still a child trying to live in an adult world, and she would read in his eyes the pity and regret.

His hand was back on her thigh, kneading it, and turn as she might she could not avoid it. She moved away so sharply, she knocked over a glass filled with dark red wine, so that it fell over on to others clattering along the length of the table, staining the rich lace cloth and dropping mercilessly on her gown and the gown of the woman sitting opposite.

Horrified, Chantal stared around her. All along the length of the table, eyes were staring at her and silence had descended. From his seat further down the table, Dieter rose to his feet and came towards her. She raised her eyes, filled with tears, staring at him helplessly and with a gentle smile he said, 'Here you are Chantal. I looked for you when I came in, but I couldn't find you.'

The Grand Duchess relaxed her haughty stare, saying. 'You two know each other? Really, Herr Steinberg, I wish you had said so earlier, I would have invited you together.

Dieter smiled. 'I only arrived back in Paris last night. Your invitation was waiting for me, Grand Duchess.'

'It appears we have had a little accident,' she said. She called to a footman standing near the door and immediately they were surrounded by others who removed the offending cloth and the glasses, and within minutes the table was put to rights. Chantal stared down at her gown ruefully and turning to the other guest murmured, 'I am so sorry, Madame.'

Count Alexandr had risen to his feet and staring haughtily at Dieter said, 'It is unfortunate that Mademoiselle Grolan is known to you, she does happen to be with me this evening.'

'There is difficulty, however,' Dieter said evenly. 'Mademoiselle Grolan does happen to be my fiancé. I returned from Vienna to ask her to marry me.'

Chantal was staring at him with wide-eyed astonishment and before the Count could say another word, the Grand Duchess said, 'It seems to be that your words have put a different complexion on events, Herr Steinberg. Perhaps we should finish our dinner and then decide who is escorting who. Count Mitriov, perhaps you would like to sit here next to Count Alexandr and Mademoiselle Grolan will be placed next to her fiancé.'

The rest of the meal progressed without interruption. For the main part Chantal sat in silence, as yet unable to collect her thoughts on the turn of events. It was evident that Dieter had come to her rescue after seeing her plight, but by doing so he had no doubt placed himself in an impossible position.

She could not think that he had come back from Vienna with a marriage proposal in mind, so what would be expected of them in the days that lay ahead?

Dieter too was troubled. He had seen the way the Russian had behaved towards Chantal, had seen the fear in her eyes, known instinctively that he was behaving outrageously. Before thinking about it, he had leapt to her rescue, and he was not sure that he was ready for such a commitment.

He was conscious of her sitting beside him. Creamy shoulders emerging from the delicate silk gown with the dark red stain spreading across the draped skirt, the gleam of jewels in her ears and round her throat, the silken porcelain skin and tendrils of golden hair. He did not need to look at the other women sitting around the table to know that she was more beautiful than any of them, but was it enough?

How well would Chantal fit into his world? Music was his life, his passion, how well would music and Chantal blend together, and how would she bear to leave France to follow him around the world from one country to another, one city to another, when all most women craved for was a settled home where there were friends and relatives?

So many questions filled his mind for the rest of that evening, and later when he sat at the piano and played for them. It was later still when they drove through the city in the early dawn that the questions had to be answered.

311

'Can we leave the carriage here and walk the rest of the way?' Chantal asked quietly.

It was a cold moonlit night with a small chill wind sweeping round the corners as they made their way along the lamplit boulevard and they walked in silence, yet they were both aware that questions had to be asked. In the end it was Chantal who said nervously, 'Thank you for what you did tonight, Dieter. I was afraid of him, he was a terrible man and I was dreading having to leave with him at the end of the evening. You knew what was happening?'

'I know Count Petronov's reputation where women are concerned. All Paris knows it. I cannot understand why the Grand Duchess asked for you, or why the Salon allowed you to go.'

'I know. The girls warned me, but with the Salon it is all business and very little else. I suppose they will know all about it in the morning.'

'Well I wouldn't worry about that, Chantal, perhaps instead we should begin to talk about us.'

'Oh Dieter, I know you didn't come back from Vienna to ask me to marry you, it was a spur of the moment thing because you saw that I was afraid and you wanted to help me. We needn't say anything just yet, and in a little while we can let it be known that you have had second thoughts. Nobody will be surprised, they will talk about me as that foolish young woman who had no more sense than attend a banquet in the company of a man who was known to be a libertine.'

'Most of those people at the Grand Duchess's banquet knew why you were there, they know that you are employed by Anton Mordant, and they know that he makes a great deal of money from allowing his models to accompany the rich and famous. He did himself no favours by allowing you to meet Count Petronov. So you think in a few weeks' time we should discreetly end our engagement by admitting it was a mistake?'

She looked up at him with eyes filled with embarrassment. She did not want to end the engagement. She wanted it to be true, but she could not take advantage of a generous gesture from an old friend, whose only wish had been to protect her. He smiled.

'I shall be here in Paris until the end of April, Chantal. After that I have been invited to visit America. I have a series of concerts lined up in several American cities and I hope to have completed the music for a new operetta before I leave. We could also spend those four months in getting to know each other.'

Her eyes opened wide. 'But we do know each other Dieter, or at least I thought we did.'

'I knew a girl who stood out like a jewel in the midst of other girls, a

312

very young girl who was infatuated with me as so many of the other girls were infatuated, with me, with other men they met during those two years, but now I am looking at a woman. The girl has grown up, and I have to be sure if that infatuation has turned to love and if my own feelings were real. Do you think we shall discover the reality in the next few months, Chantal? Do you think we should try?'

'Oh yes, Dieter, I do, I want so much for us to try.'

'What will you tell your mother?'

'My mother!'

'Why yes. I am not the English aristocrat your mother wished for. Perhaps in her eyes I shall always be the music teacher she regarded as something of a disaster in your young life.'

'I shall tell my mother when we are sure it is what we want Dieter, and nothing she can say or do will make me change my mind.'

'And will you tell her face to face or will you write to her?'

'In four months' time there may be nothing to tell her, but if there is then I shall have to make up my mind then. At the moment I would prefer to write to her. I still don't feel ready to meet my mother, but it has nothing to do with you, Dieter, it stems from all those years when she told me my father was dead and the terrible consequences her lies led me to.

'I love her very dearly, I shall always love her, but when at last we do meet, I want there to be no shadows between us, I want to believe that the past is finally behind us. Don't you understand?'

'Oh yes I understand, but you should not make your mother suffer too long. Perhaps you should try to understand that she was very much younger than you when her young life changed forever.'

His words echoed the words André de Mirandol had said to her before she left England and although she recognized the truth in them she was not yet ready to accept it.

36

Paris in the spring of 1913 was a magical time. To be young and in love, to feel a part of the warm vibrant city and to be loved by the man Paris idolized.

Women came to the Salon to buy Anton Mordant's creations but they also came to look at the woman who would marry Dieter Steinberg. Anton made the most of it. Chantal was his joy, as much his creation as the gown he clothed her with but as he and Madame fussed over her neither of them had discovered the real Chantal, the Chantal reserved exclusively for the man she loved.

They were seen together everywhere, the theatre and the opera, the racetracks and the romantic restaurants and Anton was aware that her days at the Salon were numbered.

The girls flocked round her while she showed them her engagement ring, a large sapphire surrounded by diamonds, and they showered her with questions as to when she would leave, when would they marry and where would they live?

When she told them they were going to America for twelve months at least, they were both envious and excited, and at the end of March Dieter said she should think about leaving the Salon as soon as possible.

'But we have until the end of April, Dieter,' she protested.

'I want to take you to Vienna and meet my grandmother,' he said. 'You have always said how you would like to see Vienna.'

So she broke the news to Anton the following day, and although his face was a picture of disappointment he laid on a farewell party to which he invited a good many of his best customers as well as Philippe Grimalde and kissed her hand gallantly and congratulated her on her forthcoming marriage.

Smiling down at her he said, 'When I first met you I knew that you would be a success story. Perhaps I should write to Vicomte de Mirandol and tell him how well you have prospered.'

'I would really much rather you didn't,' she said softly.

'You would prefer to tell him yourself?'

She smiled. 'Perhaps,' was all she would say on the matter.

Never in her wildest dreams had she thought she would ever be able to afford to buy Anton's gowns, but he happily reduced his prices to accommodate her, in the belief that she only had to appear in his creations to encourage women to buy from him.

On the morning she left the Salon for the last time, she stood in the doorway waiting for a cab, surrounded by innumerable boxes containing her clothes as well as hat boxes and gifts from Monsieur Anton and the girls. Celeste kissed her warmly.

'I shall miss you Chantal. I suppose I'll get your replacement but we have been good friends, haven't we?'

Chantal returned her embrace with tears in her eyes. Celeste had been her friend, always ready with good advice, often humorous, often critical, but in all Paris she was the one person she was really sad to be leaving behind.

All afternoon lay before her because she had not arranged to see Dieter until the evening, and after she had unpacked the boxes and re-packed into waiting suitcases there was nothing for her to do.

There was a new warmth in the sun and along the boulevards people were smiling at the promise of spring. Leaving the apartment she headed for the river and the terraces that lined its banks, where artists would be busy painting the life that strolled and loitered there. It was a favourite place with Celeste who had seemed to know everybody, and when Chantal had once remarked on it, the other girl had laughed delightedly.

'I know everybody in Paris capable of starving in some garret or other. They are all hoping for the fortune they'll make tomorrow, their hearts are as large as their expectations.'

Many of them greeted her as she passed among them, calling out good wishes, encouraging her to buy their work. She bought two small pictures, not because they were of exceptional beauty, but because they were the work of a young artist Celeste was particularly fond of and because they would always remind her of a part of Paris she loved.

He made a great thing of wrapping the pictures for her, and then as he passed them over, he said with a boyish smile, 'You bought them because of Celeste not because you couldn't live without them.'

She smiled. 'I did buy them because of Celeste, but I liked them, I love this place, they'll always remind me of today and this particular place.'

'You're going to America, Chantal?'

'Yes, at the end of April, but tomorrow we are going to Vienna.'

'Do you intend to waltz the next few weeks away?'

'I've never been there. I'm going to meet Dieter's grandmother but I hope we shall be able to waltz in the city of waltzes.'

He raised her hand to his lips and kissed it and as she turned to walk away, she was aware of two women waving to her from the promenade above. She turned, thinking at first that it was some other person they were trying to attract, and then she recognized Louise Darvish. Her heart sank. Why on this particular afternoon had somebody from her past come to haunt her?

Louise kissed her warmly, holding out her hand to her companion and saying, 'This is my cousin Ella, we're having a week in Paris to buy some clothes. I wanted to go to Anton Mordant's but Ella wanted to go to Pierre Boidins, when we couldn't agree we decided to have a look round here instead. Are you living here, Chantal? Amanda wrote to you in Bordeaux, didn't you get her letter?'

'I haven't been to Bordeaux for some time. I've been moving around. My mother wouldn't have known where to send Amanda's letter.'

'I must say you're looking absolutely wonderful, blooming in fact. Are you married? Do you live in Paris?'

'I have been living in Paris. I'm leaving in the morning.'

'Leaving! Where are you going?'

'To Vienna.'

'How wonderful. I spent a week in Vienna and I adored it. Are you going alone?'

'No.'

'Darling, don't be so secretive. Who is he? Is it serious?'

'Louise, I want to know about Grace. What happened was terrible.'

'Heavens yes. She had the most beautiful wedding and she looked enchanting. Everybody was so happy that day, everybody except Sebastian, he looked as though his world had come to an end. Whatever happened between you and Sebastian, Chantal?'

'I realized that I would be a very unsuitable wife for him. It was better to find out while there was still time. I hope he finds happiness with the right sort of girl.'

'Well, he's engaged to be married, some girl he's met in India. Her father's a general, Sir somebody or other. He's opted for a daughter of the regiment.'

'I'm sure he'll be happy with her. It would never have been my kind of life.'

'A lot of the guests went to see the *Titanic* sail, all those flags waving and the bands playing, and she was such a beautiful ship. Nobody could believe it, all England was in mourning.'

'And Grace's parents? I suppose they were devastated?'

'Absolutely, particularly her father. He's aged terribly these last few months. Grace was always so precious to him.'

'I know.'

'What have you been doing in Paris all these months?'

'Working.'

'Working!'

Louise said it as though work was a word she had never heard before, something she would never expect to hear from a girl who had been a guest in her home.

Chantal smiled. 'People do work, you know. I enjoyed my work and being with girls who needed to work, as I did actually.'

'But what did you do?'

'I worked as a model.'

'Gracious. Which fashion house did you model for?'

'Anton Mordant.'

'But, Chantal, he's the best. How did you manage to find work there? Oh, I'll admit you're very beautiful and with a figure to make men mad but aren't models supposed to be rather dubious?'

'Not if they work for Anton Mordant.'

Louise's eyes were bright with anticipation. What a lot she would have to tell her friends when she returned to England. Chantal Grolan had worked as a model for Anton Mordant, and she was going to Vienna with somebody she was reluctant to talk about.

'Can't we have dinner together this evening?' Louise said quickly. 'We have so much to talk about, surely you're all packed for Vienna, you can spare a little time for an old friend.'

'Actually, Louise I have another engagement this evening, I'm sorry but it won't be possible to have dinner with you.'

'Can't you tell whoever it is that you've met an old friend. We're staying at the Ritz. We'd love you to join us, wouldn't we Ella?'

Ella smiled, but Chantal shook her head. 'It really isn't possible, Louise, I'll write to you in a week or two when I know what is happening.'

'But what is happening? Why can't you tell me now?'

'Because there isn't time. I'm so glad to have seen you again and I'm sorry I can't stay with you longer.'

She embraced the two women quickly and with a farewell smile hurried away.

Louise looked after her with an exasperated frown on her pretty face.

'Well really,' she complained. 'Wouldn't you have just thought she'd have wanted to spend this evening with us. I hardly told her anything about the wedding which she was supposed to be going to. There was as much talk about her non-attendance as there was about the ceremony itself.'

Ella eyed her cousin with some amusement. Louise had a lot to say about her French schoolfriend. How badly she had let Sebastian down, how discourteously she had behaved towards them after being a guest in their house, and when Sebastian's engagement had been announced, Louise had been one of the first to say that everything had been for the best. Chantal would have been unsuitable and in time Sebastian would come to see it for himself.

'Perhaps we should go to Anton Mordant's Salon in the morning Ella,' Louise was saying. 'Surely somebody will talk about her if I say a very old friend of mine had been modelling for them.'

'I shouldn't think it very advisable to talk to the models.'

'Not the models Ella. If I'm spending money I'm talking to Anton Mordant himself. You know me, I can be very discreet when I want to be and I always get my own way.'

Ella gave a wry smile. Indeed Louise had always been the spoilt girl in the family but it was deplorable the lengths she would go to to achieve her own way. She had no doubt that in the morning they would go to the dress salon and she would have to writhe in embarrassment while she watched Louise's manipulations. She simply hoped that Anton Mordant or anybody else for that matter would prove to be a wily opponent.

Because Ella had always been the poor relation, this holiday in Paris was Louise's treat, something that happened every spring and for the next part of the year she would be conveniently forgotten until spring came along again. She was grateful to Louise. She rescued her for one week every April and it was always Paris they went to so that Louise could replenish her wardrobe. Louise would say with a bright smile, 'Isn't this better than that draughty country parsonage?'

She had heard a lot about Chantal Grolan and had envied her bitterly. She had only met Sebastian twice but he had become her idol, the sort of man she would like to marry but knew she never would. When Louise had told her that Chantal had walked out of their engagement she had hated her. She had built up an image of a haughty self-centred girl whom Sebastian was well rid of, but while Louise had been talking animatedly to her old friend Ella had been sizing her up. She was not in the least how she had pictured her. For one thing she had not been ashamed to admit that she had worked, and she was beautiful in a restrained elegant way.

318

As they walked along the boulevard Louise was saying airily, 'Of course there was always something different about Chantal, not because she was French but she never talked much about her home-life. When she first came to Madame Lafayette's her mother lived in Dijon, her father was dead. Then her mother got married again and went to live in Bordeaux. Amanda Wentworth went to stay there, she said her mother was quite beautiful and they lived in a small château overlooking the river.'

She prattled on remorselessly about Chantal during her schooldays. Her infatuation for Dieter Steinberg, her artistic flair, saying at last, 'I wonder who she is going to Vienna with, didn't you get the impression that she didn't want to tell me?'

'Perhaps she didn't, after all why should she?'

'It's probably somebody quite bohemian and she wouldn't like to admit it. I'm so annoyed that we were unable to get tickets for Steinberg's concert. Apparently they were sold out weeks ago and from last night he's doing no more in Europe. I believe he's going to America.'

'It must be wonderful to be so handsome and talented.'

'And to think he wasted his time on a group of dizzy teenagers. All we could see were his looks, never his talent.'

Her meeting with Louise had disturbed Chantal considerably. It had brought back memories she had pushed to the back of her mind, and stirred feelings burdened with regret. She ached for Andrew grieving over Grace's death, oblivious to the face that he had another daughter he must never know. She was glad that Sebastian had found consolation with a girl eminently suitable, a girl who would further his chosen career. Louise had called her a daughter of the regiment and Chantal knew she could never have been that. It was something essentially British, and she said a silent prayer for Sebastian's happiness.

She recounted her meeting with Louise to Dieter over dinner that evening and with a little smile he said, 'Why didn't you tell her you were going to Vienna with me, why are you so afraid?'

'I think all my life I've been afraid. Every time I found some sort of stability we were moving on, now I'm afraid to believe that you really want to marry me, that it's all going to come true.'

He reached out across the table and covered her hand with his own.

'This time, Chantal try to think that dreams do come true. Tomorrow we'll take the train to Vienna and when we get there we will drive through the Vienna woods and I will introduce you to my grandmother.'

'Will she like me, do you think, will she think I'm good enough for her grandson?'

'She will adore you. She is my mother's mother, my mother was her youngest daughter. Her name is Baroness Bruchner.'

'Baroness!'

Dieter smiled. 'My grandmother never liked my father. He was an officer in the Royal Hussars, overbearing, dictatorial, exceedingly pompous. My two older brothers followed him into the regiment, I preferred writing music and playing the piano. My mother died young, and for a while I lived with my grandmother, largely I think because I was her favourite, my two brothers were too much like my father.'

'Are they still alive?'

'The elder was killed in Slovenia, I haven't heard from the other for a great many years. We were never close. Perhaps my grandmother will know.'

As she stepped down from the carriage on to the forecourt of Baroness Bruchner's house, several days later, Chantal looked round with delighted anticipation. The house overlooked a scene of pastoral beauty and Chantal had been enchanted with their drive through the Vienna woods. It was a large stone house tinged pink with the rays of the afternoon sun. Virginia creeper decorated the walls and as they crossed the cobbled courtyard an old man came out of a side door, raising his hat in greeting, his face wreathed in smiles.

Dieter went to shake hands with him and the old man held on to it joyfully.

Turning to Chantal, Dieter said, 'This is Hans, he has worked for my grandmother for as long as I can remember.'

He held out his hand and Chantal went forward to take it while the old man smiled down at her with obvious delight.

'He knows only German I'm afraid, Liebchen, but he is delighted to meet you.'

After the old man had shuffled off across the courtyard Dieter said, 'When I was a little boy he made boats for me and donkey carts. He took me skating on the lake and climbing in the mountains, he was a good person in my childhood. I think we will find my grandmother in the tower room. It is her favourite place.'

She was aware of stone floors and warm exquisite rugs, of dark oak beams and the sun slanting down from tall small paned windows. Together they climbed up a flight of shallow stairs that led upwards to a balcony that ran round the hall, then to another flight of stairs that led to a stout oak door which Dieter opened, calling out as he did so, 'Are you in there, grandmother?'

Chantal was aware of firelight and the scent of pinelogs, then she saw that an elderly lady had risen from a chair across the room and was clasped in Dieter's embrace before he brought her forward to meet her.

Chantal noticed the older woman's smile which was warm and embracing in a face of singular beauty. Her hair was silver white, her face hardly lined. Dieter was so much like her. They had the same eyes, dark grey-blue eyes, the same mouth which was capable of embracing whoever they met with the charm of its smile.

She was small and fragile, and yet there was grace in every movement, and in that first instance of their meeting Chantal thought my mother would like her. This is true nobility, real and genuine charm.

'We must have tea,' the Baroness said. 'It is a custom I adopted when I stayed with friends in England many years ago. I only drink China tea so I hope it is to your palate. Ring for the servant Dieter, we will have it here sitting in the window.'

She returned to her seat and after Dieter had summoned the servant he pulled two chairs forward so that they could sit with her looking out across the gardens.

'Have you enjoyed your ride through the woods?' the Baroness asked her.

'Oh yes, they're very beautiful, but so is Vienna, I've loved all of it.'

'Yes, Vienna is beautiful but I do not go into the city at all these days. Life there is too hectic for me. The shops are always crowded and the streets are so busy.'

'You should get a motorcar, grandmother,' Dieter said, 'They are all the rage. You could get around more.'

'My dear boy, I don't want to get around. I like my carriage, besides what would I do with my horses? Motorcars are noisy and smelly.'

'Alas I didn't think you would approve.'

The tea arrived on a huge silver tray laid out with delicate china cups and saucers and a silver cake stand piled with tiny cakes. The Baroness asked if they would prefer milk or lemon, and they watched while she seemingly enjoyed the ceremony of afternoon tea.

They talked about old times but Chantal never felt that they were excluding her from their conversation because every now and again the Baroness would lean forward and explain things about the people they were discussing.

'We always have too much to talk about,' she said at last. 'Our meetings are always so fleeting these days, he has to get back to Vienna or some other place, I can never catch up with him.'

There was so much pride in her voice however, and with a gentle smile she said, 'My other grandsons were all so forceful, they wanted to conquer the world that was waiting for them when all Dieter wanted to do was play his piano. They teased him unmercifully and I used to say to them, "What is so wonderful about wanting to be a soldier and go to war for some cause you are totally unsure of?" Dieter was always so very sure that one day the world would recognize his music and now that it has I am so very proud of him. Are you musical, my dear?'

'No. I am not a performer, but I do love music. I too am very proud of him.'

The old lady smiled. 'He tells me you met when you were one of his pupils in that school in Switzerland. I never liked him being there, he was worth so much more.'

'I know. We were never worthy of him.'

'Tell me, my dear, why did you fall in love with my grandson, surely not when you were one of his pupils?'

'Yes I did fall in love with him then, but I was too young, I thought it was puppy love, something I would recover from, but when we met again I knew that I never had. The most wonderful thing of all is that Dieter loves me.'

'And now you are to go to America with him.'

Chantal looked at Dieter with wide questioning eyes. It was something they hadn't discussed even though she had hoped. Now he was smiling at her reassuringly.

'I wanted Chantal to meet you, grandmother, then I wanted us to discuss our marriage with you. I would like it to be here in Vienna so that we can go to America together at the end of the month.'

The old lady's eyes filled with tears. 'Oh, that is kind of you Dieter, I've never been consulted about anything by any of the others, they've all gone their own ways oblivious of anything I thought, but I do want you to marry here in Austria, so that I can come to your wedding and spend some time with you before you leave for America. It could be a very long time before we meet again.'

Chantal's heart was singing with happiness. In just over two weeks they would sail on the *Ile de France* as man and wife and there would be stability and security in her life. It was much later when she lay in bed that she thought about her mother.

It would be the hardest letter she had ever needed to write in her life. Her poor mother who had thought to shine at her daughter's marriage to an English nobleman, the one dream in her life that was fated to end in disappointment, and all she could hope was that one day her mother would forgive her. She did not know how long they would remain in America but she resolved that on their return they would go to Bordeaux.

Marie Claire would like Dieter. She would understand why Chantal had fallen in love with him and she would glory in his success and the knowledge that her daughter had not married a nobody after all.

322

37

Marie Claire stared down at the two envelopes beside her breakfast plate with some misgiving. One bore the Paris postmark, the other was from Burgundy, bearing her sister Jeanne's writing.

Chantal's letters were always the same, the good life in Paris, the friends she had made and the excitement to be found in the city. Jeanne wrote very seldom and she never had any good news. It was always about her sister Margot's short temper, childish ailments and her mother's increasing problems with old age.

She decided to open Jeanne's letter first. It informed her briefly that their mother had died peacefully in her sleep, with details of the funeral, and the hope that Marie-Claire would be able to attend.

She wept as she laid it back on the table. She had not seen much of her mother over the years but she remembered the happy times of her childhood and the way her mother had worked to give them a happy home. She would go to the funeral of course, but she would not ask Henri to go with her. He did not know them and he was busy at the château.

She opened her daughter's letter and sat back in amazement. Chantal was leaving her job in Paris and going for a few days to Vienna to stay with her fiancé's grandmother. She hoped to marry Dieter Steinberg before they set sail for America at the end of April and she was very, very happy. She hoped her mother would give them her blessing and when they returned from America she would bring Dieter to meet her.

Her first thoughts were of anger. All the long years of plotting and scheming were lost and now Chantal was to marry her music teacher, and in Vienna of all places. Why were they going to America, supposedly so that he could teach music in some school or other, and what sort of a life would it be for Chantal when she could have had something much better?

323

It was only later in the day when she went into the town and met a group of women friends for afternoon tea in one of the fashionable cafés there that she received the surprise of her life.

When her friend Annette commented on her sad expression she told them about Chantal and passed over the letter so that they could read it for themselves.

'Dieter Steinberg!' Marie Dupont exclaimed.

The rest of them squealed with excitement and Marie Claire stared at them in hurt surprise.

'Why are you so angry?' Annette said, 'Steinberg is famous. Don't you read your papers or magazines?'

Marie Claire continued to stare at them stupidly and the three of them hurried to tell her why Dieter Steinberg was famous and why he wa going to America.

'Chérie, you should be delighted, he's incredibly handsome and so talented. He's played before all the crowned heads of Europe and great orchestras all over the world are playing his music. You should be thrilled and excited for Chantal.'

When she recounted the conversation to Henri over dinner that evening he could only smile at her excitement as well as her anger.

'We should be at her wedding,' Marie Claire complained bitterly, 'I'm her mother. Why is it such a hole-and-corner affair?'

'But it isn't,' Henri said reasonably, 'Doesn't she say they are visiting his grandmother.'

'All the same, why couldn't she have told us months ago that she was meeting him again, and why Vienna? She says she will bring him here when they return from America but it will be like meeting two strangers.'

'There is nothing we can do about it, Chérie, we have to accept it.'

Her mother's death was remembered much later and Marie Claire said tearfully, 'Two shocks in one morning was terrible. I have to go to Burgundy for mother's funeral, they're expecting me.'

'Well of course you must go. Spend a little time with them. There will be a great deal to discuss.'

Henri was so nice. He was kind, always understanding. She had been lucky this time.

Chantal was to be married in the tiny church near Dieter's grandmother's house, where the old lady herself had been married years before.

There were few guests. The village doctor who was Dieter's friend from childhood, and the villagers who had welcomed him home, as well as his grandmother's servants.

She stared at her reflection in the long cheval mirror in her bedroom. For years she had stared with her mother at frothy wedding gowns in expensive magazines and Marie Claire had said that one day she would be married in such a gown. Now in the elegant simplicity of her pure silk cream gown she had to admit reality was a far cry from those distant dreams.

She had purchased her gown in Vienna as well as the wide brimmed hat with its sweeping ostrich feathers. She looked beautiful, even Anton Mordant would have agreed that the graceful folds of the gown on her slender figure was more distinctive than yards of frothy lace.

Minutes before, she had seen Dieter setting out for the church in the company of his friend, and when she looked down the window she could see Hans escorting his grandmother through two lines of villagers who had come to watch.

As she walked down the stairs to the hallway she was greeted with delighted smiles from the young girl standing at the bottom of the stairs. The doctor's young daughter Elizabeth who was to act as her bridesmaid. Her pretty face was alive with excitement.

'You look so beautiful Chantal,' she said. 'Are we ready to leave?'

She nodded, and as they walked the short distance to the church she was aware of the smiling faces and expressions of admiration.

The service was simple, the banquet at the house a delight, and the Baroness's face a picture of happiness. It was later as they were about to leave for a few days in the city, that she was handed her mother's letter. She sent her love and her good wishes and a hope that they would all meet very soon. That letter seemed to put the seal on her day's happiness.

At the end of April they boarded the *Ile de France* at Le Havre on a day of bright sunshine and white scudding clouds. It would have been strange if she had not thought of Grace as she stood in the middle of their stateroom with its exquisite ornamentation and the masses of flowers that well wishers had sent them.

Grace must have started her voyage on the *Titanic* amid such spendour and she could not help the small shiver of fear that swept over her. The *Ile de France* was small in comparison to the *Titanic*, but Dieter smiled at her fears. 'She's a beautiful ship,' he said, 'The fact that she is smaller doesn't really matter, Liebschen. The Ritz is not the largest hotel in the world.'

'I can't help thinking about Grace and her husband, they must have been as happy as we are on the morning they sailed.'

'Nothing is going to happen to us, Chantal, the *Ile de France* has made the crossing many times, and we have an adequate supply of lifeboats.' He laughed. 'We are not going to need them, I promise.'

Her fears subsided as they entered into the life of the ship. They danced the nights away and they were treated as celebrities by the other passengers until she wondered if it was always going to be like that.

Dieter was quick to allay her fears. 'There will be times when fame catches up on us, but we have to accept it and leave it alone. When we return to Europe we have to look for a house well away from the city and a lot of people, somewhere we can relax and be ourselves,' he said gently.

'How long are we to stay in America?' she asked him.

'About a year. I have engagements that cover a year, it's difficult to say.

Neither of them visualized that the enormity of events in Europe would change their plans and the lives of a great many people on both sides of the Atlantic.

In Burgundy Marie Claire stood with her family as her mother was laid to rest. The priest had said kind words about her devotion to her children, her example as a loving and caring woman and how much she would be missed by all who knew her, but all Marie Claire remembered of the day was that rain fell from grey leaded skies and around the grave her feet were squelching in clay.

Jeanne's children stood clutching their posy offerings, their small faces curious about the day's events but oblivious of its gravity. Margot had received her coldly, eyeing her fashionable clothing with thinly disguised disdain and ignoring Marcel who stood clutching his hat at the edge of the crowd.

Marie Claire was surprised to see him there. Jeanne had told her he was living with a woman in the village and that he was not even on speaking terms with his wife. That he had come to pay his last respects to her mother lifted him slightly in her estimation. After the committal he sidled over to her and her first reaction was that his bold good looks had gone. His face was lined and thin, his shoulders stooped and his teeth badly needed attention when he smiled.

'We're honoured to see you in these parts, Marie Claire,' he said. 'I wondered if you'd come.'

'I wouldn't not come to my mother's funeral,' she answered dryly.

'I suppose things will be different up at the farm, now the old lady's gone.'

'I don't see why. My mother had little interest in the farm for years. Marc has run it very well.'

'With help from his wife and Margot.'

'Of course. It's their bread and butter too.'

'You're not expecting anything I suppose?'

'No, of course not. I've done nothing for the farm, the people who have worked on it deserve everything.'

'I worked on it for a time.'

'In between your other nefarious pursuits.'

He grinned. 'Well, you have to admit your sister Margot wasn't the easiest woman to live with. She was jealous and domineering, what she said was so, and a man can only take so much.'

'If you'd been different Marcel, perhaps Margot would have been different.'

'Not very likely. She was born difficult.'

'Didn't you know that when you married her, or did you simply want an interest in the farm.'

'I have to admit that entered into it. I liked farming, I just didn't like being married to your sister.'

'Are you happy now, Marcel?'

'Enough, how about you, why isn't your husband here with you?'

'He never met my mother, I didn't expect him to come. Besides he has a great deal to do in Bordeaux.'

'What has happened to that daughter of yours? I expect that school in Switzerland ensured she had the right sort of husband.'

'Chantal is married and living in America.'

'America!'

She smiled without enlightening him further.

'I must go now, Marcel. They are ready to go back to the farm. Where are you working these days?'

'Here and there. I'd like to get back into farming, perhaps I'll speak to Marc.'

She smiled and moved away. She did not think Marc would consider taking him back, Margot would have something to say about that.

Nothing at the farm seemed to have changed. The furniture, the layout of the kitchen, the cooking utensils were exactly as she remembered them as a child and she wondered why Jeanne didn't look for something more modern to surround herself with.

She hated her bedroom. It brought back too many memories of a life she had tried to forget.

She would stay three or four days. She longed for the comfort of her home near Bordeaux, the views of the gently meandering river, the beautiful rooms tastefully furnished and her husband's smile across the dinner table. Life was good, but better than that it was stable. It isn't great wealth, passion or fame that really makes life good, she reflected, it is stability, the knowledge that come hell or high water nothing will change.

327

On the second day of her visit the rain had stopped and a pale watery sun shone out of a delicate blue sky. She shrugged her arms into a warm camel-haired coat and her feet into walking shoes and decided to walk down the lane as far as the château gates. She did not expect to meet people on her walk, the lane belonged to the farm and the people from the château never used the gates leading to it. It was only when she neared the stile that she paused. Beyond it lay the field that had once blazed with the gold of sunflowers and at that moment the memory of it was so intense it brought the tears into her eyes.

She climbed the stile and looked out across the field, bare and empty without its crop of vegetables, and the memory of the sunflowers long gone. Without hesitation she walked along the narrow path towards the hill where she had once loved to sit, sketching the flowers and then she saw the man.

He stood looking out across the field, one hand shading his eyes from the sun, leaning idly on his walking stick and her heart missed a beat. He was tall and slender, dressed in country tweeds and there was something in the intensity of his gaze that made her stand suddenly still. She knew him instantly, she would have recognized him in a crowd, in a hundred years time, and she stood still on the path. He had come back again but it was too late for both of them.

Her gaze never wavered as she watched the sunlight gleaming in his silvered hair and his attitude there was a strange look of sadness, a regret for something irretrievably lost. He turned away suddenly and moved towards the gate, then as he reached it he turned once more to look back and then he saw her.

She did not move. She was aware of her heart beating painfully and her mouth felt suddenly dry with anxiety. For what seemed an eternity they stared at each other and then he raised his hat and turned away. She did not know whether to be angry or relieved, but after he had passed through the gate she walked back until she reached the stile and climbed over it.

He was walking up the lane towards her and she could not avoid him. Their eyes met again and he was suddenly aware that she was afraid, that she wanted to run from him, then like a sudden flash of lightning he recognized her and his face lit up with such a smile of welcome she went forward instinctively to take his hand.

He smiled down at her and, oh, she remembered the charm of his smile, the warmth in his blue-grey eyes, the feel of his hand around hers.

'Marie-Claire!' he exclaimed. 'By all that's wonderful. I've been here often over the years, why is it we never met before?'

'I haven't lived here for a great many years,' she answered.

'I know, you went to the Sorbonne and set Paris alight. That was your ambition, wasn't it?'

She smiled.

'What have you done with your life Marie Claire?'

'I never got to university. I am married to a wonderful man and we grow grapes in the region of Bordeaux.'

'Why Bordeaux, I wonder?'

'Because we live there. Unlike you I was not tied to an ancestral home and a way of life.'

'Of course not.'

'And you Andrew, what have you done since we last met?'

'I married a girl I'd known a long time, my eldest brother died of cholera in India and I came in for his title and eventually my father's. Do you have children?'

'I have a daughter, and you?'

'Yes, we had twins, Grace and Sebastian, then we had Alice. She was born some years after the other two.'

She was suddenly aware of a deep penetrating sadness as he looked over her head towards the fields beyond, and seeing her looking at him searchingly he said, 'My daughter Grace and her new husband went down on the *Titanic*. They were on their honeymoon.'

Pity filled her heart. 'Oh Andrew, I am sorry.' She thought then of all the years when she had wanted to hurt him, when she had prayed that he would suffer, and now all she could feel was this all-absorbing pity for a hurt that had been too punishing, too drastic.

'I don't suppose we'll ever really get over it. Constance fills her time with a great many things, which leave her little time to think and there are whole days when I seem incapable of thinking about anything else. Grace and I were very close, my son is in the Indian army so we see very little of him, there's Alice of course, we have to be very careful that we don't cosset Alice too much. Is your daughter married?'

'Yes. She's in America at the moment.'

'So you won't be seeing much of her.'

'No. Are you here on holiday?'

'For a few days, staying with my sister Vivienne at the château.'

'You're not painting pictures then?'

'Every day I say I must start again but I never do. I still have that picture of you among the sunflowers, what a pity that they're no longer there.'

'I know. My father wouldn't sow them any more.'

'The picture is in my study, I look at it often. I remembered you every time I looked at it, the sunshine during that lovely August and those long lovely days we had, how wonderful to meet you again like

329

this. The number of times I've hoped we might meet somewhere around here.'

He was staring down at her and his thoughts were that she was still beautiful, still the enchanting girl who had filled his days in that long lost summer.

'I take it you are visiting your family here?'

'I came home for my mother's funeral.'

'Oh I'm sorry. So this is a very sad visit?'

'In some respects yes. My mother was quite old and had not been well for some time. I haven't paid them many visits over the years. At this time of sorrow it is something I regret.'

'Yes indeed. Is your father still alive?'

'No. I have two sisters, I am closer to one than the other.'

'That does happen in families. When are you returning to Bordeaux?'

'I'm not sure, soon though. There is really nothing for me here any more.'

'Would you like me to walk back to the farm with you, the lane is lonely?'

'No, really there is no need. I have walked this lane alone a great many times. I am glad I met you, Andrew, and I hope there are happier times in store for you, when time has healed the grief you feel over your daughter.'

He smiled. 'Thank you, I too hope so.'

He raised her hand and brushed it with his lips, then after looking long and deeply in her eyes he turned and walked away. For several minutes she did not move but stared after him as he walked back towards the château, and it was only when he reached the gates that he turned and raised his hand in farewell.

For many years she had agonized on what she would do if they ever met again. Once she had hidden behind a mask, but she had foolishly believed that she would meet him in England when Chantal had found some English nobleman to marry. How foolish it had all been and she had been the loser.

Andrew remembered her as a girl he had loved for a brief month in the summer with memories of sunflowers and roses, the warm sun and heady fleeting passions, but he had soon forgotten when reality entered his life. She was the one who had remembered because there had been Chantal. She had been the one to pay most dearly for those few brief weeks of bliss.

Jeanne smiled at her when she let herself in by the kitchen door. 'There's fresh coffee on the stove, Marie Claire. How far did you walk?'

'Down the lane as far as the château gates, nothing very much changes around here.'

'No, except the sunflowers, they're long gone.'

'I think I may go back to Bordeaux the day after tomorrow Jeanne. This is a busy time for Henri and he's probably feeling rather lonely.'

'I thought you might have stayed a little while.'

Marie Claire smiled. 'Why don't you and the children spend some time with us in the summer? They would love the river and it is a beautiful part of France. Marc too if possible.'

'It won't be possible for Marc, Marie Claire, the farm seems to take all his time, remember how it was with Papa.'

'Yes. I never remember him taking a holiday.'

Just then the door opened and Margot came in carrying a shopping basket which she laid down heavily on the kitchen table.

'I saw you in the lane,' she said sharply. 'Who was that man you were talking to?'

'The Vicomtesse's brother from England. I met him before.'

'When you were guests at the château I suppose, and when you were rather more than a guest to the Vicomte de Mirandol.'

Marie Claire finished her coffee and, turning to her sister Jeanne, said, 'I think I'll go upstairs and start packing my suitcase, will you call me when you're preparing dinner and I'll give you a hand.'

'There's really no need, Chérie, I can manage, I have to do it every day.'

Margot was unloading her shopping basket, placing things heavy-handed on the table top, but as Marie Claire turned to go out of the room she snapped, 'What were you and Marcel talking about at the funeral. I'm still his wife, I have a right to know.'

'Nothing very much Margot. He offered his condolences about our mother and said he missed farming, that's all.'

'Missed farming! He was always too busy in the wine taverns to do much farming. Did he say anything about that woman he's living with?'

'Nothing at all. Surely he would not discuss her with me.'

Her sister frowned but said nothing more, and after she turned away, Jeanne said, 'I'll call you when dinner's ready, Margot and I can cope.'

Not to be outdone, Margot said acidly, 'We've had to cope, haven't we? It wouldn't have done any of us any good to rely on Marie Claire.'

As she set about packing her suitcase, she knew she could never have come back to the farm to live. Her childhood memories were happy, but they had been quickly overtaken by the trauma and hostility of the years that came later. Now she felt an urgent and desperate need to get home to the château she had made her own and to Henri's delighted welcome that she had returned early.

38

Vivienne de Mirandol stood at the window watching her brother walking across the courtyard towards the door. He had been with them for three weeks while his wife was with her mother in Cannes. Since Grace's death Constance had hardly been at home, it had been the South of France or Italy, Switzerland or Madeira and always with her mother, since Andrew preferred to stay close to home with his memories.

She did not blame Constance. Sometimes it paid to get on a merry-go-round that didn't stop, only in the end one had to get off and face one's personal disasters.

He seemed more distracted than ever over dinner until even André commented on it.

'I really thought you were coming to terms with it Andrew,' he said, 'but today you seem sadder than ever.'

Andrew smiled. 'I'm sorry to be such a wet blanket,' he said gently. 'I've been walking along the lanes round here, a journey of nostalgia if you like. It brought back many memories.'

André and Vivienne exchanged glances and changing the conversation Vivienne said, 'Have you heard from Constance, Andrew?'

'Oh the usual postcard. She's not a great correspondent. They seem to be enjoying themselves in Cannes.'

'I'm glad.'

'I can't think what they find to do, over-rich people in expensive hotels, all doing the same sort of thing. Your mother loved it, didn't she André?'

'Well yes. She loved the life in the casinos and she simply loved Provence. My father was like you. He could take it or leave it. When my mother loved Deauville he loved Cannes, when she loved Cannes he preferred Trouville.'

'Convenient in an arranged marriage, I think.'

'Of course. It was amazing how well it worked.'

It was later in the evening when Vivienne found her brother alone in the library that she broached his faraway preoccupation with other things for most of the evening.

'Something has upset you, Andrew,' she said anxiously. 'I had thought you were coming to terms with Grace's death, at least if one can ever be said to come to terms with something so tragic, but this evening something has unsettled you.'

Andrew smiled. 'It has nothing to do with Grace, Vivienne, actually I met a woman in the lane this afternoon. I hadn't seen her for years, the woman who was once the subject of my painting hanging in the study.'

Vivienne's heart jumped alarmingly. 'You spoke to her?'

'Yes, we came face to face in the field that once was filled with sunflowers. I didn't recognize her at first, then that summer came flooding back to me. She's beautiful. The girl was lovely, I never really forgot her.'

'What did you talk about?'

'Our lives and what fate had done to us. She was here for her mother's funeral, she now lives in Bordeaux with her husband. I told her about Grace, she was sympathetic of course.'

'Did she say if she had children?'

'A daughter. In America at present.'

'Did she say what Cha . . . her daughter was doing in America?'

'No. I don't suppose she thought it important, for me at any rate.'

For the first time Vivienne understood why Marie Claire had always been different in André's estimation. This had been her chance to tell Andrew that her daughter was his daughter, but she had not done so. But if she had, what would have been the outcome? Andrew would know that the Chantal who Sebastian had been in love with was one and the same, and his guilt would have been insupportable.

At that moment she breathed a silent prayer of gratitude to Marie Claire.

Henri was waiting for her train to arrive, his smile warm and welcoming and Marie Claire went forward into his embrace with a feeling of great tenderness. This was reality, the sun shining on the Gironde river, busy with tiny boats and the uphill drive to the pretty château standing firm but unpretentious on the hillside.

She had been born in the farmhouse in Burgundy but during the last few days it had meant nothing to her. This was home, this house she loved and which Henri had allowed her to adorn with every luxury they had been able to afford.

Nothing at the farm had altered, it still bore the imprint of her parents' life, her father's frugality and her mother's acceptance, Jeanne and Marc's honest toil and Margot's bitterness. She had tried her best to persuade Jeanne to visit her and to bring the children with her but she did not think they would come.

Jeanne's life was firmly entrenched in her own world, she had never known any other, and perhaps it would be unwise to open her eyes to an existence that would never be hers.

She had thought about Andrew constantly since their meeting and more and more she began to acknowledge the folly surrounding much of her life. For a few brief weeks, Andrew had been in love with her but he had never loved her, his love had been reserved for an English girl he had never forgotten. By her stupidity she had hurt a great many people, Vivienne de Mirandol and Maurice, her daughter, even the Reverend Mother at the convent who had tried to tell her she was so wrong about a great many things but she had not believed her.

Chantal had promised that when they returned from America they would visit, but could things between them be the same? Chantal had married the man she had cautioned her against marrying. Would Chantal forgive her for that even now when they were together?

Chantal had elected to marry in Vienna which surely was proof that there was some intangible barrier between them still.

Chantal was loving America, its vastness and the pace of existence. A new young country with an exciting awareness of life that the old world had taken for granted. This was a world forging ahead without restricting memories of past glories that had gone for ever, young America was living in the present and creating future glories and America opened its warm heart to Dieter's music so that they were welcomed and fêted wherever it was heard.

If she had been asked to choose a favourite city she would have found it difficult, she loved them all because each one was different but the Christmas of 1913 they decided to spend in New England and she fell in love with it.

On Christmas morning they went by sleigh to the pretty wooden church near to their hotel, where carols were sung in a church decorated with holly and garlands of scarlet berries and silver baubles.

Outside, people were embracing and greeting one another and Chantal said happily, 'Oh Dieter I could live in this beautiful place, I shall hate going home at the end of April.'

Dieter smiled down at her and said gently, 'I'm afraid it won't be the end of April Leibchen, I have engagements for at least another year. If you like, we could look for a house in Vermont so that at least there is some sense of permanency in our lives.'

She looked at him doubtfully. 'Perhaps we could find somewhere to come to when you are not working, but if you are working I want to be with you wherever it is.'

He squeezed her hand and smiled down at her. 'Your mother will be disappointed Chantal, how will you break the news to her?'

'I don't know. I do send her copies of everything I can find about you in the newspapers, and copies of your programmes when you are performing. She tells me she is very thrilled for us but she will be disappointed, I'm sure.'

They never found their house in Vermont because they never seemed to have the time to settle in one place for longer than a few days. Engagements poured in and Dieter's new operetta was performed to rave reviews in New York in June.

At the banquet after its first performance she saw Dieter in earnest conversation with a tall military gentleman and their host said to her, 'Dieter is talking to an English general, and looking very serious whatever they're discussing.'

She stared across the room at them, and their host said, 'I expect they're discussing the news from Sarajevo, nothing for us to worry about.'

It was later in their hotel room that she asked Dieter why he had seemed so preoccupied for most of the evening.

'The heir to the Austrian throne has been assassinated in Sarajevo by Bosnian Serbs. The entire area is a hotbed of trouble, I can't think that it will stop here.'

'But it's nothing for us to worry about, surely Dieter?'

'Have you forgotten, Liebchen, that I am Austrian and a subject of Emperor Franz Joseph.'

She stared at him in surprise. She had forgotten, but she still couldn't see how that assassination in a far distant country could alter their life in new and exciting America.

Dieter took her into his arms and gently kissed the top of her head, and anxiously Chantal said, 'What do you think will happen?'

'I don't know. It could be very far-reaching. Germany has been spoiling for trouble, Russia is demoralized and Turkey an uncertainty. I have an awful fear that life as we know it is soon to be seriously threatened.'

Chantal had never concerned herself with life outside France. Paris was Paris and could never be threatened by other people's quarrels, and life in Vienna had seemed too joyful with its palaces and ballrooms, the heady sweep of its music and the Hapsburgs who seemed to have been on the Austrian throne for ever.

She was writing to her mother often now. Long letters filled with American scenes and sights, Dieter's popularity and his success, and in return Marie Claire wrote of her fears that the old world was changing and that now there was fear in people's hearts that something dreadful was hanging over all of them.

When she passed her mother's letters over for Dieter to read, he said sadly, 'I'm very much afraid that she is right. Here in America we are a long way from what is happening in Europe, but trouble never stays for long in one place, it has a nasty habit of spreading. I think in the end America too will be aware of it.'

But between America and strife-torn Europe stretched the Atlantic Ocean and not even the German invasion of little Belgium convinced them that they had anything to fear. Germany defeated Russia and began their advance on Paris which fortunately was repulsed at great cost to the Allied armies in the battle on the Marne.

Dieter played night after night for some charity or another in aid of the European War Effort but Chantal knew he was unhappy. He felt he had no business to be enjoying the luxury of life in America when in Europe his compatriots were fighting and dying for a cause that was already lost.

What could he do in Austria, an Austrian with a French wife, and when everything he loved and believed in his native land was over-powered by the dominance of Germany? He rejoiced when America declared war on Germany in 1917, telling Chantal that with half the world ranged against her, Germany must know the end was in sight.

When they finally sailed into the harbour at Le Havre on their return to France the world as they had known it was no more. The Tsar and his entire family had been assassinated in Russia, Austria and Germany had become republics and the fields of northern France were still ridged with mile upon mile of trenches, trenches where millions had died in the name of pride, greed and stupidity.

Chantal telephoned her mother from Paris and Marie Claire, beside herself with joy, asked quickly, 'When are you coming home?'

In the end Chantal went alone to Bordeaux because Dieter decided to go to Vienna to see what he could salvage from the life he had known. When Chantal said she would go with him, he said, 'Go home to your mother, Chantal. I'll come to Bordeaux as soon as I can, but I think this is a time when we have to face our past in our different ways.'

Her mother and stepfather were there to meet her when she stepped down from the train, and her mother asked anxiously, 'Isn't your husband with you, Chantal. Isn't he coming?'

'He's gone to Vienna, mother, but he will come when he's satisfied

336

himself that he can do nothing there. I think he is very anxious about his grandmother.'

Marie Claire was delighted with her daughter's appearance. She was beautifully dressed in the latest American fashion and there was an aura of contentment about her as she chatted happily on their way to the château.

'Nothing seems to have changed here,' she said. 'I remember the river and the vineyards along its banks. Did the war touch you at all?'

'Well, of course,' Marie Claire said sadly. 'We lost friends and our friends lost sons fighting in the north. We lived off the land and there was nothing in the shops, but we always knew that in the end we would win, we had to. There were a pile of letters waiting for you at the château from England, from the friends you had there I expect.'

It was much later that Chantal opened them, watched by her mother, but not too avidly as she had once done.

'I hope none of them have lost people,' her mother said at last. 'The toll of British lives was terrible.'

'Amanda's husband was killed on the Somme, mother, so her little boy has the title now. I liked him enormously. I am so sad for Amanda. . . . Louise's husband was wounded but has now recovered and . . . her voice tailed off and she looked up at her mother uncertainly.

'What is it, Chérie?' her mother asked.

'Sebastian is now Earl of Westmond.'

In that first brief moment she saw the raw pain in her mother's eyes to be quickly replaced by her voice saying quickly, 'Sebastian? Sebastian Martindale?'

'Yes, mother. His father was killed at Verdun in 1916. Sebastian has left the Indian Army and he and his wife are now living at Blaire. His mother is living somewhere in London with his grandmother.'

Marie Claire didn't speak. She wanted desperately to change the subject but she could find nothing to say, nothing at least that was important, and the bleak expression in her eyes prompted Chantal to say, 'Mother, I know that the Earl of Westmond was my father, I have known for a long time. I wish you had told me the truth, it would have saved me and Sebastian a great deal of heartache.'

'You and Sebastian, why you and Sebastian?'

'Because there was a time when we thought we were in love. I didn't know he was my half-brother, it was the Vicomtesse de Mirandol who showed me the picture my father painted of you in the sunflower field. We both of us knew the truth.'

She watched the tears falling helplessly down her mother's cheeks and she took her in her arms until the sobs subsided.

337

'Mother, why did you lie to me all those years? Why did you tell me my father was dead? Was it pride, that he never came back to you, that he married somebody else?'

'It was a mixture of so many things, pride and anger, sadness and despair. I met him, you know, when I went to your grandmother's funeral. We talked for a little while, there was no animosity on my part, no anger, it was as if we'd met often over the years, a feeling that he'd never been far from that cottage in the woods. I was glad that we had been able to meet like that, it meant that I could come back here to Bordeaux and thank God for what I had.'

'Oh, mother, don't you think it could all have been so very different?'

'I don't know. I could never have gone on living at the farm because they made me so unhappy there and I had to find work. It could have been different if I'd accepted it, but there always seemed to be something pushing me on. I couldn't let go, Chantal, it was as though I had to show the world that I had lost out but my daughter wouldn't.'

'But you hadn't lost out, mother. You had Maurice and you had a good life in Dijon with him. It always seemed to me that just when we were happy in our life we had to move on. I loved the convent but I had to go to Switzerland. I had friends in Burgundy but I had to make new ones in England. I never understood you until that morning when the Vicomtesse showed me the painting.'

'And you were so terribly angry with me, you didn't come home?'

'I knew I couldn't accuse you openly, I knew if I did there would be tears, and words might have been said that neither of us would forgive. I needed time.'

'Have you forgiven me now, Chantal?'

'Yes, I'm sure I have. There is a contentment about you I never saw before. I want Dieter to see you like this, my real mother who was always there under the façade.'

Dieter arrived several days later and when Marie Claire looked into his eyes she knew that he was right for Chantal. She found she could talk to him and that he understood her, she admired his maturity and his unaffected delight in his success and when they left to fulfil several pressing engagements in Paris their promise to come back at the first chance they got reassured her.

She stood with Henri on the terrace watching Dieter and Chantal climb into the cab, responding to their waving hands and smiling faces until the cab left the gates, then with Henri's arm around her waist they walked back into the house.

There had been many times over the last two weeks when she had felt a rush of gratitude for all that she had and a tremor of anguish that she had almost lost it.

She could think about Andrew dispassionately now, a man she had loved desperately when she was too young and the price she had been asked to pay too high. It seemed to her now that Andrew too had paid but in those quiet moments when she thought about him he seemed as close as the sunflowers that had once turned the long grey field into a blaze of sunlight.